Marmaduke Charles Frederick Morris

Yorkshire Folk-Talk

With Characteristics of those who speak it in the North and East Ridings

Marmaduke Charles Frederick Morris

Yorkshire Folk-Talk
With Characteristics of those who speak it in the North and East Ridings

ISBN/EAN: 9783744767521

Printed in Europe, USA, Canada, Australia, Japan

Cover: Foto ©Andreas Hilbeck / pixelio.de

More available books at **www.hansebooks.com**

YORKSHIRE FOLK-TALK

WITH

CHARACTERISTICS OF THOSE WHO SPEAK IT
IN THE NORTH AND EAST RIDINGS

BY THE

REV. M. C. F. MORRIS, B.C.L., M.A.

Vicar of Newton-on-Ouse, Yorkshire.

London

HENRY FROWDE, AMEN CORNER

York

JOHN SAMPSON

1892

PREFACE

FOUR years have now gone by since I circulated a letter among those who, so far as I knew, took an interest in the subject of our East Yorkshire dialect. The main object aimed at in the following pages will perhaps be best understood if I in part repeat what I said at that time. I will quote my own words :—

'Those who have made a study of the English dialects, and have listened attentively to them as they have been spoken, cannot but have noticed that a considerable change has taken place in the ordinary language of our country-folk during the last twenty years. The North and East Ridings of Yorkshire are no exception to the rule. Railways and certifi-cated schoolmasters, despite their advantages, are making sad havoc of much that is interesting and worth preserving in the mother tongue of the people. This is to be regretted. It is with the object of collecting any such relics of the past, which would otherwise be doomed to oblivion, that I make the following appeal to my brother Yorkshiremen, many

a 3

of whom, I know, must have a sort of affection for
the rich and powerful dialects of the Eastern half of
the County.   These sound like music in the ears of
many of us.   I am well aware that much valuable
work has been already done in this direction, and
that by more able hands than mine.   Still, it is probable that the mine is not exhausted; and if, as
Professor Max Müller observes, in his *Lectures on
the Science of Language*, "some of the local dialects
of England, as spoken at the present day, are of
great importance for a critical study of English,"
surely no stone should be left unturned for discovering any particles of ore which still exist in out of the
way places, and for thus rescuing what can still be
saved of our decaying dialect.

Not only, however, am I desirous of gathering
together any lingering traces of bygone words, but
also of collecting peculiar Yorkshire phrases, sayings,
modes of expression, and grammatical usages.   Far
less has been written about these than about mere
dialectic vocabularies, and yet I think it will be
admitted that to a Yorkshireman, at all events, they
possess a certain interest.   There are, I believe, still
a vast number of such more or less local peculiarities
of expression which are worthy of being preserved.

'But there is a further branch of enquiry which
may well be pursued.   It has been said that every
other Yorkshireman you meet is a character.   There
is truth in this remark.   A healthy independence,
originality, and sense of humour meet one at every
turn.   Many are the Yorkshire stories that can be

related to illustrate such independence and originality—stories which have never yet been placed on
record. Very grateful shall I be, then, to those who
will be good enough to furnish me with any such, together with any dialectic peculiarities that come before
their notice ; and in the case of these latter, it will
add greatly to their value if the name of the district,
or better still the exact place where they are known
to have been used, is mentioned. I feel sure there
is sufficient material of this kind to fill many a volume,
if only it could be collected.'

This request met with a willing response in many
quarters, and I have much pleasure in acknowledging
my obligations for the assistance I have received
from others. These are too numerous to name in-
dividually. But my thanks are due in a special way
to Hr. Pastor Feilberg, of Darum Præstegård, Denmark, the learned author of the *Jutlandic Dictionary*,
whose kindly and ever-ready help was invaluable ;
also to Mr. R. H. Lipscomb, of East Budleigh, Devon-
shire ; Mr. E. P. Allanson, of York ; Mr. G. Frank,
of Kirby Moorside ; and the Rev. D. S. Hodgson, late
of Helmsley, for many interesting literary contribu-
tions. To Canon Atkinson, of Danby, for those examples of the dialect from the *Cleveland Glossary*,
which I have quoted with his permission in a few
cases, as well as for other valued aid, I must express my gratitude. But lastly, and it may also be
said mainly, am I indebted to my friend the Rev. E. S.
Carter, of York, without whose hearty support and
able co-operation, especially at the outset, I should

scarcely have ventured on my undertaking. To him I accord my best thanks.

It will be at once seen that many words, idioms, and grammatical as well as other usages, noticed in these pages, may be found in other parts of England also. To have inserted those which are peculiar to East Yorkshire only would have been wellnigh an impossibility : my rule, therefore, has been to give any which deviated in some way from the usage of ordinary English ; even thus difficulties arose, for it was not in every case apparent whether a word or phrase should be reckoned as dialectic or not. On this point opinions will differ.

The Glossary will be found to contain not far short of two thousand words, and there are throughout the volume about twelve hundred original examples of the dialect. By far the greater portion of these I have heard at various times from the lips of the country-folk themselves, many of whom have most willingly given me information in cases of doubt.

After each word in the Glossary I have indicated by a distinguishing letter whether it is commonly, fairly commonly, or only rarely used at the present date in the folk-speech. A word is given as in common usage if it is so in any locality in the North or East Riding, and not necessarily throughout the whole of that district. I am not aware that this has formed a feature of any previous Glossary; I have, however, made this addition because it seemed to me likely to give greater interest to a work of this kind. A few obsolete words are also inserted : these are cases

which have either only .recently fallen out of use, or
else are connected with observations which have been
made in the earlier pages of the volume.

In a large number of instances the Danish equivalents or derivations are given, and as often as possible
I have connected the Jutlandic words with our own,
bearing as they do such a close likeness, not to say
identity with them, in many cases.

In a treatise on Yorkshire Folk-talk, many pages
can hardly be otherwise than dull to any but enthu-
siasts : it has been my aim, therefore, to break the
monotony in some sort by introducing lighter touches
here and there; in the hope of making the whole more
varied and readable.

Many Yorkshiremen are seeking their fortunes or
are settled down for life in places far away from the
haunts of their younger days. Should this book fall
into the hands of any such, I shall consider myself
well repaid if it calls up before them pleasant recollections of their youth, or brings back to their
minds the familiar and well-loved tones of our rugged,
but racy and 'strengthy' folk-talk.

M. C. F. M.

Newton-on-Ouse,
        January 14th, 1892.

CONTENTS

CHAPTER VIII.

CHAPTER IX.

CHAPTER X.

CHAPTER XI.

CHAPTER XII.

YORKSHIRE FOLK-TALK.

CHAPTER I.

INTRODUCTORY.

' He gav oot sikan a stevn,' said an old man to me one day in the course of a conversation in which he was describing certain events and reminiscences of his early days. This he did in words of great force and interest. He was a Yorkshireman of the old school, and spoke the dialect in all its richness, raciness, and purity : he poured it forth as if he revelled in its very broadness, though there was in fact not a sentence but what was perfectly free and natural : it was his mother-tongue, and so best told his thoughts. To many his talk would sound almost like a foreign tongue, but his English was better than a great deal that passes for such at the present day : it is true his words and modes of expression were archaic, but it was that that gave them their charm ; they were always clear, pointed, and incisive ; it was a treat as well as a lesson to listen to him. My old friend was approaching fourscore years and ten, and when speaking of his age he would often say, 'Aye, ah think ah 's ommost gitten ti t' far end,' or 'Ah doct ah 's gannin' fast.' Nevertheless, for his years he was wonderfully hale and hearty ; he had a rich profusion

B

of silvery hair and an undimmed eye, and though
troubled with rheumatism he was still able to get about.
He had never travelled more than a few miles from the
place where he was born, or, as he quaintly expressed it,
'Ah deean't gan bauboskin aboot leyke sum on 'em ; ah
sticks ti t' heeaf.' His own 'coonthry' or 'heeaf'—
that is, the immediate neighbourhood of his home—was
to him his world, and of that he knew every inch. He
was honest as the day, and as true as steel. The likes
of him are not now often to be met. They are relics of
a bygone time.

It was the last word of the first above-quoted sentence
that chiefly arrested my attention on 'this occasion.
Yorkshireman though I was, I did not remember to
have heard it spoken before, though formerly 'stevn'
was well understood as a literary, and till lately as a
dialectic word also. The same word occurs, for instance, in *The Owl and the Nightingale*, a poem attributed
to Nicholas de Guildford, about the year 1250, where
we read at line 229,

> 'That nis noght soth, ich singe efne
>   Mid full dreme and lud stefne.'

Although this poem is written in one of the (so-called)
dialects of the South of England, we may find in it
many of our East Yorkshire words. Two occur in one
of the lines just quoted, viz. *dreme* and that just alluded
to ; the former is found in our word *dream-holes*, as
applied to the slits or holes in church towers for letting
out the sound of the bells, *dreme* or *dream* meaning
song, or musical sound ; while the latter is, as I have
observed, though rare, still current coin, and means a
loud shout, and may be connected with the modern
Danish word *stævne*, to summon or cite.

It is indeed only seldom that one hears such out-of-the-way words as these spoken in the ordinary flow of human talk; the channels in which they have for centuries run their course are wellnigh dried up. No language or dialect can ever be permanent; but with regard to our own folk-talk, it has never received such a shock as in the last quarter of a century. The language of the country people of fifty years ago is very different from what it is at the present time : much of it remains, it is true, and will remain for years to come, but much is being lost, and that speedily. As an old dame with whom I was once speaking on this point said with manifest tokens of regret, in which I fully shared, in alluding to the speech of the young folks of the present day, they 'prim it doon noo.' When I make use of the term dialect or folk-talk throughout these pages, I mean the mother-tongue of the elder portion of the community which is spoken freely among one another, but which is widely different from that which they speak before strangers or those of a different social status from themselves. No doubt all their speech has a character of its own, but that which they speak on all occasions, except when they are perfectly at their ease, is always more or less toned down. It would be thought too familiar and very unbecoming to address a stranger in their broadest speech.

It is not perhaps always understood how much is involved in the word 'dialect,' at least if we may judge by our own in East Yorkshire. It does not mean merely that a certain number, or even a large number, of peculiar out-of-the-way words are used which one does not hear elsewhere ; nor yet besides, that ordinary English words are pronounced with a strong accent, but it means, in addition to the fact of every vowel having other treatment from what it has in ordinary English, that the whole structure of sentences and modes of expression are different from what we hear elsewhere. It is scarcely too much to say that there are very few sentences of ordinary English beyond the briefest that in the mouth of Yorkshire folk of the old school would not be recast in a different mould. An example or two will illustrate my meaning. ' It is impossible ' is not a long sentence, neither is it an out-of-the-way one, but short and simple though it appears, the Yorkshireman would not so express himself; there is the Latin word *impossible*, and he does not like it, and so he says instead 'there isn't such a thing.' Or let us take such a common expression as 'he spread a report that'; here again is the Latin derivative *report*, which would be avoided thus—'he set it about that.' Yet once more, the Yorkshire way of expressing 'remind me of it' would be 'think me on about‚ it,' or again 'since I can remember,' 'since I can *tell*.'

It is remarkable, though easily accountable, how very few words other than those of Anglian or Norse extraction are made use of by our elderly people when conversing freely together. It is to be feared that in days gone by my brother clergy have not sufficiently borne this in mind in their preaching. No doubt this difficulty grows less as education spreads itself, but some half century ago the Sunday discourses in our churches must have been to many practically as an unknown tongue. In those days it is probable that not a few were like an old lady in the parish of a friend of mine in the East Riding who had invited a stranger to preach for him on one occasion. Meeting his aged parishioner in the village a few days afterwards, he enquired in the course of conversation ;—'And how did you like the sermon last Sunday, Betty?' 'Aw,' she replied, 'it wer a varry good 'un.' 'Do you think you could tell me what it was about, Betty?' asked the Vicar. 'Naw,' she says, 'ah 's seear ah can't, bud ah felt it wer varry good!' As with her, so with others: they had often to be satisfied with a sentence here and there which they could follow, and imagined the rest from the preacher's voice, intonation, and manner, which, if impressive, went a long way with them.

In days when schooling was but little thought of, some of the less educated preachers in various religious com-munities showed no little common sense in that they made no attempt whatever at fine language in their oratory, but addressed their hearers in a tongue 'under-standed of the people,' that tongue being downright good incisive broad Yorkshire; they did not beat about the bush, but went straight to the point and hit hard. I remember hearing many years ago of some preacher in the East Riding who was discoursing upon the duty of Christian forbearance, and by way of summing up some previous remarks said, with much emphasis, 'If they call ya (i.e. if they call you names) tak neea heed on 't; bud if they bunch ya or cobble ya wi steeans, gan ti t' justice, an' a'e deean wi 't at yance.' How much more forcible is this than the same idea would be when clothed in the ordinary language of the pulpit of a generation ago, which might be somewhat as follows :—' If you are brought into contact with those who make use of oppro-brious epithets towards you, remain absolutely passive with regard to them ; but if they inflict upon you griev-ous bodily injury, it may then be expedient, with a view to preventing a recurrence of similar conduct, to seek redress through the ordinary channels of legal procedure.' On another occasion, also in the East

Riding, I remember as a boy hearing of a certain preacher who worked himself to a high pitch of excitement, and who, after extending his vocal organs 'fortissimo' for a considerable length of time, found at last his throat failing him, and by degrees became so hoarse that his words were wellnigh inaudible : he went on, however, as long as possible, but ultimately had to give in, which he did with the singularly brief apology, 'Ah 's roopy,' whereupon he retired and let someone else finish. His explanation, though brief, was intelligible, and so sufficient. And this reminds me of a story of a clergyman who, in the middle of the service, found his voice giving way, and was compelled to announce to the congregation that he was 'physically incapable of proceeding,' an expression which was amusingly misunderstood by one of his hearers, who met the Vicar a few days afterwards, and in alluding to the incident, condoled with him in the following terms, ' Well, ya see, sorr, we all on us a'e ti tak physic noos an' thens !' Our roopy friend knew better than to make use of such circuitous verbiage as this clergyman did, and there could at least be no mistake with his hearers as to what he meant when he announced his incapacity to continue his discourse.

The good old-fashioned Yorkshire dialect of former days possessed so many features of its own, and such interesting features too, that the question naturally suggests itself, what account can it give of itself? in other words, what is its history? A general survey of its vocabulary, structure, and pronunciation points mainly in one direction. The home of our folk-talk lies on the other side of the North Sea. It is to the land of the Norseman that we must look for nearly all the component elements of our dialect, those elements of course I mean which may strictly be called dialectical. Speaking roughly, I should say that at least three-fourths of our Yorkshire words may be traced either directly or indirectly to Scandinavian origin. It is impossible to say when the Scandinavian adventurers first began their incursions upon this north-eastern part of the country. Ethelred began his reign in 866, but long before that time there must have been inroads made upon the country by ruthless Vikings with more or less of success, though their foothold in this part of England was not a firm and wide-spread one till after the year just named. It was not until the death of Ethelred that the Danes had strongly established themselves in Northumbria and elsewhere. The multitude of lands called after them in East Yorkshire and Lincolnshire proves the thoroughness of their conquest and the permanence of their occupation.

The great Anglian settlement which preceded that from more northerly shores has also left its traces upon the present day folk-speech of East Yorkshire, though it is by comparison only faintly defined. It is sometimes hard, if not impossible, to determine whether words still in use in Yorkshire are vestiges of the Angle or the Norseman. And then again, who can say exactly what the Anglian tongue was? Whether it was composed mainly of Western Teutonic dialects or others of Scandinavian growth, or again a mingling of these two, philologists must decide : most probably the latter is nearest the mark. That the Anglian tongue contained at least some Norse elements there can be no doubt. And so even long before the great Danish stream set in there must have been in the folk-speech of Northumbria and East Anglia at least traces of the language of the pitiless pirates who afterwards

made the country from the Tees to the Wash the
main centre of their conquests and devastations.

During the lengthy period over which the Viking
invasions extended themselves, it was East Yorkshire
and Lincolnshire especially that formed as it were the
fulcrum through which their overwhelming force was
exerted :. it was here that the pressure, so to speak,
was strongest; and to this day there is no part of
England where their impress upon the folk-talk is more
strongly marked than in these two counties.

Two Norse streams have in short poured in upon
this part of England : the first, a more or less diluted
one through the Anglian invaders; the second, an
undiluted and stronger one through the savage Viking
marauders. Whatever we may say of other parts of
England, the strongly prevailing element in our East
Yorkshire folk-talk has for wellnigh a thousand years
been Norse. What it was before that is less certain.

It would be an interesting if a laborious study to
compare the dialects of Jutland, Slesvig, Holstein, and
Holland, to say nothing of parts of Sweden. A wide
philological field here lies open from which a rich
harvest might be gathered. Let us hope that at no
distant day students will be forthcoming to take such
a work in hand. Much new light might thus be shed
on our own Yorkshire dialect.

It is asserted by writers on early English that in the
thirteenth century the speech of the country was divided
into three main dialects, viz. the Northern, the Midland,
and the Southern ; the former of these being spoken
throughout the greater part of Northumbria, as well
as in the Lowlands of Scotland, the North and East
Ridings would consequently be included within the
range of its influence.

Anyone acquainted with the Yorkshire dialect who has read my namesake Dr. R. Morris' *Specimens of Early English*, which contains numerous extracts from standard English authors from the year 1250 to 1400, cannot but be struck with the large number of words and phrases identical with those in constant use at this day among our Yorkshire country folk, but which have become rare or obsolete as literary English. When it is stated, as it has been stated, that certain of these examples are written in the Northumbrian dialect, we must clearly understand what that statement means. To suppose that these authors who are quoted wrote in the Northumbrian dialect, as we understand the word dialect, is quite misleading : they are merely specimens of English of that date, with a certain admixture of local peculiarities ; so that they give us little or no idea of what the actual speech of the country folk was. In reading through these and such-like examples, we hardly find three consecutive words of what may be called dialect pure and simple. It is unfortunate that we have so few examples recorded of what the actual folk-talk of that or a much later period was. I do not remember to have seen any at all earlier than the sixteenth century, if so early. But that there was a distinct folk-talk then, as now, none will doubt, and it is scarcely less doubtful that the speech of the tillers and the masters of the soil was much more widely separated than it is at the present day.

It is worth noticing in what a comparatively straight course the folk-speech of East Yorkshire—we might rather say of East Anglia—has seemingly run during the last thousand years. Influences which told so strongly on the state language itself seem to have made comparatively little impression upon the mother-tongue of the Northumbrian people.

In his grammatical introduction to the work just referred to, the author points out a number of differences between the northern and southern, so-called, dialects. It is interesting to see that many of these northern peculiarities still survive in full force. Thus, for instance, there is the dropping of the final *e* in irregular verbs, as in *spak* for spakest. *Sal* and *suld* (pr. sud) for *shall* and *should*. Again, the final *en* in past participles is never dropped ; thus we say *putten, ho'dden, fowten, letten,* &c., in our every-day speech for *put, held, fought, let,* &c. ; this is quite a feature in our dialect. *Fra* (from), *til* (to), though still very common in East Yorkshire, are unknown in the southern dialects ; the substitution of *k* for *ch* in such words as *bink* (bench), *kist* (chest), *skrike* (shriek), *birk* (birch), is common. Dr. Morris says, p. xix, 'As early as the latter part of the twelfth century we find a tendency in northern writers to adopt the *es* as the genitive inflexion of feminine as well as of masculine nouns.' This may be so, but whatever northern writers in the twelfth century may have done in adopting the *es* in the genitive, Northern speakers at the close of the nineteenth century very commonly do not adopt it, but continue to say, e. g., *the dog tail, the cat back*, for the dog's tail, the cat's back. The personal pronouns are frequently used reflexively, as *I rest me* (I rest myself), *sit you* (sit yourself, used actively). The northern dialect employed *gate* (way) as a suffix ; we still retain it in certain cases, e. g. *neea-gates* (no-how), *onny-gates* (any-how). *No-but* (only), so common to this day in the north, was not found in the southern dialect, and the same may be said of *at* (that). A glance at the copious notes at the end of the *Specimens of Early English*, shows how many of the old English and Anglo-Saxon words may still be heard in the folk-speech of East Yorkshire, some being identical with the mediæval usage, and others slightly changed ; as examples we may take *funden* (found), *gret* (cried`, *lathes* (barns), *bleike* (pale`, *reke* (smoke), *settle* (a seat`, *litel* (little`, *to dark* (to hide, or lie motionless).

Among the verbal inheritances from the past, we might at first sight expect to find in our Yorkshire folk-talk many vestiges of ecclesiastical terms, for in no part of England it would seem was the influence of the Church so great as in Northumbria ; and yet, if we may judge by what we know of the dialect at the present day, it is remarkable how very few words traceable to ecclesiastical sources have been introduced into it, though some there clearly are : it can have assimilated but little at any time from that quarter ; while upon the language of the country at large ecclesiastical influences made themselves felt to an extent both wide and deep. Words of Romance origin, even at the present day, are scarcely used at all by our older country people, and when they are used, their meaning is frequently misunderstood, and so they are often employed very inappropriately. It is unfortunate that they ever attempt to use them when they can express themselves more simply and plainly by the phraseology of their traditional tongue, which is so essentially a northern one.

It was the same with regard to the Norman Conquest. Words which, after that far-reaching event had taken place, were forced by the prevailing Court influence upon the language of the State into legal proceedings and documents, and which were so univer-

sally adopted by the aristocracy of the country, scarcely
touched the old and homely language of the inhabitants
of Northumbria. These were a different race, and
clung tenaciously to their Norse or Northern tongue.
It was they who influenced the language of the rest of
the country, rather than that they were influenced by it
or others. In the standard English of the present day
there is a very considerable admixture of words of
Scandinavian origin, while the proportion of words
other than Norse in the pure dialect of East Yorkshire
is, comparatively speaking, but small. This anyone
may examine for himself by studying any good philological dictionary of the English language.

As compared with Queen's English, it is not easy to
say what constitutes a dialect. To hear some discourse,
it would seem as if a mere disregard of the main rules
of English grammar, with the introduction of a sprinkling of mispronunciations, was sufficient to enable anyone to imitate the dialect of a district such as that of
which we are speaking in these pages. I need hardly
point out that such an idea is absurd and erroneous.
Dialect is far other than that. It may be said to be the
traditional unwritten speech of the people of any district. It is folk-talk as distinguished from the language
of the Court or the Government ; it is a mother-tongue,
rather than a scholastic or written tongue ; it is local
speech as distinct from national speech. I will quote
two or three words here by way of illustration. Thus
in our dialect we call a house a *hoos*, or, as it might be
written, *hus*. This, the Yorkshire pronunciation of the
word, is the traditional pronunciation. It is the ancient
sounding of the word, as it was uttered when it was
first introduced into this country, as it is still the orthodox pronunciation of it in the region from whence it

came to us. If some Member of Parliament, in address-
ing the House of Commons, were to· speak about this
Hoos, he would assuredly bring ridicule upon himself.
And yet, on philological grounds, he would be quite
within his rights in calling it *Hoos*. But, on the other
hand, if one of our native country-folk were to say to
a friend and neighbour who had just called, ' gan inti
t' *house*,' he would be considered to be *knacking*, that is,
talking in an affected, mincing manner; or, as we
sometimes express it, *scraping his tongue*. The fact is
that *hoos* is as good or better than *house*, and as there
are a considerable number of Yorkshire Members of
Parliament, possibly if they all agreed among themselves
always to call it *Hoos* instead of House, something
might be done towards restoring to the word its rightful
vowel sound.

On the same principle we say *noo* instead of *now*;
this, again, is merely a retention of the old form of the
word, and we pronounce it to this day as they do in
Scandinavia; nevertheless, *noo* would be considered
vulgar in polite society, while *now* among the country
people would be thought ridiculous. Or, again, *ah* is
the equivalent for *I* in the dialect ; it is a more euphonious vowel-sound than the generally received i-sound,
as every vocalist well knows ; but yet *ah* is dialectical,
and so is thought vulgar, coarse, and barbarous ; still
for all that, it possesses a certain interest, for to this
day over a great part of West Jutland it is preserved
as the pronunciation or an old form of the personal
pronoun.

It would not be thought the thing, in the language of
the court, to pronounce *come* as *kom* ; and yet in the
dialect we always so pronounce it, and, I may add,
quite correctly ; for thus the word has been handed

down to us from the times of the Danish settlement in
East Anglia, and so it is now pronounced in modern
Danish.

The same remarks might be repeated with regard to
the Yorkshire for *home* and *again*, which we commonly
pronounce *heeam* and *ageean*; these two words being
almost in exact agreement as to sound with their
Danish equivalents *hjem* and *igjen*. So that when we
say, as we might say, *Noo ah's kom heeam ageean*
(now I have come home again), the sentence should
not be regarded as a mere vulgar pronunciation of
standard English, which it is not, but as a really correct
Norse form of the words handed down from father to
son through ten centuries, while the classical English
equivalent is so far a deviation from its Norse
original.

I think we may say that our dialect of East Yorkshire is something very much more worthy of study
than some are apt to suppose. It is true that a great
amount of its individuality has in the course of years
been lost; still, it is not a little surprising that so much
remains, especially when we consider how small an
attempt has been made to consolidate it by men of a
poetical or literary turn of mind. What Professor Earle
says in his learned work—*The Philology of the English
Tongue*—of dialects generally is to a great extent true
of our own. He writes (p. 94):—

'Even so it is with the dialects—all their goodness is gone
into the King's English, and little remains but their vener-
able forms. Such power and beauty as they still possess
they cannot get credit for, *carent quia vate sacro*, because they
want a poet to present them at their full advantage. Where,
in some remoter county, a poet has appeared to adorn his
local dialect, we find ourselves surprised at the effect produced out of materials that we might else have deemed

contemptible. A splendid example of this is furnished by the poems of Mr. Barnes in the Dorset dialect; unless a Southern fondness misleads us, he has affiliated to our language a second Doric, and won a more than alliterative right to be quoted along with Burns.'

With these remarks I cordially agree. Our own dialect possesses power, but for this it gets but little credit with the outside world; nor will it, till some Yorkshire Burns or Barnes is raised up to show it to the world in whatever of force or beauty belongs to it.

But although, from a literary point of view, our dialect, in common with others, is so little appreciated— at least, not to the extent it might be—by any beyond a comparatively few who still take delight in it, and who are enthusiastic about it from old associations or on other grounds, yet it may be studied with interest and advantage by those of philological inclinations. In this respect a special charm seems to attach to it. And it is surprising how this pursuit grows upon the student of the dialect. At first he is only a casual observer, and his ear is slow to catch any unusual word or phrase; but his faculties are wondrously quickened in the use, and he becomes more earnest and more accurate as time goes on. It is one of the delights of the country to hear country talk as well as to see country sights. Nevertheless, how frequently it happens that those who live in the country know but little about country things, country habits of life, country work, and especially of country speech. I know that there are often difficulties in the way of a comparative stranger getting at a thorough know- ledge of the folk-talk, to which difficulties I have elsewhere alluded; still there is abundant scope for the exercise of his faculties, if he is so minded, with the means generally at his disposal. But, like everything else, the study requires perseverance, care, and accuracy of observation.

I have frequently met with persons who have lived all their lives in Yorkshire, who know little or nothing of the phraseology that is daily being uttered around them by thousands of voices,—a phraseology which will well repay investigation. And again, there are others who, though they may have a wide knowledge of the peculiar words which are in every day use with our people, are yet ignorant of those idiomatic usages and modes of expression which differ more or less from those of ordinary English.

It has been my aim in writing these pages to awaken, if it may be, a keener interest in the study of our dialect, which I believe every true Yorkshireman has an affection for, and which, when spoken in its purity, sounds like melody in his ears.

CHAPTER II.

ONE needs some apology for speaking about Grammar: of all dry and unpalatable subjects, whether for the schoolboy, or for those of maturer years, English Grammar is the driest. It has always been a marvel to me that our hard-worked schoolmasters in the Elementary Schools can ever get the country lads to learn it at all. A few years ago there were ugly rumours of strikes even among the scholars of some of our schools : I cannot but think that English Grammar must have been at the bottom of all that ! What can the ideas of the children be of Greek and Latin affixes, prefixes, and suffixes ? Multiplication no doubt vexes their youthful minds, division may do the same, rule of three may puzzle them at times, especially if it be 'double'; still even those horrors may be endured, and the young folks may perhaps come out of the ordeal all the clearer headed for it ; but of all maddening things, English Grammar must be to them the most maddening. The one consolation to them is that the Education Department, with its attendant Code, cannot follow them beyond the school precincts, that they can leave their Greek and Latin affixes, prefixes, and suffixes behind them upon the desks as soon as they get outside the

c

school doors and return—relapse or retrogress if you
like—to Yorkshire Grammar once more. I confess
that I cannot refrain from a sort of inward satisfaction
when I hear, as I have so often heard, at the close of
a long three hours in school on some fine summer day,
the sudden and joyous transition on the part of the
scholars as they rush into the fresh air, from 'Depart-
mental' to Yorkshire Grammar; it is a regular trans-
formation scene. They drop as they would a hot
potato their Greek and Latin derivations and forms,
they scatter to the four winds their distinctions between
strong verbs and weak verbs, between even singular
and plural, and fall back with evident delight and relief
to their traditional and homelier rules of speech. And
small blame to them for it. What though they say, the
moment their backs are turned upon the school, *Ah is* or
Thoo tell'd or *He ho'ded*; is not this what their fathers and
mothers have spoken before them? After all is said and
done, Grammar is but, in some sort, a fashion; and the
worst that can be said of Yorkshire Grammar is that
it is old-fashioned: to ordinary ears no doubt it may
sound barbarous or even ridiculous, but I can assure
the most rigid English grammarian that if only he could
live for a few years among a people who always prefer
to say *Ah 's* to *I am*, the former would in time sound
quite as much 'de rigueur' as the latter. It is not,
after all, such a long step from *Ah is* to *he is*; and at
least our use has the merit of uniformity; it is, moreover, quite as intelligible as what is generally deemed
the correct form.

However, in spite of outside pressure and the great
educational movement of late years, Yorkshire Grammar
is not yet quite a thing of the past, and I daresay it may
still be some little time before it is so. I have, there-

fore, given in this chapter, for the sake of those who may wish to know something of our rules of speech and to speak or write the dialect more correctly, a very brief outline of some of its more salient grammatical peculiarities. I can only hope that I shall not have ' my Lords ' of the Department down upon me for presuming to encourage or give countenance to a code of grammar antagonistic to their own, or for wishing their grammatical syllabus at a place not many miles from Jerusalem; for, as far as our dialect is concerned, I confess I do so wish it ! In any case, however, I venture to think that the scholars themselves will not quarrel with me for desiring longer life to the old rules of Yorkshire folk-talk.

The Article.

The indefinite article has the same usage as in standard English.

The definite article should be invariably written *t'*, whether before a vowel or consonant, e. g. *T' airm* (the arm), *t' hoos* (the house), *t' bairn* (the child).

It is sometimes asserted that the article is omitted before a consonant : this, I venture to think, is quite a mistake; it is not omitted in 'classical' Yorkshire, though frequently it is scarcely audible.

Sometimes (and this is especially the case in the Holderness district), the *t'* is softened down to *d'*, thus, *gan inti d' hoos* (go into the house).

The only exception to the abbreviated form of the definite article is when used before *Lord*, as applied to the Deity.

This shortening of the definite article is quite a leading feature in the dialect, and makes words which would

otherwise sound familiar become almost unintelligible
to strangers : it scarcely needs any examples to illustrate this, for it can be seen at a glance that such a
question of the tailor for instance as, *Is t' wax i·t'
windther?* would hardly be understood by a 'foreigner'
as the equivalent for 'Is the wax in the window?' Of
course the article thus abbreviated is much more clearly
heard before a vowel or *w* than before a consonant, and
again more clearly before some consonants than others :
thus, for example, it would be plainly audible before *f*,
l, or *s*; not so plainly before *b*, *m*, or *n*; while before
words beginning with *d* or *t* its presence would not be
detected except by practised ears; still, under all circumstances, it is there, and in writing the dialect as
spoken at the present day, it should never be omitted.

Number.

The plural number is formed in the ordinary way by
adding *s* to the singular; but *eye* makes *een*, *child*
becomes *childer* in the plural, and *shoe* is changed to
shoon, though in this word the old form is not now so
often used as formerly; while *hoosen* (houses) is now
but rarely heard, though even quite recently I have had
sensible proof of its lingering hold with old people in
the north-east corner of the county. In the plural of
certain words denoting space of time or quantity the
final *s* is omitted, e. g. *fo'tty year* (forty years), *fower-
teen yakker* (fourteen acres), *fahve shillin'* (five shillings).

Case.

The possessive case in *s* is not used; the simple
nouns or pronouns in juxtaposition is all that is required
to denote possession ; thus, *t' hoss heead* (the horse's
head), *t' dog wags it taal* (its tail), *Bill book* (Bill's book).

The same rule applies when more than one possessor is involved; thus, if we wished to express in correct dialectical form such a phrase as 'the dress belonging to the wife of Tom Harrison's son Peter,' we should say *Tom Harrison Pĕtther weyfe dhriss*.

Gender.

There is no deviation from the ordinary rules of gender, except that all implements, mechanical contrivances even of the simplest kind, and many tools, are of the feminine gender; thus, a watch, an oven, a scythe, a plane, &c., are all feminine, and are spoken of as 'she.'

In certain parts of the East Riding bordering on the coast, I am informed on good authority that the sea is spoken of in the feminine gender. I do not remember to have heard it myself, and so possibly this usage is only a local one.

The Adjective.

Many adjectives form their comparative and superlative by adding *er* and *est* or *r* and *st* to the positive, which in standard English would be compared by prefixing *more* and *most* to the positive. Thus :—

POSITIVE.	COMPARATIVE.	SUPERLATIVE.
Awkard.	Awkarder.	Awkardest.
Backard.	Backarder.	Backardest.
Comfortable.	Comfortabler.	Comfortablest.
Menseful.	Mensefuller.	Mensefullest.

Sometimes also an adjective which is compared irregularly will adopt the same form; as, *Lahtle, lahtler, lahtlest*.

The numeral adjective *monny* (many) is seldom used in the ordinary sense, *a deal* or *a vast* being the usual expressions. When, however, it is so used, the indefinite article is prefixed ; thus the equivalent for *many of them* is either *a deal on 'em* or *a monny on 'em.* *Great* is not used in conjunction with *deal*, the necessary intensive of it being supplied by *varry*, e.g. *a varry deal* is used for 'a great deal.'

In the same way the indefinite article is often placed before *much* without change of meaning, e.g., *There 'll be a mich ti tell*; this, however, is by no means so common as *a deal* or *a vast.*

In the termination *th* of the ordinal numerals the final *h* is always omitted in the dialect ; or perhaps it would be more correct to say that the *th* is here pronounced as *t.* Thus 'fourth, fifth, sixth,' &c., are pronounced *fowert, fift, sixt,* &c.

Frequently the adjective is used as an adverb : e.g. *yan mud easy fall* (one might easily fall) ; *it gans varry whisht* (it goes very quietly). It may be noted that the word *bettermy*, which is commonly used in the expression *bettermy folks*, is a curious example of a comparative formed by the addition of *more* (of which *my* is a corruption) to that which is already a comparative, thus forming a double comparative. It would be more correct perhaps to write the word *bettermer*, though the pronunciation is more in harmony with the other form.

The Pronoun.

The personal pronoun *I* is used as follows :—

SINGULAR.	PLURAL.
Nom. *Ah* and *I* (short) (I).	*Wǎ* (we).
Acc. *Mǎ* (me).	*Uz* (us).

The form of the nominative singular varies according to the sense and the position it occupies in a sentence, being generally *ah*, but sometimes short *i*. Thus we say *Ah mun cum* (I must come), whereas 'must I come ? ' would be expressed by *mun i cum ?* When any degree of emphasis is requisite, *ah* is always used ; thus we should say *mun ah cum or Dick ?* (must I come or Dick ?)

Thou is an important word, and in familiar speech between equals it is invariably used rather than the *you* of modern English. It is thus declined :—

SINGULAR.	PLURAL.
Nom. *Thoo, Tha* or *Ta* (thou).	*Ya* (*a*-short) (you).
Acc. *Thǎ* (thee).	*Ya* (*a*-short) (you).

In the nominative singular *thoo* is always used when it is the first word in the sentence, or elsewhere when special emphasis is required, as :—*thoo knaws* (you know), *dust thoo think at thoo can skelp mah bairn* (said in anger).

Ta is used after an auxiliary verb in ordinary familiar conversation ; as, *wilt ta cum wi ma ?* and in all questions in the second person *ta* is closely connected with the verb, so as to form part of it, as *sa'nt-ta ?* (shall you not ?), *harks-ta* (listen), *leeaks-ta* (look).

Tha is also used instead of *ta*, but no rule can be laid down with regard to the interchange of these forms.

The nominative form *thoo* is used for the accusative when stress is intended to be laid upon that word ; thus, *he 's com for thoo* and *he 's com for tha* would have a well understood distinction of meaning, the former implying that the person sought was one of many, the latter without regard to others. It is sometimes supposed that *ta* or *tha* (thou and thee) is not used except in the objective case, but as a matter of fact it is used both in the nominative and accusative cases : thus, we have the expressions *wilt tha ?* (will you ?) and *he sent tha* (he sent you).

. *He, she,* and *it* are declined in the ordinary way. *It,* however, is generally abbreviated to *'t,* especially at the end of a word, as *on 't* (of it), *wi 't* (with it) *til 't* or *tul 't* (to it), &c.

It is to be noted that in certain parts of the North Riding the abbreviation *'t* for *it* is always made, e.g. *he brak 't i two* (he broke it in two); *fettle 't up* (put it into order). The usage is not so common in other districts.

The accusatives *him, her, them* are often used for the nominative, as e.g. *him (her* or *them) at wants can gan* (he who wishes can go).

The peculiar use of the pronouns *he* and *sha* to denote 'husband' and 'wife' should be noticed. Thus the husband or wife would say in speaking of the other, *sha* (or *he) 's nut i 't hoos* (she is not in the house), neither the name nor the relationship having been previously mentioned.

Possessive Pronouns.

The possessive pronouns *mah* (my), *thah* (thy), *oor* or *wer* (our), &c., do not deviate in their use from ordinary rules. There is, however, a use of *oor* in the sense of 'belonging to our family' which is to be noted, e.g. *oor Bet* (our daughter Bet).

The compound personal and possessive pronouns most commonly in use are as follows :—*mysen* and *mysel* (myself) ; *thysen, thysel* (thyself) ; *hissen, hissel* (himself); *hersen, hersel* (herself) ; *itssen itssel* (itself); *wersens, wersels* (ourselves) ; *yersen, yersel* (yourself); *yersens, yersels* (yourselves) ; *thersens, thersels* (themselves). Of these forms, those ending in *en* and *ens* are commoner than those in *el* and *els*, though these latter are by no means infrequent, especially in the North Riding.

The personals *thoo* and *tha*, and the possessives *thah* or *thi* (thy) and *thahn* (thine), are always used in the folk-talk, *you*, *your* and *yours* being reserved for that of a supposed more refined style of speech.

As in other parts of the country, so in Yorkshire, *me* is often used for *I*; as, *John an' me's gitten across* (John and I are not on good terms).

Relative Pronouns.

The relative pronouns *who* and *which* are seldom used, *at* being substituted. *At* may be merely an abbreviation of 'that'; but with more probability it is the old Norse relative pronoun *at* unaltered.

When *who* is used relatively, which it is sometimes, the *w* is always sounded, so that *who* is pronounced sometimes as *whau* and sometimes as *wheea*; thus, *Ah deean't knaw wheea* (or *whau*)*'s gitten 't* (I don't know who has got it). Whenever used relatively, *wheea* and *whau* are employed indiscriminately.

Interrogative Pronouns.

The dialectical form of the interrogative *who* is either *wheea* or *whau*; as, *wheea's yon?* (who is that there?) *whau telled ya?* (who told you?)

Which is unchanged; as, *which on 'em is 't?* (which of them is it?)

'Whose' is pronounced *wheeas*. This word is seldom used by itself as an interrogative. For instance, it would be incorrect to say *wheeas is 't skep?* (whose is the basket?), a slight periphrasis would be adopted which requires explanation. The Yorkshire for *whose is the basket?* would be either *wheea's owes 't skep?* or *wheea belangs t' skep?* The latter of these is the simpler, and is merely a curious attaching of the greater to the smaller, a rule which holds good in all cases. With regard to the former, this written in plain English is *who is owns the skep?*—a phrase which is unintelligible grammatically, unless we supply the missing link, which is as follows : *who is (it that) owns the skep?* And this is further simplified when we bear in mind that *as* is frequently substituted for *who*, e.g. we say *them as likes* (those who like.)

In parts of the North Riding the interrogative phrase above cited would take the form, *wheea owes t' skep?* This, though less common, is plainer, and merely represents, *who owns the skep?* The word *owe* (to own) was formerly in common use ; examples of this may be found in Shakespeare, thus :—

'To parley with the sole inheritor of all perfections that a man may owe.'—*Love's Labour's Lost*, Act II, Sc. 1.

Demonstrative Pronouns.

The pronouns *this, that, these, those,* are used dialectically much in the manner of standard English, except that *yon* is generally substituted for 'that,' and *them* for 'those,' as *yon man* (that man), *them yows* (those ewes). *Yon* is seldom used with a plural noun ; though, in order to give *them* a more demonstrative force, *yonder* is frequently added, as—*them bo'ds yonder* (those birds there).

Indefinite Pronouns.

The indefinite pronouns commonly in use are the following :—*All*, *beeath* (both), *few*, *mich*, and *mickle* (much), *monny* (many), *neean* (none), *onny* (any), *sich*, *sikan*, and *sike* (such), *uther* (other), *yan* (one).

It may be noted that the old form *mich* is now much more frequently used than *mickle* (Old Norse mikill); indeed this latter is rapidly becoming obsolete.

Care must be taken to distinguish *yan* from *yah* (one). Southerners, in endeavouring to learn the dialect, frequently make mistakes over these words. *Yah* is a numeral adjective, *yan* an indefinite pronoun. Thus we should say, *yan on 'em seed nobbut yah coo i t' pastur* (one of them saw only one cow in the pasture). It would be an unpardonable mistake to say *yah on 'em*, or *yan coo.* To avoid errors of this kind it should be borne in mind that *yah* must always have another word agreeing with it, whereas *yan* may stand alone ; thus, *nobbut yan.*

It should be observed that *sike* or *sich* is used before a consonant, and *sikan* before a vowel ; as, *sike deed* (such doings), *sikan a vast on 'em* (so many of them). Sometimes, however, *sike* or *sich* is found before a vowel, as *sike yal* (such ale), and while they are used with words of both the singular and plural numbers, *sikan* is restricted to those of the singular. It often happens that in modern speech *sich* is followed by *an*, either as part of it or as a separate word, but in either case it is merely another form of *sikan.*

The Verb.

The grammatical peculiarities under this head are so numerous that it will not be possible to do more than point out some few of the principal of them. Let us begin with

The auxiliary verb TO BE.

Indicative Mood.

Present Tense.

Singular.	Plural.
Ah is (I am).	We arc.
Thoo is.	You are.
Hc is.	They arc *or* is.

In the third person plural *is* is pretty frequently used instead of *are*, e. g. *them 's good uns. T' folks is startin ti flit* (the people are beginning to remove from their house).

The ordinary English ' I am' is never heard from one end of the district to the other with those who are speaking in the dialect.

Imperfect Tense.

Singular.	Plural.
Ah wur *or* was (I was).	We wur *or* was.
Thoo wur *or* was.	You wur *or* was.
He wur *or* was.	They wur *or* was.

Future Tense.

Ah sal *or* will be (I shall *or* will be)	We sal *or* will be.
Thoo sal *or* will be	You sal *or* will be.
He sal *or* will be.	They sal *or* will be.

There is an old form of the future still in use, but dying out, which should be noted, viz. *Ah 's, Thoo 's,* &c. (I shall, thou shalt, &c.). EXAMPLE :—*Ah 's wesh ti-morn* (I shall wash to-morrow).

The distinction between *am* or *is* and *be* is pretty clearly defined, the latter being always preferred in the conditional mood. We should not say *if ah is*, but *if ah be*. Sometimes, however, *be* is used in the indicative mood, as, *theer it be* (there it is).

The imperfect *wur* might perhaps more correctly be written *wer*; it is sounded short, and the *r* is scarcely heard.

Infinitive Mood.

Present.	*Perfect.*
Ti be (to be).	Ti a'e been (to have been).

MAY.

Present Tense.

SINGULAR.	PLURAL.
Ah maay *or* mă (I may).	We maay *or* mă.
Thoo maay *or* mă.	You maay *or* mă.
He maay *or* mă.	They maay *or* mă.

Imperfect Tense.

Ah mud (I might).	We mud.
Thoo mud.	You mud.
He mud.	They mud.

Maay is more emphatic than *ma* generally, though often it is used when no emphasis is intended.

MUST.

SINGULAR.	PLURAL.
Ah mun (I must).	We mun.
Thoo mun.	You mun.
He mun.	They mun.

We may note that the negative *mun not* is always contracted into *maun't*.

HAVE.

The usages of the auxiliary 'have' are peculiar, and require some care in treatment.

The simple form of the present tense is as follows :—

SINGULAR.	PLURAL.
Ah a'e *or* ev (I have).	We a'e *or* ev.
Thoo ez *or* es.	You a'e *or* ev.
He ez.	They a'e *or* ev.

As the form of the verb varies in affirmative, negative, and interrogative phrases, it will make it clearer if we illustrate this by a simple example ; for this purpose let us give 'have taken' as a model.

SINGULAR.

Affirmative.	*Negative.*	*Interrogative.*
Ah 've ta'en (I have taken).	Ah a'e n't ta'en (I have not taken).	Ev ah ta'en ? (Have I taken ?).
Thoo 'z ta'en.	Thoo ez n't ta'en.	Es ta ta'en ?
He 'z ta'en.	He ez n't ta'en.	Ez a ta'en ?

PLURAL.

We 've ta'èn (We have taken).	We a'e n't ta'en (I have not taken).	A'e wă ta'en ? (Hav we taken ?)
You 've ta'en.	You a'e n't ta'en.	A'e yă ta'en ?
They 've ta'en.	They a'e n't ta'en.	A'e thă ta'en ?

It should be observed that the 1st pers. plur. of the negative is sometimes *we ev n't ta'en.*

In the 3rd pers. sing., and in the 1st, 2nd, and 3rd pers. plur. interrogative, I have preferred to write *ă, wă, yă, thă,* instead of *he, we, you, they,* in these cases the pronouns being pronounced short.

Imperfect Tense.

SINGULAR.	PLURAL.
Ah ed *or* ad (I had).	We ed *or* ad.
Thoo ed, ad, edst, *or* adst.	You ed *or* ad.
He ed *or* ad.	They ed *or* ad.

Imperative Mood.

Ev (have) *or* a'e.

Infinitive Mood.

Ti a'e *or* ev (to have).

PRESENT PARTICIPLE.   PAST PARTICIPLE.

Evvin' (having).   Ed *or* ad (had).

In the imperative, *ev* is used before a vowel, and *a'e* before a consonant ; as, *ev it riddy* (have it ready) ; *a'e nowt ti deea wiv 'em* (have nothing to do with them). *Ev*, however, is sometimes used before a consonant instead of *a'e*, but there is no rule as to when it shall be so used.

SHALL.

The verb *s'al* (shall) requires no special remark, except that with a negative it becomes *sahn't*, and sometimes *sal nut*: thus, *ah s'al rahd* (I shall ride), *ah sahn't rahd*, or *ah sal nut rahd* (I shall not ride).

The Conditional Mood.

The use of the conditional form of the verb 'to be' in any sentence has been already noticed. I may here repeat, however, that *if I be* is always preferred to 'if I am'; thus—*If ah be owt leyke* (if I am fairly well). The conditional form of a verb is often introduced by *nobbut*; thus in the last example it would be equally correct to say *nobbut ah be owt leyke*.

In order further to illustrate the peculiarities of the verb, we will here add one or two tenses of the verb 'to do.'

Indicative Mood.

Present Tense.

SINGULAR.	PLURAL.
Ah deea *or* diz (I do).	We deea.
Thoo diz.	You deea.
He diz.	They deea.

Perfect Definite Tense.

SINGULAR.	PLURAL.
Ah 's *or* ah 've deean (I have done).	We a'e *or* 've deean.
Thoo 's deean.	You a'e *or* 've deean.
He 's deean.	They a'e *or* 've deean.

It should be noted that in the 1st, 2nd and 3rd pers. plur. *we 've*, &c., are used affirmatively, and *we a'e*, &c., negatively and interrogatively, e.g., *we 've deean ; we a'e n't deean ; a'e wa deean ?*

The first future, *Ah s'al deea*, or *Ah 'll deea*, and the second future, *Ah s'al a'e deean*, are declined regularly.

General Remarks.

As has been already observed, the adoption of *is* for 'am', admits of no exception ; its use is often very deliberate and emphatic. EXAMPLE :—*Ah is glad.* Again, Q. Are you John Smith ? A. *Ah is.*

The future tense is frequently used for the present. Thus : Q. Is William younger than Dick ? A. *Ah se think he will. Yon 'll be John* (that no doubt is John).

The other most common verbal divergences from standard English in the dialect are to be found in the formation of the perfect and of the participle, especially the latter.

The vowel-changes here, as compared with standard English, are numerous and irregular ; it would be difficult to classify these deviations from ordinary usage ; it will, therefore, be sufficient merely to add a list of some of the more ordinary ones.

By far the commonest change is the addition of *en* to the past participle ; indeed, it may be said to be the rule for the past participle to take this form.

Thus we have :—

PRESENT.	PERFECT.	PARTICIPLE.
A'e or Ev (have).	Ed.	Ed.
Beeat (beat).	Bet.	Bet *or* Betten.
Beeld (build).	Belt.	Belt.
Bid (bid).	Bad.	Bidden *or* Bodden.
Binnd (bind)	Bun.	Bun.
Bleead (bleed).	Blid, bled, *or* blaad.	Bledden.
Brek *or* Breke (break).	Brak.	Brokken.
Brust (burst).	Brast.	Brussen *or* Brossen.
Checas (choose).	Choaze.	Chozzen.
Creeap (creep).	Crep *or* crop.	Croppen.
Cum (come).	Cam *or* com.	Cum'd.
Cut (cut).	Cut.	Cutten.
Ding (throw down).	Ding'd *or* dang.	Ding'd.
Drahve (drive).	Drave.	Drovven.
Fele (hide).	Felt.	Felten.
Feyght (fight).	Fowt.	Fowten.
Finnd (find).	Fan.	Fun.
Flig (fly).	Fligg'd.	Fligg'd.
Fling (fling).	Flang.	Flung.
Flit (change one's abode).	Flitted.	Flitten.
Freeze (freeze).	Fraze.	Frozzen.
Gi'e (give).	Gav.	Gi'en (pr. geen).
Git (get).	Gat.	Gitten, getten, *or* gotten.
Grave (dig).	Grave.	Grovven.
Greeap (grope).	Grape.	Groppen.
Grund *or* Grahnd (grind).	Grund.	Grunded *or* Grun'.
Hear (hear).	Heerd.	Heerd.
Hing (hang).	Hang *or* hung.	Hung *or* Hing'd.
Ho'd (hold).	Ho'ded.	Ho'dden.
Ho't (hurt).	Ho't.	Ho'tten.
Kep *or* kip (catch).	Kept *or* kipt.	Keppen, kippen, kept *or* kipt.
Lig (lay).	Lig'd *or* Lihd.	Lihn.

D

PRESENT.	PERFECT.	PARTICIPLE.
Lig (lie).	Lig'd.	Liggen or Lig'd.
Lit (let).	Lit or let.	Litten or letten.
Leet (light).	Let.	Letten.
Loss (lose).	Lost.	Lossen.
Mow (mow).	Mew.	Mow'd or mown.
Preeave (prove).	Preeav'd.	Provven.
Put (put).	Put.	Putten.
Rahd (ride).	Rade.	Ridden.
Rahse (rise).	Rase.	Risen.
Rahve (tear).	Rave.	Rovven.
Saw (saw).	Sew (pr. sue).	Saw'd or Sawn.
See (see).	Seed.	Seen.
Sell (sell).	Sell'd.	Sell'd.
Sew (sew).	Siew.	Sew'd or sewn.
Set or sit (set).	Set.	Setten.
Shak (shake).	Shak't.	Shak't or shakken.
Shoe (shoe, as e.g. of a horse).	Shod.	Shodden.
Shut (shut).	Shut.	Shutten.
Sit (sit).	Sat.	Sitten.
Smit (infect).	Smitted.	Smitted or smitten.
Snaw (snow).	Snew.	Snaw'd or snawn.
Speak (speak).	Spak.	Spokken.
Splet (split).	Splet.	Spletten.
Spreed (spread).	Sprade.	Spridden.
Stan' (stand).	Stood.	Stooden.
Stick (stick).	Stack.	Stucken.
Strahd (stride).	Strade.	Strodden.
Strahve (strive).	Strave.	Strovven.
Strike (strike).	Strake or strak.	Strukken.
Sweer (swear).	Sware or swar.	Sworn.
Tak (take).	Teeak or teuk.	Ta'en.
Tell (tell).	Telled.	Telled.
Thrahve (thrive).	Thrave.	Throvven.
Thrust (thrust).	Thrast.	Thrussen.
Treead (tread).	Trade.	Trodden.
Win (win).	Wan.	Won.
Worrk (work).	Wrowt.	Wrowt.
Wreyte (write).	Wrate.	Written.

The verb is frequently placed at the end of a sentence when ordinarily it would occupy another position. No rule can be given on this point; it will best be illustrated by a few examples: thus the common Yorkshire equivalent for 'it has turned very cold' is *it's varry cau'd tonn'd.* Or again, 'Harry had to go to York,' would very generally be thus expressed: *Harry had ti York ti gan.* Frequently we find the verb reiterated at the end of a sentence, e.g. *it's a useful thing is a laatie*; or again, *Sha wer nobbut an oot o' t' waay body was n't Mary.*

The Adverb.

The adverbial peculiarities are numerous, some of which will be noticed here.

The following are some of the adverbs most commonly in use, with their equivalents :—

ADVERBS OF TIME.

Afoor (before), *allus* or *awlus* (always); *for awlus* is equivalent to 'continually'; *eftther* (after), *i'-noo* (soon), *mostlins* (generally); sometimes 'in general' is used, but 'generally' is not heard in the dialect; *nivver* (never), *sen* (since), *ti-morn* (to-morrow), *yesternect* (last night). We may observe that *yance ower* is the equivalent for 'once,' 'on one occasion,' 'at one time'; thus—*Ah thowt ah wer boun ti be badly yance ower* (I thought I was going to be ill at one time). *Tahm by chance* is used for 'occasionally.'

ADVERBS OF PLACE.

Aback (behind), *aboon* (above), *ahint* (behind), *atwixt* (between), *onywheers* (anywhere), *sumwheers* (somewhere).

ADVERBS OF MANNER, DEGREE, NUMBER, &c.

Ablins (possibly), *aye* (yes, indeed), *eneeaf* (enough), *fair* (quite). EXAMPLE :—*Ah 's fair bet*, i.e. I am quite beaten, *ginner, as lief, liefer* (rather, sooner), *happen* (perhaps), *mebbe* (perhaps), *mich* (much ; 'too' is never used before 'much,' but always *ower*), *naw, neea, nooa, naay* (no), *nobbut* (only), *part* (many, much, a large quantity of anything), *partlins* (partly), *reetlins* (rightly), *seemlins* (seemingly), *varry* (very). *Strange* is also commonly used for 'very,' as *stthrange queer deed.* *Despert* again, is used in the same way. *Sairly* has a like meaning, for which the corresponding adjective with *and* is sometimes substituted ; thus we may say, *he wer sairly vexed*, or, *he wer sair an' vexed.* *Weel* (well), *what for?* (why ?), *whya* (well—in assent).

The ordinary adverbial termination *ly* is not so common in the dialect as in ordinary English, *lins* sometimes taking its place, and sometimes the adjective is used instead of the adverb. *That, whahl* take the place of *so, that*; thus—*Ah 's that badly whahl ah can deea nowt* (I am so poorly that I can do nothing).

Better is often used for 'more,' e.g. *he 's been oot o' work better 'an a fo'tnith* (he has been out of work more than a fortnight).

The adverbs of affirmation and negation require notice. *Yes* is not used in familiar speech, but when employed otherwise it is pronounced *yis*; the wellnigh universal equivalent is *aye*.

The adverb of negation has four forms, all of which are in more or less common use, viz. *naw, neea, nooa*, and *naay.* That in most general use is *naw ; naay* is seldom used except when accompanied by a phrase following in close connection, e.g. *naay, noo, thoo maunt git that inti yer heead*; in such connections it is very common.

The Conjunction.

The conjunctions most commonly in use are the following :—*an'* (and), the *d* being never sounded ; *'an* (than), *an' all* (also, as well)—this last is a word of very general use ; it is also used as an adverb in the sense of 'indeed,' e.g. *ah did an' all*, i.e. 'I did indeed'; in the same sense *that* is used, e.g. *ah did that*; *at* (that), *bud owivver* (still, nevertheless), *if in case, if so be* (common redundancies for 'if'), *nowther* (neither), *seea* (so), *sen* (since). *Withoot, wi'oot, widoot, bedoot* (unless), *whahl* (until).

NOTE. *As* is used instead of 'rather than'; thus, *ah thowt he'd betther cum yam as staay wheer he was* (I thought he had better come home rather than stay where he was).

For to is commonly used for 'in order to,' thus :—*ah 's here for ti deea t' job* (I am here in order to do the job).

The Preposition.

Some of the prepositions most commonly in use in the dialect are given below, together with a few illustrative examples.

Aboon (above). EXAMPLE:—*It leeaks bad aboon heead* (it looks bad above head).

Afoor (before). EXAMPLE :—*Afoor lang* (before long).

Again (against).

Ahint (behind).

Amang, sometimes abbreviated to *mang* (among).

Fra, frev (from): *fra* is used before a consonant or *y*;

frev, before a vowel. EXAMPLE :—*Ah cums fra York ;
ah cums frev 'Ull* (I come from York—Hull).

Inti, intiv, intil, intul (into). *Intil* and *intul* are more
prevalent in the North than in the East Riding. *Intiv*
is only used before a vowel. EXAMPLE :—*He cam intiv
oor toon* (he came into our village); *ah didn't put nowt
intul 't* (I did not put anything into it).

Nearhand (near). The preposition *near* is never
used without the suffix *hand*. *Nearhand* is also used in
the sense of 'nearly,' e.g. *nearhand fahve pund* (nearly
five pounds).

Ower (over).

Ower-anenst (over against).

Wi, wiv (with . *Wiv* is only used before a vowel ;
wi before a consonant and occasionally before a vowel
also. EXAMPLE :—*Wi sum on 'em* (with some of them) ;
ah wrowt wiv 'im, or *ah wrowt wi 'im* (I worked with
him).

With is always used instead of *by* in the sense of
by means of; thus, *ah 'll send it wi t' carrier,* by the carrier;
also for *by* simply, as, *he lives wiv hissen,* i.e. by himself.

At is used for *on* when it signifies point of time, e.g.
ah seed him at Settherda (I saw him on Saturday). The
curious use of this preposition must not be mistaken for
an abbreviated form of *on 't,* from which it is wholly
distinct. In the southern part of the North Riding this
usage of *at* is exceedingly common.

Of instead of 'for' is found in the expressions *of a long
while, of a good bit,* &c., meaning 'for a long time.'

The Interjection.

The noteworthy interjections are the following :—
Aa! (oh), expressive of admiration.
Aw! (oh).

Ger awaa ! or *ger awaa wi' ya !* (pooh !), literally ' get away with you !' said especially to throw disbelief or doubt on an assertion.

Noo ! (well !), the common form of salutation made by two friends on meeting.

Sitha, lo' tha, lo' ya, leeaks ta ! (lo ! look !)

Well-owivver ! (indeed !), an expression of surprise.

Whisht, whisht wi' ya ! (hush !).

For other grammatical usages and examples of rules already given, I must refer the reader to the specimens of the dialect to be found in the body of the work as well as to those in the Glossary.

CHAPTER III.

FEW writers ever had a closer acquaintance with the folk-speech of their country than Sir Walter Scott. The frequent illustrations he gives of the Lowland Scottish tongue, so closely allied to our East Yorkshire vernacular, give additional life and interest to his ever-fresh writings. Another Sir Walter Scott there can never be again; still, it may be wished that we had some native Yorkshireman of literary fame who would take up our own folk-talk somewhat in the same spirit at least as the author of *Waverley* did that of his country.

The attempts which authors sometimes make to introduce touches of the Yorkshire tongue into their writings are, it must be confessed, for the most part failures; the older country-folk would, I feel sure, be generally at a loss to know what such parodies of their parlance were meant for. This failure can only be explained by the fact that it is not altogether an easy thing for those who live at a distance from it to know any country speech well. Even the mighty literary gifts of Sir Walter Scott would have failed him in this particular had he not lived all his life among the people whose language he so often reproduced; nor would that have sufficed had he not besides constantly held intercourse with the country folk themselves, and so become at first hand thoroughly in touch with their habits of life as well as with their modes of thought and expression ; in short, had he not been perfectly 'at home' with them. In this way, and in this way only, can a folk-talk be really known.

Our country people here are in a sense bi-lingual, like the Welsh ; with this difference, that the two varieties of speech which the Yorkshireman makes use of are not so widely dissimilar as in the case of the Welshman. Still, our people have the language which they employ when talking freely among themselves and that which they make use of when conversing with strangers or those of another class than their own ; these two modes of speech are quite distirct. And here one of the great—perhaps I should say the great—difficulty in acquiring a thorough mastery of the Yorkshire dialect presents itself. The people are most reluctant to address an outsider, so to speak, in terms they would employ amongst themselves ; as before stated, to do so would be thought disrespectful. I am speaking now, be it observed, of what remains of the dialect in all its purity, which is quite another thing from indifferent English with a strong provincial accent and a quaint word or two thrown in here and there. It is only by stealth as it were, and that 'by habs and nabs,' as we say, that a stranger can learn much of the true folk-talk of the country ; and even then his ear must be quick and sensitive, for the chances are ten to one if you ask a Yorkshireman to repeat again a sentence containing some out-of-the-way word or phrase which you failed at first to catch, that on the second occasion he will make use of a different word altogether, and perhaps will reconstruct his sentence in the mould of every-day English.

And further, your difficulties will not be lessened if your
friend has the least inkling that you are attempting to
extract information of a literary kind from him ; in that
case your chance is wellnigh hopeless, and you may as
well *lap up* at once : it is only when they are absolutely
at their ease that they will converse freely in their
mother-tongue. Sometimes too their homelier phrases
may be best heard when under the influence of excitement or strong emotion. Frequently has it occurred to
me, in the ordinary course of conversation with our
country-folk, that I have caught the first syllable or
perhaps only the first letter of some every-day and
familiar word which, before the utterance was completed,
has been replaced by some supposed more polite but,
perhaps, in reality far less expressive one. It is naturally, as I have said, when under excitement or the
influence of deep feeling that their language is of the
purest.

A rather remarkable instance of this I well remember.
I was visiting a poor woman some years ago, whose son
had recently died : she was describing to me minutely
the course of the lad's long illness, and especially the
final phases of it ; but when she came to tell me of his
last moments, what he said to her and she to him, her
words suddenly changed from those of more or less
ordinary English, in which she had up to that point been
speaking, to those of the broadest dialect : her deep
feeling seemingly drew forth the language of her heart,
and she fell back instantly and unconsciously upon her
mother-tongue.

Another case comes to me which further illustrates
the point. On this occasion I was visiting a parishioner
who was dangerously ill. The aged mother of the sick
man was standing by as I was enquiring about his

malady. He was in a very weak state : he could do scarcely anything for himself. Says the mother, 'he 's neca f—— : he can deea nowt for hissen.' There was a sudden pull up at the letter f. I knew what it meant : she was going to say 'he 's neea fend aboot him ' ; only she thought it would be a little more polite to turn the expression in the way she did.

In speech the utterance of the Yorkshire people is for the most part somewhat slow and deliberate. Words are not wasted in the expression of thought ; and although the vocabulary of the older people may be rather limited, yet this deficiency is more than made up for by the force of the words which they have at command, and by the manner and intonation with which they are spoken. In the language of the blue jacket, they may not have many shot in their locker, but every shot tells.

In the following remarks upon the pronunciation of our dialect I cannot hope to do more than give but a very imperfect idea, to those unacquainted with it, of what it sounds like. It must be heard to be appreciated : no amount of explanation of which my limited powers are capable can convey an absolutely correct impression of certain of the vowel-sounds : they can only be approximated by the ordinary methods of pen and ink.

A former Bishop of St. David's, so the story goes, on first coming to take up his abode in Wales, was wishful to learn something of the language. The pronunciation proved a difficulty, and especially that of the Welsh *ll*. It was a veritable *crux*. The learned prelate did not like to be beaten, and so with a view to overcoming, as he thought, all obstacles, he engaged a native Welsh scholar to give him instruction in the language. The Welshman, who was very obsequious in manner, saw

that the Bishop had great difficulty with the *ll*, but how
to explain accurately the lingual process by which this
formidable sound was to be correctly uttered he knew
not. He was almost at his wits' end for an explanation.
At last a bright thought struck him, though he felt a
little shy in putting it point-blank to his illustrious
pupil; accordingly, he coated the pill with as much
sweetness as he was able, and with deferential utterance
addressed the Bishop thus: 'Your Lordship must please
to put your episcopal tongue to the roof of your apostolic
mouth, and then hiss like a goose!' I do not think we
have anything quite as bad in the Yorkshire dialect as
the Cymric *ll*; still, the same kind of difficulty attends it
that there does any foreign tongue; the southerners can
never frame to pronounce it aright, or as I once saw it
rather oddly expressed somewhere, 'It takes a Yorkshireman to talk Yorkshire.'

By no ordinary method of spelling is it possible, as I
observed, in all cases to give the true and exact pronunciation of our folk-talk, and the scientific devices
adopted by modern philologists in recording the finer
gradations of the vowel-sounds, valuable though they
might be, would be out of place in these pages; but even
with these aids errors are liable to creep in, for the specimens given in those philological treatises dealing with
the subject are often of necessity received second or
third hand. Some of those interested in the dialect
have suggested half-jokingly that the phonograph should
be brought into requisition in registering the tones of
the folk-speech. The idea is a delightful one, no doubt,
but there is one insuperable difficulty in the way of its
being carried out. It is no easy matter to get the old
folks to talk their broadest every-day speech to you in
the ordinary interchange of ideas; there is always a

certain unwillingness about it; and I am thoroughly
convinced that one would have about as much chance
of inducing them to talk their archaic Yorkshire into
a phonograph as of getting them to play a sonata of
Beethoven.

And so I have fallen back upon the more easily
understood, if less scientific, plan of using the ordinary
letters and spelling in writing the dialect. This, I
admit, is not always satisfactory, for some of the dialectical vowel-sounds are so unlike anything we find in
standard English that it requires a certain amount of
artifice to indicate them. Let me, by way of explanation,
take a single example. There are few vowel-sounds
more difficult to pronounce than that in the common
word *owt* (anything). This word is not pronounced as
out, nor as *ought*, nor yet as *ote* in *wrote*. The best
indication I can give of the true sound is to say that it
is about half way between *ote* and *out*. It is a very
shibboleth. The pronunciation of the following short
sentence would be no bad test as to whether a man is a
native or not: *Dust thoo knaw owt aboot it?* (Do you
know anything about it?)

There is, unfortunately, no recognised system of
spelling in the dialect. It is hardly to be looked for
that there should be. Our native writers of the folk-
speech are few and far between, at least those of any
note. Of dialect poets worthy of the name we have
none. In our wide county and with our rich vocabulary
this failure is rather remarkable: but with a people so
eminently practical and matter-of-fact as the Yorkshire
folk are there is perhaps not so much room for wonder
after all. This lack of high-class dialectical literature
throws one upon one's own resources a good deal in the
matter of orthography.

My aim on this point has been to give, by aid of the spelling, some indication of the pronunciation by a comparison with a corresponding spelling in 'Queen's English.' I am afraid that the spelling may not be found to be quite consistent throughout. Still, I trust it may be thought sufficiently so, and that it may be easily read, at least by those who are acquainted with the dialect at all.

The letter-sounds will be briefly touched upon presently; but there is one letter so especially characteristic of the dialect, that a few preliminary words may be said upon it. That letter is *a*. I know of no other part of England where it is pronounced exactly as it is in Yorkshire. It is heard to greatest advantage when uttered by itself as an interjection expressive of admiration.

I remember very well a woman once describing to me a big Sunday School gathering which she had seen when on a visit to a relative in the West Riding. It was a gigantic affair ; and the children, dressed in a sort of uniform, passed by her in hundreds, if not thousands. From the way she spoke I imagined my friend had never before witnessed such a spectacle. She described minutely every detail, and summed up with the remark, '*Aa! they did leeak bonny.*' The words were simple, but there was an indescribable expressiveness in the pronunciation of the introductory interjection which spoke volumes. It was drawn out to a great length, and in sound approached closely the *a* in 'air,' care being taken to detach it from the 'ir.' I draw special attention to this letter-sound and the description of it, because essentially the same, though not so extended a pronunciation of it, takes place in every word where the *a*-sound, as in 'rate,' occurs : of such words there are, of course, a large number. The pronunciation in these cases is generally indicated by *aa*, c. g. *laate, braad, maade, flaad, 'caashon, raade, saave, braay, a-gaat, waay, saay*, &c.

The ordinary middle *a* which is found in such words as 'back,' 'man,' 'hand,' is in the dialect changed to a broader sound, not easy to indicate accurately, but unmistakeable when heard; it is not so extended as *ah*, nor yet is it by any means equivalent to the short *o*, as is sometimes supposed : it may be best likened to the short *ah*, only that the sound is abrupt; so that 'back,' 'man,' 'hand,' and all similar words might be written *băhk, măhn, hăhnd*, &c. But this spelling looks awkward, and might easily be misunderstood ; I have therefore adopted the ordinary spelling in these cases.

The *ah*-sound pure and simple occurs very frequently ; we have it in *ah* (I), *mah* (my), *thahn* (thine), also in *wahrm* (warm\), *dwahrf* (dwarf), *tahm* (time), *stthrahd* (stride), *rahd* (ride), and in numberless other words.

The short *a*-sound is also of frequent occurrence; we meet with it, for instance, in *ma* (me), *tha* (thee), *wa* (we), *fra* (from) ; also very generally in all words ending in *ay* or *ey*, as *Sunda* (Sunday), *Bev'la* (Beverley), &c. : in all such cases it is sounded rather abruptly, as in 'enigma.'

A great amount of expression can be thrown into the Yorkshire *a* by the modulation of the voice ; so much so as to give quite a different meaning to the same word when it occurs. This, for instance, is the case with *naay* in such sentences as '*Naay, ah deean't knaw*' (I am sure I cannot tell), and '*Naay, noo, ah's nut boun' ti beleeave that*' (you are mistaken if you suppose I am going to believe that). The difference in the modulation of the voice in pronouncing the word *naay* in these

two examples at once prepares us for a different frame
of mind in each case.   In fact, the altered tone gives
practically an altered meaning to the word.   The same
thing occurs in ordinary English.   There are many
ways, for example, of saying 'yes'; it may be pronounced so as to mean 'I assent to that,' or 'I am
doubtful,' or 'indeed ?' and so forth.   Professor Max
Müller, in alluding to this point, in his *Lectures on the
Science of Language,* gives an amusing illustration of
these modulations in the Annamitic language, where
the word 'ba' pronounced with a grave accent means
a lady, an ancestor ; pronounced with the sharp accent it
means the favourite of a prince ; pronounced with the
semi-grave accent it means what has been thrown away ;
pronounced with the grave circumflex it means what is
left of a fruit after the juice has been squeezed out ;
pronounced with no accent it means three ; pronounced
with the ascending or interrogation accent, it means
a box on the ear.

Thus 'Ba bà bâ bá,' is said to mean, if properly
pronounced, 'Three ladies gave a box on the ear to
the favourite of a prince.'

Now, although the modulations of the voice of the
Yorkshireman are said to be expressive, yet I think it
will be admitted that he must yield to the men of Annam
in that respect.   Still, in our dialect a good deal may be
expressed in a small compass by merely giving different
modulations to the letter *a* for instance ; and the different gradations of the vowel-sound are numerous.   These
will be alluded to presently.   In our every-day speech
we might have at least three different *a*-sounds in one
short sentence, thus :—

A, bud a an 't.

This would be equivalent to, 'Indeed I have not.' The first *a* is the peculiar Yorkshire *a*, the pronunciation of which is indicated on another page, and for convenience might be written *aa* ; the second is the ordinary Italian *a*, and may be written *ah* ; the third is shorter than the first, and is perhaps best described in writing as *ae*, though it should be noted that there is here but one vowel-sound. It may be observed that none of the three *a*-sounds Here given is anything like the ordinary English *a* ; that sound does not exist in the dialect at all : it is quite foreign to it. All the different gradations of this vowel in our folk-speech are single, and therefore purer vowels than the ordinary English *a*. We may illustrate this by a single instance. Take, for example, the word 'made' ; here the *a* is pronounced as a double vowel, the latter part of which is a distinct *e* or *ee* ; but in the Yorkshire form of the word *maade* there is but one vowel-sound pure and simple. It is the same in principle with the other two examples given above. In the latter of them the sound corresponds very closely with that of the Danish *æ*. It is important to notice these distinctions in pronouncing the dialect, for mistakes are frequently made on this point.

In so large an area as that comprised within the limits of the North and East Ridings, one might reasonably expect certain diversities of pronunciation and expression ; nor are such diversities wanting : still, they are, comparatively speaking, few, and need not be dwelt upon. The main features of the dialect are identical all the district through.

What then, it may be asked, are the leading characteristics of the dialect ? I will try and point them out.

E

First, *the pronunciation of the letter ' u.'*   In no part of
England is this vowel uttered with a closer adhesion to
its correct and ancient sound than here; it is the true
u-sound, and cannot be mistaken.   We have it indeed
in certain words still in standard English, e. g. full,
pull, bull, put, push, &c., but these instances are, comparatively speaking, few ; the sound is quite lost in such
words as sun, must, run, but, rub, up, under, hunt, and
many other which might be named ; but in Yorkshire
the genuine *u*-sound is retained in all these words without exception ; we delight in it.   In some words it is
rather more strongly marked than in others, especially,
e.g., in *bud* (but), where the *u* treads closely upon the
heels of the *oo*-sound, but never quite reaches that limit.
Who that has ever heard the expression, *Cum thi
waays, huney*, as spoken by a mother to her bairn, can
doubt for a moment what the true pronunciation of the
old English, or Norse, or Anglo-Saxon *u* must have
been ?

One of my early recollections when coming home
from school was to hear called out at Milford Junction
' Change here for Hull,' the *u* being always given with
its characteristic Northern accent.   The pronunciation
of that single vowel told me that I was not far from the
borders of Northumbria.

Closely connected with the *u*-sound pure and simple
is the *oo*-sound, which may be regarded as an extension
of it.   A large number of words which in standard
English take the *ou*-sound, as in 'out,' in the dialect
rigidly keep to the *oo* or *u*-sound.   Such, e. g., is the
case with cow, now, house, ground, mouse, town,
gown, found, round, out, brown, &c. ; in all such
words the *oo*-sound predominates over the *u*, but in
these cases it is not easy to draw the line which

separates the two, so gradually do they shade off into one another.

It may, however, be said without hesitation that the *ou*-sound of standard English is never heard in the dialect at all ; the nearest approach to it is perhaps in the isolated word *pownd* (a pond), the pronunciation of which is peculiar and exceptional, the *ow* being like neither that in 'own' nor in 'frown,' but between the two. The pronunciation of *owt* (anything), already alluded to, and *lowze* (to loose), are also approximations to the *ou*-sound, but yet quite distinct in each case. On the other hand, by a strange perversity, certain words which in ordinary English possess the true *u*-sound, are in the dialect changed variously. Take, for instance, such words as book, cook, foot, &c. The first of these has no less than three pronunciations, viz. *beeak, bewk,* and *book,* in which last the *oo* is pronounced as in 'root'; 'cook' has two pronunciations, viz. *ceeak* and *cook,* the *oo* being here again long. 'Foot' is invariably pronounced *feeat.*

As a general rule, then, the pure *u*-sound is retained in the dialect in all those words which in standard English are spelt with a *u,* and adopted or preserved in many others which are spelt with *ou* or simple *o.* This, as I said, forms a very marked feature of our dialect, and not the least pleasing one ; for when the ordinary *ow*-sound, as in 'how,' and the Yorkshire *u* or *oo* are sounded side by side, it is not difficult to decide which of the two is the more euphonious.

The second strong characteristic of the pronunciation of the dialect is *the prevalence of the eea-sound.* It is quite remarkable what a large proportion of our vowel-sounds take this form. Nearly all standard English words in which the *e* and *a* are found in juxtaposition

and form one syllable, are in the dialect distinctly and
almost invariably sounded as two syllables, a certain
amount of stress or accent being laid upon the *e*.

It would perhaps be more correct to say that formerly
the *ea* was pronounced as two syllables, and while in
course of time this double sound has gradually merged
into one in the English language of the present day, in
the Yorkshire dialect the old double sound goes on as
of yore.

The word 'meat,' for example, is in the dialect pronounced *meeat*; so too, dread, dream, head, bread,
instead, lean, mean, speak, team, leave, leaf, &c.,
become *dreead, dreeam, heead, breead, insteead, leean,
meean, speeak, teeam, leeave, leeaf*, &c. 'Lead' (the verb)
is generally, however, pronounced in the ordinary way,
while 'learn' and 'earn' are changed to *larn* and *arn*
in the dialect.   Again, words having the ordinary
English *a*-sound generally, but not invariably, come
under this head, and take the *eea*-sound in the folk-
speech.   For instance, cake, dame, name, lame, same,
safe, tale, waste, &c., are changed to *cceak, deeam,
neeam, leeam, seeam, seeaf, teeal, weeaste*, &c.   Sometimes, when the pronunciation is very broad, the *eea*
almost develops into a *y*-sound; but it is incorrect to
write it so; I have therefore in all cases disregarded
this tendency in the examples given.   But a much
larger class of words, containing the vowel-sounds *o* or
oo, are attracted as it were by main force to the *eea*-
sound.   Thus 'stone' becomes *steean* (though *stane*, and
very rarely *stein*, are also used), 'fool' becomes *feeal*,
and floor, roof, door, noon, school, soon, no, do, so,
spoke (of a wheel), bone, cool, whole, boot, foot, root,
look, home, proof, with many others that might be
named, are pronounced *fleear, reeaf, deear, neean, scheeal*,

seean, neea, deea, seea, speeak, beean, keeal, heeal, beeat, feeat, reeat, leeak, heeam (also *yam*), *preeaf.*

Again, some words in 'ough'—namely, enough, plough, tough, bough, &c., in the dialect must be written as they are pronounced, *eneeaf, pleeaf, teeaf, beeaf* (also *bew*), &c. ' Rough ' is, however, pronounced with the *u*-sound, and the same may be said of *brough.* From the above few examples I have given, it will be seen what a strong leaning there is in our dialect towards this *eea*-sound ; so much so, indeed, that I have no hesitation in regarding it as one of its three most salient marks.

The third feature of the dialect to which I shall draw attention, is the very peculiar use of an abbreviated form of the definite article in particular, *and of abbreviations generally.* The abbreviation of ' the ' to *t'* is practically a universal rule.

It is scarcely to be wondered at that strangers are given to think that the definite article is omitted in our dialect, if not generally, at least in a great number of cases, for it has that effect with south-countrymen. The truth is that their ears being unused to this shortening of the article, they fail to catch the *t'*-sound, lightly touched by the tongue as it generally is, especially before consonants. I grant that sometimes it may be omitted in rapid speech, just as in ordinary English words and letters are not unfrequently slurred. But that is not the rule. The rule is in all cases to sound it, and sounded it always should be, however lightly in some connections. In the following sentence it may be thought difficult to pronounce the article before each word, where it occurs, e.g. *T' bairns drave t' coo ti t' pastur aback o' t' toon* ; but even where the word following begins with *t,* the article may be invariably detected, not indeed by a double movement of the tongue, but, as in the two words *t' toon* in this sentence, by a very slight and almost imperceptible pause between the *t* and *toon*.

As regards abbreviations generally, I need hardly do more here than merely allude to them ; they will be best understood by examining the numerous examples of the dialect I have given in the vocabulary at the end, and in other specimens of the folk-talk throughout the volume. Let the following instances suffice to indicate what is meant. The conjunction 'and' and the noun 'hand' always have the *d* elided ; 'than' becomes *an* ; 'with' is changed to *wi*; ' it ' is shortened to '*t*, especially at the end of a sentence ; but in Cleveland this abbreviation is universal : 'of' very commonly becomes *o*' and 'have,' *a'e*. It would perhaps be incorrect to say that our Yorkshire *at* is an abbreviated form of 'that' e.g. *ah tell'd him at*, &c., for it is by no means improbable that this may be the traditional usage of the old Norse or Danish *at* in the same sense. That *i* is not an abbreviation of 'in,' but the Danish *i* pure and simple, I have no doubt ; this con-clusion becomes almost irresistible when one hears such a sentence as *T'keeam brak itu i t' bairn han'* (the comb broke in two in the child's hand).

It may lead to a more correct idea of the pronuncia-tion of the dialect if under the head of each letter a few of the peculiarities are pointed out, and their correct rendering illustrated by examples, though in many cases the true pronunciation can only be approximated by this means.

A.

There are several sounds belonging to this vowel, which is one that is never pronounced as in ordinary

English. The principal of these sounds are the following :—

(1) The long *a* (*aa*) in such words as grate, slate, wait, ail, which may be written for convenience *graate, slaate, waate, aal.* The expression of the 'tone-hold' of this vowel has been alluded to on another page.

(2) The middle *a*, as in can, ran, gan, &c. This sound is broader than the common English *a* as in 'man,' but not equivalent to *ah.* Its pronunciation has been explained above.

(3) The short *a*, as in the abbreviated form for 'have' (*a'e*); this is sounded without any of the *e*-sound, as in the ordinary English *a*, thus *a'e ya ?* (have you ?)

(4) *A* followed by *r*, as in part, arm, park, &c. In such cases the *r* is scarcely, if at all, heard, and the vowel-sound corresponds to something between *aa* and *ai.*

The words just quoted might perhaps best be written *pairt, airm, pairk*, &c. 'Dark' and 'hark,' however, do not follow this rule, but more nearly approach the ordinary pronunciation.

(5) *A* in the sense of *I* is sounded as in the standard English word 'father,' and is generally written *ah*; the *a* in 'father' (dialectic) is pronounced almost as in (4).

B.

This consonant follows the rule of ordinary English, except that it is not heard in such words as tumble, nimble, bramble, thimble, tremble, ramble, gamble, &c., which are pronounced *tumm'l, nimm'l, bramm'l, thimm'l, tthrimm'l, ramm'l, gamm'l*, &c.

In the word 'hobble,' the equivalent for which in the dialect is *hopple*, *b* is changed into *p*; but in 'cobble' the *b* is retained.

C.

C followed by *h* is sometimes pronounced hard, as *k*. This is the case in the following words :—bench, chaff, churn, chest, thatch, birch ; these are changed to *bink, kaff, ke'n* (the *r* not being sounded) *kist, theeak, birk.*

D.

The *d*-sound plays a distinctive part in the dialect, especially in connection with *th* and *t,* which it very frequently takes the place of. Thus, e. g., 'without' becomes *bedoot* or *widoot* ; 'but' is changed to *bud*; and 'bottom,' 'farthing,' are sounded *boddom, fardin.*

In the middle of a word *d* is often pronounced like a soft *th* (as in 'then ') which we may call *dh* or *dth.* For instance, nidder, murder, binder, under, wonder, window, &c., become in the dialect *nidther, mo'dther, bindther, undther, wondther, windther,* &c.

It is difficult to describe accurately the precise rules of pronunciation of this letter, but it will be alluded to subsequently.

D final is frequently suppressed: thus *fand* (the perfect tense of 'find') is pronounced *fan'* ; so too 'bound' is *boun'* ; also stand, and, hand, grand, &c., are changed to *stan', an', han', gran',* &c.

When preceded by *n* and followed by *l*, *d* is mute, as in candle, handle, randle-bauk, &c., which are sounded *cann'l, hann'l, rann'l-bauk.* On the whole, there is a decided tendency for the *d* to be softened or omitted altogether in folk-speech, thus following a general rule with regard to it in Danish.

E.

There are not such marked changes in this vowel·

sound as in *a* or *o*; still we have several variations from ordinary rules.

They are as follows :—

(1) In the pronouns me, she, we, the *e* is changed to short *a*, as *mă, shă, wă.*

(2) The *e*-sound when followed by *r* is changed into long *a* in some words : for instance, serve, certainly, discern are pronounced *sarve, sartainly, disarn.*

(3) In the word 'errand,' *e* becomes *ea.*

(4) In a large class of words, of which get, yet, dress, ready, friend may be quoted as examples, the *e* is changed to a distinct *i,* and these words should be written *git, yit, dhriss, riddy, frinnd.*

(5) Words or names ending in *el* or *ell,* of more than one syllable, change the *e* into *i*; thus Morrell, parcel, chancel, chisel, garsel, are pronounced *Morrill, parcil, chancil, chisil, garsil.*

(6) There is a strong tendency to drop the *e*-final in monosyllables ; thus, make, game, take, shame, gate, wake, came, shake, ale, &c., are pronounced *mak, gam, tak, sham, yat, wak, cam, shak, yal,* &c., but no general rule on this point can be laid down, many of these forms being Norse derivatives. In tame, mane, and some others, the *e*-final is retained.

G.

The following are some of the changes under this head.

(1) *G* preceded by *n* is never sounded as in 'finger,' but as in 'singer'; that is to say, the *g* is not dwelt upon or doubled. Such words as anger, monger, longer, single, swingle, mangle, new-fangled, and all words of more than one syllable, follow this rule, which admits of no exception.

(2) In the words 'length,' 'strength,' and any others like them, the *g* is omitted, and the words pronounced *lenth, strenth,* &c.

(3) *G*-final preceded by *n* is generally mute in words of more than one syllable; thus middling, parting, reading, &c., are pronounced *middlin', partin', readin',* &c., while ling, ding, bring, &c., are sounded as written.

(4) In adverbs ending in *ings,* as *partlings, mostlings, aiblings,* &c., the *g* is mute.

H.

As a rule, the aspirate is omitted in words requiring it, but not by any means so invariably as in some parts of England, and it is seldom inserted in words that do not need it: where it is so inserted the object apparently is to give additional emphasis, e. g. *hivvry yan on 'em* (every one of them); not infrequently the aspirate is prefixed to the affirmative *aye* (yes), though it is not strongly sounded.

A peculiar aspirate is given to some words beginning with *ho,* e.g. 'hope,' 'hole,' &c.; these are pronounced somewhat as *whooap, whooal,* &c., and although *yam* and *heeam* are the usual and more correct equivalents of 'home,' yet in the East Riding *wom* is also frequently heard.

I.

The principal sounds of this vowel are the following:—

(1) *Ah;* as in the equivalent for 'I' (pers.pron.), 'mind,' 'mine,' &c., which are pronounced *ah, mahnd, mahn,* &c., though in the case of 'mind,' *minnd* is also heard.

(2) *ah;* as in fine, line, wine, &c., pronounced almost as *fahin, lahin, wahin,* &c., the *ah* not being very strongly

emphasized : thus, for instance, it would be wrong to pronounce ' fine ' as *fahn* pure and simple, the *ah*-sound not being simply open.

The border-line between (1) and (2) is sometimes not very clearly defined : it is only use that can give the true pronunciation in every case. Thus, in the case of 'mine' the pronunciation is *mahn*, without any trace of the *i*-sound, while in the case of 'fine' the *i* is distinctly blended with the *ah*-sound.

(3) *Ey* ; as in kite, like, sike, lite, hipe, wipe, pipe, ripe, &c., which are pronounced somewhat as *keyte, leyke, seyke, leyte, heype, weype, reype,* &c., or approximately so.

Certain words in which *ight* is a component part follow this pronunciation, e. g. fight, might, blight, &c. ; others take the *ee*-sound ; *vide infra*.

(4) *Ee* ; as in bright, frighten, light, night, right, &c., which are sounded *breet, freeten, leet, neet, reet,* &c. Certain words in which *ia* occur in juxtaposition also follow this rule, as e. g. briar, liar.

(5) Words in which the *i* is long frequently take short *i* in the dialect; thus bind, blind, climb, find, &c., are changed to *binnd, blinnd, climm, finnd,* &c. ; while on the other hand, 'little' is pronounced *lile* as well as *lahtle,* and 'wind' is pretty often pronounced *wind.*

(6) *I* followed by *r* is pronounced nearly as *o*. Thus, first, third, bird, dirt, thirty, mirth, &c., become *fo'st, tho'd, bo'd, do't, tho't-ty, mo'th,* &c. On the other hand, as exceptions to this rule we have girl, girth, and girn pronounced *gell, geth,* and *gen.*

It should be borne in mind that the description of the pronunciation given above is only an approximate one, the actual utterance in these cases being by no means in perfect unison with the ordinary *o*-sound ; it is something between that and a very short *au*-sound.

J.

This letter follows the ordinary pronunciation.

K.

K before *s* is sometimes omitted, especially in place-names, as ' Stokesley,' *Stowsla.*

As observed above, this letter-sound is retained in the dialect in certain words which in standard English begin or end with *ch* ; these words are for the most part of Norse origin.

L.

When *l* precedes *d, t, f, k*, especially when it follows *a, o, u*, and the diphthongs *au* and *ou*, it is silent : thus, salt, cold, old, bulk, fault, shoulder, &c., are pronounced *sau't, cau'd, au'd, boo'k, fau't, shoo'dher*, &c.

M and *N.*

(No change).

O.

The principal changes of this vowel are the following :—

(1) *Eea* ; for instance, words ending in *o*, as who, do, so, two, &c., are sounded *wheea, deea, seea, tweea*, &c.

(2) *A* ; thus, long, among, wrong, &c., are changed to *lang, amang, wrang*, &c.

(3) *Aw* ; thus, low, toe, snow, crow, blow, row, &c., are pronounced *law, taw, snaw, craw, blaw, raw*, &c.

(4) Long *o* is sometimes changed to short *o*, as 'pōst,' *pŏst.*

Also in a large class of words, such as lost, tossed, frost, cost, &c., the *o* is pronounced perceptibly shorter than in ordinary, especially Southern, English.

(5) The diphthong *oa* is generally pronounced *aw*; for instance, foal, load, toad, road, &c., become *fawl, lawd, tawd, rawd,* &c.

(6) *Ow*, pronounced as in 'how' in the dialect, is changed to *oo*; thus bow (a salute), brow, now, &c., are changed to *boo, broo, noo,* &c.

(7) *Oo* becomes *eea*, e. g. (look) *leeak*, (crook) *creeak*, (took) *teeak*, (fool) *feeal*, (soon) *seean*.

(8) *Ou* becomes *oo*; e. g. thou, round, sound, hound, &c., are pronounced *thoo, roond, soond, hoond,* &c.

P.

(No change.)

Q.

Qu is sometimes changed to *w*, as in 'quick' (*wick*), 'quaint' (*waint* or *went*), 'quean' (*weean*).

R.

The nasal *r*, so common in the South of England, is a sound quite unknown among Yorkshire folk; indeed, this letter is but little heard at all, and is hardly ever rolled or trilled.

In such words as 'bairn' or 'arm' the *r* is mute, and the *a* is changed to *aa* or *ay*. Again, it is silent in such words as forty, word, world, burnt, &c.: the pronunciation of these has been already described. At the end of a word the *r* is sometimes doubled, as e. g. *what forr?*

In words where the vowels *e, i,* or *u* are followed by *r*, these are often transposed, thus, e. g. lantern, curd, burst, &c., are pronounced *lantthron, crud, brust,* &c.

S.

The sibilant, so unpleasant a feature in English generally, is slightly toned down in the dialect :—

(1) By the omission of the *s* altogether in the posses-sive case, as *William hat, Mary book*, for 'William's hat,' 'Mary's book.'

(2) In certain words where the sibilant is a very pronounced feature it is somewhat mitigated or evaded in the folk-talk; thus the place-name 'Sessay' is sounded *Sezza*, and 'scissors' is pronounced *sithers*.

T.

T in the middle of a word is frequently changed to *th*, or, to speak more correctly, *th* is added to the *t*-sound, which is very lightly touched with the tongue; thus 'water' becomes *watther*, 'alter' *altther*, 'enter' *entther*, &c.: this pronunciation is a universal and strongly marked characteristic in the folk-speech.

Th is not heard in 'than,' 'them' (except at the begin-ning of a sentence), and 'that' (except as a demonstra-tive pronoun). Participles ending in *pt*, as kept, slept, crept, &c., sometimes have the *t* omitted.

The interchanges of *t* with *th* and *dh* are so numerous and various, that it is impossible to formulate rules with regard to them.

U.

This vowel has the following sounds:—

(1) As in the ordinary pronunciation of 'full' in all words where *u* occurs; which is quite one of the most striking points in the dialectical pronunciation.

(2) The *o*-sound (approximately) when followed by *r*, as in 'hurt,' 'durst,' &c., which are sounded somewhat as *ho't, do'st*, &c.

(3) The *i*-sound, as *mich* (much), *sich* (such) or *sike*.

(4) The *eea*-sound, as *seeagar* (sugar), *seear* (sure).

(5) The *oo*-sound, as *boo'k* (bulk).

(6) The *iew*-sound, as *fliewte* (flute), *rhiewbub* (rhubarb). Many words in *ue* or *ui* also take this sound; thus, *triew* (true), *bliew* (blue), *friewt* (fruit), &c.

V.

Sometimes this letter is substituted for *f*, as in *shav* (sheaf). In 'over' and its compounds *v* is always changed to *w*.

The *v*-sound in 'of' is omitted, thus following the rule of Danish speech.

W.

In the words 'who' and 'whose' the *w* is very distinctly pronounced; the dialectical forms of these words are *wheea* and *wheeas*.

X.

In some words this letter is changed to the *s*-sound simply, as e. g. *ass'l* (axle).

And the same remark applies to place-names in which *x* occurs, as *Asby* (Haxby), *Wheesla* (Whixley).

Y.

Some words beginning with *a*, *o*, or *ho* prefix *y* before the vowel-sound, as *yal* (ale), *yance* (once), *yat* (hot), &c.

Ey or *ay* final is generally pronounced as short *a*, especially in place-names or surnames, as *Harlsa, Helmsla, Pockla, Bev'la, Sprautla, Yearsla, Hartla, Bentla, Payla*, &c.

The old pronunciation of 'oven' was *yewn*; it is still occasionally heard.

Z.

This letter sometimes takes the place of *s*, as *doze* (dose), *uz* (us); but in such cases it is only lightly sounded, and the *z*-sound, which is a leading feature in some of the Southern dialects, is by no means so in our own.

In the above alphabetical summary I have only been able to give a very brief and imperfect outline of the pronunciation of the folk-speech in some of its leading features and other peculiarities. I have but one or two further remarks to make here.

It should be observed that the *e*-sound as in *me* is comparatively seldom heard in the dialect; a somewhat shortened use of it occurs in the case of the personal pronoun *I*, in place of the ordinary *ah*, the rule being that *ah* is always used at the beginning of a sentence and generally elsewhere, though occasionally the short *e*-sound takes its place. Thus, *ah 'll cum if ĭ can*, the *i* being sounded as a short *e*.

Again, the *e*-sound in *friend* is changed into short *i*, and that in *settle* into *a*.

The two-fold pronunciation of *wind* has been already alluded to; it may be noted however that the verb *to wind*, is pronounced *winnd*, while the noun wavers, perhaps not inappropriately, between *winnd* and *wīnd*, the former being somewhat the commoner, though Dr. Johnson seemed to prefer the other when he said, on being questioned on the point, ' I cannot finnd it in my minnd to call it winnd, but I can find it in my mind to call it wind.' This argument by alliteration falls to the ground, however, with the Yorkshireman, who always pronounces 'find' as *finnd*, 'mind' sometimes as *minnd*, but never as *mind*, and 'wind' about equally as *winnd* and *wīnd*.

Eight and *weight* are pronounced as *height* in ordinary English, while in the dialect this latter word is sounded as *heyte*, or nearly so. The *i*-sound pure and simple, as in *pine*, is very rarely, if ever, used. The pronunciation of *o* as *aw* has been mentioned above. But before concluding my remarks on the pronunciation of the dialect, I will give a little incident which came under my own observation, and which illustrates the strong leaning there is towards this treatment of the vowel-sound. It was at a school inspection not far from York. The inspector was giving a class of eleven boys a test in dictation; the subject was the Bear, and the beast's claws were not unnaturally spoken about several times in the passage read. When all was done, and the work was being looked over, the inspector (who, by the way, was from the South of England), was 'stagnated,' as we say, to find that four out of the eleven boys, whenever the word *claws* was read, invariably wrote it *clothes*. The poor lads must have been sorely puzzled to think what a bear could possibly require clothes for, but on this occasion their mother-tongue overpowered their reasoning faculties. I confess I felt, as a Yorkshireman, not altogether displeased at this indication that the old speech had not quite lost its hold on the rising generation, even though it might be the means of bringing some of the youngsters to grief on the day of the school inspection.

There is one rule of pronunciation which admits of scarcely an exception, and that is with regard to the *a* in such words as fast, glass, grass, grant, nasty, answer, draft, laugh, task, &c.; in these and in all similar cases the *a* is sounded as in *gas* or *mass*. *Master*, however, is pronounced *maasther*.

The *o*-sound in lost, cost, foster, and all words of that kind, is short, and is never heard as if spelt *au*, which is so universally the case in Southern England.

I must conclude this chapter with a few words as to

F

the way in which *th* is treated in our folk-talk. Speaking generally, there is a decided tendency to evade its use. Apart from the fact that the definite article is always abbreviated to *t'*, whether before a vowel or consonant, there are other usages which lead to a similar elision of the aspirate; for instance, as already mentioned, *than* is shortened to *'an*, *them* into *'em*, though this latter is not peculiar to the district, and *smother* is pronounced *smoor*.

On the other hand, a sound approaching the *th* is introduced into a large class of words which do not ordinarily contain it; thus the Yorkshire for strong, stride, strange, &c., is *stthrang, stthrahd, stthraange*, &c. It is not easy to make clear in writing what this sound is; it may be said, however, that the aspirate is made with the extreme tip of the tongue, and that only very slightly, while the closely preceding *t*-sound is also distinctly heard. Also in words beginning with *dr*, such as drain, dream, dress, &c., the *d* is changed to soft *dh* or *ddh—dhreean, dhreeam, dhriss,* &c. There is again in these cases a doubling of the *d*, like that of *t* in words beginning with *thr*.

It is no easy matter for educated people to learn the pronunciation of our vowel-sounds unless they have from their earliest years been in the way of hearing them; for not only are they quite unlike those of ordinary English in many cases, both in their formation and the way they are applied, but, as I have said, the difficulty of hearing the dialect spoken in its freedom and fulness is also an obstacle. Education too, is doing its work, and among other results the young people are many of them, I regret to say, ashamed of their mother-tongue. And what is the consequence? Frequently either a mongrel, nondescript, neither-fish-

flesh-nor-fowl, semi-slang kind of lingo, hateful to hear,
or else a hum-drum, matter-of-fact, education-depart-
ment English, as dull and uninteresting as the Fens,
with no ups and downs, such as we find in our Yorkshire folk-talk, to break the monotony of things. In
either case the result is not satisfactory. I remember
once speaking to an old Yorkshire body about the
speech of the present day as compared with what it was
half a century back. 'Aye,' said she, 't' yung 'uns
dizn't talk noo leyke what tha did when ah wer a lass ;
there 's ower mich o' this knackin' noo : bud, as ah tells
'em, fooaks spoils thersens sadly wi' knackin. An' then
there's anuther thing ;—when deean, *they can mak nowt
bud mashelshon on't!*' She said truly, and the metaphor
was an apt one ; it is only too often the case that the
rising generation make nothing but 'mashelshon of
their 'knackin,' or fine-talk. The 'mashelshon' is a
mixture of wheat and rye, and like it, much of the
young folks' speech now-a-days is neither one thing
nor the other. I for one, at all events, prefer the racy
and forcible old folk-talk of Yorkshire as it is still here
and there spoken by natives who have seen three score
and ten or four score summers, have not had to submit
to the tortures of English grammar, and who have
never wandered far from their own *heeaf.*

CHAPTER IV.

LIKE every other kind of speech the Yorkshire dialect has its idioms. Without a knowledge of these it is impossible to write it correctly or to speak it as it should be spoken. Some of these usages differ but slightly from ordinary English, but these may be said to form the niceties of the folk-talk, and it is here that the difficulty in acquiring it mainly lies.

It may possibly be found of interest if I give a few examples of our idioms and modes of expression, though they can only be taken as samples of hundreds of others, and I shall not be able here to arrange them in any kind of order.

Perhaps I can begin with no better instance than our peculiar use of the verb 'to call.' In asking a person his name, the Yorkshire form of the question is not 'what is your name?' but 'what do they call you?' When examining school children in the country districts it frequently happened in putting this, the first question in the Catechism, to them, that I was met only with vacant stares; but the moment the form was changed to that in common dialectical use the answer was invariably given. For some reason or other this first question in the Church Catechism is often omitted by the teacher—a mistake surely, for many a lesson may be taught from the meaning or use of a name ; and to those who are inclined to pass over this important question in the Catechism and who ask 'what's in a name,' I reply, often a great deal. But I must not wander off into by-paths.

There is another meaning of 'to call' which is of universal use throughout the district. 'To call' people means to abuse them to their faces (to abuse behind their backs is *to illify*), to call them bad names. Often when words run high the pronoun *thoo* is interspersed with great emphasis, thus indicating supreme contempt, while in cooler moments and without emphasis it is but the sign of close familiarity and friendship. There is, for instance, all the difference in the world, in com- mencing a sentence, between *Dust ta think?* &c. and *Dust thoo think?* &c. The Yorkshire equivalent for 'to call' anyone, in the sense of attracting their attention, is 'to call of' him ; thus we should say *Noo, Polly, be sharp; run an' call of Tom.* Similarly we say 'wait of' a person, never 'wait for' him.

There are two expressions in connection with the verb 'to think' which deserve notice, viz. 'think to' and 'think on.' ' Think to' is equivalent to 'think of' in standard English, as in the phrase 'what do you think to it?' 'Think on' signifies the same as 're- member,' as in the sentence, *Noo, thoo mun think on.* This idiom is also used actively as *Think ma on,* i.e. 'remind me.'

The double negative is in universal use : it is no uncommon thing to hear three or even four negatives in succession where one only is required ; thus, *He nivver said nowt neeaways ti neean on 'em* (He never said any- thing one way or another to any of them). Again, the

double negative would be used in such an expression
as the following—*He'd nut putten a deal o' nowt inti t'
land* (He had not put much of anything into the land).
Times and oft when I was Inspector of Schools
have I heard and seen written 'Lead us not into no
temptation'; and this, perhaps, is as good an example as
any, because here the negative is thrown in when there
is no corresponding affirmative in the sentence, thus
showing what a strong tendency there is to use it. The
following example I cannot refrain from quoting : it
was said by an irate owner of a garden when peeping
over the wall after the reception of a few stones or other
missiles, and seeing a boy standing demurely, looking
as if butter would not melt in his mouth—*neeabody's
neea bisniss ti thraw nowt inti neeabody's gardin !*

There is a peculiar use of the verb 'to be' which may
here be noticed. The ordinary construction of the past
participle passive is changed to the infinitive active with
'be.' Thus the expression 'it will have to be taken up'
becomes in dialectical form *it'll be ti tak up.* Or again,
at a game at cricket, for instance, some one disputes the
word of the umpire, and indignantly exclaims : *Whya! if
ah's oot, ah s'all be ti hug oot* (Well ! if I'm out, I shall
have to be carried out). Or perhaps the ball is lost,
whereupon the fielder calls out that *it'll be ti finnd,* not
'it will have to be found.'

Again, we frequently find words verbalised, and not
seldom fittingly and forcibly so. Let me give one or two
specimens : a good example is that formed from 'over'
to be *overed* means to be finished, and is one of our
commonest usages. Or take the case of the word
'meat,' which in the dialect, as in the Bible (Lev. xiv. 10;
St. Luke xxiv. 41, &c.), means any kind of food, and not
simply flesh meat—which, by the way, is called butcher's

meat : to *meat mysen* simply means to find my own food.
A relative of mine once went into the cottage of a widow
who was very badly off: to eke out a living she took in
a lodger ; the house was small and the visitor expressed
surprise that the arrangement could be carried out, and
enquired how it was managed ; whereto the widow made
answer : *Well ya see, ma'am, he meats hissen an' ah weshes
him*, i. e. 'he finds his own food, and I wash for him.' *To
reet* means 'to set to rights,' and is used in a variety of
ways : sometimes 'up' is added to the verbal form, and
to reet up means 'to correct,' or, as we say in Yorkshire,
ti stthraiten. Thus it was said to me once with reference
to a troublesome boy : *Ah can't deea nowt wi t' lad, he
wants sum yan ti reet him up.* *To hot* and *to bath*
are substituted for 'to heat,' and 'to bathe ' ; even such
phrases as *to potato* and *to strawberry* would be
commonly used to express to plant with potatoes or
strawberries. *To voice* a person is to make him hear
by calling to him, to make the voice reach him.

'Good' and 'bad' have their peculiar treatment. In
the first place, they have the meaning of 'easy' and 'difficult' ; e.g. we say *good ti see* or *bad ti see*; *good ti tell*
or *bad ti tell.* Again, *good* often signifies 'well,' e. g.
yan mud as good stop at yam (one might as well stay at
home). If a thing is well made it is said to be *good
made ;* or if a sheep has a thick fleece, it is said to be *good
wool'd,* this expression being also used figuratively in the
sense of plucky or brave. Also we must note the verbal
use of the same word, which is curious ; thus *ah gooded
mysen* means 'I raised my hopes'; it would be used in
such a sentence as the following : *Ah gooded mysen at ah
could git ti t' chetch ov Eeastther Day.* And lastly, we
have the phrase *a good few,* meaning 'a considerable
number.'

There's nowt aboot that is an expression used in an argument, and signifies 'there is nothing to be said against that'; i. e. I admit that point. *He's going in twenty, thirty,* &c., i. e. 'he is in his twentieth, thirtieth, &c. year.'

The dialect is prolific in words that relate to the state of a person's health or bodily condition—medical terms, as we may call them. In visiting the sick, a clergyman is naturally in the way of hearing many words of this class, some of them very peculiar. I scarcely know how a south-country man who comes suddenly to practise in Yorkshire escapes making an occasional blunder in prescribing for his patients, at least in the case of many of the old folks.

You ask a man how he is, and he says, *ah's betther* or *ah's quiet betther*; this does not mean that he is improving, but that he is quite well again ; if he wished to express that he was only improving, he would say *ah's betther 'an what ah a'e been*, and he might add *bud ah's nobbut badly yit.*

Let us take an imaginary case which will illustrate a few of these medical words and phrases.

The mother says to her neighbour, *Oor Joe's leeaked a bad leeak of a lang whahl*, and they agree that the doctor should be sent for. He comes ; and they explain that poor Joe *catch'd cau'd t' last backend*; it was perhaps *a varry blethery tahm, an' t' lad teeak neea tent of hissen* ; the cold *clap'd on tiv his chist* and he has *nivver fair kested it yit*, he *mended* a bit *aboot Kessmas*, and then after a week or two he had some *sad backenins*. The doctor then asks a few questions as to how the patient is affected, and the mother describes that at *t' fost end* the lad was *nobbut a bit hoarst*, but that he rapidly *warsened* till at length he was *fair closed up*. After that,

she might go on to say, he had some *despert bad coughin'*
bouts ; that he was *bedfast for a fo't-nith*, and that the
cough *tewed him seea whahl he couldn't git neea rust*
neeaways. This went on till the unfortunate Joe got *that*
waakly an' doddhery whahl he could hardlins trail hissen
across t' chaam'r fleear ; at times he would be full of
pain, perhaps his back would *wark whahl he didn't knaw*
hoo ti bahd ; they tried oils and all manner of *stuff* to
try to *dill* the pain when it was on him, but it was *all ti*
neea use. The mother would perhaps relate that she
herself had been poorly with nursing her son, and had
got a cough ; but she did not think the complaint was
smitting, but that, what with one thing or another, she
was *quiet stall'd oot*, that she had now *gotten ti t' far end*,
and send for the Doctor she must ; and when he had
come and examined her son she might ask him if he
thought the illness had not *sadly fleeced* the invalid, and,
·if the case was serious, whether he thought there was
still *onny mends for him*. He takes the doctor's medicine,
and for a time possibly there is no visible improvement,
he *nowther dees nor dows*, or he *maks poorly oot*; but
after a time a change takes place ; after several bottles
of *stuff*, another is sent which *caps* him, and in the end
he *nips aboot as cobby as owt*.

A severe pain would not be said to be hard to bear,
but *bad ti bahd*. If one feels shivery and shaky, as if
some poisonous matter had got into one's very bones
and blood, we sometimes say that we are *all iv a atterill*.
Many other examples under this head might be quoted,
but these must suffice.

In no department does the dialect retain such a strong
hold as in agricultural terms. Whether we look at the
fields, the plants, tools, implements, work, men, horses,
cattle, sheep, poultry, carts, harvest, corn, the dairy, or

anything else connected with the farm, we find any
number of quaint words and phrases, most of which
have been handed down from father to son through
many long year-hundreds.

Let us walk through *t' staggarth yat* and take our
stand there for a moment. What do we see? There
lies before us the good *au'd swath* which is used for *t'*
coo-pastur; beyond on one side is another *swath-garth*
which has just been *mucked ower wi good manishment*
preparatory for *hay-tahm*, and in hope of a good *fog*
afterwards; on the left hand is *t' au'd twenty yacker*
liggin i faugh, in which two ploughs are now at work,
and being strongish land and hot weather the horses
are *weeantly tew'd*; but it is now *lowsin tahm*, and *t'*
hames and barfams will shortly be hung up till next
morning, when the horses will again be *yoked*. There on
the ground lie the *gearing* and *swingle-trees*, and hard
by is an old harrow with its *bulls brokken.*

At the *far-end* of the field is Ned, *yan o' t' daytal men*,
liggin a hedge; although *gallick-handed* he is a *don hand*
at t' job. Not far off is his young son coming home after
flaayin' creeaks all day long, while his still younger
brother has been *tentin' t' coos i t' looans*. The hedges,
whether 'laid' in the ordinary way, or whether in *stake*
an' yether, all look neat, and the *cam-sides* are well
cleaned. But we must take a look at the dairy, and on
our way back through the *staggarth* we see some nice
cletches of chickens picking away at the remains of some
hinder-ends and *caff*. The dairy is well kept, with its
cream pankins, siles, briggs, skeels, piggins, and all the
rest of it, though now-a-days *skeels* and *piggins* have
given place to cans of a different sort. Perhaps one of
the cows has just *cau'ven* and there are some jars of
beeas'lins with which to make puddings for the household.

The newly-made butter is well *blaked,* but some of the cream looks *a bit bratty.*

No better Yorkshire was spoken than in the hay-field or harvest-field before machinery was as much used as it is now. How delightful on the early morn-ing in July to hear the music of the *strickle* against the old *leea;* in other words, the sharpening—*sharping* as we call it—of the scythe, made by three or four stalwart mowers. The *gess* as it lay *i sweeath* caught the rays of the rising sun, which, aided by the *spreedin* of the hay-makers, quickly did its work ; then some of the hands would *put in* to pave the way for the rakers, and thus the hay in time was got into *windrow* preparatory to being put into cock or *pike ;* or, if the weather happens to be *wankle,* all the hands are at work to get the partly-made hay *off t' grunnd* and into *lap-cock,* which was a sort of twisted armful lightly laid on the ground.

If a 'foreigner' were to go about among the men, he might catch such words as *limmers, leading, shelvins, skell up, teeam, bleck, thill-horse,* or *snubbits,* and perhaps he might not be much the wiser. The *hales* or *steer-tree* of a plough might even sound strange to him, if he happened to get upon that subject.

Possibly one field on the farm is *nowt bud reins an geirs,* another is *seeavy* or *sumpy,* or others full of *bull fronts, brassics, ketlocks, kelks* or weeds of some kind or other, which require *hand-lukin* at times.

If, at another time of the year, the stranger were to look for a moment towards the stacks, he might see here on the ground a *dess* or two of hay ready to be put into the *heck,* or there, a *bottle* of straw for bedding. Away in a grip in one of the fields the *hind* sees *yan o' t' yows rigg-welted,* and quickly sets her on her feet again : he looks at her with some interest, for it is near *clippin-*

tahm; he finds that the *hogs* will require well *weshing ti year*, for there's *a vast o' cotty 'uns amang 'em*.

Many old words keep dropping out of use in the speech of the country folk, but perhaps not quite so rapidly as some suppose. The dialect is not quite dead yet. Let us take as a test of this the Glossary at the end of vol. ii. of Marshall's *Rural Economy of Yorkshire*, 2nd edition, 1796. This work concerns the North and East Ridings, so that it is well suited for our purpose.

A correspondent from the neighbourhood of Kirby Moorside, whose memory ranges over the past forty years, has given me, firstly, a list of those words which during that period (1851–1891) he does not remember ever to have heard at all, and secondly those which have become obsolete in his district during the same interval. It must be borne in mind that this is but a rough-and-ready test, and only applies to a very limited area.

1. *Words not heard from* 1851 *to* 1891.

Addiwissen : a fool's errand (nearly obsolete in 1796).
Aiger : a tide wave.
Aither : a flowing.
Angles : the holes or runs of moles, field-mice, &c.
Ass-card : fire shovel.
Aumas : an alms.
Average : the pasturage of common fields and other stubbles after harvest.
Badger : a huckster.
Bauf : well-grown, lusty.
Beesucken : applied to the ash when its bark is cankerous.

Belive : in the evening.
Booac : to reach.
Boorly : gross or large made.
Bride-door.
Bride-wain.
Bun : a hollow stalk.
Buver : the gnat.
Canty : lively.
Capes : ears of corn broken off in thrashing.
Clapperclaw : to beat with the open hand.
Clavver : to clamber as children.
Dindle : to experience a sort

of tremulous sensation after a blow.

Dordum : a riotous noise.

Dorman : the beam of a bed-room floor.

Dove : to doze,

Dowled : flat (of liquor).

Droke : darnel.

Eased : dirtied.

Elsin : an awl.

Falter : to thrash barley in the chaff in order to break off the awns.

Fastness-een : Shrove Tues-day.

Fey : to winnow with the natural wind.

Fezzon-on : to seize fiercely.

Fleaks : hurdles woven with twigs.

Flig : able to fly.

Fooaz : to level the top of a fleece of wool with shears.

Frag : to fill full.

Frem : strange.

Fruggan : an oven poker.

Gammer : to idle.

Garfits : garbage.

Glead : the kite.

Glut : a large wooden wedge.

God sharld : God forbid.

Gossip : a godfather.

Groze : to save money.

Hagsnare ; a stub.

Heap : a quarter of a peck.

Hip : to skip in reading.

Hurn : the space between the sides of an open chimney and the roof of the house.

Jaup : to make a noise like

liquor agitated in a close vessel.

Keeans : scum of ale.

Kimlin : a large dough-tub.

Kin : a chop in the hand.

Lafter : all the eggs laid be-tween two separate brood-ings.

Lairock : the skylark.

Leap : a large deep basket.

Leathe : to relax.

Leathwake : lithe, flexible.

Leaze : to pick out by the hand.

Leeav : to walk heavily.

Leeavlang : oblong.

Leer : a barn.

Maiz : a kind of large light hay basket.

Mang : a mash of bran, malt, &c.

Mauf : a brother-in-law.

Maul : a beetle.

Mauls : mallows.

Maund : a large basket.

Meals : mould, earth, &c.

Mealin : an oven broom.

Moot out : to break out into holes as old clothes.

Murl : to crumble as bread (verb active).

Nat : a straw mattress.

Neeze : to sneeze.

Nowt-herd : a keeper of cat-tle.

Orling : a stinted child.

Osken : an ox-gang.

Owerwelt : laid on the back (of a sheep).

Pannel : a soft packsaddle.

Pick up : to vomit.

Picks : the suit of diamonds in cards.

Piggin : a small wooden drinking-vessel.

Pot-kelps : the loose bow or handle of a porridge-pot.

Prood-tailier : the goldfinch.

Pubble : plump, full-bodied (as corn).

Reeang'd : discoloured in stripes.

Renky : tall and athletic.

Rie : to turn corn in a sieve.

Roil : to romp as a boy.

Rowt : to low as cattle.

Rassell'd : withered, as an apple.

Sark : a shirt.

Saul : a kind of moth.

Scalderings : the under-burnt cores of stone lime.

Shandy : somewhat crazy.

Side : long, deep.

Sind : to rinse, or wash out.

Snooac : to smell in a snuffing manner.

Sowl : to pull about in water.

Spaw : the spit of a pen.

Speng'd : pied, as cattle.

Spires : timber stands (not common).

Spittle : a little spade.

Spoil : the weaver's quill.

Stife : strong tasted.

Stoven : a sapling shoot.

Strum : the hose used in brewing, &c., to keep the tap free.

Swatch : a pattern of cloth.

Teylpeyat : a tell-tale.

Twitters : thread unevenly spun is said to be in twitters.

Uvver : upper.

Wallaneering : an expression of pity.

Wazistheart : an expression of condolence.

Wead : very angry.

Whittle : a pocket-knife.

Wike : the corner of the mouth or eye.

Wun : to live or abide.

Yowl : to howl as a dog.

Now it may happen that words which have fallen out of use in one district survive in another. It is so in the present instance. In this parish, Newton-on-Ouse, eight miles north-west of York, the following from the above list are still, even at this date (1891), current coin, though it is true some are interchanged but seldom.

Aumas, Beesucken, Booac *or* Boak, Buver *or* Buer, Canty, Dordum, Elsin, Falter, Fezzon on, Flig, Gammer, Garfits, Glut, Jaup, Lafter, Leap (a fisherman's basket), Leathwake,

Leeavlang, Piggin (a milking-pail), Renky, Sark, Sind, Sowl Spittle, Teylpeyat (now pronounced Tellpyat), Wike, Yowl.

It is possible that others might be added to these, for in certain cases, unless special enquiry were made, they might easily escape notice. The word *aiger* would hardly be heard except on a tidal river, but the cry *wahr aiger* raised by the boatmen when the approaching tidal wave is visible, is still common on the lower part of the river Ouse.

Other of the words quoted may retain their hold in other parts, e. g. *doven*, another form of *dove* (to slumber), is still heard in the Wold country, and in one locality in the East Riding *nowttherer*, another form of *nowtherd*, is also in use.

2. *Words gradually fallen out of use in the interval*
1851–1891 (*as above stated*).

Ananters : lest, in case.
Ar : a scar.
Arf : afraid.
Ark : a large chest.
Backbecaraway : the bat.
Blendings : peas and beans grown together.
Botchet : mead.
Breea : the brink of a river.
Broach : the spire of a church.
Bummle-kites : blackberries.
Burden-band : a hempen hay band.
Cake : to cackle as geese.
Cazzons : dried dung of cattle.
Char : to chide.
Chunter : to repine at trifles.
Clavver : clover.

Cod : a pod.
Coop : an ox-cart without shelvings.
Coor : to crouch.
Cowdy : pert.
Cowstriplings : cowslips.
Cruse : pleased.
Cushia : cow-parsnip.
Dessably : orderly.
Doory : very little.
Dow : to thrive.
Downdinner : afternoon luncheon.
Draff : brewer's grains.
Duds : clothes.
Faantickles : freckles on the face.
Faff : to blow in puffs.
Fixfax : the sinews of the neck of cattle.

Fowt : a fool.
Gad : a long rod or whip.
Gallick-handed : left-handed.
Gamashes : gaiters.
Gauve : to stare vacantly.
Glorfat : very fat.
Gotherly : affable.
Gowpen : two hands together full.
Graith : riches.
Har : a strong fog.
Haver : oats.
Hotter : to shake.
Hurple : to stick up the back (of cattle).
Kelter : state.
Mainswear : to swear falsely.
Met : two bushels.
Mint : to make a feint.
Moy : muggy.
Nithered : perishing with cold.
Old farrand : old-fashioned.
Over get : to overtake on a road.
Owergait : a gap in a hedge.
Pulsey : a poultice.

Purely : pretty well.
Ripple : to scratch as with a pin.
Rooter : a kind of rushing noise.
Rush : a meeting.
Scaldered : chafed.
Scug : to hide.
Sidelong : to fetter cattle.
Sie : to stretch.
Scraffle : to crawl in haste.
Skeller : to squint.
Snevver : slender and neat.
Speck : the heel-piece of a shoe.
Spalder : to spell.
Stark : tight.
Sunder : to air.
Swaimish : bashful.
Taal : to settle in a place.
Thaavle : a pot-stick.
Unkard : strange.
Weea (to be) : to be sorry.
Whimly : softly.
Woonkers : an exclamation.
Yaud : a riding-horse.

The same remark applies to this as to the former list of words. Many of them are at this time in common, or fairly common, use in the district where I live. The following are some such :—

Arf, Blendings, Chunter, Cod, Cruse, Deeary (another form of Doory), Dow, Duds, Faantickles, Fowt, Gallick-handed, Gauve, Glorfat, Hurple, Kelter, Mint, Nithered, Old-farrand, Sie.

I am strongly of opinion that, in spite of the great tendency to decay in our dialect during recent years, there are still many more archaic words and expressions in use in certain parts here and there than some of us have any idea of. I know by my own experience in one district at least that this is the case. It is true the old words and phrases are not now so often heard by educated people as they used to be ; the country folk are much more shy of using them before strangers than they were ; but for all that, they are used largely by many of the elderly inhabitants when conversing freely among themselves.

It only remains for me to add a few idioms and verbal usages of a general character, most of which have occurred to me in conversation with our folk from time to time, some of them very frequently.

Miscellaneous examples of idioms and verbal usages.

To. This preposition has one or two peculiar usages : thus, instead of 'of no use' we say *to no use.* Also we say, What will you take *to your dinner ?* instead of *for* your dinner. Or again, Do you take butter *to* your bread ?

There isn't sich (or *sikan*) *a thing.* It is impossible.

It means nowt. It matters nothing.

T' au'd man, t' au'd woman. These are synonymous with Father and Mother, and are not so used with any idea of disrespect, but merely in a matter-of-fact way.

Other tweea, three, &c. Two, three, &c., more.

Consider of it. Consider it.

To happen·an accident. To have an accident.

Ah'll tell ya. I assure you ; or as an intensive, e. g. ' bud ah 'll tell ya, sha's that badly whahl she can tak nowt ' (but I assure you she is so poorly that she can take nothing). ' Ah had ti run, ah 'll tell ya ' (I had to run hard).

Recollect. The verb *remember* is seldom used, *recollect* being generally substituted ; though *tell* is common also, as in the phrase ' Sen ah can tell ' (Since I can remember).

G

To have a right is equivalent to 'ought,' or 'in duty bound,' in such a phrase as the following : 'He 's gotten a weyfe an' bairns, an' he 's a right ti keep 'em.'

To take. To look, to consider, e. g. 'Tak it this waay,' i. e. consider it in this light.

All as one. One and the same thing.

Satisfied. Certain : e. g. 'noo, ah 's satisfied it 's reet.'

To show. To appear : e. g. 'He shows a decent lad.'

Want. The use of this word is peculiar ; it is almost equivalent to 'ought': for instance, 'Do those letters want posting ?' is equivalent to 'Ought those letters to be posted ?' Again, 'Does that parcel want to go ?' is the same as saying 'Has, or ought, that parcel to go ?' I may add that this usage is not confined to country folk only, but applies more or less to all classes ; it is a north-country idiom.

Good thowt. Presence of mind. Such an expression as 'presence of mind' would not be used by our older country folk, the nearest equivalent being that here given.

Best ends. Best sample of anything, as apples, potatoes, &c.

What. Used interjectionally to express uncertainty ; e. g. 'There 'll be—what—mebbe a scoqre.'

Forced. Obliged.

Start. Begin. These two last-named equivalents, 'obliged' and 'begin,' are never used in the dialect.

Oor. Our ; in the sense of belonging to the family of the speaker : e. g. 'Ah seed oor Sam' (I saw my brother Sam).

Hard eneeaf. Without doubt. *Example* : 'Yon 'll be him hard eneeaf.'

Not suited. Not pleased, or greatly displeased ; e. g. 'He wasn't seea varry weel suited.'

By noo. By this time.

Hard an' fast asleep. Fast asleep.

T' len'th on 't. The extent of it.

It meead us 'at wa couldn't. It was impossible for us.

To tell of. To tell.

He and *she.* It is very common for the husband or wife to be alluded to by this pronoun without any kind of previous mention that it is the husband or wife that is being spoken of : thus the wife would say of her husband, 'He 'll be here inoo,' instead of calling him by his Christian name or 'my husband.'

Went foreign. Went to foreign parts; went abroad.

A deal. Many; e.g. ' a deal on 'em diz it.' ' A varry deal ' is equivalent to ' a great many.'

To reckon nowt on. To think lightly of; e. g. ' Ah reckons nowt on 't.'

He is sairly off on 't. He is very ill.

We are off away. We are going away from home.

Ah thowt for ti cum. I thought about coming, or intended to come.

Year upon year. Year after year.

Ah unbethowt mysen. I thought it over again, and found out my mistake.

Along of or *All along of.* In consequence of ; e. g. ' It warn't along o' me, it wer all along of him.'

Ah deean't want nobbut yan. This is a common way of expressing ' I only want one.'

To fare on. To manage, to carry on, to do; e. g. it would be said *we fared on* in such and such a way for a time.

To. This preposition is sometimes used in the sense of ' except' or ' all but '; e. g. We lost them *to three or four*, i. e. all but three or four.

To lay out. To explain; e. g. 'When he laid it oot tiv her sha could mak nowt on 't.'

To set it aboot. To spread a report; e. g. ' Sha set it aboot 'at ah 'd taen t' childer fra t' skeeal.'

To'n ti t' deear. To turn out of doors.

Aleean. This is an abbreviation for ' let aleean,' i. e. to say nothing of : e. g. *Q.* ' Is 't teeaf?' *A.* ' Aye, it 's bad ti pull, aleean choppin.'

To get up. To become fine (of the weather); e. g. ' Will t' daay git up, thinks-ta?'

Nowt seea and *Neean seea.* Not so, not so much; literally, nothing so : e. g. ' Ah 's nowt seea leeam bud what ah can gan ti t' chetch.' ' There 's neean seea monny on 'em.'

To have it over with. To talk it over with.

Nookin or *neeakin.* Sitting in a chimney corner.

Ginger hair. This is the invariable expression for red or light hair.

Putten oot o' t' rooad. Buried (of people or animals).

To put sideways or *sideway.* To put aside.

To jump with. To meet by chance.

A week was last Thursday. A periphrasis for last Thursday week.

Some, other some. Some, some. Also used as an equivalent for ' others '; e. g. ' Some leeaked betther 'an other some.'

Aether thruff or by. Either through or by the side of; an expression equivalent to ' by hook or by crook.'

T' bairns could tell t' keeak fra t' piece on 't. This was said to me by an old man when describing the dearness of bread in former days, implying that they had to be very careful.

Seea thoo knaws. Commonly said as a *finale* after two parties have come to high words.

Noo ah 'll tell ya what. Used in beginning a story introduced into a conversation ; a new start or departure.

Good ti nowt. Of no use, good for nothing.

Like all that. Like anything ; e. g. ' He row'd amang 'em like all that.'

Ah can't deea reet. This expression is used in the sense of ' I fail to please ' (as a servant, for instance).

Ah leyke nowther t'egg nor shell on 't. I don't like the look of it at all.

It's weel spokken 'at 's weel ta'en. (Old Yorkshire.)

When a man tries to talk in a more refined way than he is accustomed, he is said to *knack* ; but there is another mode of expressing the same thing, which is by saying that he is *scraping his tongue.*

It rains heavens high. It pours in torrents, especially if accompanied by wind.

It hardens oot. It is taking up ; said of the weather clearing up after a heavy rain, and especially after one of long continuance : the idea is that before the weather can become settled, there must be an interval during which the ' hardening out ' process goes on.

I add here a few sayings that have been communicated to me by a correspondent.

That 's what ah wared on 't, nowther a hau'penny mair ner

a farden less.' (To *ware* is the common expression for to
'spend.')

A labourer being asked whether a speculation which he
had made in hay answered, said, ' Ah nivver reckoned it ; if
ah lost, it wer nowt ti neeabody, an' if ah gaaned ah warn't
boun ti give it away.'

' If he can't lead he weean't pull i t' pin.' Said of a head-
strong man who wants it all his own way. The allusion is
to the old-fashioned way of yoking horses in a cart, the *pin*
being the middle place of three horses in line.

' Ah can hardlins addle mysen heat,' said by an old stone-
breaker as he sat on his heap of stones one cold November
day.

' Ah can't mak good breead when t' beeans is i flooer.'
This is a common saying, the idea being that the smell from
the bean-flowers affects the yeast, and so the bread cannot
be good at that time !

' Ah deean't want ti teeam wahrm watther doon his back ' ;
that is, I don't want to praise him.

' Yan can't mak a sho't keeak oot of a watther skeel,' said
of a stingy person.

' He started on wi vulgar fractions, an' catch'd him yan on
t' heck.' Part of the description of a row that took place at
an inn in the old coaching days.

' He 's a neyce young man, but he hezn't lost t' yalla off his
neb ' ; i. e. he is very green.

' It 's leyke gittin' a-gait ti mend au'd cleeas ; there 's mair
hooals 'an yan thinks for i t' lahinin.' Said of cutting some
dead boughs out of a tree.

CHAPTER V.

THE old-fashioned Yorkshireman can best express himself in his own dialect ; he at all events can make it cut deeper than any attempts at Queen's English. There are scores of words and phrases in daily use among our country folk which appear to me, and I believe to most lovers of the old Yorkshire folk-talk, to carry with them a strong expressiveness, a raciness, perhaps I should rather say, which their equivalents in ordinary English certainly do not seem to possess in like degree. Any person who will take the trouble to investigate and study our Northern dialect as it deserves to be studied, will find in it much to repay him ; and unless I am mis-taken, he will be surprised what a rich storehouse of words full of power and interest, of terse and quaint expressions, and of forcible phraseology, lies concealed in the unwritten traditional mother-tongue of our sturdy Yorkshire folk. It is a subject to which too little atten-tion has been given in days gone by. The English Dialect Society was not established a day too soon. It has done a great deal, and will no doubt do more. One of the latest outcomes of the work of the English Dialect Society is the making up of a Dialect Dictionary, which of itself is no small result of its labours, and cannot but prove a valuable addition to dialectical literature. It is, however, very desirable that those who are engaged in any such work should, as far as may be, gain or verify their information at first hand, I mean from the lips of the country folk themselves. This, through the rapid spread of education, is daily becoming more and more difficult; but still, even at this time of day, a great deal may be learnt from them which is worth noting, in the lingering archaicisms of the country speech.

I should like to illustrate my meaning by a few examples; though among so many that occur, it is hard to make a choice.

Perhaps I cannot give a better example by way of beginning than one alluded to in the last chapter; I mean the very frequent use that is made of the expression *to think on* in the sense of 'to keep in mind,' 'to remember,' 'not to forget.' I may observe that the stress in uttering it is laid on the last word. This phrase has always seemed to me to be full of force. We say in common parlance 'hold on,' as when a man lays hold on the end of a rope and is bidden not to let it go: he has to keep it in his hand. So here: when a child is told something by its parent, the command is frequently added that it is to mind and *think on*; it has, that is to say, to keep what it has been told in the grasp of the memory and not let it go. And while on the subject of the memory I will mention another word which I do not think is common to the rest of England, but rather peculiar to the North; I mean *off* in the sense of 'by heart.' When a teacher, for instance, has given a child something to commit to memory, he will ask after a time if the youngster has it *off,* by which he means, is he able to repeat it by heart? There is also another sense in which the word *off* is used. When a man, for example, wishes to say that he is on the point of going somewhere, that he is just going to depart, the common phrase is *ah 's for off.*

Another word which expresses a great deal in small compass is *fend* : you see perhaps a poor helpless crea-ture in a household who never can do anything for herself, and who is a hindrance rather than a help in the work of the house ; of such an one we say that she can't *fend* for herself. And so, too, we use the same expression of one who is clumsy or awkward in moving about and gets in the way of others ; of such it would be said that she has no *fend* about her. The word is also used very aptly of a person making his own way in the world ; or again, of an animal which no longer requires the care of its mother. It is hard to see why so good a word as this does not find a place in the literary language, and it is not to be forgotten that we have our country folk to thank for preserving it to us.

As a further illustration we might take the verb *tew*, which is universally used throughout the district, and in a great variety of ways. It is in its idea closely associated with any kind of unusual exertion or work to which the agent or workman has applied himself with more than ordinary vigour. If, for instance, a child is restless and fidgetty in bed, the mother complains that it is *tewing* itself. If a man is anxious about his crops in a *wankle* time, he will bestow such extra labour upon them as to *tew* himself; or if a farmer's horses are ploughing in strong land that is *clum*, they will *tew* them-selves till they get into what is called a *muck lather*.

Again, as to other forceful expressions : when a place is conveniently situated and easy of access, it is said to be *gain hand*; and similarly, a place that is awkwardly situated or un-get-at-able is said to be an *ungain* spot ; and further, a *gain* road is a short road.

If a workman is at a standstill in his work from any
cause—as, for example, a bricklayer for want of mortar—
he is said to be *fast* for mortar ; and if the same workman
does not take kindly to his occupation, he would say that
he did not *matter* it much.   Or again, when a person is
much occupied with work, he is *throng*; and if others are
busily engaged with him, we say that there is *throng
deed*; while the same expression would be used if there
were unusual stir or business going on of any kind.   In
ordinary English we say that a person is greatly disappointed when he finds out that he is mistaken about
some matter ; in Yorkshire, when this is the case, he
is said to be *sadly begone*.   To take away persons'
characters, to abuse them behind their backs, and the
like, is to *illify* them.   A dull, stupid, senseless sort of
person is called *daft* or a *dafty*; and from the same word
we have *daft-heead*, meaning 'a blockhead,' together
with *daft-like*, *daftness*, and *daftish*, which speak for
themselves.   The dialectical equivalent for 'to inform a
man about anything,' i. e. to explain matters to him, is to
insense him ; the word implies more than merely telling,
it rather signifies to give complete information upon any
matter so that it can be fully comprehended : a man
would say that he did not understand how to do a certain piece of work because he was not properly *insensed*
into it : when we are fully *insensed* upon a subject we
know how to act.   This old word occurs in Shakespeare,
although it is sometimes wrongly spelt, viz. *incensed*--at
least so it would seem.   The following passage from
Richard III, Act iii. Sc. 1, appears to be a case in point.

'Think you, my lord, this little prating York
Was not insensed by his subtle mother
To taunt and scorn you thus opprobriously?'

Read by the light of our dialectical usage, may not this be the right interpretation and spelling of the word? It is curious that a word which expresses so much should now only survive in an unwritten tongue. Or again, take the word *hefted*, which almost tells its own tale. In Danish and other languages a *hefte* means a handle, as of a knife or sword. In our dialect we speak about a man being *weel hefted wi' brass*: this surely is a more forcible expression than simply saying that a man has a good fortune, or that he is well off. Riches imply power and influence, and he who is possessed of them can wield them as a man wields a weapon or implement either for defence or attack, or for accomplishing some great work or end. This word, too, is to be found in Shakespeare, in the expression 'tender-hefted nature' (*Lear*, ii. 4).

When a person attempts anything for the first time, or is only beginning to get accustomed to some new work or duty, we ask how he *frames*; that is to say, how does he adapt himself to it? what kind of promise does he give of succeeding in his endeavour? The expression is wide in its application, and extends to animals as well as people. A horse might *frame* to make a good hunter, or a dog to be clever with the gun. A boy who is working in a careless or slovenly manner is sharply pulled up and told to *frame*, by which he understands that he is to do better, or at least make a better attempt. I have even heard it said of a clergyman coming to work in a new parish that he *fraames middlin'*, which in a Yorkshireman's lips is high praise. So useful is this word found to be, that a substantive corresponding to it has been coined, and although *framation* is not quite so commonly heard as the verb from which it is derived, still its meaning is well understood; we should say, for instance, of a lad undertaking some work and not succeeding in it, that he had no *framation* about him.

When a man is in low spirits he is said to feel *dowly*; this, too, is a word which does duty in a variety of ways, and is most expressive : it is applied to things, conditions, and places, as well as to people.

Often the employment of an appropriate word will add singular force to a remark which would else be comparatively tame. Thus, *graithing* is a vocable not uncommon in our folk-speech; it is used in the sense of clothing, fittings, furnishings, and the like. This same word was once applied in a telling manner by one who had taken out a summons against a labourer for some offence. The offended party was returning from the magistrate who had issued the required mandate. On the road he meets his antagonist, who eyed him with some malevolence and curiosity. The plaintiff returned the look, and called out triumphantly to the other, 'Aye ! ah 've been gittin sum graithin for tha !' Under the circumstances, I do not know of any word that would better express the state of things than that used on this occasion.

Our Yorkshire folk are fond of sport, and many a forcible expression might be picked up in connection therewith by those who are thrown in the way of it. For instance, on the morning of the day of the harriers coming to the place of meeting, one man would say to another in bated breath, ' We 'ev her set '; there would be no mention of the word hare. It would be perfectly understood that the speaker had been out with others, ranging, and knew where the hare was on her ' form.'

As a rule, my fellow ' countrymen ' are supposed to be pretty good judges of character, and they can sometimes express the good or bad side of a man in a few

but telling words. I remember being told of an old stable-
man who, in speaking of a fellow-workman who had
died rather suddenly, said that John H. was one of the
best men that ever ate 'butter and bread'; he had *no
back-door ways about him.* And I have heard of another
whose pithy reply to a question as to character took the
following form, 'Whya, there 's nut mich on him, bud
ivvry bit on him 's stthraight !' The subject was, I need
hardly add, not a big man.

The Yorkshireman is often wont to make a statement
indirectly with no little force, whereas it would ordinarily be expressed in a plain matter-of-fact sort of way.
To give a single example. I am reminded by a correspondent of an old man who wished to explain that it
was a long time since a certain event had taken place.
It would have been enough if he had said so in so
many words, but he chose rather to word it thus, 'Aye !
there 's been a deal o' coorse weather sen then': in
this way an edge was given to his remark which made
it much more telling. Just in the same way, *bunch* is
the common word for 'kick,' but if the kicker wishes to
give a little extra force to his words, he sometimes says,
' Noo ah 'll gie tha mi feeat if thoo dcean't mahnd.'

Stthrovven, thrussen, and *thruff* are rather queer-
looking words to occur in close proximity in a short
sentence, but they may be 'rapped off,' as we say, quite
naturally by a native of the North Riding; they were
so in the example I am about to give, and, I may add,
with considerable effect. An old dame, who had
received some coals from a ·charity, finding that a
smaller quantity had been allotted to her than her
neighbour, who was in worse circumstances, became
mightily indignant, and poured out the vials of her
wrath in no measured terms, adding as a condensed

summary of her state of mind, 'If ah 'd a'e thowt 'at it
wad a'e cum ti this, ah 'd a'e sthrovven ti a'e thrussen
thruff widoot 'em.'   Even in Yorkshire, it is to be
feared, pride, jealousy, and ingratitude are not absolutely unknown ; and it must be confessed that there was
just a pinch of all three in this old lady's cutting words. ᾽

Under the existing state of things, the payment of
taxes is no doubt a necessity, but to be overtaxed is not
only not a necessity, but is to some natures specially
irritating.   Nevertheless, rather than that their purse
should suffer, or still more their principles, such sensitive people will from time to time be found to take any
amount of trouble to try and get their grievances re-
dressed ; and who can blame them ?   The sense of
justice is strong in all of us.   It was so, beyond doubt,
in the case of a certain old woman from one of the dales
of the North Riding, of whom I was told that she one
day appeared before the Commissioners of Income
and Assessed Taxes for the district in which she lived.
It seems she had been surcharged for a riding-horse,
to her great annoyance.   And so she donned her Sunday best, and in due time appeared before the said
Commissioners to appeal against the charge.   Either
there was a flaw in the formalities, or she did not state
her case intelligibly, or something else was wrong ; at
all events she did not succeed in making good her claim,
and she left the room somewhat crestfallen, and in a
very agitated frame of mind.   Meeting an acquaintance
shortly afterwards, he asked her how it could possibly
be that she had not gained her point.   'Whya,' she replied, angrily and excitedly, 'ah 'd ower good a hackle
o' my back ; bud ah 'll git a proper hoss, an' ah 'll rahd
awlus ! '

In another chapter I have drawn attention to the

leading features of our dialectical vowel-sounds, and among them the common change of *o* and *oo* into *eea*, as 'do,' *deea*; 'root,' *reeat*. This often puzzles Southerners when they hear the dialect spoken, for it frequently makes words so pronounced sound like others with a different meaning. For instance, a pauper in a Union Workhouse was showing a person the beds provided for the casuals, and pointing out the wooden bed, and pillow of the same material, remarked, with a twinkle of his eye betokening a certain amount of glee : 'Aye ! they weean't scrat their teeas thruff t' bedding.' If the visitor was from a distant county, I am afraid the force of the remark would be lost upon him ; he would naturally wonder what possible connection weeping had with the matter. The real meaning of the word would probably not occur to him.

In the dialect a *cloot* is generally applied to a cloth of limited dimensions ; it may, however, do duty under circumstances for quite a large table-cloth, in which case it seems to have a force which it did not have before. A clergyman's son, Robert L., tells me he remembers in his young days a servant lad being allowed in his father's house to come into the dining-room to learn to wait, and saying to him, after vainly endeavouring to fold up the table-cloth, 'Tak ho'd o' t' cloot, Bobby, will ya ?' The same gentleman, too, remembered their housemaid, on the occasion of a dinner-party, opening the dining-room door slightly, and without even looking into the room, proclaiming through the chink, 'Pleeas, we're fast for cann'ls.' This expressed a good deal. It implied more than the bare fact that they were without candles ; it meant that no further progress could be made with the preparations for dinner without the said candles. The need was imperative.

Sometimes a strong bit of Yorkshire, when accompanied with a threat, is almost overpowering. It has
even been known to bring a love affair to a sudden
termination. A story is told of a sawny old bachelor
in a village not far from Northallerton, who was in love
with a lass in a neighbouring place. He came home
one day to his aged mother, a black-eyed, spirited old .
soul, whom he maintained, and who saw her home im-
perilled. It was late one Sunday night after meeting
the girl. He thus briefly described what took place.
'Muther was set ower t' fire ; sha click'd up pooaker
an' com at ma, an' sha says, " If ivver thoo gans efther
that lass ageean, ah'll fell tha." 'An',' he added, 'ah
nivver do'st.'

Every Yorkshireman knows what *warming* a child
means ; perhaps not a few have good reason to remember the force of this expression by bitter experience.
I do not know whether my brother 'countrymen'
require more flogging than other people, but it is a
remarkable fact that our dialect is peculiarly rich and
forcible in what a Winchester School boy would call
'tunding' phrases. *Ah'll gie tha thi bats; he bensill'd
him weel; she bray'd ma; if thoo bunches ah'll gie tha
a cloot ower t' heead; a daffener; a good eshin'* (or
hezzlein') ; *ah'll dhriss* (or *sttrighten*) *tha; ti ding doon ;
he fetch'd him a kelk ower t' shoodthers; he leead'd his
jacket; ti nevill, skelp, bazzak, pick, yenk,* &c. These, and
many more like them, will be familiar to many of us.

A clergyman of my acquaintance was visiting an old
man, who enlarged, among other things, on the devo-
tion of his daughter to her only child, John Robert. He
gave him to understand that she fairly idolised the
child ; and there and then seeing the boy in the street,
he called to him in tender tones, 'John Robert, yer

muther wants ya.' But John Robert was not to be
caught without first ascertaining that the coast was
clear. 'Will sha wahrm ma?' was the lad's cautious
reply. The grandfather's annoyance may be better
imagined than described.

Occasionally in the course of conversation on the
most ordinary and trivial topics, we hear bits of Yorkshire which arrest our attention by reason of their
raciness. Thus a Bilsdale man, in speaking of a storm
he was once out in while grouse driving, forcibly
described it as follows : he said, 'It fair teeam'd doon,
it stower'd, an' it reek'd, an' it drazzl'd, whahl ah was
wet ti t' skin an' hed'nt a dhry threed aboot ma.'

A resident in Whitby gave me some time ago an
account of an amusing conversation about a new-
coming parson into his neighbourhood. Like many
other clergy, he found it necessary to make a few
changes on coming to the parish. In the present case
the changes do not appear to have been of a very
violent character, but they were enough seemingly to
excite a few of the older inhabitants : 'Well,' was asked
of one of the parishioners, 'and how do you like your
new clergyman?' 'Whya, he's a quiet man, bud
folks disn't knaw what ti mak on him; he's rovven
doon t' Ten Commandments an' the Loord's Prayer
an' sell'd 'em ti Tommy Tranmer for fahve shillin'; an'
he wanted ti hev them uther boords doon an' all—what
di ya call 'em—them 'at tells what folks hez gi'en ti t'
chetch; bud Jamie Smith (that's him 'at 's chetch-
warner, ya knaw), he wadn't hev that ; naw, Jamie went
clean wahld at that'!

My Whitby friend also tells me of another characteristic bit of 'Yorkshire,' which a farmer from the
neighbourhood once treated him to when he was apolo-

gising to the other for his ignorance about agricultural matters, but who after all was not quite so ignorant as the apology seemed to imply, 'Bud,' says the farmer, 'thoo knaws a vast aboot it ; ah do'st ventther wi' thee for a hind.' This was taken as a high compliment, and it is probable that a look of satisfaction passed over the face of him who had just before professed himself unskilled in the work of the farm; whereupon, the other, thinking that he had perhaps gone rather too far in his remark, and that his words might conceivably be taken advantage of, promptly added, with true Yorkshire caution, 'Ah sud mebbe a'e ti back tha oot a bit t' fo'st year ! '

The love which every Yorkshireman has for an old favourite horse is strong indeed, and when an animal of this kind goes the way of all flesh the owner is often wellnigh moved to tears. ' I shall never forget,' writes a correspondent, 'the broken voice of my father's bailiff when he came to report the death of a favourite mare after a long watching ; he simply said, "it 's owered," and turned away.' That announcement, brief though it was, told a great deal more, so it seems to me, than if expressed in any other way.

H

CHAPTER VI.

SPECIMENS OF THE FOLK-TALK.

IN giving examples of the traditional speech of our
Yorkshire country folk, one naturally searches in the
first instance as far back as possible for specimens or
even traces of it; such searching, however, is productive
of only meagre results. To anyone who has at all
studied our dialect it would be deeply interesting to have
before him in black and white, if it might be but a few
pages of a really reliable description of the unadul-
terated folk-talk of, say, four hundred years ago. Specimens of Early English we have an abundant supply of;
but specimens of early folk-talk we have absolutely none,
so far as I am aware. We have nothing, for instance, to
show us how the sons of the soil spoke with one another
in the year 1500, in the dales of the East Riding or of
Cleveland. Whether such linguistic studies were ever
seriously taken in hand is doubtful; at all events, it
seems that nothing of the kind has come down to us.
One of the earliest approaches to anything of this
nature is a Lowland Scottish Glossary which dates from
the year 1595. This Glossary was appended to a Latin
Grammar, and the Grammar is supposed to have been
written by one Andrew Duncan, Rector of Dundee

Grammar School. Extracts from this Glossary are published in an early number of the reprinted Glossaries of the English Dialect Society. The folk-speech of the Lowlands of Scotland bears such a strong affinity to that of East Yorkshire, that a glance at Duncan's Glossary is not without interest, albeit that its scope is contracted and defective. Still, we may learn a few facts from it that bear upon our subject. Thus, for example, we find that certain of our Yorkshire pronunciations of the present day are identical with those of the South of Scotland at the close of the sixteenth century: as instances we may quote *brek* for 'break,' *chow* for 'chew,' *snaw* for 'snow,' *blaw* for 'blow,' *threed* for 'thread,' *meer* for 'mare,' and so forth; but the list of words is so limited that we cannot draw many conclusions from it. A few familiar words appear among the number given, viz. *slope, pig* (Yorks. *piggin*), *bladder* (mud), *carlish* (Yorks. *chollous*), *clap, headstall, sneck, imp* (to insert), *sheerer* (harvester), with some others.

What is most desired is however not found in Duncan's Glossary, viz. a few sentences to indicate the pronunciation at that date of ordinary vowel-sounds. One would like to know, for instance, if in the folk-speech of that date 'do' was pronounced *deea*, (look) *leeak*, (dame) *deeam*, (lame) *leeam*, (plough) *pleeaf*, (tough) *teeaf*, and so on. One would be curious to ascertain if the abbreviated definite article was in full force in the middle ages as it is now; if the personal pronoun *ah* (I) was universally used as at the present day, whether the *tth* or *ddh*, another strong peculiarity of our present pronunciation, was a strong peculiarity in those days. Whatever our own opinions may be on these and many other questions of the kind, we are in the dark as to positive proof.

H 2

The earliest example of the folk-talk in anything like
the true sense of the word, with which I am acquainted,
was written nearly a century later than the publication
of Duncan's Glossary.

The passage which I shall quote is from a dialogue
by G. M. Gent, published in York in 1685, and described
on the title-page as 'a Yorkshire Dialogue in its pure
natural dialect, as it is now commonly spoken in the
North parts of Yorkshire.' I cannot give the entire
production; the lines I quote form part of a conversation between a farmer, his wife, and son on agricultural
work. Pegg, who is first addressed, is either the
daughter or servant lass. The extract I have made
runs as follows :—

> ' *Mother.*—You set yan on unscape an' than you rewe
> Greeat matters of an angry word I trowe.
> Strahd, lass, an' clawt sum eldin oot o t' hurne,
> Then gan thy ways an' fetch a skeel o' burn,
> An' hing t' pan ower t' fire i t' reckon crewk
> An' ah 'se wesh t' sahl an dishes up i t' neuk.
>> *Father.*—Pray thee deea, Pegg; then ah 'se get up
>> i t' morn
> An' late sum pokes, an' put up wer seed corn :
> Then thoo may sarra t' gawts an' gilts wi draff,
> An' ah 'se give t' yawds sum hinderends an' caff :
> Then for wer breeakasts thoo may heeat sum cael
> Till ah lie by my shack-fork an' my flail;
> An', John, mak riddy my harrows an' my plewgh,
> An', he an ah, Pegg, sall deea weel eneugh.
> Ah 've heeard it talk'd an' noo t' trewth ah 've funnd,
> Amell tweea steeals t' tail may fall ti t' grunnd.
> Ah lited on Hobb, an he lited on me,
> An' nowt at all is riddy, that ah see ;
> Nowther traces, hames, nor barfans ti finnd,
> Swingle-trees nor helters, all 's made an ill end.
> Bud tweea days sen ah 'se seear they wer all here,
> Hung on an heeap i t' midst of oor laer fleear.

Son.—Faether, they 're liggin all on oor faugh lands;
Ah trailed 'em theer mysell wi my awn hands.
    Father.—Thoo 's a good lad, my Hobb, that teeak
sike care :
Is t' yoaks an' bows an' gad an yoaksticks theer?
    Son.—Aye, Aye ; an' t' plewgh-staff teea, hopper
an' teems ;
Wa lack nowt bud a bay stag o' min eems
'At we 're ti yoak i t' plewgh afoor wer yawds,
An' then ah 'se seear we 'se rahve up all adawds.
    Father.—Ne'er rack, ne'er rack ; we 'se tak neea thowt
for that ;
Ah 'se seear 'at it 'll bahd us billing at.
Oor land is tewgh, an' full o' strang wickens,
Cat whins, an seeavy furs, an monny breckins :
It 's nowt bud gorr, it ploshes under feeat ;
Wa 'se finnd trouble eneugh when wa cum ti it.
    Son.—Lythe ya, lythe ya, how fondly you talk
You think we 'se mak monny ill-favart bawke.
When wa do plew, wa mun tak tahm ah reed ;
Ah 've heeard folks offens say mair heeast warse speed.
T' feck on 't 's gripp'd, an t' watther runs away ;
Ah was at t' field mysell, and saw 't ti-day.
It 'll bring as good blendings ah dar say
As ivver grew a reeat in onny clay.'

In the original, from which this is taken, there are
misleading spellings and slight omissions of letters, some
of which I have corrected. There are still a few evident
inaccuracies in the text : in the last line, e. g., *in* would
no doubt be more correctly written *iv* ; *ti it* in the
original is written *teaut* ; *tiv it* or *tul 't* would be more
consistent with modern usage, and I suspect with that
of the period of the writing ; but I have written *ti it* as
adhering more closely to what was before me.

The above is a valuable example of the dialect .as
spoken in the North Riding more than two hundred years
ago, and, beyond all reasonable doubt, for centuries before

that, without material alteration. It must have been written by one who knew the folk-talk of that day well, but probably had not been much accustomed to writing it. It is noteworthy how slight have been the changes in the dialect, until the last few years, during the past two centuries. Indeed I venture to maintain that the written language has changed more than that spoken by the country folk. Take the example just quoted. In the main it would be perfectly understood by many of our older people at the present time. A few expressions and words have apparently fallen out of use altogether; but the dialect is essentially unaltered. The quotation will repay some study.

The opening expression, *you set yan on unscape*, has died out; it means you put one in mind of a thing that is not convenient.

Hurne is a word that has vanished, though but lately; it signified a hollow place near the chimney or *hood-end* in old-fashioned cottages, where the kindling was kept.

It would not now probably be understood what *mine eem* meant; the word, however, occurs in several glossaries of comparatively recent date, and signifies an uncle on the mother's side.

Gorr is now nearly obsolete; but Feilberg, in his Jutlandic Dialect Dictionary, gives the word as in use in parts of Denmark in the sense of slime, or filth; it is so used in the passage before us. The word is still in use in standard English under the form of *gore*, and in the restricted sense of clotted blood. It is curious that in Icelandic the same word is used for half-digested food, and in Swedish in a somewhat similar sense, as also for matter or 'stuff' generally. Whether *bows*, i.e. hoops for carrying fodder, are still used under that

term in any part of the district I cannot say with cer-
tainty; in Jutland the word under the form *bue* is
commonly used, with a like meaning, by the cowboys and
others for carrying fodder from the barns to the places
where the cattle may happen to be.

The other less common words will be found in the
glossary at the end of the volume.

For the sake of those who are not so familiar with
our folk-talk I will add a ' translation ' of the above passage.

Mother. — You annoy one, and then, I trow, you greatly
regret an angry word. Go, my lass, and gather some firewood from the kindling hole, then go and fetch a pail of
water and hang the pan over the fire on the hook, and I will
wash up the milk strainer and dishes in the corner.

Father.— Pray do so, Pegg : then I will get up in the morning and look out some sacks and put up our seed corn ; then
you may feed the pigs with grains, and I will give the horses
some tail-corn and chaff. Then you may make hot some
porridge for our breakfast until I put away my threshing
fork and flail : and, John, do you make ready my harrows
and plough, and he and I, Pegg, will manage well enough.
I have heard it said, and now I have discovered the truth
of it, between two stools the tail may fall to the ground. I
depended on Hobb and he depended on me, and I see that
nothing whatever is ready; no traces, hames, or collars to
be found ; no swingle-trees or halters; everything is out of
its place. Only two days since I am sure they were all here
thrown on a heap in the middle of our barn floor.

Son.—Father, they are all lying on our fallow ; I took
them there myself with my own hands.

Father.—You are a good lad, Hobb, to take so much care ;
are the yokes, and fodder hoops, and long whip and yoke-
sticks there ?

Son.—Yes ! and the plough staff as well, seed basket, and
teams ; we want nothing but a bay horse of my uncle's that
we must harness to the plough before our old animals, and
then I am sure we shall tear up everything to pieces.

Father.—No fear, no fear! we will not trouble our heads about that; I am sure it will require our working it well. Our land is strong and full of coarse couch grass, briars, rushes, and plenty of ferns. It is nothing but slimy mud, it splashes under foot; we shall find trouble enough when we come to it.

Son.—How foolishly you talk; you think we shall make many poor looking ridges. When we plough I advise our taking time; I have often heard people say 'more haste worse speed'; the greater part of it has channels cut in it and the water runs away; I was at the field myself to-day and saw it. It will produce as good a mixed crop of wheat and rye, I dare say, as ever grew a root in any clay.

A wide interval of time separates the next specimen of the dialect from that which goes before it. I hesitated whether or not to insert this extract as an example of the North Riding folk-talk, for it has now been published many years and has not seldom been quoted. But the piece is so well written throughout, and is such an admirable sample of the Yorkshire tongue, that I cannot refrain from giving the main portions of the dialogue. It was said, when the pamphlet was published, that the writer was a south-country man; if so, the production did him credit; in any case it could only have been composed by one who had heard the dialect spoken for some considerable time.

One or two words by way of preface are necessary to explain the drift of the conversation.

Towards the early part of the present century an agitation was set on foot to remove the chancel screen in York Minster. It was thought by some that its removal would open out the full view of the great building from west to east, and so a grand effect would be produced. Others argued that the screen was such a beautiful work in itself that to remove it would be a mistake. The point was hotly contested. Meetings were held, and letters written on the subject without end. The writer of the dialogue thus describes the state of things at the time in a foot-note. 'To such a pitch was the discussion respecting the screen carried on in York about this time, that nothing else was heard, spoken, or thought of. Footmen picking up scattered arguments in the dining-room debated together furiously in the servants' hall ; while in the kitchen the cook, housemaid, and scullion were all engaged in the dispute. At a dinner party given by Mr. C., a gentleman who sat with his back to the fire, feeling rather cold, requested a servant, whose head was full of the argu-ment, to *remove the screen*—meaning the one at the back of his chair. John started from his reverie at once, and quite forgetting where he was, called out that he would be hanged if it should be *stoored* for any man.'

Even the farm labourers got to hear tell about the Minster screen ; and being just then, as it happened, rather a *slack tahm* on his farm, one of these, Bob Jackson by name, takes it into his head to go and have a look at the screen for himself. As he rides along Goodram-gate he falls in with his friend Mike Dobson, and at first would have ridden past him, but Mike calls out to him, and after exchanging a few words of saluta-tion, they converse with one another thus :—

'*Mike.*—Bud what brings thee ti York this tahm o'
t' yeer,
Ah 's scear it diz yan good ti see tha heer.
Hez ta browt owt ti t' market, owr 's thi teeam ?
Are all thi bairns quiet fresh at yam an' t' De'ame ?
Ah sud a'e thowt you 'd all been thrang at t' farm
Mang t' haay an' coorn, for this is t' thrangest tahm.
    Bob.—Wi sum folks it may be ; bud, bairn, mah haay
Hez all been steck'd an theeak'd this monny a day ;

An' as t' wheeat weean't be ripe a fo'tnith yit,
An glooarin at it weean't mak it fit,
Ah 's cum'd ti Yorrk ti weeast an hoor or seea,
Sin' ah had nowt partik'lar else ti deea;
An', mun, for sum tahm past ah 's seear ah 's been
Just crazed ti knaw aboot this 'Minstther Screen.'
T' newspapers used ti talk o' nowt mich else,
It meead mair noise 'an yan o' t' Minstther bells;
An' seea ah 's cum'd ti see what it be leyke;
Diz thoo knaw owt at all aboot it, Meyke?'

Mike hereupon assures his friend that he is just the man
to act as guide; the nag is put up at a stable hard by and
carefully looked after; the two then enter the Minster
together.

'*Bob.*—Bon! it 's a stthrange greeat pleeace, an'
    dash it, Meyke,
It maks a chap feel desprit lahtle leyke;
Ah feels all iv a tthrimml with the dreead
Lest onny bad thowt noo sud fill mah heead.
Bud show us owre this Screen is ti be funnd;
Is 't summat up o' t' reeaf or doon o' t' gruund?
    Mike.—Whah! sootha, lootha, leeaks tha, theer it stan's,
T' bonniest wark ere meead by mottal han's;
That thing all claam'd wi lahtle dolls is t' Screen,
Aboot which all this noise an' worrk hez been;
An' if thoo 'll whisht a minnit, mun, or seea,
Ah 'll seean insense tha inti t' yal ti deea.

Thoo sees when Martin wiv his crackbraan'd tthricks
Set fire t' Minstther leyke a heeap o' wicks,
Fooaks frev all pairts o' t' coontthry varry seean
Clubb'd brass ti pay for reetin it ageean;
Seea ah, mang t' rest o' quality, put doon
(For ivvry lahtle helps thoo knaws) a croon.
Noo seean as t' brass was getten, afoor lang
Frev ivvry pairt a soort o' chaps did thrang;
Steean-meeasins, airtchitecks, an' sike like straight
All clustthered roond leyke mennies at a bait,
Sum ti leeak on an' give advice, bud Bob,
Neea doot meeast on 'em com ti laate a job.

Bud when ti leeak thruff t' Minstther they began,
They started ti finnd fau't wi 't tiv a man ;
This thing wer ower big, that ower small,
Whahl t' uther had neea business theer at all.
If ivver thoo did tiv a cobbler send
A pair o' sheun he did nut mak, ti mend,
Thoo 's heeard what scoores o' fau'ts he varry seean
Wad start ti finnd oot wi thae poor o'ad sheun ;
T' sowing wad be bad, an' seea wad t' mak,
An' t' leather good ti nowt at all bud crack.
Just seea theeas chaps funnd fau't wi neea pretense
Bud just 'at t' pleeace was nut belt by thersens;
Noo when they com ti t' Screen it strake 'em blinnd,
For nut yah sing'l fau't wi 't could they finnd,
Until yah cunning chap ti show his teeaste
Threeap'd oot leyke mad 'at it wer *wrangly pleeaced.*
He said it sud a'e been thrast fodther back,
For t' Neeave leeak ower lahtle it did mak,
An' that it seea confahn'd his view o' t' pleeace
Ti let it bahd wad be a sair disgreeace.
  Bob.—Whya, sike a feeal as that sud nivver stop
Doon heer belaw, bud gan an' glooar fra t' top ;
Ah mud as weel ding mah back deear off t' creeaks
An' then tell t' weyfe 'at it confahn'd mah leeaks ;
Mah wo'd sha 'd seean confahn mah leeaks for me
Wiv what ah weel sud merit—a black ee.
  Mike.—Yah feeal maks monny is a thing weel knawn,
An' t' trewth on it was heer meeast tthrewly shown ;
A soort o' chaps 'at scarcelins could desarn
T' diff'rence twixt an o'ad chetch an' a barn
Fra t' cuntthry sahd all roond aboot did thrang,
An swar it sud be shifted reet or wrang.
Noo deean't thoo think 'at ah had nowt ti say,
Bud just did let 'em hev ther oan fond way ;
Nay; hundhreds, bairn, o' foo'aks agreed wi me
'At stoored it owt nut, an' sud nivver be.
Disputes an' diff'rences 'at had neea end
Began ti start, frinnd quarrelled seean wi frinnd;
Mair non-sense teea aboot it, bairn, was writ,
'An ivver hez been fairly read thruff yit,

For monny a feeal his help each way ti lend
Geease quills an' feealscap weeasted bedoot end.
Meetins were held, men spak whahl they gat hoo'arse
An' barley-seeager rase i price o' coo'arse,
Whahl sum fooaks ti ther frinnds said seca mich then
Yah wo'd togither they 've nut spokken sen.
Bud thaugh seea dispritly they talked an' fowt,
Neean o' theeas meetins ivver com ti owt.
At last they did resolve ti call anuther,
Ti sattle t' quesh'n at yah way or t' uther;
When eftther beeals an shoots an' claps an' greeans
E neeaf ti wakken t' varry to'npike steeans,
T' quesh'n ti t' subscrahbers theer was put
Whether it sud be shifted or sud nut.
   Wa gat it, mun, as seeaf as seeaf could be;
For ivvry man o' sense did vooat wi me;
When lo! t' oad chairman frev his pocket beuk
A lot o' vooats lapt up i paper teuk,
Wi which i speyte of all 'at we could say
He to'nn'd t' quesh'n cleean ti t' other way,
An thus desahded it sud shifted be;
Bud *shifted* 't nivver was, as thoo may see.

.   .   .   .

Bud what did seeam ti me uncommon hard
An vexed ma seea ah knew nut hoo ti bahd,
Was 'at mah moncy, dash it, sud be ta'en
Ti deea that wi, ah wished sud nut be deean.
Could ah a'e gitten mah croon back, ah sware
'At egg nor shell on 't they sud nut see mair.
Bob.—Thah keeas just maks ma think o' Jamie Broon,
T' o'ad dhrunken carpentther of oor toon.
Thoo sees yah day ti Jamie's hoose ah went
An' fan' he'd gitten t' bailiers in for rent:
His weyfe, poor thing, was ommost flay'd ti deead,
An' rahv'd off t' hair by neeavesful frev her heead,
An' t' bairns all roored ti see ther muther roor,
Ah nivver i my leyfe seed sike a stoore.
O'ad Jamie he was set i t' ingle neuk
Glooarin at t' fire wiv a hauf fond leuk.

.   .   .   .

For him thoo sees ah caredn't hauf a pin,
For dhrink had browt him ti t' staate he was in;
Bud mah heart warked ti see t' poor bairns an t'
    deeame;
An' seea ah moonted t' meer an' skelped off heeame,
An' theer ah teuk fahve poond, pairt of a hooard
Ah 'd felt i t' Bahble ti be oot o' t' rooad
(For ah 's yan o' thor chaps at 's ommost seeaf
Ti spend all t' brass at 's handy ti my neeaf),
An' sent it tiv him by wer dowtther Nance
'At he mud pay off t' bailiers at yance.
Wad you believe as seean as t' brass he gat
He off ti t' public-hoos, an' theer he sat,
An' sat an.smeuk'd, an' smeuk'd an' dhrank away
Fra two'alve o'clock ti two'alve o'clock next day.
Just then ah enttherd t' hoose as ah past by
Ti git a dhrink, for ah wer desprit dhry;
An' theer ah fan t' oad raggil ti be seear
Stthritch'd ov his back deead dhrunk o' t' parlour fleear.
Ah thrast mah han' intiv his pocket neuk
An' back ageean-mah fahve poond nooate ah teuk;
For when ah gav him 't it wer mah intent
'At he sud deca nowt wi 't bud pay his rent.
Just seea ah think thoo had a rect ti tak
T' croon thoo subscrahbed, could thoo a'e gitten 't back,
Sen they ti whom t'was gi'en had got neea reet
Ti deea owt else bud what t'was gi'en for wi 't.

.   .   .   .

Mike.—An noo ah thinks ah 've tell'd tha all ah ken
An meead tha just as wahse, mun, as mysen;
Seea cum thoo yam wi me an see t' oad lass
An' git a beyte o' summat an' a glass;
For ah 's se'a hungered t'onnd ah scarce can bahd,
Ah 've gitten quiet a whemlin i t' insahd.
Bob.—Ah 've neea objections, bud afoor ah wag
A single leg ah 's tied ti see mah nag.
Mike.—Thoo needn't, mun, i Moss's yard he 's seeaf,
Ah 's warrant, ti get haay an' coorn eneeaf;
His isn't t' inn wheer rogueish hostlers cheeat,
An' greease t' hoss mooths ti set 'em past ther meeat.

Nay, Moss's man 'll tak mair tent o' t' bceast
'An onny muther of her bairn ommeeast.
  Bob.—Neea doot, neea doot he 'll tent it weel, bud, bon,
Ah mud as weel just see hoo he gits on ;
He may a'e slipp'd his heltther wiv a tug
Or gitten yah leg owr 't ti scrat his lug.
  Mike.—Aweel, leeak sharp, an deeant be owr lang,
Or yam bedoot tha ah 'se be foorc'd ti gang.
  Bob.—Yah minnit for ma, bairn, thoo needn't stop,
For ah 'll be back i t' crackin' of a lop.'

I may observe in passing, that the author of the
above dialogue gives it as a specimen of the North
Riding dialect ; but beyond one or two words, such as
bedoot and *heeame*, which are confined to that division
of the county, it might as appropriately be assigned to
the East Riding, thus confirming the opinion I have
expressed elsewhere, that the dialectical usages peculiar
to either Riding are, comparatively speaking, few.

The following example of the country talk which I
give, consists of an absurd story I heard told many
years ago by the master of a well-known grammar
school in the East Riding, whose capacity for relating
amusing incidents and reminiscences of various kinds
was quite phenomenal, and whose presence at a dinner
party was a guarantee to its success.   His only fault
was that he was not a Yorkshireman, and do what he
would he could not frame to pronounce our vernacular
aright.   I have therefore been compelled to turn the
language into as 'classical' Yorkshire as my limited
powers would allow.   I never heard any title given to
the story, and so for lack of a better, let us call it *Bill
and I*, or, *Drinkers, beware!*   The scene of the incident
is laid at a wayside inn.   One of the eye-witnesses
of the event described it in his own way pretty much as
follows :—

'Yah day ah wer gannin doon t' rooad ti Bo'lli'ton wi Bill, an' Bill wer gannin wi me, an' seea wa beeath on us wer gannin wi yan anuther. It wer a varry wahrm day, an' efthur a bit wa com tiv a public-hoos : seea Bill says ti ma, " wilt ta com in, mi lad, an' git a glass o' summat ? "

' " Whya," ah says, " it 's varry wahrm an' ah 's dhry : ah 's neea objections."

' An' seea wa beeath on us gans in ti t' public-hoos. An' as wa was set suppin wer yal an' ho'ddin a bit o' pross wi yan anuther, ah seed a greeat lang swanky chap set i t' lang-settle ower anenst us. Noo ah seed him all t' tahm gloorin at us despert hard ; an' eftther a bit ah says tiv him :

' " Noo, mi lad, what 's ta gloorin at si hard forr ? "

' " Whya," says he, " when yan hez'nt nowt ti sup yans-sen, ah thinks 'at t' next best thing ti deea is ti leeak at them 'at hez."

' Wa laff'd, an' ah says, " Whya ; bud wa can seean mend that : what wilt tha tak ? "

' " Aw," says he, " ah 's nowt partiklar."

' " Whya, bud thoo mun give it a neeam," ah says.

' " Then," says t' man, " ah 'll tak a quahrt o' yal."

' " A quahrt ! " ah says, " wad n't a pahint sarve ya ? "

' " Ah deean't think it wad," says he ; " thoo sees ah 's gitten sikan a greeat thropple 'at a pahint nobbut wets yah sahd."

' Seea ah tells t' sarvant-lass an' sha fetches him a quahrt o' yal.'

' Noo t' man had gitten sikan a mooth as ah nivver seed ; it *war* a mooth ; it war a reg'lar frunt deear : an' he oppens his mooth an' he sups t' quahrt o' yal at yah slowp. Noo ah seed him deea it, an' Bill seed him an' all ; wa beeath on us seed him, an' seea what ah 's tellin o' ya 's reet.

' He sets t' mug doon, an' ah leeaks at him ; an' ah says tiv him ; " Noo, my lad, dost ta think thoo could deea that ageean ? "

' " Whya," says he, " ah thinks ah mebbe mud "

' " Then thoo s'al." An' seea ah gans mysen an' ah fetches him anuther quahrt o' yal. An' as ah wer cumin' thruff t' deear-steead ah seed a moose-trap setten aback o' t' deear, an' there wer a moose, iv it an' all ; it warn't a varry big moose, an' it warn't a varry lahtle moose, it wer just a middlinish sahz'd soort of a moose ; an' ah taks up t' trap an' ah pops t' moose inti t' jug, an' ah teeams t' yal inti t mug, an' froths it weel up, an' ah gi'es it ti t' man. Then he taks t' mug intiv his han' an' oppens his mooth—(noo ah seed him, an' Bill seed him an' all ; wa beeath on us seed him, an' seea what ah 's tellin' o' ya 's reet)—aye ; he oppens his mooth an' sups off t' yal, moose an' all, at yah slowp. An' then ah leeaks at him, an' ah says tiv him, " Noo, my lad, hoo didst ta leyke *that* yal ? "

' " Aw," he says, " t' yal aals nowt ; varry good yal ; *bud ah thinks there wer a bit o' hops i that last !* " '

A correspondent from the Holderness district, whose knowledge of the dialect is well known by what he has written on it and in it, was good enough to send me a number of his compositions, among which was an account of a visit to the country of a quick-witted little lame laddie, whose lot had been cast in a dingy alley of a large town. He gives a description of what the boy saw, and tells some of his impressions of country life, and how he revelled in it.

I will only here quote a short extract which refers to what Tommy thought about the country talk which was so strange to him. It aptly illustrates a few homely words and expressions. He says :—

' The words that they use are so funny,
   I laugh very much at their talking.
When a woman is dressed up a fright,
   They say—" Sha 's a greeat mollymawkin."
If you spill any soup on the table,
   They cry out " Aw ! leeak hoo thoo 's slutherin."
And if anyone's weeping and wailing
   She 's sure to be " blairin' an' blutherin."
Whenever I laugh very much ;—
   " Aw ! leeak hoo he werricks an' gizzens."
And a shirt that is scorched at the fire ;—
   " Diz tha see ? Lawks a massy ! it swizzens ! "

When anyone shivers with cold,
    " He's all of a ditherum dotherum,"
And when you're a tease or a plague
    They say that you "werrit an' bother 'em."
A door never creaks on its hinge,
    It always "beeals oot on it jimmer,"
And a pot always " gallops an' boils "
    When it gets much beyond a good simmer.
If you walk pretty hard round the house
    They say that you " rammack an' cluntther,"
And a woman who's not very neat
    Is a " macktubs, a bummax, a buntther."
A blow on the nose is a " snevitt,"
    And scissors are always called " sithers,"
Whenever the road's very dirty
    They say that it " closhes an' slithers."
A man never grumbles and growls,
    Though he frequently " chitthers an' chuntthers,"
And pigs are called " nackies " and " chackies "
    Before they grow into big grunters.
Dull people are said to feel " dowly,"
    A spendthrift is always a " weeastther,"
And when you don't walk very smart
    They say that you " slammock an' sleeastther."
A trap for a hare is a " snickle,"
    A thing that is brittle is " smopple,"
And when they are milking a cow
    They tie her hind legs with a " hopple."
They say that a man's in a " pankin "
    Whenever he flies in a passion,
And an old woman dressed like a girl
    Is described as " oa'd yow i lamb fashion."
I could tell you some scores of queer words,
    And I would if my paper was longer,
So I'll keep 'em until I come home,
    As soon as I grow a bit stronger.'

It will be found that a few of the words in the above extract are not contained in the Glossary; for, interesting though they may be, they seem to partake of the

I

nature of many other terms of a similar, scarcely 'classical,' character, which might be almost indefinitely multiplied. I have consequently thought it better to omit them.

A good bit of Yorkshire is that which I heard told about twenty years ago by a gentleman whose powers of imitation in the dialect were remarkable. It was called *Nannie Nicholson Taatie Pie.* The said Nannie Nicholson had a potato 'pie' in her garden: one morning, to her dismay, she found her store of potatoes in sad disorder, holes and rents were made in it, and the potatoes were strewn in all directions; it was in, fact 'a bull in a china shop' sort of business. To make matters worse, she could not tell how it had happened. At length one of her neighbours volunteered to make enquiries, and after minute and careful investigation, he came to the old lady and said that *he 'd fan' it oot*, and he thus related the concatenation of circumstances that led to the disaster :—

'It wer all along o' t' rezzil a scrattin' under t' hen bauk : t' rezzil flaayed t' au'd cock, t' cock flakkered ower t' wall an' flaayed t' bull, an' t' bull rooam'd agaan t' yat-stowp an' deng'd t' staggarth yat off t' creeaks an' went beldherin doon t' looanin leyk owt mad; then he met Jamie Broon wi a lahtle yeffin dog, t' dog yeff'd, an' he flaay'd t' bull, an' t' bull teeak ower t' hedge an' lowped reet inti Nannie Nicholson taatie pie.'

Other versions of this well-known story have been circulated, one at considerably greater length, which records some additional exploits of the bull, how that after 'lowping' the hedge he made a 'bonny blash i t' dike' and then got on to a moor and 'tthrade an au'd steg ti deeath,' and how that the lads gave chase and ultimately captured him. But I have recorded the story almost *verbatim* as it was told me.

As a rider upon the following example, I will add one of a similar kind which I have received from Holderness. A countryman of that district once related how a wasp made the churning of butter too salt, and so spoilt it : this he described as follows, in answer to a question how such a thing could possibly be :—

'Whya, t' wasp teng'd t' dog, an t' dog hanched at t' cat, an' t' cat ran owerquart t' staggarth an' flaay'd t' cockerill, an' t' cockerill fligg'd ower t' wall an' flaay'd yan o' t' beeos, an' t' beeos beeal'd an' stack it heead thruff t' dairy windther an' flustthered t' lass seea awhahl sha let t' sau't-kit tumm'l inti t' kennin' o' butther.'

It is matter for regret that any of our folk should ever be ashamed of their broad speech, which they have inherited from their fore-elders; but this not infrequently is so. An acquaintance of mine, who till lately lived in Hull, one day took a walk to a village a few miles distant from that busy centre. Being a native York-shireman himself, he always enjoyed hearing the, to him, familiar and expressive cadences and phrases of the Holderness vernacular. One good old soul whom he visited on this occasion, thinking his ears might be shocked by her every-day rough honest speech, made some attempts to refine herself into polite English, which were as needless as they were laughable. The father was nursing his child, and telling it he 'wad a'e ti be up afoor t' craaks i t' mornin' an' tak his braykus wiv him.' Says the wife, 'nut *braykus*, faether, say *breekus*; wa maun't a'e t' bairn browt up broad spok-ken ; naw, bliss her, she shan't be browt up broad spokken.' At another house our friend heard an irate parent threatening to 'sowle' his refractory son 'like a dog sowlin a pig.'

Let me here insert a very typical piece from the Pickering Moors; it was sent to me from that neighbourhood by one whose knowledge of the Yorkshire tongue is well known.

The dialogue is between two farm labourers in the ploughing field, during a short pause in their work:—

Assy Gooadge.—What 's tha want noo, sum bacca ?

Mate.—Naw. We 'r gahin' ti a'e waint deed seean, a'e n't wa ?

Assy G.—Aye, ah heeard seea mysen. What 's it all aboot ?

Mate.—Whya, ther nobbut hez ti be yah guardian for oor toon, an' ther 's tweea on 'em wants ti be in, seea ther 'll be a contest.

Assy G.—Sall *we* a'e ti deea owt ?

Mate.—Aye ; ther 'll be paapers sent roond, an' then thoo 'll a'e ti vooat wheea thoo 's forr.

Assy G.—Bud ah can't reyte. Canst ta giv uz a leet ?

Mate. Here 's a match. Ah gi'en ower smeukin' mysen ommost. T' weyfe can sahn thi vooat fo' tha, ah 's think.

Assy G.—Aye, sha 's a good scholar, an' lahrnt hersen ; sha reytes all oor letthers, sumtahmes gans ti t' skeealmaastther ti ax him ti dhriss t' onvallops for her. Bud what deea tha git for bein' guardian ah wundher ?

Mate.—Aw; nowt 'at ah knaw on.

Assy G.—Well howivver ! That caps owt, it diz ah 's seear. Wheea 'll a'e ti pay t' expenses o' t' election then ?

Mate.—It 'll a'e ti cum oot o' sike feeals as us mebbe. Ah 's feelin' cau'd. Gee-up, hoss !

Assy G.—Aye ; it 's snahrly an' cau'd ti-day, bud it 'll' seean be lowsin' tahm noo. Cum here, ahrve ; wo-hop !

A man at Ampleforth some years ago attended the funeral of an old friend there who was a Roman Catholic, and was buried with the usual ceremonial of that

Church. The somewhat ornate ritual and the, to him, unusual length of the service, exercised the poor man's mind a good deal; in fact, he was profane enough to describe the ceremony as a whole, as 'weeant gannins on,' and as to some of the details he expressed himself somewhat thus : -

'Aye, they've gitten poor au'd Kit (Christopher) sahded at last. They wur a long whahl ower t' job, bud they've deean it at last. They had sum lahtle lads i wheyte goons; an' they put t' coffin upon a bink i t' Chetch, an' read summat 'at ah could mak nowt on. Then t' lads started ti reek t' preeast, an' they reek'd t' ain t' uther an' they reek'd au'd Kit ; an' then they all bood ti t' preeast. Eftther a bit they started ti degg t' preeast, then they degg'd t' ain t' uther, an' they degg'd au'd Kit. Bless ya, bairn, it wer a lang job, bud they 've gitten him happ'd up at last.'

It need hardly be observed that the 'reeking' and the 'degging' referred to the use of incense and holy water at certain parts of the impressive service.

It is not often that one forgets the stories of one's childhood. There is a bit I heard my father tell as it was told to him many years ago by a North Riding rector. The said clergyman was standing talking to a parishioner one day when a lad passed on the other side of the 'toon stthreet' that he did not recognise. Enquiring of the woman to whom he was speaking who it was she soon 'insensed' him.

'Whya, Sorr,' says she, 'deeant ya knaw? They call him *Timmy James's cute lad.'*
'And what do they call him Timmy James's cute lad for?'
'Whya ! then ah 's leyke ti tell ya. Ya see yah day his meeastther sent him ti Hoonton wiv a cart wi a toop ; an' as he wer gannin doon t' lonnin he meets yan o' thor Pedlars wi seein-glasses. Says t' chap, "mah lad, wilt ta bahy a seein-glass ?" "Naay," says t' lad, " ah a'e na brass for

seein-glasses." Seea then they gans banttherin along wi
yan anuther. Says t' lad, " Nobbut thoo 'llt let mah toop see
hissen iv a seein-glass, ah 'll gie tha saxpence." (Noo he
kenn'd 'at t' toop wer varry guilty o' buttin.) An' seea he
said he mud. An' t' lad ho'ds yan o' t' seein-glasses up
afoor t' toop, an' t' toop runs at it wi sikan a mash ! Says t'
chap, " Thoo young raggil, bud ah 'll mak tha pay for this."
Seea he gans eftther him ti Hoonton an' he plecans tiv his
maastther on him. Bud t' lad varry seean cums in an' he
shoots out " Maastther, Maastther, gi'e him nowt ; a
bargin 's a bargin ; ah gav him saxpence ti let t' toop sec
hissen iv a seein-glass." An' seea t' oa'd chap went away
an' he gat nowt.'

The story of the cat and the drowning mouse has
been frequently told, but I give it here as another short
example of Yorkshire, 'as she is spoke.' I have not
seen it written, and so I write it from memory. There
may be other versions in existence, but the moral of
the story is in all cases one and the same.

'Ther wer yance a moos 'at had gitten it hooal just agaan
a greeat vat iv a briewery ; t' vat wer full o' liquor iv a gen'ral
waay, an' yah day t' lahtle moos chanced ti tumm'l in an'
wer leyke ti be dhroonded. An' seea, says t' moos tiv itsen,
what mun i deea ? T' sahds is seea slaap an' brant ah doot
ah sa'll nivver git yam na mair; ah 's flaayed ah sa'll a'e ti
gan roond an' roond whahl ah 's dhroonded. Bud eftther a
bit t' cat pops it heead ower t' top o' t' vat, an' sha leeaks at
t' moos an' says, what wilt tha gie ma if ah git tha oot o' t'
vat ? Whya, says t' moos, thoo s'all a'e ma. Varry weel, says t'
cat, an' seea sha hings hersen doon o' t' insahd ; t' moos varry
seean ran up t' cat back and lowp'd reet fra t' top o' t' vat
intiv it hooal an' t' cat eftther it ; bud t' moos wer ower sharp
an' gat fo'st ti t' hooal, an' then to'ns roond an starts ti laff at
t' cat ; t' cat wer ommost wahld at that, an' shoots oot, did'nt
thoo saay 'at if ah gat tha oot o' t' vat ah sud a'e tha. Aay,
bud, says t' moos, *folks 'll saay owt when they 're i dhrink!*'

The following short passage is a specimen of our

dialect, in which a farm lad attempts to describe to his friend the symptoms of an attack of the influenza, and how he contracted the ailment, or rather, we should say, how it was brought to a crisis.

This friend, whom we will call Dick, remarked how, a month ago, with some concern, he had noticed that Jack, the other *dramatis persona*, had 'leeak'd a bad leeak'; whereupon Jack gives an account of himself in these words :—

'Whya ! noo then ah 'll tell tha hoo ah is. Thoo sez 'at ah leeak'd a bad leeak when thoo seed ma a bit sen. Ah ' laay thoo wad a'e leeak'd a bad leeak an' all if thoo'd been hann'ld as ah 've been hann'ld. Fooaks calls this complaint 'at 's stirrin t' inflewenza ; but as ah tells 'em, it 's neean it ; it 's summat a vast warse. Thoo knaws yah day at t' forend o' t' year ah 'ed ti tak fower beeos for oor maastther ti Bev'la : it wer a varry cau'd daay, an' afoor ah gat ti t' far end it startcd an' it fair teeam'd doon wi raan, an' varry seean ah 'ed n't a dhry threed ti mi sark.

' When ah gat ti t' spot, t' man war n't theer ; an' seea ah gans ti t' hoos ti see t' missis, an' sha sends a lahtle lad ti laate him. Noo then, as ah was stood i t' deear-steead wi t' missis, yan o' t' beeos see'd t' coos iv a pastur, an' afoor ah could git tiv im he was ower t' hcdge an' dyke an' intiv a seed clooas, an' went beealin an' lowpin' ower t' lan's fit ti rahve up t' grund : ah eftther him wi t' dog, an' he runs fo'st ti yah sahd o' t' clooas an' then ti t' uther, whahl ah thowt ah wer boun ti be fair bet wiv him, bud at last wa gat him thruff t' yat an' back ti t' uthers. Ah left mi beeos and started back for yam.

' Noo, bairn, when ah gat tiv oor pleeacc, ah felt mysen iv a varry queer waay. T' cau'd had clapp'd on ti ma, an when neet com ah wer all iv a atterill : an' seea ah varry seean fligged up ti t' bauks as t' au'd hens diz ; an' then ah wer bed-fast for ommost a fo'tnith. Tahm 'at ah wer liggin i bed ah could hardlins bahd ; mi heead wark'd an' mi beeans wark'd ; bud ah was t' warst i mi limbs reet fra mi lisk ti mi teeas. T' doctther com, an' he ga' ma sum stuff ti dill t' paan, bud next daay 't wer as bad as ivver ageean. T' Settherda eftther t' Doctther com'd, ah started ti boaken hard, an' ah think 'at that did ma t' maist good of owt, bud all t' tahm ah felt that waak an waffy an' doddery whahl ah thowt yance ower at it wer boun ti be owered wi ma. Bud howivver, at t' week end ah started ti mend, an' ah teeak anuther bottle o' stuff an that meead ma 'at ah could eeat a bit, and then ah teeak anuther an' that just capp'd ma ; an' noo thoo sees ah 's aboot at t' aud bat : bud mahnd ya, Dick, ah a'e n't fair kessen 't yit. Sum fooaks says at it 's smittin, bud ah 's seear ah knaw nowt aboot that neeways. Bud ah'll tell ya, lad ; thoo maunt git it yoursen, or else it 'll fleeace ya, an' varry sharp an' all.'

Although the scene of what I am next going to relate is, strictly speaking, beyond the border of the North and East Ridings, though still in the county of broad acres, I cannot withhold it. I am indebted to a correspondent for it.

Among the inhabitants of a country village in the West Riding, were a goodly number of folk whom Apollo had inspired to tune a variety of instruments of music, both for strings and wind, as well as to make melody with the voice. And so it came to pass that these good people determined to give a concert. A conductor was invited from a neighbouring town, and after much practising a night was fixed, and the performance came off. Among the attractions of the programme was an orchestral piece, which everybody was looking forward to with intense pleasure. All went in splendid style until the fourth movement, an *adagio*. In the middle of this the trombone all by himself, gave out a sound almost loud enough to blow the roof off. The audience were startled, while the conductor looked furious ; and when the grand *finale* of the piece was reached, he took the trombone-player to

task, and blew *him* up sky high for such erratic conduct ;
'Why,' said the man, by way of apology, 'ah thowt it
wur a nooat, an' it wur nobbut a fly—*bud ah plaayd it!*'

Nothing illustrates our folk-speech better than those
short, homely, every-day phrases and sayings which
may be constantly heard round cottage doors, or in the
fields, by those whose ears are open for them. With
few exceptions, all the short sentences which are here
added I have myself heard at various times, and I give
them as they were spoken.

1. Cum thi ways in an' sit ya doon.

2. T' hosses was good 'uns ; they 'd buckle undher wi ther
bellies ommost ti t' grunnd when wi was teeaglin up t' tim'er
on ti t' waggin ; aye, poor things, they was grand 'uns.

3. Ah deean't gan bauboskin' aboot leyke sum on 'em ; ah
sticks ti t' heeaf.

4. Ah 'll wahrm tha thi jacket if thoo deean't give ower this
minnit —— noo, ah 's tellin o' ya.

5. T' pales has ommost whemm'ld ower inti t' plantin.

6. When t' hoss wer new yauk'd it lowp'd reet on end.

7. Hoo 's yoor fooaks?

8. Ah 's sadly tew'd aboot oor Dick ; he gits set i t' public-
hoos of a neet, an' then he cums yam as meean as muck,
whahl he 's fit ti rahve all afoor him.

9. T' pigs has been makkin sad deed reeatin up t' swath.

10. Yan 'll nivver see t' marrow tiv him.

11. Sum daays ah 's middlin' ; an' uther sum ah 's as waffy
an' waake as owt.

12. Ah put a bit o' ass uppo t' cauzer—au'd fooaks falls
numb. (Said by one who had strewn ashes on the foot-path
in frosty weather.)

13. *Q.*—What sort of work had you to do ?
A.—Wa striked, an' lowsd shaffs an' helped ti windher
lahn an' all soorts ; we was nivver fast.

14. Is ta laatin oor maastther ?

15. He nips aboot as cobby as can be.

16. Ah wrowght an' tew'd amang t' taaties an' wezzels ti
scrat eneeaf ti feed t' pig.

17. Wa didn't want ti hing him oot o' t' way. (Spoken with reference to hanging a dog.)

18. Wheer a'c ya felt yoursell ; we 've laated ya all ower.

19. Thoo fraames leyke an au'd woman i stthraw boots. (Said of one working indolently.)

20. *A*.—I am sorry to hear your husband has been getting drunk frequently lately.

      B.—He did cum yam a bit fresh yah neet ; bud ya see it 's Kessmas tahm !

21. They meead nowther end nor sahd oot ; it was nowt bud differin' an' threeapin.

22. Pleeas 'm will ya wakken us at fower, acoz it 's weshin mornin.

23. Ah s'all nivver mannish widoot Jack gans an' all.

24. Stop a bit whahl wa git wer dinners.

25. Sha tell'd sike teeals as nivver you heeard.

26. Noo deean't be neyce (i. e. shy) ; help yoursells.

27. Pleeas, we're oot o' streea ; there 's nowt bud a bit o' mushy stuff at t' far end o' t' loft fleear.

28. Nowt o' t' sooart.

29. T' lass sets her ti t' stee, an' her muther taks her t' rest o' t' waay yam.

30. Ah teeak cramp i mi leg, an' all t' guidhers cotthered up all ov a lump.

31. Sha dhropt t' pankin uppo t' fleear an' pashed it all i bits.

32. He was bitten wiv a ratten an' gat prood flish intiv it, an' his hand was all ov a atterill.

33. Baa'n, ah was ommost mafted, it wer that wahrm : ah did feel putten oot o' t' waay, it was seea maftin'.

34. They 'd mutton ti ther dinners, bud it wer nowt bud glorr.

35. Ah 'll gie tha yan on thi nappercracker (head).

36. He hackered an' stammered leyke an au'd ganthert ' chooakin wi bran.

37. T' craws is varry throng ; they 're fettlin up ther nests ageean ; bud sum on' em 's been rahvin 'em all i bits leyke all that, an' they 've been feyghtin yan anuther reet doon ti t' grunnd.

38. *Q*.—Is there much corn out northwards?

A.—Aye, a vast; ah seed sum i peyke, an' sum i sweeathe, an' sum i all forrms.

39. T' lahtle lass is nobbut badly; sha 's cuttin' her assel teeth.

40. Tak t' bands off t' shelvin' an' ah 'll fetch t' lad ti tak t' au'd meer yam.

41. Thoo hang-gallas thief, thoo, ah 'll wahrm tha thi jacket fo' tha, nobbut ah could catch tha.

42. Let 's feeal it, an' gang laat it. (Let us hide it and go and seek it.)

43. *Jack, standing among a group of lads, loq.* Jim; a'e ya a bit o' bacca on ya?

Jim.—Naw, ah 's seear ah a'e n't.

Jack.—A'e ya ony o' ya ony on 't on ya? (This specimen was told me many years ago.)

44. *Q.*—Well, N., how do you manage to get your pigs to look so well?

A.—Whya, ah gi'es 'em a bit o' slap i t' mornins' an' a bit o' wo'zz'l at neets, an' they corresponds wi yan anuther.

45. Thoo 's a dossel-heead. (Dossel is the straw knob on the top of a stack.)

46. Ah 've stthraan'd t' guidhers o' my shackle.

47. We 've gotten him neycely sahded, i. e. we have got him decently buried.

48. He stack t' au'd ass wi t' shill (shaft) end.

49. He gans wiv his nooaze uppo t' grunnd. (Said of a man who was very much bent.)

50. Whyah, noo! ah think this dinner tahm 'll set him, (Said of one who was lying *in extremis.*)

51. Sha hings an' trails aboot t' hoos; sha 's sadly oot on 't.

52. Cloot his lugs. (Box his ears.)

53. Wheea 's owes ya, an' wheer deea ya cum fra? (Said to a small boy by a stranger.)

54. *Q.*—Well, how are you to-day?

A.—Whya! ah 's aboot at t' au'd spot; ah 's neea forrarder, ah 's backarder if owt.

55. *Q.*—Now, A., how is your wife this morning?

A. It 's ti neea use tellin o' ya a stooary; sha 's been i bed a good bit an' ah think sha 'll nivver cum oot neea mair awhahl sha 's hugg'd oot; ya see sha 's been a woman 'at 's wrowght hard an' had a stthrang fam'ly.

56. *Q.*—Are you still at the same work, John ?

A.—Naw ; ah 've lapp'd up wi Joe ; ah seean lowsened fra t' job.

57. In a former parish of my father's an old woman fell down and broke her leg, and on his asking her how it happened, she said, ' Ah chipp'd ma teea i t' pooak on t' fleear.' (I tripped up, or caught, my toe in the sack on the floor.)

58. They weean't a'e ti be varry numb-heeaded uns ti start at that job.

59. *Q.*—Well, William, what 's it gahin ti deea ?

A.—Whya, ah doot it 's gahin ti be blethery.

60. Ah nivver sees him noo bedoot ah git a glent on him ov a Sunda as he passes.

61. Thoo leeaks as thoff thi poddish was welsh (i. e. you put on a wry face).

62. What wi coughin' an' spittin' ah 's kept agait.

63. *Q.*—But who is to pay for the pump being mended ?

A.—Wa s'all a'e ti mak a getherin.

64. *Q.*—How is your husband ?

A.—He 's gotten ti worrk ageean, an' ah thinks he betther for 't ; ya see, when he 's set i t' hoos he gits agait o' studyin', an' he maks hissen that nerrvous whahl yan dizn't knaw what ti deea.

65. When ah wed mah missis sha wer a lahtle cobby lass, bud noo sha 's a greeat poshy body.

66. They went thruff t' hooals at t' backsahd o' t' hoosen. (This was heard by me not long since near Whitby ; the old plural *hoosen* is now rarely used.)

67. We 've awlus letten him mootther oor bit o' stuff. (Said of a miller grinding corn for a farmer, which he did by multure, i. e. taking a portion of the corn as payment for grinding.)

68. Thoo mun think ma on ti remmon it.

69. Ah doot thoo 'll nut a'e tahm ti put t' bell in for au'd John afoor t' Chetch.

70. They yan lited on t' uther ti deea 't. (They depended on one another to do it).

71. Are t' broth cau'd eneeaf ti sup. (Broth is always spoken of in the plural number.)

72. Ah 've ta'en t' top off'n t' clock; ah 's freetened o' nappin' t' glass.

73. You 've gitten a grand leeak-on o' gess ti year (i.e. there is every prospect of a good crop).

74. What 's ta nestlin at? Wheer ivver is t' meer gahin ti git crowled teea? (Blacksmith to a mare he is shoeing.)

75. They nivver diz neea good eftther they git ankled in wi them lot.

76. Deean't fash thysel ower 't.

77. Tak care t' hansel thi new bonnet o' Eeastther Sunda; it suits tha tiv a pop.

78. Ah weean't a'e ya scrattin up mah new tthrod; noo then, ah 's tellin o' ya.

79. Ah 's had a weary whahl on her, bud ah 's gitten shot on her noo. (Said by a man who had recently lost his wife !)

80. Ah 's jealous ah sal nivver be quiet betther.

81. Thoo mucky bairn ! what hivver hez ta been deeain' ti git thi feeace all setten in wi muck leyke that : gan thi waays ti t' beck an git thisen weshed, or ah 'll help tha.

82. Mah wo'd, bud them 's gran' uns. .

83. Noo he did leeak sadly begone did poor au'd Frank as seean as he fan' it oot.

84. *Jack.*—Bill, what tahm hez 't gitten teea? *Bill.*—If ah 's reet it 'll be fahve or a bit betther mebbe. *Jack.*—Then ah mun lap up, an' away an' git t' beeos foddhered.

85. Dick; whau 's yon? *Dick.*—Ah 's seear ah deean't knaw ; ah 's neea kennin for him.

86. They 're awlus differin' an threeapin aboot summat.

87. Au'd Mary 's gotten t' heart diseeas : an' sha can't bahd ti be clash'd or putten aboot or owt; it tews her sadly.

88. Ah leeamed mysen sadly wi t' axe, bud ah lapp'd t' pleeace up : it blooded t' clout despertly at fo'st, bud it varry seean mended.

Examples of this kind might be indefinitely multi-plied, but enough perhaps have been cited to show the general character of the folk-talk at the present date.

CHAPTER VII.

To anyone who is acquainted with the folk-speech of East Yorkshire a visit to Denmark cannot but be deeply interesting. Everyone knows that the languages of the two peoples have much in common ; nay, it is not too much to say that the backbone of the Yorkshire dialect is Danish pure and simple. This has been from time to time brought out and exemplified by others who have written upon the subject. When one hears Danish spoken in some of the country districts, the likeness is in some respects still more striking than it appears when written, as I will presently briefly draw attention to in one or two particulars. A Danish friend of mine, an artist, told me some years ago that when he first came to England to sketch and study on our Yorkshire coast, he knew but little of our language, and absolutely nothing of our Northern dialects : he took up his abode for a time near Flamborough, and used frequently to listen attentively to the broad speech of the Flamborough fishermen, which contained so many Danish words and modes of expression that he could at once make out much of what they were talking about without any difficulty. I subsequently sent my friend a specimen of our North Riding dialect, requesting him to make notes of words and expressions therein that were familiar to him in Denmark. When he returned the document the notes were so numerous as quite to surprise me at first ; though when we consider the extent and character of the Danish occupation of this part of England, it is hardly to be wondered at that its indelible impression upon the language of the people still remains so clearly and deeply marked ; in fact it would have been strange had it been otherwise. During the year 1890 I made two journeys to Denmark to stay with Danish friends ; once to the extreme East of the country within a few miles of the Swedish coast, and once to the extreme West, within hearing of the roar of ' Vesterhavet ' as it lashes in its fury the long low sandy shores of Jutland. To me these visits were full of interest. My friend in the West was unsurpassed in his knowledge of the Danish dialects and folk-lore, and being an excellent English scholar, I learnt much from him. I had, too, an opportunity of hearing the Danish folk-talk spoken in its fulness, for the people of that part had mixed but little with the outer world, and in their speech and customs were not far removed from their fore-elders of former centuries.

Almost the first place I visited in the neighbourhood was the island of Fanö. This is the most northerly of the Frisian group, and the only one of them which still belongs to Denmark. It was a sunny day in July when I crossed over the narrow belt of water which separates Fanö from the mainland. The impressions made by what I saw on this quaint little island I shall not easily forget. In days gone by, each of the different islands had its own peculiar costumes ; but, sad to say, the irresistible force of fashion has broken through traditional usage, and Fanö alone remains faithful to its old and pretty fancy in the matter of dress. The Fanö folk have nothing to say to the latest Paris novelties; they know better what suits them : it is a picturesque sight on a Sunday morning to see the streams of people—men, women, and children, book in hand, scrupulously tidy and clean in appearance, wending their way to the Kirk, the women clad in costumes and decked with adorn-ments similar to those of generations long passed away, which I will not attempt here to describe, while the children are taught to know or at least to like no other garb. I will only add in passing that it requires seven *ske'ts*, as we call them in Yorkshire, of fourteen feet each, in order to make a dress for a Fanö woman—that is, nearly thirty-three yards of material, which seemed to be somewhat in excess of what is usually thought enough in this part of the country ; but these ample folds contribute to the appearance as well as to the warmth of the dress.

My return journey from Fanö to the mainland was attended with some little risk of being stranded. There were two Danes with me when we hired the boat to take us across. We delayed starting beyond the appointed hour, and the tide was rapidly ebbing. The skipper, a fine specimen of a sailor of the old school, who must have seen more than seventy summers, assured us with some anxiety that it would be as much as we could do to get over the strait, even if we started at once. We made haste and jumped into the boat : the sail was hoisted, and we were under way in less than a minute. A stiffish breeze was blowing at the time, and we made rapid headway, though not without once or twice touching the bottom with the keel ; in fact so little water

was there to spare that one of the party had to sit in
the bows to trim the boat, with two of us amidships and
the skipper astern. At length we were nearing the
opposite shore in safety, and the passenger in the bows,
thinking that all cause for anxiety was over, made a
motion to alter his position in the boat, whereupon the
old Viking shouts excitedly with the true Jutlandic .
accent ' Du maa ei komme endnu.' To my ear this
sounded as much like our Yorkshire dialect as anything
could do that was not it ; and I feel sure that any
Yorkshireman on hearing it would have at once understood it. It is true we have no negative like *ei* in our
folk-speech ; *endnu* is pronounced precisely as our *inow*,
which had perhaps better be written *inu* ; and although
the meanings of *endnu* and *inu* are not quite identical,
yet I cannot but think these two words are in reality the
same in their origin, the transition of meaning from ' at
present ' to 'almost at present ' or ' shortly,' being an
easy one.

The similarity between the Danish dialects and our
own is to be seen in a great variety of ways over and
above the form of the words themselves.

In a single chapter it would be impossible to draw
out the points of resemblance at any great length ; I
must be content with touching upon a very few of them
which may be taken as types of others not less interesting.

Turning our eyes homewards, we see that the whole
face of the country from the Tees to the Humber, to
say nothing of East Lincolnshire, is thickly covered
with Scandinavian names, and no inconsiderable part
of the ancient language is spoken even at this day, and
with the old traditional pronunciation. Before proceeding further, however, I will give a single, but what

K

seems to me a very remarkable example of the numerous survivals of the Northern tongue of a thousand years ago.

There is a word in our Yorkshire folk-talk still current, which I have repeatedly heard used by some of our older people to express the corners of the mouth or the eyes—I mean the word *weeks*. *T' weeks o' yer mooth* or *t' weeks o' yer een* are expressions well understood at this time in the North Riding. Who would suppose at first sight that the corners of one's mouth and eyes had any· thing in common with the word universally employed to designate the bands of savage marauders or pirates who for centuries devastated our shores—the Vikings? Yet so it is. We sometimes hear this word pronounced Vi-kings, as if these invaders of our shores were a sort of petty kings or chiefs instead of merely Vik-ings, that is to say; inhabitants of the Viks—the bays or creeks of the shores of various corners of Scandinavia, and specially, as it would seem, of the southern parts of the peninsula and of Denmark. Our word *week* above mentioned, and Vik or Vig, are the same word, and uttered, be it observed, with exactly the same pronunciation as is preserved in Denmark at the present day. So that, instead of calling the hardy yet cruel Norse pirates Vi-kings, we ought rather to term them Veek-ings or Week-ings, just as in modern Danish a man from the Faröes is called a Faröing. The same word appears over and over again as a place-name, sometimes under the form *wick* and sometimes as *Wyke*, in the latter case pronounced as it is spelt ; and in other parts—Lincolnshire, to wit— the word appears again as *Wig*, which, substituting *v* for *w*, is the Danish spelling of the old Norse Vik. The form *wyke* can be nothing more than a corruption of the original word. I have long regarded this Yorkshire

word *weeks*, as applied to the corners of the mouth and
eyes, as one of our most interesting relics; for the true
Norse vowel-sound of *Vik* is preserved with singular
clearness by means of that solitary word in our dialect,
although there are other words where the same sound
is drawn near to.

When it is observed that the surface of the country
is covered with names of Scandinavian origin, I do not
refer only to place-names, our *bys* and our *thorpes*,
though these are as 'common as peas,' as the saying is,
but to words which give us an insight into the nature or
surroundings of the land, as well as to terms that pertain
to the settlement upon, and the cultivation of the soil.

On the subject of place-names commonly so called, I
do not propose to dwell, although much might be said
about them; I may, however, mention in passing, that
any one who has travelled in the West of Denmark
may easily imagine how the *by* originated. It is one of
the most striking features of that region to see the
numerous farmsteads with their enclosures dotted about
over the country : a single rude farmstead at the time
of the Danish colonisation of Northumbria would con-
stitute a *by*, and by degrees other houses clustered round
or near them ; a *by* was in fact in the first instance a
settlement, and afterwards a village or town. As regards
thorpe it is worth notice that in our Yorkshire pronunciation of that word is conserved its Danish form
very closely. *Tthrup* represents as nearly as may be
the dialectic rendering of the word, the aspiration being
very slight, and this is nothing more nor less than the
Norse termination *trup*.

But what about our Yorkshire *ings* and *carrs*, our
dales and *riggs*, our *ridings* or *ruddings* and *reins*, our
rakes and *gaits*, *dykes* and *becks*, *stells* and *kelds* ?

K 2

These and many other like words carry on their face their Norse complexion—nay, their Norse essence. Nearly every parish in the district that has a river flowing through it possesses its *ings*, which is the same word as the Danish *enge*, *eng* being a generic word signifying low ground, flooded now at times or not as the case may be, but always near water, and divided by ditches into *fenner* varying considerably in size. These *fenner* or fens are so called, as far as I could understand from the people in Denmark of whom I made enquiry, not in consequence of the character of the land itself, but because of the way in which it is divided by ditches or rather trenches. We in this country always associate moisture with the fens, but it does not appear that that is the primary meaning of the word. In this district of East Yorkshire at the present day *ings* are what they are in Denmark, meadow land near water ; and although in our own country it does not of necessity follow that they are on low-lying ground—for there are cases where they are found on higher situations, even on the high ground in the Wolds sometimes—yet these instances are comparatively rare. Neither is it a matter of course that all meadow lands near water are called *ings* ; many are not, though how it is there are these distinc‧tions I am at a loss to determine, unless it be that the meadows have been brought under cultivation subse‧quently to the Danish settlement, or that the old term has been gradually superseded by others. I may add that as the *enge* are divided by *fenner*, so also are the *agre* (fields) divided by *rener* or narrow balks, our Yorkshire word *rein*, which I will again refer to presently.

There are many parishes, especially in the East Riding, which have their *carrs*—a word quite familiar to every farmer in those parts. The word comes from the old Norse *kjarr*, and in modern Danish is spelt *kjœr* or *kœr* (pronounced *care*), and in Jutlandic *kjar*. In Denmark at the present day the term is used in two senses, viz. either for a village horsepond, called a *gadekjœr*, or for moist, boggy rough meadow land made 'sour' by standing water and overgrown with what are called in Danish *halvgrœsser*, or reeds. In this sense the word exactly corresponds with the Yorkshire use of it at the present date, except that with us the land so named need not necessarily be meadow. Land of this character is for the most part what we call in the folk-speech *soor* (sour), a pronunciation identical with *sur*, which is in Denmark applied in precisely the same way; perhaps I should rather say such *was* the character of the *carr* land, for in recent years drainage has done much to alter the face of the country and the character of the land. There can be no doubt that in former times the *carrs* were little better than swamps over-grown with brushwood, the happy resorts of numberless waterfowl, but of small value for the farmer.

At the present date the *carrs*, although drained, are not as a rule good land, being greatly beholden to the season for anything like a full crop. The soil is for the most part peaty; and in working the land large stumps of trees, which have lain there for ages, are frequently brought to the surface. The dark-coloured wood is still hard when first dug out of the ground, and not unfrequently the farmers make gate posts of it; they do not, however, prove very durable—exposure to the air soon causing the wood to rot.

I need not go beyond the limits of this parish of Newton-on-Ouse for additional traces of the old Danish settlements of more than a thousand years ago. Every

cleared way through a wood is called a *riding*; and
there is a field in the parish which always goes by the
name of the *ruddings*: this word indicates clearances
from forest land. *Royd* and *rod*, like *röd* in Denmark, are
elsewhere common terminations, all implying the same
thing. The old Norse *rydja* meant to clear land, especially of wood, the modern Danish form of the word
being *rydde*, and a clearance of anything is a *rydning*.
It need hardly be pointed out that the word *riding*, or
ridding, in the sense of a wood clearance, has nothing
to do with the divisions of the county into Ridings, a
term which has reference to the tripartite division of
it : the origin of this word, however, is Norse, coming
from the Icelandic *thridjungr*.

Less common, but still in usage in our folk-speech, is
the word *rein*, meaning a strip of land at the edge of a
field, so rough and overgrown with brushwood that it
cannot be cultivated. Thus, sometimes a man will complain in ploughing a field, that it is difficult to do,
because it is *nowt bud reins an' geirs*: that is to say,
that it is full of coarse or thorny strips and triangular
bits at the corners, awkwardly shaped, being too narrow
for the plough to be turned round in them. In that
short phrase, which happened to be said to a friend of
mine in conversation with a farmer, we have two interesting old Norse words, *rein* and *geir*: the former of
these is derived from the Icelandic *rein*, a strip of
land.; while *geir* is the same word as the Icelandic
gejr, an arrow-head. Thus, too, an eel-spear is called
aalegejr, because of the triangular shaped end to each
prong.

Again, another field or fields in this parish is called
the *Sheep-rakes*; so it has been called from time out of
mind, though none of our people know why it is thus

designated. Here, also, is evidence of the old Norse tongue, for a cattle-rake or sheep-rake signifies a right or place of pasturage for cattle or sheep, a *stray*, as we should now call it, from Icelandic *reika*, 'to wander.' In much the same sense at the present time do we use the word *gait*; we speak about *gaits* for cattle, *cow-gaits*, and so forth, meaning right of pasture for them. The derivation from Icelandic *gata* is obvious.

To go from land to water : our Yorkshire country-folk scarcely, if ever, make use of the word stream, *beck* is used instead ; *dyke* has a wide application, being sometimes employed with reference to a ditch, or, as I have frequently heard it, to the river Ouse ; a *stell* is a wide open drain, and though *keld* has passed out of the dialect as an ordinarily used word, it is to be found in many place-names.

Turn which way you will, old Norse and Danish words meet us everywhere. In agricultural nomenclature especially are they noticeable ; indeed, it is hardly straining a point to say that it is difficult to find words that spring from any other source, and which, when used, are at once understood. Go into a hind's cottage with its farm-yard close by, either in Holderness or in Cleveland, and in talking with any native of middle or advanced age you may, if you are so minded, practically bid good-bye to Queen's English and converse in the Danish tongue. The time of your visit may be either at the *forend*[1] of the year, or at *clippin tahm*[2], or at the *backend*[3], or when the *yule clog*[4] stands ready for the fire with the other *eldin*[5] ; you go into the *hoos*[6] (or, as we should more properly spell it, *hus*, or you turn and

---

[1] Danish Forende (front part).
[2] D. Klippe (to cut).
[3] D. Bagende (hind part).
[4] D. Jul (Christmas).
[5] D. Ild (fire).
[6] D. Hus (house).

meet the *husband*[1] in the *garth*[2]. Possibly you may be
sensibly reminded of the nearness of the *muck-midden*[3]
and *myg*[4], which have not yet been *scaled*[5], over the
swath[6]. Hard by is the *lathe*[7], and on the floor there
ligs[8] some *bigg*[9] barley or *blend-corn*[10]. Hanging on
the wall is the *ley*[11], with its accompanying *strickle*[12],
and an old flail with its *swipple*[13] bent. Out in the fields
or in the fold-garth are the *stots*[14] and the *wyes*[15] and
the *gimmers*[16], together with one or two *drapes*[17] and
stags[18], while some species of the very flies that *teng*[19]
them are called *clegs*[20]. *Near hand*[21] is the *coo-byre*[22],
and the milk-maid has just done *stripping*[23] the *kye*[24],
and is coming with her pails to the dairy. The old
skeels[25] and *kits*[26] have gone out of fashion, but the
sile[27] is still in use. You may see perhaps some of the
men on the farm *scruffling*[28] turnips or cleaning the *kam-
sides*[29] and *balks*[30], or burning old *garsel*[31] which the
hask[32] wind helps to consume. The *bairns*[33] may be

---

[1] D. Husband (master of a house).
[2] D. Gaard (a farmstead).
[3] Jutl. D. Mog (manure) mödding (manure heap).
[4] D. Mog (manure).
[5] D. Skille (to separate).
[6] D. Svær (rind).
[7] D. Lade (a barn).
[8] D. Ligge (to lie).
[9] D. Byg (barley).
[10] Jutl. D. Blandkorn (a mixture of barley, oats, peas, and vetches).
[11] D. Le (a scythe).
[12] D. Strygc (to rub).
[13] D. Svippe (to crack a whip).
[14] D. Stud (a bullock over four years old).
[15] D. Kvie (a young heifer).
[16] Jutl. D. Gimmer (a ewe lamb).

[17] O. N. Driopa (?)
[18] D. Steg (a male, applied to certain birds and animals).
[19] D. Tænger (tongs).
[20] N. Klæg (a horse-fly).
[21] Jutl. D Nærhaand (near, applied to a horse in a pair).
[22] D. Ko (cow), Bo (to dwell).
[23] D. Strippe (to strip).
[24] D. Köer (cows).
[25] O. N. Skiola (a milk-pail), D. Skaal (a bowl).
[26] Dutch; Kit (a small tub).
[27] N. Sil (a strainer).
[28] D. Skralle (to pare).
[29] D. Kam (a comb or crest).
[30] D. Bjalke (a balk).
[31] D. Gjærdsel (dead hedge wood).
[32] D. Harsk (rusty, rancid).
[33] D. Barn (a child).

flayin kreeaks[1], or tenting the *geslins*[2], or pulling *ket-locks* and what not called *lukin*[3]; or it may be Martinmas time, and the lads and lasses have returned from the neighbouring town, where they have just got hired, and have brought back their *fest* or *gods penny*[4], after having deposited the *addlins* of the previous twelve months in the bank.

Words and expressions like these might be added by the score; but the agency of the Northern tongue may be seen in an even more interesting manner when we consider the way in which it has preserved to us certain vowel-sounds in words which differ only slightly from the standard pronunciation. Take, for instance, such a word as *leck*, which in the dialect is the common pro-nunciation of 'leak'; *leck* comes much more nearly to the Danish pronunciation of its own word *læk* than does 'leak.' Again, when we speak about a 'sack,' it is true we as often as not call it a *poke*, which is probably one of the comparatively few words the dialect has grafted into its vocabulary from the French; only, be it observed, when we do make use of the other term, we invariably pronounce it *seck*; or, to speak more cor-rectly, we retain the old pronunciation of the Icelandic form of the word *sekkr*, wherefrom comes the Danish *sæk*, and from which 'sack' is a deviation. It is as easy to say 'sack' as *seck*, but the traditional and correct vowel-sound of this word has been preserved in the folk-talk from time immemorial.

Again, in the Yorkshire pronunciation of 'building' we have a key to the true meaning and origin of the word. In the dialect the word is distinctly sounded

[1] O. N. Flaja (to frighten).
D. Krage (a crow).
[2] D. Gjæsling (a gosling).
[3] Icel. Lok (a weed).
[4] D. Fæste (to secure). Jutl. D. Gudspenge (earnest money).

beelding, and a *beeld* is a shelter of any kind from the weather ; it need not necessarily consist of bricks and mortar ; a tree or a hedge might, and often do, act as a *beeld* for the traveller against wind and rain, and in that sense the word is very commonly used. Here, again, we have an inheritance from the Norsemen care-fully preserved in the unwritten folk-speech. Some raised object there must be to form a building, but it would seem from our dialectical form of the word that the fundamental idea contained in it was that of a shelter, and not necessarily a structure of masonry, as we now generally understand the term, this latter being only a secondary or subordinate meaning.

The children who watch the geese in the lanes in the summer days call the young birds *geslins* ; it is not a long march from 'gosling' to *gesling*, but in this our Northern pronunciation of the word we cling to the ancient vowel-sound, and in *gesling* we have precisely the pronunciation as in the modern Danish *gjæsling*. Here we may see another example of the undeviating transmission of sound in the mother tongue of the people through a series of long centuries, despite the many literary changes that have passed over the English language during such an epoch of time.

The old tinder-box of our grandfathers' time has now been cast aside. Messrs. Bryant and May, and a host of other 'match-makers' after their sort, have done away with the necessity for such a tedious operation in striking a light as that which accompanied the tinder-box. But the old folks, in speaking about this antiquated article of the domestic furniture of their childhood, always call it *tunder* instead of 'tinder.' This also falls in with ancient usage, for in Icelandic the word is *tundr*; while the modern Danish form is *tönder*, both of which sounds are much more in harmony with our York-shire pronunciation of the word than 'tinder.'

These latter few instances I have given may seem to some but trivial matters, scarcely worth speaking about ; but as straws show from which *airt* the wind blows, so do these words by their peculiar vowel-sounds show the source from which the language of the people has in the main been drawn, even if there were no other traces. The mighty Northern stream which swept over ·Northumbria may still be traced by means of these and other similar tiny distillations which have not yet quite evaporated into thin air.

The following are a few examples taken indiscrimin-ately, which will perhaps help further to illustrate the point aimed at in this chapter. They might be added to indefinitely.

Yorkshire Dialect.	*Danish.*
The use of *with* for *by* means ' of,' e. g. *Ah com wi t' traan* (I came by the train.)	The same usage is com-mon, e. g. *Jeg kom med toget* (I came by the train).
The employment of *to* for *of* in the phrase, *Ti neea use* (of no use).	*Det er til ingen nytte* (lit. It is to no use).
A *piece* of way, e. g. *gan a piece o' way wi ma* (go a part of the distance with me).	*Gaae et stykke vei med mig.* (Go a piece of way with me.)
Ah gav him 't (I gave it to him). In this particular phrase the *v* is retained in *gav*, but in *He ga' mooth* (He uttered a shout) it is omitted, as frequently before a con-sonant.	*A (jeg) ga' ham et* (I gave him it).
Til and *Ti* (To).	*Til* (To). In ordinary con-versation this preposition is

Yorkshire Dialect.	*Danish.*
	frequently pronounced *Ti*, which is in accordance with the Yorkshire usage.
A-gait (on the go ; in operation).	*I gang* (in motion, in operation).
Ta'en or *Teean* (an abbreviation for 'taken').	*Tein* (Dialectical abbreviation for *tagen*).
Brek, a common pronunciation of *break,* perfect tense *Brak.*	*Brække* (pr. *Brekke*, perf. tense *Brak*).
Sikan (such).	, *Sikken* (such a).
The frequent use of *k* for *ch* in such words, e. g., as *skrike* (shriek), *busk* (bush), *skimmer* (shimmer), *bink* (bench), *flick* (flitch), *kist* (chest).	*Skrige* (shriek), *busk* (bush), *skimte* (to gleam forth), *bænk* (bench), *flik* (patch), *kist* (chest).
What do they call you? (What is your name ?) This expression is invariable.	*Hvad hedder De?* (lit. What be called you ?)
Folk, Folks. The word 'people' is not used in the dialect.	*Folk* (people).
Thoo (Thou). This word is always used colloquially and familiarly instead of *you.*	*Du* (Thou) ; also similarly used and pronounced.
He teeak off (He ran away from home or situation).	*Han tog til* (He went to).
He's browt ti t' beggar staff (He is utterly ruined).	*Han er bragt til Tigger-staven* (He is utterly ruined).
Ti brek i two (to break in two). This pronunciation is identical with the Danish : and the letter *i* in such words as *finnd, minnd, blinnd,* &c., is much nearer the Danish sound than is the ordinary English sound in these words.	*At brekke i tu* (to break in two). *Finde, minde, blinde,* &c.
He com (He came). This	*Han kom* (He came).

Yorkshire Dialect.   *Danish.*

form of the perfect of *come* is very common.

Like to: although used in other senses, there is one which may here be noted, viz. *on the point of*, e. g. it would be used in such a phrase as *Ah wer like to tumm'l* (I was on the point of tumbling).

Lige ved at (on the point of), e. g. *Jeg var lige ved at tumle* (I was on the point of tumbling).

The pronunciation of modern Danish, and especially that of the West Jutland dialect, bears, as has been already remarked, many striking resemblances to corresponding utterances in our own East Yorkshire folk-talk. To one or two of these let me briefly allude. As I have elsewhere observed, the *u*-sound is one of the leading characteristics of our dialect. This sound, as we utter it, exactly accords with the Danish pronunciation. *Nu, hus, ung, muld, muge, brun, rund*, are strikingly parallel as to the vowel-sound with the Yorkshire pronunciation of now, house, young, mould, muck (verb), brown, round; and cases of this kind might be indefinitely multiplied.

The treatment of the letter *d* in Danish ˉagrees in a remarkable manner with the Yorkshire usage. In the middle or at the end of a word it is very frequently omitted in speech; thus in such words as *hund, kunde, manden, gloende, bunden, handel*, the *d* is mute; similarly in the East Yorkshire dialect this letter is silent in stand, fand, landing, windle, thunder, meddle, and many like words, these being pronounced *stan, fan, lannin, winn'l, thunner, mel*.

The letter *v* is also another case in point; the Jutlandic utterance of that letter being in unison with our pronunciation. In the dialect, 'over' is pronounced *ower*, which accords precisely with the Danish pronunciation of the same word. *Ovn* (oven) is pronounced *own*, the *ow* being sounded as in 'how'; this again, is almost identical with *yewn* or *yown*, which is the Yorkshire rendering of the word. Another strikingly parallel case is to be found in the word *dovter*, the Jutlandic for daughter; this is pronounced as our *dowtther*.

Although the Danish dialects when written appear at first sight so different from what we are accustomed in Yorkshire, yet a close examination of them discloses many points of resemblance. I here give two examples of Danish folk-talk, the first from the borderland of Slesvig and Jutland, the other from the parish of Ulvborg in North Jutland. They will prove, I trust, not uninteresting to the student of our Yorkshire dialect.

Specimens of Danish Dialect.

I.

Dær war engang æn kong ; han haai æn kauk au æn sket som hir Jæp. Saa blöw æ kongs kauk au Jæp ujæns faa de han kom et mæ vilt ; so saa Jæp a kun gan skyr æn las vilt o æ daẃ ; sau gek æ kauk in au saa de te æ kong. Haar han saai er, saa skal han o gyer er ; læ ham kom in. So saa han te Jæp ; haar do saai do kun skyr an las vilt o æ daw ? Han saai naai ; men æ kong saa ; do har saai er, o do skal o gyer er, hæjsen ska do taas te faang, mæn kommer do mæ en las ska do fo di fö an blyw fri faar o vær sket.

Jæp gaa sæ te o skrol, sau gek han. Sau fon han æn gamm'l piv, sau blæst han i dæn, sau kam dær vilt fræ aal fi værens hjörner, sau skör han saalæng te hen fæk æn las.

Sau skul han hen atter æn uwen te au kyr hans vilt hjem o. Sau kam han faabi nawe skælebasier dær sor i naat hæstsnaws. Godaw, saa Jæp ; hwa besteler i ? Vi hoker o æn uwen do skal ha o kyr di vilt hjem o. Tak skal i ha ; sau behewer a et au go længer. Sau gek han en let ; sau

kam han te tow jererkauper dær sor o spon. Godaw, saa
Jæp; hwa spiner ı te? Vi spiner o naat töj do skal ha tc
hæsttöj au kyr di vilt hjem mæ.

Sau gek han en let, sau kam han te tow myk dær kam
skænen. Godaw saa Jæp; hur vel i skæn o? Vi el skæn
hæn au kyr di vilt hjem. Tak skal i ha, sau behewer a et o
go længer.

Sau kam an te æ jerekauper o fæk æ hæsttöj, au sau kam
han te æ skælebasier o fæk æ uwen, sau laser han æ vilt o
sau kor han hjem i kongens gor te de skralerer i æ baarcgor.
Sau kam æ kong ur au sij æ vilt. Sau saa han; no æ do fri
nær do steer mæ æn anen sket. Sau gek han ur faar o ste
æn skct. Dæn föst han kam te han saa han tur et, faa han
war ræj han ku et. Sau saa Jæp; jaaw, de kan do gaat;
kan do et fo vilt, sau ka do faatæl ham nyt. Hur skul a fo
nyt nær a gor i æ vil mark? Ka do et fo san sau ka do brug
löwn, de haar a gor sau mane gaang.

Sau kam han dær. Dæn föst daw han gek ur o jawt fæk
han slæt et. A kong kam te ham ar æ awten au saa; haar
do faat naat vilt? Sau saa han næj. Haar do hör naat nyt?
Han saa ja; a haar hör to æ væsterhaw war bræn aw o di
slöt er mæ byghalm. Dæn anen daw fæk han hæjer et vilt,
mæn da haaj han nyt: dær war flöwen æn stuwer faawl
öwer æn kærk o dæn gor æn æk, o aal dæm faalk dær war i
æ kærk o æn hal mil nær ve en di draawner i dæn æk.

Sau blöw æ kong vre au gek op te dæn gamm'l slöt o saa;
de ær æn snaws kaal a haar faat; vilt for han et aw, löwn
haar han naak aw. Hwa haar han da saaj? Dæn föst daw
han kam hjæm, da saa han, æ væsterhaw war bræn aw o di
haaj slot er mæ byghalm. De ka vær san; dær æ komen
mane las bode kogt o stæjt fesk hær faabi, saa Jæp. Dæn
anen daw, saa han, dær war flöwen æn stuwer faawel öwer
æn kærk, o aal dæm faalk dær war i æ kærk o æn hal mil
nær ve en di draawner i dæn æk.

No kan a faasto de, saa Jæp, faa dær æ komen baaj om
aal dæm snæjker dær vil kom di kun fo arber au gyr ligkister,
au di sku vær spes te æ æn au drywes i æ juwer mæ æn
rænbok, faar hæjsen ku dær et blyw plas te dæm.

Sau trowe æ kong dc. Ater dæn tij ku han gaat go; fæk han
vilt, sau war er guwe; o fæk han nyt sau trowe æc kong er.

Translation.

There was once a king; he had a cook, and a gamekeeper who was called Yep. The king's cook and Yep came to loggerheads because he did not come with any game; accordingly Yep said, 'I could easily shoot a load of game in a day.' So the cook went in and told this to the king. 'If he has said this he shall also do it; let him come in.' Then he said to Yep, 'Have you said you could shoot a load of game in a day?' He said 'No.' But the king said 'You have said it, and you shall also do it, or else you shall be taken to prison; but if you come with a load you shall get your food, and become free from being a gamekeeper. Yep uttered a cry and departed.

Then he found an old pipe and blew into it, and game came from all four quarters of the globe; so he shot long enough to get a load.

Next he would go in search of a waggon to drive his game home on, and came past some black beetles which lodged in some horse manure. 'Good day,' said Yep, 'what are you doing?' 'We chop on the waggon you shall have to carry your game home on.' 'Thank you; then I need not go any longer.' Then he went on a little and came to two spiders who sat and spun. 'Good day,' said Yep, 'what are you spinning for?' 'We are spinning some things you shall have as harness to drive your game home with.'

Then he went on a little and so came to two gnats which came running. 'Good day,' said Yep, 'where will you run to?' 'We will run away and drive your game home.' 'Thank you; then I need not go further.'

Then he came to the spiders and got the harness, and so on to the beetles and got the waggon. Afterwards he loads the game and drives home to the king's palace so as to make a rattling in the courtyard. Then the king came out to see the game, and he said, 'Now you are free when you engage me another gamekeeper.'

Accordingly he went out to engage a gamekeeper. The first he came to said he did not dare (to engage himself) for he was afraid he could not (do the work). But said Yep, 'Yes, that you can very well. If you cannot get game, at all events you can tell him news.' 'How shall I get news when I go into the rough country?' 'If you cannot make up what is true, you must tell lies; I have done that ever so many times.'

So he came to the palace. The first day he went out to hunt he got nothing at all. The king came to him in the evening and said to him, 'Have you not got any game?' He said 'No.' 'Have you heard any news?' He said, 'Yes; I heard that the Western sea was burning up, and that they quenched it with barley straw.' The next day he got no game again ; but then he had news (to tell). A great bird had flown over the church, and it laid an egg, and all the people who were in the church and half a mile near to it were drowned in that egg.

Now I can understand that, said Yep, for word is come that all the carpenters who would, could come and get work to make coffins which should be pointed at the end and be driven into the ground with a mallet, for otherwise there would not be room for them. So the king believed it. After that time he could manage well : if he got game, then it was satisfactory, and if he got news, then the king believed it.

II.

' Dær waar æn præst aap ve Tyner i gamm'l daw ; han waa grow gere, au ku aler ŏwn aa gi hans faalk naawe.

Saa kam dær æn gaang i æ slæt æn kal te ham aa tow tjænest ; han skul vær dæn fŏst a æ slæterer, aa om æ awtener ful han mæ dæm ur o æ æng. Saa snar di waa komen dærur saa gu kal te dæm, de ær aler vær aa slo græjs, no'll vi er aa drek saa læng vi har naawe, aa sau'll vi leg waas te aa sow bag æter, aa hæt saa howres som vi ka. Di gŏr da som han saa, aa haj aal slas lŏstehier a væn di blŏw kŏw aet lo di dæm ti aa sow oner æ vun. Om æ maaner væn di blŏw vagen, mien han igæn te no kun et aler betal sæ aa begyn mæ æ orber han vil tæj æ hiele ansver o sæ ; aa sau' or di hwa dær waa tebag aa haj et howres somel te her a merestier ; sau saat di dæm o æ vun aa kŏr hjæm ; mæn aal tesam'ls waa di da rej faar hwa far vil sæj væn di kam hjæm aa aler haj bestilt æn smiten ; mæn æ kal saa di skul et vær rej, han skul naak sŏre faa di hiele.

L

O æ vej kam di faabi æn stej hwo. dær lo grow mane
skælebaser; æ kal saa di skul haal stel, han sprang a æ vun
aa samlet æ mælmaskaare hal ful a skælebaser. Omsier
kam di da hjæm, aa æ præst kam rænen ur imuer dæm, aa
no waar et atal te æ kal skul snak faa di aner. Naa, hvordan
gaar det? har I faaet hele engen slaaet? saa æ præst. Ja
væl ha vi de, swar gu kal, æ har da ejsen fonen naawe o æ
vej æ gæn vil bej far om. Naa, har du det, hvad er det
min sön? Ja, far, æ har fonen æn swarm bi. Det var
da godt, det er bestemt mine; der er i dag flöjet en swærm
bort fra mig. Ja mæn æ vil gæn bej far om aa gi mæ dæn
swarm : far har sau mane; æ ær æn fate kal aa har slæt ene.
Nej, det kan jeg paa ingen maade, min sön! Aa jow far ku
gæn gi mæ no dæn jæn swarm. Nej paa ingen maade, hvor
er de henne jeg maa straks have dem. Ja, svar æ kal, vel far
ha dæm, sau har æ em i mi mælmaskaare; mæn faa de far
et ku la mæ ha em—æ har sjæl fonen em aa ær ekkons æn
fate kal;—sau el a önsk te aal æ bi maa blyw te skælebaser
aa aal æ græjs vi har slowen i nat maa res sæ o æ ruer
igæn.

A præst fæk æ kaare aa lot en op; dæ waa jo et ant som
skælebaser. No blöw han rej faa si græjs aa skeket æn
dreng hæn faar aa sije huren et gek mæ æ æng. Han rænt
dænier aa so laant hæn te æ vin blest æ græjs aap hwor di
haj lo om æ nat, aa sau stræft han aa ræn hjæm aa roft læng
för han haj naaj æ præst som kam imuer ham : Far, far æ
græjs æ rest snar aalsamel, aa de res ino stærk i dæn jæn
hjön.

Translation.

There was a priest up by Tönder in olden days : he was
very greedy, and could never afford to give his servants anything.

There came then once in hay harvest a man to him and
entered his service. He wished to be the first of the mowers,
and in the evening he followed the others out on to the
meadow. As soon as they were come there the good man
said to them, it is never worth while to cut grass : now we
will eat and drink as long as we have anything, and then we
will lay us down to sleep afterwards, and enjoy ourselves as

pleasantly as we can. They did then as he said, and had all kinds of diversion, and when they were tired of it they laid themselves to sleep under the waggon. In the morning when they were awake he declared again that now it could not be worth while to begin with the work : he would take the whole responsibility upon himself; and so they ate what there was left and enjoyed themselves together up to dinner-time; then they sat themselves on the waggon and drove home; but they then became anxious among themselves for what father (the priest) would say when they came home and never had done a stroke of work ; but the man said they need not be anxious, for he would certainly manage the whole affair.

On the way they came by a place where there lay a great many black beetles ; the man said they were to stop ; he jumped from the waggon and collected the luncheon basket half full of black beetles. At length they came home, and the priest came running out towards them, and now it was agreed that the man should speak for the others. ' Well, how are you getting on ? Have you got all the meadow cut ? ' So said the priest. ' Yes, it is all right,' answered the man, ' I have, moreover, found something on the road I would fain ask father about.' ' Indeed, have you so ? What is it, my son ? ' ' Yes, father, I have found a swarm of bees.' ' That was fortunate ; it is certainly mine ; there is to-day a swarm flown away from me.' ' Yes, but I would fain ask father to give me that swarm : father has so many ; I am a poor fellow, and have none at all.' ' No, that I can on no account do, my son.' ' Oh, yes, father could now kindly give me this one swarm.' ' No, on no account ; wherever they are I must instantly have them.' ' Very well,' answered the man, ' if father will take them, I have them in my luncheon-basket; but for that, father could not let me have them—I have myself found them, and am but a poor man—so I will wish that all the bees may become black beetles, and all the grass we have cut down during the night may rise on its roots again.'

The priest got the basket and opened it ; there was nothing whatever but black beetles. Now he became anxious for his grass, and sent a boy off to see how it fared with the meadow. He ran down there, and saw far away that the wind blew the grass up where it had lain during the night, and then he hastened and ran home and cried, long before he had reached the priest who went towards him : 'Father, father, the grass has risen almost all at once, and it is rising now rapidly in the one corner.'

Through the help of a Danish friend I have translated the above story as literally as might be, so that the two may be compared together.

On a careful examination it will be seen that there are many words and expressions which bear a close likeness to those corresponding with them in our own dialect. For instance :—*war* (wer), *engang* (yan gang), *saa* or *sau* (seea), *kom* (kom), *a* (ah), *te* (ti), *haar do* (ha'e tha), *gaa sæ ti o skrol* (lit. gav hissen ti a skirl—gave himself to a shriek), *fon* (fan), *fræ* (fra), *hjörner* (hurnes, i. e. corners, an old Yorkshire word ; vide Glossary), *hiele* (heeal, i.e. whole), *længer* (langer). Let these suffice as examples of many others which might be given. The words in brackets are the Yorkshire equivalents to the Jutlandic. It must be borne in mind that the Jutlandic *d* is frequently pronounced as our soft *th* ; *æ* is sounded very much as our Yorkshire *a* described in another chapter—thus the word *æ* (hay) in one of the foregoing passages harmonises exactly with our pronunciation of the word. The *aa* varies between *o* and *au*, but more closely approaches the latter than the former: thus *faalk* is the exact equivalent of our Yorkshire way of pronouncing *folk*; *faawel* similarly of *fowl*. The Jutlandic *i* agrees in sound with the Yorkshire very generally, which is so different from that of ordinary English, being equal to *ee* in most cases: and closely connected with this sound is that of the Danish *j*: indeed it is the combination or interchanging of these

two sounds that go to make up that strongly marked
feature of our dialect, the *eea* sound—*egjen, hjem, hjæm,
jen* or *æn*, for example, are nothing more nor less than
our Yorkshire forms *ageean, yam, heeam, yan.* The
Danish *j*, when it occurs elsewhere than as the first
letter of a word, is by no means always sounded: thus
in *gjöre* (to do or make) the *j* is mute, and in the Jutlandic dialect the word assumes various forms, such as
gör, ger, gyr, with many others. This word was retained, almost in one of its modern Jutlandic forms, till
recently in our Yorkshire folk-speech as *gar*: for instance, our old people used to say *it gars ma paan* (it
causes me pain), *it gars ma greet* (it makes me weep).
The same remark applies to the word *gjæk* from which
our *gicken* or *gecken* is derived.

With the exception possibly of certain districts in
Sweden there is no part of Scandinavia where the folk-
speech so nearly approaches that of East Yorkshire as
in West Jutland and North Slesvig. Any student of our
own dialect who wishes to investigate the matter more
deeply for himself cannot do better than refer to Mr.
H. F. Feilberg's learned and elaborate Jutlandic Dictionary, entitled *Ordbog over jyske Almuesmål,* now going
through the press, which is the most complete and
valuable work of the kind that has ever been compiled.
It is written by one who knows the folk-speech as well
as his own, and who has spent a life-time upon this
and kindred studies. One great merit of the work
lies in the fact that the information is mainly drawn from
the most reliable source—the people themselves.

Before I conclude this chapter I would just remark
that there is one peculiar feature in the West Jutland
dialect which I have not seen noticed elsewhere, and
for which it is difficult to account; I mean the pro-

nunciation of the letter *r*.   This sound is in that region
identical with the nasal *r* of the dialects of Southern
England.   It is quite universal in south-west Jutland,
while in Yorkshire there is not even the faintest trace of
it.   On hearing the Danish dialect spoken for the first
time, this remarkable peculiarity struck me very much.
I do not know over what extent of country this sound is
heard, but from the fact that we have not a vestige of it
in Yorkshire, I imagine it must be an importation and
probably a comparatively recent one ; but this is a point
that requires investigation.

For further comparison of the folk-talk of the two
districts, I must refer the reader to the derivations,
incomplete as they are, which are given in the Glossary
at the end of this volume.

CHAPTER VIII.

WHATEVER difficulties may surround the derivation of place-names, those of some of our field-names are not less perplexing. A large number of these have become so torn and twisted in the course of ages that their first shape is almost past recognition. Still, perhaps I should say therefore, they prove an interesting study to those who are able to give themselves to it. What an amount of physical geography they unfold. They tell very often, too, of stirring events, of battles and invasions, of camps and settlements; they record something of the natural history and botany of the district, of animals now no more to be found in their old haunts, and of plants and flowers that no longer deck the ground; they speak of families who had perhaps for generations inhabited the spot, but whose place now knows them no more. Although many of these old field-names are so mangled that they can with difficulty tell their own tale, yet it is surprising what a history is revealed by those which can speak. Not to go beyond the boundaries of this parish of Newton-on-Ouse; here nearly every field has a name, and although many are of no special interest, sometimes merely recording the name of a recent occupier, yet a large proportion have held their ground for many centuries and afford food for thought and study.

This parish consists of three townships, and in one of these—Linton-on-Ouse—I felt that without much difficulty I could get a fairly complete list of the old field-names. This I did by the aid of one of my elderly parishioners, of whose accurate knowledge of local geography I had heard, but which in reality far exceeded my expectations. He knew the name and the characteristics of every field in the township, and being a thorough Yorkshireman, he was able to give the designation in each case with the correct traditional pronunciation. Accordingly, I invited him to come to my house one evening and he began at one end of the place, and without note of any kind, went through the whole township of about 2,300 acres, giving the name of every field.' These I took down one by one carefully, with the exact pronunciation, as far as I could, as he uttered it. He never hesitated for a moment, and to the best of my knowledge and belief not more than one close was omitted. Such a list not having been previously made, as far as I know, and some of the field-names being curious, I will give the list *in extenso*, only omitting those names which merely described the field by the number of acres it contained, of which there were a fair sprinkling, though these have a special interest of their own. He took the township farm by farm, and I have kept to the same grouping.

The names are as follows :—

Farm No. 1.—Roger wood, Tom wood, T' carr, T' clay pownd, Spring Wood clooas, Mark hill, Jack wood, T' bull garth, Ned Paak, T' hag, T' fo'st branfits, T' middle branfits, T' far branfits, Mill clooas.

No. 2.—By hoos field, Mill clooas, Middle ings, Far ings,

T' fox heeads, T' field i t' front o' t' hoos, T' fo'st branfits, T' far branfits, Hall garth ingses.

No. 3.—T' corner field, T' fo'st branfits, T' second branfits, Gowly field, T' hag, Gibson hill, T' boddums, T' brig field, T' high garth, T' low garth.

No. 4.—T' fo'st hag, T' fox hag, T' field i t' front o' t' staable, T' field aback o' t' staable, T' hag just ower t' brig, T' boddums, T' corner field, T' ooak-tree field, Nor' crovs (crofts), Harry Dunnington clooas, T' coo-pastur.

No. 5.—Rush clooas, T' hill clooas, Dawson corner clooas, T' fo'st (or girt) sumlers (or sumleys), T' second sumlers, T' field aback o' t' brick garth, Middle field, Far field, Dawson hill, T' clay field ower t' brig, T' boddums, T' corner clooas, T' hall garth, T' ingses, T' croft, T' toon-end piece. Moor end.

No. 6.—Spring wood clooas, T' far-oot wood, Snahry clooas, T' dreean sumlers, Girt sandwith, Robison clooas, T' clooas at t' front o' t' barn, T' shoodther o' mutton, T' sumlers, Charles garth, T' ingses, T' law (low) bell garth, T' high bell garth, Grassin sumlers, Sumlers hill, T' girt hag.

No. 7.—T' fo'st field agaan t' rooad, Tommy Reet hill, T' far clooas joinin' Smith's, Six yakker joining t' plantin', Snahry clooas, T' fo'st sandwith, T' second sandwith, Nor' crovs, T' au'd hoos garth, T' seed clooas, Corner clooas.

No. 8. Linton lane, Broon clooas, Girt sandwith, Girt ling clooas, T' whinny garth, T' avvy lings (*or* T' avvyl ings), T' au'd twenty yakker, West field, Field top.

No. 9.—Reet clooas, Tommy son clooas, T' Ruddings, T' rush, Frank garth, New clooas, T' field, Nor' crovs, T' bull garth, Field top, T' lang field, T' fo'st flats, T' far flats, T' ingses.

No. 10.—Fox cover clooas, Margery well, T' clooas aback o' t' hoos, Peckitt wood field, T' clooas aback o' t' wood, T' wights garth, T' plaans, T' whale jaws clooas, Gowlan field, T' coo-pastur, Seeavy flats, T' hut clooas, Girt flats, T' ingses, T' plewin ings, Gowlan hill, Mörrill clooas, T' lahtle galls, Girt galls, Corner clooas, T' parson clooas.

No. 11.—Mowin' ings, T' bull paddock, Girt sheep rakes, Lahtle sheep rakes, T' staggarth clooas, Little wo'th, Wood sahd clooas, Peg dike, Lahtle Thackra, Girt Tha:kra, Corner clooas, T' coo-pastur.

Odd fields.—Billy Keeak clooas, Pidner croft, High garth, Watther mill field, Bland field, T' galls, T' lock ings, Apple garth, Law (low) Priest garth.

A glance at the above names shows us that a considerable portion of the area described must in former years have been covered with wood. Such appellations as *Hag, Snahry Clooas, Ruddings, Sandwith,* &c., clearly indicate this ; indeed, a certain part of the township, and that not a small one, still goes by the name of Linton Woods.

A *Hag* is a wood of some kind, not one probably with large trees in it, but partaking of the nature of low brushwood or stumpy trees, something like a rough overgrown hedge ; the Danish word for a hedge is *Hegn* or *Hæk,* which is probably connected with our word *Hag.*

Snahry Clooas is a field which contains *snars,* or, as they are or were sometimes called, *hag-snars.* This is a ploughing field, and although it has been for some time under cultivation, there are still so many old stumps or *snars* that the plough is sometimes broken by striking against them. The *Ruddings,* as before stated, tell us that there has been a *rydning* or clearance from the ancient forest. *Carrs* are seldom met with in this part of the country, but the *carr* at Linton, as elsewhere, indicates a combination of wood and moisture in that particular spot. *Paak* is our Yorkshire pronunciation of 'park,' and a park may be either a pond or an enclosure, while *ned,* which precedes it, may be connected with our word *nether* (lower). ' Mark Hill' may simply be so-called after a man's name, or it may be the Danish word for a field or collection of fields. *Branfits* is a word which it is difficult to trace. There is the old word *fittis* or *fitts,* which is applied to low-lying strips of land beside a river, which may probably account for the latter part of the word. Being near a river we have our *ings* in all directions ; it is, however, very seldom that one hears of *plewin* (ploughing) *ings*, these being almost always meadow land. *T' fox heeads* has nothing to do with heads, *heeads* being our local pronunciation of earths. *Gowly field* may be so called from the corn-marigold, which goes by the name of *gowlan* in the dialect. *T' boddoms*, I take it, are merely low-lying fields ; some connect the word with the Icelandic *botn* : this no doubt might apply in a hilly country, but these *boddoms* are surrounded by no rising ground whatever, beyond the gentlest slope.

A field which is now called the *Hag* has a *rush* or narrow strip of wood or rough ground at the end of it, hence the name *Rush clooas*. *Sumlers*, it would seem, might be Summerleys, or summer pasture land, though the derivation of the word is by no means clear ; the *Dreean sumlers*, I imagine, are so-called from the fact of their having been drained at some time, or from having a drain running through them. *Spring wood clooas* lies adjacent to a wood which has a *runnel* going through it, which may give the name to the wood ; this, however, is not the only place in the neighbour-hood where the word 'spring' is associated with wood, and which may have nothing to do with water. The two *bell garths* are probably named after some previous owner or occupier, at least I can account for the name on no other supposition.

The designations *Girt ling clooas* and *t' whinny garth* tell us that that part of the township at least was covered at one time with heather and gorse. The name of the next field to these is the most puzzling in the list. Beyond doubt the exact traditional pronunciation is as

I have given it, but whether the orthography is *t' avvy lings*, or *t' avvyl ings*, I cannot say ; it is possible, too, that the first letter may not be the definite article at all, in which case two further suppositions arise as to the name, which are *tavvy lings* or *tavvyl ings* : one has but little to go upon in this case, but on the whole *t' avvyl ings* seems to me the most probable. It has been suggested that *avvyl* may be a corruption of *avril*, which is a common north-country pronunciation of April, so that the name might simply be 'the April meadows,' a parallel case with ' May Fields' of other districts ; the field, however, is a late one as to season, which militates against this idea. *Reet clooas* is a field no doubt which formerly belonged to a man called Wright. Why out of hundreds of neighbouring fields there should be one that goes by the general title of *t' field* I cannot explain. *Nor' crovs* will be easily recognised as North Crofts.

It may seem strange that within such a contracted area there should be so many generic appellations for the now enclosed fields. Thus we have in this average-sized township the following: *field, clooas, garth, boddums, crofts, pastur, ings, yakker, plaans, rakes,* and *flats*. With regard to the two latter, *rakes* is clearly from the Icelandic word *reika* or *reka*, to drive, so that sheep-rakes are wide spaces for the sheep to stray in. The word *flats* almost speaks for itself, being simply level pastures.

To proceed : *T' wight's garth* would seem to indicate that this was a field supposed for ages to be haunted by some unknown beings. *Seeavy flats* are merely the level pastures which are moist, and consequently grow an abundance of *seeaves* or *seves,* the common soft rush. *Galls* are described in Halliwell as 'springs, or wet places in a field.' If this be so, then the *galls* have in course of time given the name to the whole field in this case, which indeed is highly probable. *Peg dike* and *Thackra* are both uncertain in their derivations ; the latter looks like a man's name, and yet in the other cases of that kind, some generic field-name is invariably added. *Billy Keeak Clooas* is nothing more than our Yorkshire way of writing ' William Cook's Close,' and *Pidner* is a common corruption of ' Pinder.'

I have had neither the opportunity, nor, I fear, the training to become learned in the subject of field-names, interesting though it be ; I have made this scanty allu-sion to it in the hope that others, who have not already done so, may be induced to take up the matter with more earnestness. It is one which will well repay study, and will tend to give those who apply themselves to it and kindred subjects additional interest in country life, which, after all, has some attractions over that of the town, notwithstanding what some may say. Much may be learnt from the examination of old maps and other documents ; still it must be borne in mind that we go nearer to the fountain-head in gaining our knowledge of local geography by examining the localities for our-selves, and learning what we can about them, both as regards traditional nomenclature and physical character-istics, from those whose forelders have lived for ages on the spot or in the immediate neighbourhood.

There are some interesting terms connected with the natural features and peculiarities of the course of rivers, which may not be generally known. Thus, in our own river, the Ouse, we have our *canshes* and *clay-huts*, as well as our *showds* and *gyme-holes*, our *racks* and *nabs*; but as these words are noticed at the end of the volume, I need not dilate upon them here.

It is surprising what a minute and accurate knowledge of local geography many of our country-folk have. They may not be able to tell you the name of a single river or mountain in Asia, nor could some of the older of them tell you the name of the capital of Germany or France, but every scrap of their own 'country' or immediate neighbourhood they know, and know in such a way that they can not only give you the name of everything that has a name, but also are so thoroughly familiar with the nature of the soil as to be able to state the crops which each field or part of a field is best suited for, to describe exactly where the unsound places are, and what makes them so, which pastures are best for feeding cattle, and which for dairy purposes; in short, to have a thorough and practical acquaintance with the physical characteristics of every acre of every farm in the township.

When my old friend just alluded to gave me the list of field-names which I quoted, I mentioned the fact of his having done so to one of our farmers, who remarked, 'Yes; and he could have told where every drain was laid if you had asked him.' Here was geography, with a vengeance. Surely knowledge of this kind was of far greater importance to this man than if he could have described to me the course of the Rhine, or told me the whereabouts of the Falkland Islands. In the matter of geography in schools, I am afraid we generally begin at the wrong end. Why we teach our country lads the geography of Africa before they have learnt that of their own parishes or neighbourhood, I am at a loss to know; it is not so interesting to them, neither is it so useful. There is an outcry just now for technical instruction. So be it; ought not then those who will be called to the work of husbandry to be, before all things, instructed in a knowledge of the land they will in all human probability have to cultivate, rather than be made to learn a few general facts, soon to be forgotten, about countries thousands of miles away, which they will never see, and seldom even hear of?

Having said this much, I must not be misunderstood. I would not by any means have our school children utterly ignorant of the geography of the world, but I would put local geography into the first place.

No doubt in days gone by the local knowledge was often acquired at the expense of the general, as what here follows will indicate. The moorland district north of Helmsley is a wild, out-of-the-way region, where old customs were kept up till lately with great tenacity, and where the folk-speech is rich in archaic words and forms. The people there seldom travelled far from their own homesteads, which were to them their world. A former assistant Curate of Helmsley informed me that he used to hear moorland farmers speak of Helmsley 'as 't' coontthry.' They would sometimes complain, for instance, that the farmers in 'the country,' that is to say, round about Helmsley and the more lowland parts, could feed their beasts and get better prices at the markets than they themselves could. He has even heard Helmsley spoken of as ' England ' ; in speaking, for example, of the doings of their neighbours a few miles below them, they would talk of that district as 'doon iv England.'

This reminds me of something I once heard, which shows the exalted ideas that we Yorkshiremen have of our own county ; and just as the designers of the ' Mappa Mundi ' at Hereford Cathedral placed Jerusalem as the centre of the world, so a Yorkshireman, if he were to construct a ' Mappa Mundi ' after his own ideas, would doubtless place Yorkshire as the great

centre of all things; and his own 'toon' as the heart
of Yorkshire itself!

The groom of a gentleman living near York was on
one occasion sent up to London with some yearlings
for sale at Tattersall's. He had never been far from
home before, and the great metropolis was utterly
strange to him; he felt like a fish out of water. A
friend happening to meet him at the great horse mart,
began by asking him how he liked London. 'Whya,'
said the Yorkshireman, 'ah deean't matter it mich.'
'You don't?' added the other. 'Naw,' said the groom,
'ah 's seear ah deean't, an' what 's mair, ah s'all be
varry glad when ah 's back iv oa'd England ageean.'

If the geographical knowledge of the people of a
generation or two ago with regard to regions comparatively near home was vague, that of more distant
places was vaguer still.

The faith which some of our country folk place in
almanacular prognostications is quite implicit. These
annual publications are held in high esteem. There is
nothing like a good comet year for the sale of them.
On such occasions alarmist predictions are wont to
swell the pages of these productions. And not a few
of the more nervous portion of the community wellnigh tremble and quake with fear. An amusing instance
of this kind was told me about twenty years ago by a
friend whose ability for telling Yorkshire stories was
remarkable. My only regret is that I cannot remember
more of them.

The gallant Colonel, for such he was, went one day
to call and see an old woman in the place where he
lived. It was in the year of the great comet, 1874. He
found the old lady in rather a perturbed state of mind;
in fact, she had just been studying carefully her favour-

ite almanack, and taking in every sensational rumour of the dire disasters which the comet would bring upon certain parts of the world, and especially upon France.

After exchanging a few commonplace remarks, the old lady proceeded to unburden her mind.

'They tell me, Conneril, 'at folks is leeavin' France,' she observed, with a concerned look.

'Leaving France?' replied the Colonel, 'what are they leaving France for, Betty?'

'Aw! Sir, deean't ya know?'

'No, indeed I don't ; what 's the matter then?' said the other.

'Whya,' adds Betty, 'they say 'at this greeat comet's boun ti bo'n ivvry yan on 'cm up.'

The Colonel saw that he was in for a little entertaining talk, and kept the old dame on the track of the comet, and so continues :—

'Well but, Betty, perhaps the comet will come to England ; and if it does, what shall you do?'

Whether such a possibility had ever occurred to Betty's mind it is hard to say ; she was at all events ready with her resolve, which she thus expressed :—

'Ah sud gan tiv America.'

'That' says the Colonel, 'is a great way off, and it would take a long time to get there ; and then, you know, there's the water to cross ; you wouldn't like that, I'm sure.'

The water, however, presented no difficulty to Betty's scheme, for she added at once,

'Bud ah sud gan roond by t' banks!'

The old soldier could scarce restrain his laughter, and he thought it prudent not to interfere with these quaint geographical notions, and so he allowed Betty

M

fondly to imagine that by some circuitous route along unknown shores she might eventually arrive in America.

' But, Betty,' continues her friend, 'what if the comet gets to America ? '

He looked eagerly for her reply, thinking that now she must be driven into a corner.   Not a bit of it; she rose to the occasion, saying with a slight jerk of the head and a sparkle in her eye,—

' Aye, bud ah lay t' comet wad git weel sleck'd afoor it gat tiv America.'

The Colonel felt that there was nothing more to be said after this, and he left Betty in her imagination on American soil defying all comets.

If I remember rightly, it was the same old woman who was holding a conversation with my friend about Shetland ponies.   He asked her slyly, knowing that geography was not her strong point, if she could tell him whereabouts Shetland was ; she gave him to understand she could not tell to a few miles, ' bud,' says she, 'ah yam it 's sumwheers up agaan Roosha !'

It is said that in 1851 people could travel by rail from York to London and back for the surprisingly small charge of five shillings, and many thousands availed themselves of this opportunity to go and see the first great Exhibition, opened in that year.   Many of those who went had no conception of the distance London was from Yorkshire ; possibly the extreme lowness of the railway fare may have thrown not a few out of their calculations, but whatever ideas as to distance they may have had in their minds, there were those who took it for granted that the London policemen would at once be able to ' challenge ' stray visitors from Yorkshire villages, however remote.   A case of

this kind is recorded of two friends from the neighbourhood of Pickering, who thus journeyed to the
metropolis on the occasion referred to. On their
arrival they in due course, along with crowds of sight-
seers, made their way to the Exhibition. At the turn-
stiles the crush was so great that the two companions
got separated, and for a time they lost one another.
Immediately on discovering this, the one last to enter
became rather concerned and flustered, and seeing a
policeman near the entrance, he rushed up excitedly
to him, exclaiming in tones of anxious enquiry, 'A'e ya
seen owt o' Smith o' Marishes?' London policemen
have much to put up with, but at times their minds
even when on duty are unbent by little diversions of
this kind ; and well may they be.

CHAPTER IX.

WHEN it is asserted, as it has been with much truth, that every other Yorkshireman you meet is a character, it must be borne in mind that over and above isolated peculiarities, there are certain characteristics attaching to the people generally who inhabit this part of England; indeed, it may be doubted if there is any county where the country-folk are so much *sui generis* as they are in Yorkshire. Although, I had almost said because *yan on em* myself, I feel it no easy matter to do them justice in attempting to delineate a few of the leading traits in their character. Born in the North Riding, living the chief portion of my life in the East, and now for the last twelve years having taken up my abode again in my native Riding, I have spent the main part of my time in the midst of Yorkshire folk. A six-years work as Diocesan Inspector of Schools took me to nearly every parish on this eastern side of the county, and brought me into contact with people of almost every sort and condition; my work, too, as a country clergyman has thrown me not a little into the society of my brother Yorshiremen, and afforded opportunities which no other calling in life can give so favourably (unless it be the medical profession), of learning something of the ways, habits, modes of thought, customs, virtues, faults, failings, peculiarities, in short the character of the people among whom I have lived. It is inexcusable if by this time one has not learnt something of their ways.

It is allowed that Yorkshiremen are, as we say, *good ti challenge*: this saying is true more especially of that which presents itself to the eye and the ear; but I think the expression may be in a sense extended to the deeper and more real qualities of their nature, which certainly seem to possess features that mark them out as somewhat different from others. I have repeatedly noticed that when south-country people take up their abode with us in Yorkshire, they do not, as a rule, get on well with our people. The people do not take to them, and they do not like the people. For this, as for everything else, there must be a reason.

It is in the first place instructive to see how the Yorkshire character strikes the south-country man. Now there is a question which I have for years asked of my southern friends residing amongst us; it is this: 'What struck you most in the character of the Yorkshire people on coming to live amongst them?' I need hardly say that the replies have been varied; sometimes pointed, sometimes amusing, and generally more or less instructive. But out of them all there were two or three so oft repeated that I take it they were unmistakeably warranted by the fact of the case, and so make clear to us what some of our main characteristics really are.

To begin with what is unfavourable to us. Nearly all Southerners agree that our manners are not good. We are supposed to be rough and rude. 'Yorkshire people do say such rude things, and then they expect

us not to mind it,' said a south-country lady to me one
day in some distress of mind. I endeavoured to
console her by reminding her that the rudeness could
not have been intended, but was merely a straightforward way of putting things, which was after all more
to be wished for than mere polish. No doubt the
happy combination of *fortiter in re* and *suaviter in modo*
is the state of things the most to be desired; but I
think it must candidly be admitted that the latter is not
one of our strong points. William of Wykeham's
motto, 'Manners makyth man,' is not the typical
Yorkshireman's motto; to say the least of it, he values
what are generally deemed good manners very cheaply,
though I am certain there is no one more quick to
appreciate good breeding, not only in horseflesh, but
in human kind, than he. The Yorkshireman has, no
doubt, a way of speaking his mind very freely, and
telling you what he thinks, even if his opinion be never
so contrary to your own; what others would let you
know by an innuendo or side-wind, he makes known
to you without the slightest reserve or disguise. However unpleasant this habit may be at times, it has its
advantages; you at least know where you are with
them; you can always tell whether a Yorkshireman
likes or dislikes what you do; he as good as tells you.
I must add, however, that this bluntness of manner is
more marked as between Yorkshiremen and strangers
than as between themselves. Very frequently, too, it
is aggravated or accentuated by the south-countryman's
way of dealing with us: we are independent people,
and any kind of interference with the free exercise of
that independence is quickly resented. I have not
unfrequently seen cases where Southerners, when in
positions of authority, have treated our Yorkshire folk

in a patronising spirit, and as if incapable of knowing their own minds. Few independent people like such treatment, but to Yorkshiremen this is especially galling: they like to be approached on equal terms of manhood. This in no way interferes with their willing-ness to treat others with respect; they will always respect any man whom they have proved to be worthy of respect. But prove him they must, before he can win their confidence or esteem; but having won it, it is a man's own fault if he forfeits it. The Yorkshireman's independence is of the most healthy kind; it is not only a good thing in itself, but it also fits a man for making his way in the world, and struggling with the battles of life. And yet I have very often heard this very quality spoken of as if it were something to be deplored. 'You Yorkshiremen' are such an inde-pendent lot'; 'I never came across such independent, ill-mannered people'; 'They are so independent, they don't seem to care for anybody';—these are the kind of remarks I have had to put up with in speaking with strangers about my fellow Yorkshiremen. This does not hurt us much; they do not understand us, that is all.

But yet it is not quite all; for outsiders have other dreadful things to say in answer to my stereotyped question. 'Yorkshiremen are such money-lovers'; 'They keep such a tight grip over their purses'; 'It is uncommonly hard to get any money out of them.' Well, I daresay it is true that we, like a great many others, know the value of money fairly well. Perhaps even we attach a greater value to such a small sum as twopence than the Londoner does; still for all that, the Yorkshireman can be, and is, most liberal with his money when the reason for laying it out seems to him clearly to be a strong and a valid one. And this brings me to perhaps his most strongly marked characteristic, I mean his practicality. A more practical people do not exist than Yorkshire people. They look at everything from a practical point of view. What is best to be done under the circumstances, is a question which they know well how to answer in effect at all times. When a difficulty has arisen and the Yorkshireman says *yan mun deea t' best yan can*, you feel fairly satisfied that nothing will be left undone that should have been done. Closely connected with this feature is his utilitarianism. These two qualities combined guide him as to the expenditure of money. Sentiment or taste or ornament appeal to him but feebly. Again, most cautious and circumspect is the Yorkshireman in all matters, and especially those that touch his pocket directly or indirectly. This appreciation of the power of the purse makes him shrewd at making a bargain, and economical in all his ways.

I have been told many times that Yorkshire people are 'hard to get at'; that is to say that it is hard at first to know them. I remember once speaking to a young man who had just come from the South of England to enter upon business in Yorkshire, about his impressions of the people : he came with excellent recommendations, and his character was in every way a satisfactory one. I put my old question to him in due form. The poor fellow seemed quite disheartened, 'Oh,' he said, 'they don't seem to take to me at all, although I have very good testimonials.' I felt half inclined to say, 'Of course they don't, and your testimonials might as well not have been written for all the good they will do you.' However, I encouraged him as best I could, and told him not to be too hasty in forming an opinion of the Yorkshire folk, because they were apt to be a little cold at first, but they were good at heart, and so forth. I met him again a year or so afterwards. His spirits were this time much more buoyant, and I could see that he was in an altogether happier frame of mind. He had won the confidence of those with whom he had to deal, they had treated him with kindness and con-sideration, and he said that nothing would induce him to go back to the South again. The fact was, the young man was content to do his best and wait patiently, and he found that, after all, the Yorkshiremen were not so unloveable as they at first appeared ; he found, in short, that they had not only heads, but hearts also. It is true they are suspicious and shy of strangers, but when-ever they admit another to their confidence, they are the truest and most steadfast of friends.

It is difficult to imagine two natures more opposite than those of the Irishman and the Yorkshireman ; the quick, impulsive, excitable temperament of the Celtic character is utterly foreign to that of the Clevelander or East-Ridinger. In all his dealings the York-shireman is deliberate and calculating. Even under circumstances the least expected this characteristic at times comes out. I remember once being somewhat amused by a friend telling me of a man he knew who was supposed to be courting a cook in the neighbour-hood. Mary was a young woman of excellent character, but, as is not unfrequently the way with cooks, her pro-portions were, to say the least of it, considerable. On being taxed with what was thought to be a tender feeling on his part towards Mary, the young man replied humorously that he 'thowt sha wadn't suit him'; for, he added, 'it 'll tak all mah addlins ti git her a new goon.'

I alluded just now to the Yorkshireman's cautious-
ness: strangers sometimes mistake this quality for
timidity; it causes him, moreover, to be misunderstood
in other ways. Thus a Yorkshireman, from his excessive
caution, will always understate a fact rather than the
reverse. If he likes a thing ever so much he will not
express himself accordingly, but will merely say that he
likes it *very well.* Southerners invariably misinterpret
this expression. Or if he is asked if he would like to do
so and so, and he keenly desires to do it, all he says is
'Ah deean't mahnd if ah deea.' Or again, if he says
'Ah 'll mebbe deea so and so,' it is as good as certain
that he will.

Without showing it very much, Yorkshiremen will
attach themselves most faithfully to those they can look
up to and respect, but they are slow in taking in and
acting on an abstract principle. They look at the
principle through the man who is supposed to represent
it, and if that representative disappoints them the
principle has to take care of itself. If a Member of
Parliament were unpopular with his Yorkshire con-
stituents for some purely personal or private reason,
however attentive to his public duties and true to his
principles he might be, he would stand but a poor chance
of being re-elected.

It is generally supposed that Yorkshire people are
musical. This is a statement which requires considerable qualification. Yorkshire is a large area, and there
are parts of the county of which it certainly cannot be
said that the people are musical. The most musical part of
the county is unquestionably the manufacturing district
of the West Riding: those who have been present at a
Leeds Musical Festival, for instance, can never forget
the ringing clearness of the voices there. They seem too

to possess an unlimited reserve of power which at times fairly carries one away. But of the West Riding I do not speak in these pages. In nearly every village school in East Yorkshire I have had an opportunity of testing the voices of the children. It always seemed to me that the most musical part of East Yorkshire is the Wold country, and the least so, the flat low-lying district round York. It is much more common to hear the farm lads on the Wolds singing at their work in the fields, and singing well, than in the lower country just named ; their voices too are clearer and of altogether better quality. If good air has anything to do with forming a good voice, the East Riding lads and lasses ought to be second to none as vocalists. This is a subject which has been much discussed : I cannot help thinking however that a hilly country is distinctly more favourable to vocal power than a flat country, and good air, of course, than bad air ; but perhaps race has more to do with it than either ; and if we compare the Celt with the Norseman in this respect the palm must unquestionably be given to the former.

I should give a very incomplete account of the York-shireman's character if I did not say that he is hos-pitable ; in this respect at all events he is seldom found wanting. If you enter a Yorkshireman's house, he is ever ready to welcome you to his table and to offer you the best he has ; this excellent quality pervades all classes alike.

It is sometimes instructive to know what strangers think of us. I will therefore here quote the words of two correspondents who were good enough to give me a few impressions they had formed of some of our York-shire ways. One of these, writing from a remote parish in the East Riding near the sea, speaks thus in a letter

I had from him some few years ago, of the farm servants and their work.

'The Yorkshireman of these parts appeared to me, as contrasted with the Southerner, and still more as contrasted with the Irish, rather rough and independent in their manners, but good honest men at heart. The statute hirings at Martinmas are rather injurious to the young men, who are also boarded and lodged with a hind, and thus a good deal cut off from better influences, though when they grow up they appear to improve and settle down into good industrious men. The farm labourers begin their work early in the day and are a hard-working set. As a rule they are better fed (certainly with more butcher's meat) than those in the South, and the cottager manages to have a greater variety of food, living very much on pastry in various forms, which they say " lies longer on the stomach than bread," the latter being very little used. I was struck with the fine agricultural horses generally used here, which seem to be usually of a larger size than those used by farmers in the South, the lads frequently riding as postillions on the waggon horses, which I never saw done in the South.'

I can quite corroborate what my correspondent says with regard to the food of the Yorkshire farm lads as contrasted with that of the labourers in the South. I fear our ploughboys would make a wry face if what used to be the fare of their compeers in Berkshire (say) were offered them. When at school in that county I well remember noticing the food of the husbandman there, and thinking to myself how poor it was by comparison with the workman's fare in the East Riding : bread and cheese was commonly used ; instead of which the Yorkshire farm-servant would have feasted on good wholesome beef, or pies, or something equally substantial and sustaining.

Then, as to the second of my two correspondents. One of the Helmsley clergy, himself a Lancashire man, two

or three years ago gave me the following as his experience of the Yorkshire character as compared with
that of the people of his own county. His remarks
are so much to the point that I will quote his own words.
He says :—

'Compared with Lancashire, Yorkshire folk seem money-
lovers. Perhaps in the Lancashire manufacturing districts
people used to make money easily and so learnt to spend it
as easily as they made it.

'Yorkshiremen are very hospitable. The people I visit
on the moors are poor, but invite me to tea, and offer me
the best in the house ; but if I ask for a small subscription
for some religious purpose, that is another matter.

'They are very sociable and friendly with one another,
but are suspicious of strangers.

'They seem cautious in all their sayings and doings.

'They do not like to make a definite promise or commit
themselves. When I ask a moor lad if he will come to
Church next Sunday and he says "perhaps I will," I feel it
is almost equal to other people's "you may rely upon me."

'Like Lancashire people, they are warmhearted, but it
seems to me, much more reserved.

'Having been accustomed to towns all my life, I was
greatly struck when first I came here by what seemed to me
the almost despotic authority of masters and mistresses over
their servants. They demand a strict obedience. This is so even
in small farms where there is one hired lad who eats at the
same table with his master ; yet in spite of this familiarity,
an obedience is exacted which a Lancashire lad would soon
rebel against. This stern discipline does not, however,
seem to destroy the self-reliance and independence of those
subjected to it.

'I have noticed a strong sense of quiet humour amongst
all classes. They are too simple to appreciate sarcasm.

'Their ideas of geography and history are, as one might
imagine, amusingly vague ; but they know every inch of
their own country, and treasure the biographies of their own
kin.'

From what has been already said, however briefly
and imperfectly, some little idea may be gathered, I
trust, of what a few of the leading traits in the character
of the Yorkshireman are. The rest of the chapter will
be devoted to illustrating that character by side lights as
it were, that is to say, by quoting such incidents of a
trivial nature as have been recorded and sent to me by
friends, and which may perhaps bring out with more or
less clearness one or two of our weaknesses or virtues.

The Yorkshireman in London, especially if it happens
to be his first visit to the metropolis, and he has not
travelled far from his native village before, is always
good company; his impressions of the new sights and
sounds that meet him are generally told in quaint
fashion.

It is recorded of one old Robin Wood, from a remote
moorland village, that he once took it into his head to
go to London. He had *heeard tell on 't*, and he *thowt he
mud as weel see for hissen* what there was to be seen.
What he saw does not matter. His chief delight when
he *gat ti t' far end* was to walk into any shop that seemed
specially to interest him, and air his broad Yorkshire
speech. In his wanderings through the streets he came
upon a certain store of general wares. It struck Robin
as an interesting-looking establishment. Accordingly,
he walks in, looks about him as if the place belonged to
him, and presently says to the shopman, 'What diz ta
keep here?' The collection was a truly miscellaneous
one, and so the man felt justified in replying 'Oh!
everything.' Robin looks at him and adds, 'Ah deean't
· think thoo diz: hes-ta onny *coo-tah nobs*?' (the piece of
. wood that secures the 'tie' for the legs of cows when
being milked). The shopman looked bewildered; he
had never heard of such things before, and the precise

form in which the request was made did not enlighten him much upon the point.

An old sporting character, now departed, who was always *en évidence* at the big sporting functions of the aristocracy, whether by covert, flood or field, was notorious for his brusque manner and broad Yorkshire dialect.

Once, on the occasion of a grand *battue*, luncheon was being served at the covert side, when 'Jack' was invited to partake of the unusually good things provided. Amongst delicacies of great variety, *paté de fois gras* was handed round to the members of the party, and seated on a mossy bank our friend proceeded to attack the dainty morsel with his pocket-knife. One of the sportsmen, a nobleman from the south country, seeing Jack evidently enjoying the French food he had just been introduced to, asked him what it was he was eating, when he made the following characteristic reply, 'Ah 's seear ah deean't knaw, bud it 's meeast leyke pig liver of owt!'

The same noted character had a terrier; and on one occasion he was relating an episode that took place between this favourite animal and a monkey. In the encounter, it would seem, the monkey got the worst of it, and by way of adding to the glorification of the terrier, Jack described its antagonist by saying 'He wasn't yan o' them bits o' things aboot t' boo'k o' yan's hand, bud yan o' them what di ya call 'ems, them Ryungtangs!' It is needless to say he meant ourang-outangs.

Jack used to be introduced to all the great people that came within reach of him, and made free with them. Among others, one of the royal princes came into the neighbourhood, and on being introduced, Jack seized the royal hand, exclaiming 'Ah 'av shak'd hands wi all t' greeat folks iv England, bud ah nivver thowt tì shak hands wi t' Queen's son !'

A correspondent residing in York described some few years ago an amusing scene that occurred at a farmer's 'ordinary' in a certain market town. The occasion was a Christmas rent dinner, and a relation of my informant was to preside at the table. In the earlier part of the day a farmer, who was not averse to a good dinner, came to him and thus addressed him :—' Mr. W., you 're boun' ti carve to-day, an' seea ye 'll say ti ma, " Mr. I., will ya tak some torrkey ? " an' ah s'all say "a lahtle bit if *you* pleeas, Mr. W." Bud ya maun't mahnd what ah says.' Mr. W., fully taking in this hint, gave him, when the time came and the pre-arranged farce had been duly gone through, a terrific help of turkey, which was followed by a considerable quantity of beef and plum-pudding to the same quarter. The cheese appeared; when, said Mr. W. : ' Let me give you a little cheese, Mr. I.' ' Naw, ah thenk ya, Mr. W., ah 's deean weel.' ' But you must have some cheese.' ' Naw, thenk ya, sir.' ' Now do,' says Mr. W., ' a small piece.' ' Whya, then,' adds the other,' ' a lahtle bit just to fill up t' cracks wi !'

From the same authority I learnt that at a certain village in the North Riding there lived an elderly man who had been married three times, but had been as often bereaved. Subsequently to the death of the third lady, a report was circulated to the effect that he was about to enter wedlock yet once again. One of his friends, interrogating him on this subject, he is said to have replied in the following decisive manner : ' Naay, nut ah ; what wi marryin' on 'em an' what wi burryin' on 'em, it 's ower expensive. Ah can't affo'd it nae mair.'

This correspondent also informed me that some few years ago there died at the village of W. a miser who had amassed considerable wealth. He was a blacksmith by trade, and earned about a guinea a week. He had somehow acquired a little capital, which he invested in house property at Middlesbrough when that town was rapidly rising to the height of its prosperity. At the time of his death, previously to which his houses had been sold, he was said to be worth three thousand pounds, but during his life he, after the manner of his kind, denied himself every comfort and almost every necessary as generally so deemed. In his own house he never had a fire, but at night, during the cold part of the year, would go to sit over that of some neighbour. His bread was a black-looking mixture of flour and water baked before the furnace in his smithy, and it was believed that his sole other food, besides what might be given him, consisted of potatoes boiled on the same fire.

After his demise, his wardrobe sold for three shillings and sixpence sterling, and as this included at least one good sack and several other articles not wearable but useful to the villagers, his strictly personal outfit cannot have been accounted of much value. And yet in a hole between the beam across the top of his one sitting-room and the ceiling, a hole perfectly black through continual contact with his dirty hand, there was found a bag containing eight hundred pounds. This, and the other savings, worked no benefit either to himself or his friends; for, as he was born illegitimate and died intestate, his whole property reverted to the Crown.

His cottage, after a good deal of purification and renovation, was taken by a young couple, and was one day visited by the squire's niece. She asked the bride

N

how she liked her new house. 'Aw, ah 's varra comfortable,' she said, ' an' ah isn't freetened.' ' Frightened !
why should you be frightened?' asked the lady.
'They say 'at Dick (the miser) walks,' was the reply,
' bud ah 's neean flaay'd, for if he 's gone ti heaven, he
weean't want ti cum back ; an' if he 's gitten ti t' uther
pleeace they weean't let him ! '

This village of W. must have been noted for its characters, for in the same 'toon' lived a man whose 'by-
name' was 'Coffee Jack,' who gloried in his loquacity,
or in being, as he termed it, 'raether a blatherin' sooart
ov a chap.' Having lost his first wife, and having been
deserted by his family as the several members of it
grew up and married, he, in middle life, took to himself,
by way of a second venture, a woman called Susan.
She was a tall raw-boned creature of masculine aspect,
and, like Jack, was middle-aged. In consequence of her
neither very numerous nor specially feminine attractions,
her husband was subjected to a good deal of chaff about
her ; but he used to say that ' Susie was a gay au'd lass,'
and for a time seemed quite content with his mediaeval
happiness. By and by Susie began to fall into ill health,
and also into a querulous condition of temper, so that
Jack's erewhile bliss was checked. He confided his
domestic troubles to his companions in the field, but
received not the sympathy he had a right to expect.
'Weel, Jack, hoo 's Susie?' they would cry on his
appearance among them ; to which he made some such
reply as 'Aw, sha gans graanin' an' twinin' on ; sha 's
gitten a gumbahl iv her back noo.' My informant
says : 'The poor woman grew worse, and at length
became rather an encumbrance than a helpmate.
Jack now confessed that her inability to look after
herself or perform her household duties was a sore

trouble to him, and gave it as his pious opinion that "it wad be a massy if the Lord wad tak her." His wish was shortly realised. One morning as I sat in the garden, I heard what is locally called the "death-bell." " Who is that for, John ? " I asked of the servant working close by; "Ah think it 's for Susan R., sir," he replied; and I felt that Jack was again a free man. Very soon I descried his earth-coloured smockfrock and trousers looming in the distance as he approached, presumably to tell me of his *loss*; and I at once composed my features to a due solemnity in which I might offer him my condolences. The old man came toiling along, his face down, until he was within thirty yards of me ; then stopping short and planting his curled stick on the ground firmly, he looked up and called out, " Aa, Mr. Teddy, He 's takken her at last ; ah *is* sae thankful."

'Jack continued to live on in the old place, but in course of time he grew too old for farm work " laying " hedges, and the like, and took to stone-breaking for a livelihood. Though a Yorkshireman, he was not above giving a bit of "blarney" sometimes. One day I drove past the place where he was working by the road-side, in a high and tolerably new Whitechapel, drawn by a dashing brown mare, and a day or two afterwards in a very old and well-proved phaeton, between the shafts of which shambled a grey pony with a cow-like action. On the latter occasion, I stopped for a moment to speak to him, when he said, " That isn't sikan a grand trap as ah see'd ya in t' uther daay, Mr. Teddy, bud (with great emphasis) it 's a good 'un."

'Again I passed by him when the scene of his labours was another road. The clergyman, with his brand-new light cart and highly-stepping pony had just preceded me. My own steed was the very sorry animal

just mentioned. Says Jack, " Aa, Mr. Teddy, that's a
grand pawny o' yours !—steps weel ; ah deean't leyke t'
parson's hoss a bit, gans all ower t' pleeace " (imitating
with his elbows), " ower mich daayleet undher 't."
To my modest representation that I feared my own
beast was much inferior to the parson's, he replied,
" Naay, it 's a *good 'un*." '

Along our Yorkshire coast, from Whitby to Spurn
Point, may be found as brave and hardy a race of sea-
men as any one need wish to behold ; but within the
breast of the more inland agriculturalist there is im-
planted a deeply-rooted aversion—I had almost said
dread—of going on the water : in this respect they are
in strong contrast to their seaboard brethren.

At a certain inland village in the North Riding there
dwelt a small farmer, quite the oddest fellow in the
place, who told a friend of a visit he had just paid to
a cousin at Liverpool, who, it seems, was called Eli.
After hearing a good deal of his impressions concerning
the great seaport, his friend asked him whether he had
crossed the Mersey to Birkenhead. It would appear
from his answer that he had intended to do so, but
that having been unable to strike while the iron was
hot, his courage had oozed away through his doubt as
to the capacity of the vessel to carry him. ' Me an' Eli
yam'd ti gan,' he said, ' bud when wa gat ti t' pleeace
t' booat wasn't in. Wa sat wersens doon a lahl bit, an'
sha com in efther a whahl, bud ah says tiv Eli, " We 'll
neean gan ; t' beggar 'll mebbe sink'! " '

It is a well-known fact that in making a bargain the
Yorkshireman can generally manage to sail pretty close to
the wind. The agent of a landed proprietor in the North
Riding gives me an example of this that came under his
notice, which I think would not be out of place here.

Once, when at a farmhouse, he observed a good piano-
forte by Collard in the parlour, and enquired of the
farmer where he got it. He answered :—

' Ah gat that pianna i raether a queerish sooart o' waay.
Just sit ya doon, an' ah 'll tell ya t' taal. We 'd a guverness
for mi dowtther, an' t' weyfe sha said 'at sha owt ti hev a
pianna. Varry weel, ah says, ah knaws nowt aboot sike things,
bud ah 's gahin' ti market ti-morn, an' thoo mun gan an' all,
an' we 'll see if wa can lcet o' yan. Seea t' next daay, when
ah 'd gitten mi beeas bowt, wa went ti t' pianna shop, an' ah
sez, " Noo Mr.——, ah wants a pianna, an' sha mun be
a good un' an' all, bud ah deean't want ti paay ower mich for
her thoo knaws." " Varry weel," he sez ; an' seea he starts
ti plaay on a vast o' piannas whahl he cums ti this here, an'
he said 'at sha war a varry good un." " Mebbe sha is," sez ah,
" ah knaws nowt aboot sike things, bud what 's t' muney ? "
" Well," he sez, " it had been sixty guineas, bud it had been
oot for a piece on hire, an' seea ah 'll tak fifty guineas."
" Aw ! " ah sez, " ah sees thoo 's all i t' guinea lahin ; noo, us
poor farmers is glad ti git it i punds ; seea ah' ll just tell ya
what ah 'll deea wi ya ; ah 'll just gie ya tho'tty-fahve pund
for t' pianna." " Naay, naay," he sez. Bud ah taks oot
seven fahve·pund nooats, an' ah claps 'em doon atop o' t'
pianna, an' ah sez " Noo then, theer 's t' brass ; thoo can a'e t'
muney, an' ah 'll a'e t' pianna, bud ah weean't, gi'e ya na
mair." Well then, he tewed an' he wrowt, an' he maade
sike deed as nivver was, bud at last he teeak it. Seea ah
sez " if thoo 'll send thy young man wi t' conveyance ti t'
frunt deear ah 'll help ya oot wiv her inti t' stthreet." An'
seea he did ; an' bi t' tahm wa gat yam sha wer setten up i t'
parlour.'

The same gentleman who gave me the foregoing illustration of the way we do business in Yorkshire also
sent me an account of another little experience he had.
It was this :—

' A few years ago,' he says, ' I had occasion to go into
a farmhouse in the North Riding, and I found a small pig, of

a day or two old, laid by the kitchen fire. I remarked to the
farmer's wife that it was rather an unusual place for a pig;
to which she replied, " It wer yan of eleven, an' yester morn
ah thowt it wer boun to dee; seea ah browt an' set it bi t'
fire-sahd, an' when neet-tahm com, ah teeak it ti bed wi ma,
an' ah gat up fahve times thruff t' neet ti sarve it."'

Again he adds:—

'Not long after this, on going to another house, I found two
little pigs in a hamper in the kitchen, so I told the old
woman of the incident just mentioned, and jokingly asked
her if she knew of the custom of taking pigs to bed, when
she said, " Naw, sir, ah nivver did that, bud ah awlus taks t'
geslings ti bed wi ma ; an' when mah good man wer alive,
it wer t' awnly thing him an' me used ti differ aboot ; for he
used ti saay when ah went ti bed wiv a basket full o' geslins
'at there wer neea peeace i bed at all !"'

My fellow-countrymen, shrewd as they are at making
a bargain, are not as a rule in the habit of boasting unduly of their successes in this particular, but generally
keep such matters to themselves.   It was so, at least, in
the following instance.   The son of a former Rector of
Welbury, long resident in the county, and possessing
a thorough knowledge of the Yorkshire character and
tongue, has given me, among many other of his notes,
a short one which well brings out this characteristic
feature, together with a bit of quiet humour not less
true to the life.   After market days the Rector's sons,
being at that time young lads, would discuss the affairs
of the day with their father's bailiff.   On these occasions
all manner of subjects would come up for argument,
and not a little quiet chaff was interchanged.   One day,
which is well remembered, the Rector had sold some
wheat, and after the bailiff's return from the market his
youthful friends surrounded him, to hear the news, and
particularly as to the sale of the wheat.

'Well, Jim,' says one of the lads, 'how did you sell the wheat?'

'Hoo did ah sell 't?' replied Jim, 'whya, i pooaks ti be seear.'

'No, no, Jim; what did you get for it?'

'What did ah git for 't? Whya brass!' was the old bailiff's stubborn rejoinder.

'Well, but how much brass?' urged the youngster.

'Nay, nay, noo; you want ti knaw ower mitch,' was the unanswerable stopper that was put upon the lad's inquisitiveness. Henceforth further enquiry in that quarter was hopeless.

It is well known what an affection Irishmen have for their pigs, but it must be confesssd that in that particular Yorkshiremen are scarcely behind them. I should not like to say that they very often think more of these interesting animals than they do of their children, but particular cases have been known where this would in truth almost seem to be so.

An old friend of ours used to give rather an amusing illustration of this. She was visiting a poor woman one day, and asked her,

'Well, Hannah, how are you to-day?'

'Whya! ah 's just middlin' mysen, ma'am, thank ya, bud poor Jim he 's iv a sad waay.'

'Why, what 's the matter with Jim? (her son), said the lady.

'Aw, ma'am, he 's lost two pigs an' two childer! He taks on weeantly aboot t' childer; bud as ah says tiv him, nivver heed aboot t' childer, they 're a dceal betther off 'an ivver thoo can deea for 'em: bud, ma'am, ah *is* sorry aboot t' pigs! he scratted an' scratted ti git 'em up, an' they wer wo'th two pund a-piece, an' noo they 've beeath on 'em deed.'

The same lady visited old Hannah again, when her husband was dying, when she said, in her quaint, matter-of-fact way :—

' He taks on weeantly ma'am, bud ah says tiv him, deean't tak on seea; wa didn't all on us cum inti t' wo'ld tigither, an' wa can't all on us leeave it tigither.'

The excuses which some make for non-attendance at church are at times somewhat original, if not altogether valid. A clergyman of my acquaintance was walking one day through the village where he lived, when he met a parishioner who, till a short time previously, had attended church with commendable regularity, but suddenly, from some unexplained cause, gave up attending altogether. The parson pressed the matter home, and gave his friend to understand that it would be more satisfactory if he might be favoured with some explanation of his abrupt change of custom.

' Well,' said the other, ' then ah 's leyke ti tell ya : noo ah 's nivver cummin na mair whahl au'd Izak 's theer' (Isaac being the Parish Clerk). ' How so ? ' replied the Vicar, ' what has Isaac got to do with it ? ' ' Whya, ya knaw, t' last tahm 'at ah wer at t' chetch ther was neeabody for ti sing bud me an' mah dowtther, an' seea atwixt us wa raised t' tune as neyce as could be, an' wa thowt at wa 'd deean middlin an' all ; an' when t' chetch lowsed wa met au'd Izak agaan t' deear, an' ah thowt for seear at he 'd a'e paad us a bit of a compliment for wer singin.' Bud what ivver deea ya think 'at he said ti ma ? He says " Singin' ! what, thoo buzzed leyke a bee iv a bottle, an' sha skirled leyke a pig iv a yat." Naw, naw, naw, Mistther G. ah 's nivver cummin na mair whahl au'd Izak 's theer !'

There is no meal so much thought of in Yorkshire as tea ; it is all important, and a good substantial tea is more enjoyed than anything. Sometimes circumstances of the most pressing kind have to give way to the reception of this repast. As an instance of what I mean, let me mention an incident that happened to the wife of the clergyman just alluded to. She one day went to see a woman who was dangerously ill. She arrived at the house, and without delay went upstairs. She found the poor woman much worse even than she expected to find her ; in fact, she was dying, and might breathe her last at any moment. To her surprise the husband was 'i t' hoos ' below getting his tea ready. Thinking he could not be aware of his wife's critical state, the good lady went downstairs at once to tell him how matters stood. She thought, of course, that he would immediately hasten to the bedside of the evidently dying woman. But it was not so ; and the only response she received to the earnest entreaty that he would go to the 'chamber' without delay, was, 'Whya, whya, bud ah mun a'e mi tea ! '

Among the many changes that have taken place during the present century, few are greater than those connected with our parish churches, and the manner in which the services are conducted in them. One could hardly credit the stories of neglect and irreverence of which one has heard as having taken place in former times ; and yet they were, alas, only too true. I have heard old people say that they thought no more in days gone by of going to the mother church of the district to be confirmed by the Bishop, than they did of going out for a day's pleasure. Happily that is now no more. The preparation for Confirmation in the olden days was too often of the most meagre description. To show the gross ignorance of some of those who offered themselves as candidates for Confirmation, I cannot forbear quoting an instance that was connected with a parish near Stokesley, many years ago. It was in Archbishop Harcourt's time, and an elderly woman from the parish alluded to, whose training in Church principles had been as much neglected as her education generally, expressed herself as desirous of being confirmed. For some unexplained reason she would not consent to be prepared for the rite by her own clergyman, who thereupon reported the case to the Archbishop, and asked him what was to be done. The case being such an exceptional one, the Archbishop said that he himself would examine her when he came to the place. In due course his Grace arrived, and the interview came off. Among other interrogatories, the Archbishop put the very practical question, ' Do you keep the Commandments?' 'Aye,' says the old woman, 'ah keeps Paumston Settherda at Stowsla, an' Trinity Munda at Yatton, an' Pancake Tuesda at heeam.' 'You are a poor weak woman,' remarks his Grace. 'Aye,' replies the catechumen, 'an' seea wad you be weak an' wanklin if you'd been as badly as ah 've been for t' last three weeks.' For such answers the Archbishop was not prepared, and thus the catechetical examination was brought to a sudden termination.

The country practitioner of olden days sometimes had a rough-and-ready way of dealing with patients of the humbler class. But when we are told of one who 'scraffled' in the eye of a patient whose sight was affected, the operation sounds exceptionally trying, to say the least of it. Let us hear what the patient had to say himself of the treatment he received at the hands of his medical adviser. In this case the sufferer was a besom-maker, who felt his sight failing him, and accordingly sought help from the local doctor. After his visit, he was interrogated by his friends as to how he had 'come on.' The poor fellow was rather indignant, for the manner in which he had been ' handled' was anything but comforting. He described it thus :—

'Whya! he scraffled an' wrowt i mi ee, an' then he

oppen'd t' deear an' bunched ma oot, an' said ah 'd plenty o' seet for mah tthraade.'

Possibly this doctor was the same as one of whom it used to be said that he had only two kinds of medicine, one or other of which he applied in every case. The test question which he put to all those who sought to him for relief from their maladies was to the effect as to whether the medicine required was a ' binndther '. or a ' scoorer.'

Bishop Wilberforce, of Oxford, used to be credited with telling a great many good stories, and his ready wit was well known. It is said that on one occasion, when giving a large dinner-party at Cuddesdon, he had his coachman in to help to carry out dishes, plates, &c. In the middle of the entertainment, as he was carrying a pile of plates, his foot slipped as he was going through the door, and down went all the plates with a fearful crash. The ladies of course were much startled, whereupon the Bishop pulled himself together and quietly observed, 'Ladies, don't be alarmed ; it is only my coachman going out with a break.'

It is no doubt rather dangerous work employing outsiders to do inside work to which they are not accustomed; the Cuddesdon catastrophe is an instance of this. But that was a trifle compared with what happened once at a clergyman's house near Yarm. He was about to give an extra grand spread on some great occasion, and determined to do the thing in style. Accordingly, he put his general servant-man into silk stockings, and had him in to help to wait at table. As a final preliminary this same man was told to carry in a pile of hot-water plates, while the parlour-maid went her way to announce that dinner was ready. He certainly did carry his burden in with all safety, but when the guests

paired into the dining-room they found, to their con-
sternation and intense amusement, a hot-water plate
carefully put on each chair! He probably never heard
the end of this, and on this special occasion he came in
also for no small amount of chaff anent his silk stockings; and when asked how he liked wearing them, he
would say he 'wasn't sae varry weel suited; it was
leyke being up ti yan's knees i cau'd watther!'

A Yorkshire squire, who spent part of the year in
London, used sometimes to give one or two of his servants a treat to the opera. One of them, who had a short
time before been at a great agricultural show, and had
looked with admiration and interest at the prize animals
and their owners, real or imaginary, was asked by his
master on his return from the opera what had struck
him most of all he had seen there. He expected to
hear the man loud in praise of some noted voice or
scene; instead of which, to his great amusement, his
servant said that he really thought that what struck
him most was to see among the audience the man who
had won the prize for the best bull at the great show.

I end this chapter with what was told me by a correspondent from Kirby Moorside; it well brings out a
touch of the Yorkshire character for cuteness. An old
gentleman, after the funeral of a relative, was listening
with rapt attention to the reading of the will, in which he
proved to be interested. First, it recounted how that a
certain field was willed to him; then it went on to give
the old grey mare in the said field to some one else with
whom he was on anything but friendly terms; at which
point he suddenly interrupted the proceedings by
exclaiming indignantly, 'Then sha's eeatin ma gess!'
(grass).

CHAPTER X.

IT is scarcely to be wondered at that strangers to our folk-talk should sometimes be at a loss to catch its meaning when by any chance they are brought into the way of hearing it. The words and phrases, and especially the vowel-sounds, are so different from those of ordinary English, that those who are at all new to them are at times sorely perplexed, and not unfrequently make amusing mistakes. I do not know if we in Yorkshire are more unconscious than other people of the use we make of unusual modes of expression: perhaps we are; certainly some of us are. I am reminded of an example of this which Professor Earle quotes in his *Philology of the English Tongue.* It is to the point. He alludes to it in connection with our use of the word *while,* which in Yorkshire does not have the ordinary signification of 'during the time that,' but is equivalent to 'until'; quite well-educated people will sometimes use the word in that sense. At a village in the south of the county, there lived a highly respected retired druggist. By way of making himself useful on the Sundays, he acted as superintendent of the boys' Sunday school. The lads occasionally were very uproarious, and when the din became quite unbearable, he always appealed to the scholars in the following set phrase:—'Now boys, I can't do nothing while you are quiet!'

I have from time to time heard many curious mistakes made by those from a distance, in conversing with our broad-spoken Yorkshire folk. I will briefly instance a few cases of the kind.

What amusing passages have from time to time taken place in courts of law in days when education was not so advanced as it is now, and how perplexed have judges and counsel been, who were unused to the tones and expressions of our dialect, in endeavouring to understand what witnesses have had to say! Frequent mistakes have occurred through this. One such incident is recorded by a friend of mine as having happened between counsel and a little girl, who was called upon to prove that her father's housekeeper had opened and robbed a certain box. The woman admitted having opened the box, but said she did so only from curiosity, and in the little girl's presence.

The girl detailed how the woman took her into the room where the box was and then said, *mud sha oppen i' box?* that is, 'was she to open it?' Counsel looked puzzled, and repeated the question: 'What did she say?' But the girl's reiterated answer beat him utterly: he then turned and repeated it solemnly to the judge, pronouncing *mud* as in 'blood,' and saying he really could not see what 'mud' (filth), had to do with it!

In such cases as the foregoing it is well if someone is at hand to interpose and act as an interpreter. This, no doubt, has often been done. I remember the late respected squire of the parish where I live, telling me of an example of this kind which occurred in court, when he, as High Sheriff, was sitting near the Judge, whose name he gave me ; only in this instance it was the witness who failed to understand what was said by counsel. It was an assault case. 'Was she excited?' asked the barrister. But there was no response. The question was renewed, but nothing was elicited beyond bewilderment. Whereupon the High Sheriff whispered to the Judge that he should turn the question into its Yorkshire equivalent :—*Was she put about?* This suggestion was acted upon, and the effect was, of course, instantaneous : 'Aw, sha was putten aboot sair,' was the speedy reply, and the examination went on.

As has been noticed in a previous chapter, one of the principal peculiarities of the pronunciation of the York-shire dialect is the strong tendency to adopt the *eea*-sound in certain vowels. Thus, for instance, 'same' is always sounded *seeam*, but as there is another word in common use with the like pronunciation, mistakes have been sometimes made on that score : the other word pronounced 'seeam' is *saim* (lard). As an illustration of this possible confusion of meaning, I was told not long ago of an apprentice who took out a summons against his master on the ground that, amongst other improper food, he had, as the apprentice expressed it, *seeam tiv his breead* (lard with his bread), instead of butter. The presiding Justice of the Peace, before whom the complaint was heard, not quite understand-ing the case, asked the master what he (the master) ate. 'Butter,' he replied. Turning to the lad, the question was repeated to him. He answered, *seeam*. Thinking he meant 'the same,' the magistrate dismissed the case without further enquiry, merely remarking 'why do you come here if you get *the same* to eat as your master ?'

A clergyman of my acquaintance in the East Riding, told me of an amusing interview he had when first he came to reside in Yorkshire. My friend is an Irishman, and when he accepted a living in the Wold country, was as ignorant of our folk-talk as he was of Welsh or Russian. He had but just come over from Ireland, and had not had time to make the acquaintance of any of his parishioners. If I remember rightly it was on a Saturday night, and he was to do duty at the church on the following morning, when the servant announced that a man wished to see him. The vicar went to learn what was wanted. The stranger introduced himself by bluntly ejaculating, 'ah's t' man 'at leads t' cauls for t' chetch,' adding enquiringly, 'mun ee continny ti lead t' cauls for t' chetch?' This was a poser for the new vicar; he could make nothing whatever of it; and the Yorkshireman only repeated the question, 'mun ee continny ti lead t' cauls for t' chetch?' The other only stared in mute astonishment. Thinking, however, that two heads were better than one, he retired to the drawing-room for a few minutes, to confer with his wife, to see if she could throw any ray of light upon what this 'leading t' cauls for t' chetch' could possibly be; but being equally new to the country and its speech, it was quite unintelligible to her also. At length, after revolving the strange sounding words in his mind once more, a happy thought struck him, and he decided that this man must be a sort of ecclesiastical crier, and that as the town crier gives out public notices in the streets, so this hitherto unheard-of official 'led calls,' which was interpreted to mean giving out notices, hymns, &c., in church. So, thinking that no great harm would come if the man continued in this peculiar office for another Sunday, at all events, he so far assented to the request, though somewhat hesitatingly, and the 'leader of calls' withdrew. I imagine the new vicar expected to hear some strange performances in church on the Sunday, but all went well, and on enquiry afterwards he discovered that his solicitous parishioner was no 'caller' at all, in church or out of it, but merely a poor man who had been accustomed to cart the coals for heating the church; and as he was anxious not to lose this small part of his livelihood he determined to be beforehand in securing the work under the new *régime*. It would seem therefore that a touch of the Yorkshire character came out, as well as its dialect.

Among my earliest recollections are those of fishing expeditions with my father, who at that time greatly enjoyed the sport. On the occasion to which I here allude, he had a friend with him from London, who was also a keen fisherman, and they were trying their skill in a well-known trout stream in the East Riding. The day was windy and cold. There was a little lad with us from the neighbouring village, who came to *late* a job, or merely to look on. The day wearing on, and seeing the lad crying, our south-country friend went up to him and asked him what was the matter. Whereupon he sobbed out, ' Pleeas sir, ah 's stahv'd.' Thinking that he was famished with hunger, the Londoner, in the kindness of his heart, produced his packet of sandwiches and proceeded to offer the boy some, which to his astonishment he refused. At this I ventured to intervene as interpreter, and explained that it was the cold which made the lad cry and not hunger. The incident apparently made an impression on me. I must have been about seven at the time, but it seems as fresh on my memory as yesterday.

A generation ago it was the almost universal custom for the clergy to wear bands in performing Divine Service. One Sunday a young parson from West Rounton went to preach at a neighbouring church, and on his arrival discovered that he had forgotten to bring his bands ; whereupon he suddenly turned to the clerk and asked him to try and find a pair : the clerk hurried off, and in a few minutes returned with two pieces of string, which he solemnly presented to the officiating clergyman. This reminds me of a little experience of my own : some years back I was doing duty for a friend, and on reaching the vestry I enquired of the clerk where the surplice was : ' It 's yonder, see ya,' says he, ' and there 's t' *hassock* an' all,' pointing to a cassock. There can be little doubt that if our young parson of West Rounton had asked his clerk for a cassock he would have received a hassock, and if he had demanded a hassock he would possibly have got a cassock. Such is the perversity of human nature, Yorkshire included.

Not long since I was staying with a friend near Yarm, when I was told of a ludicrous mistake made by a member of the legal profession from London, when on a visit to that neighbourhood on business. A property was for sale in the parish where my friend lives, and the said lawyer came to look over the estate for a client who had some thoughts of purchasing it. He understood but little of the Yorkshire tongue, and had no slight difficulty in understanding some of the remarks of the tenants on the estate.

On looking over the buildings of one of the farms he confronted the farmer, who, of course, instantly understood the object of the visit, and thought he would lose no time in making known some of his grievances, the chief of which seems to have been that over the gateway of the fold-yard an arch had been built, but so low that in 'leading' out manure it was sometimes impossible to take as full a load as could be wished, or, as the farmer expressed it, 'it wer varry awk'ard in leadin' oot a *laud o' manner*.' This remark was a sore puzzle to the Londoner. He naturally thought that a *laud o' manner* meant a 'lord of the manor,' but on what possible occasions, or for what possible reasons, the lord of the manor had to be carried out of this particular fold-yard on the top of a cart he could not divine, even by the aid of all the legal acumen he could command. However, it seems he took the matter into rather serious consideration, though without letting the farmer have the faintest suspicion that he thought it in any way contrary to custom that lords of manors should on certain solemn occasions be thus carted about the farm premises. He pondered the farmer's words over in his mind, and thinking that if his client should purchase the property, and the unfortunate lord of the manor should come to grief in the way he imagined, he determined to make further enquiry with regard to this hitherto unheard-of practice. He had not long to wait before he was enlightened. The same evening he met the vicar of a neighbouring parish at dinner, to whom he un-burdened his mind. Being familiar with the dialect, the clergyman at once explained that the tenant did not mean to say that the lord of the manor had to put up with any peculiar treatment whatever, but that the arch-way of the fold-yard was not sufficiently high to get an ordinary sized load of manure out conveniently ; thus, accompanied by no little merriment, was the legal mind of the stranger relieved of further anxiety on this interesting point.

It is not only entire strangers who fail sometimes to make out the peculiarities of our folk-talk: perhaps words that would be understood if spoken slowly, become unintelligible under a rapid articulation, or unusual blending of words together. As a simple example of this, I may mention a little expression that was made use of to the vicar of a parish near Whitby. He was visiting an old woman one afternoon, when she, on enquiring after the health of one of her neighbours, said something which sounded like 'dizzily gorlous?' For a moment her visitor failed to catch her meaning, but on reflection it flashed across him that the question in reality was, 'Diz a (he) lig awlus?' i.e. 'Does he lie always?' which I need hardly explain does not mean 'is he addicted to untruthfulness?' but simply, 'is he confined to his bed?'

How careful we should be to ascertain the meaning of a word addressed to us that we do not at first understand, before judging of what has been said!

A poor person speaking to a lady of her children, said by way of compliment, that she should be 'creuse on 'em'—in other words, that she ought to be very proud of them. Somehow, the lady, not understanding the dialect, could only imagine that the woman meant she should be *cursed* of them! And so she took her hasty departure quite horrified at this sudden and seemingly unaccountable imprecation.

Anyone unused to the dialectical pronunciation of our vowel-sounds might well be pardoned for misunderstanding our vocal treatment of the verb *to shout*. When our Yorkshire folk desire to attract the attention of those at a distance, they always, according to our vernacular, *shoot at them*, or *shoot on 'em*. To peaceably disposed people who are unaware of it, this local pecu-

liarity of ours in the utterance of this word might easily
be misinterpreted to mean designs of a ruffianly or
murderous character. This common way of pronouncing *shout* in these parts reminds me of a
trifling incident told me by a correspondent, which
illustrates how easily mistakes of this kind occur. A
Southern sportsman had come to have a little shooting
with a friend in the North Riding. The gamekeeper
in due course, when all was ready, led up his favourite
pointer to the gentleman, and knowing well the dog's
nature, thought it prudent to give just a word of
caution, which was merely this : 'You maun't shoot at
her, sir.' 'Shoot at her ! no,' was the astonished reply ;
whereupon the keeper added by way of explanation,
Nay, nay, sir, you mun mak on her (you must coax her).

In enquiring of a child its name, care must be taken
as to the form the question takes, or disappointing results may ensue.

Of the imprudence of seeking this information under
the ordinary form, ' What is your name ? ' I have previously spoken ; but still more rash is it, if on wishing
to find out a child's name, you break ground with, ' Who
are you ? ' for so you may meet with an answer you are
not at all prepared for.

A clergyman near Whitby went into his school one
day, and seeing a boy there whom he had not seen
before, accosted him thus :—' Well, my lad, and who
are you ? ' The boy, thinking that the rector was
making an enquiry as to the general state of his health,
gave back as his response in true Yorkshire fashion,
'Aw, ah 's middlin' : hoo 's yoursen ? '

Many an absurd mistake has been made over our
word *a-gait*. I was once told of a farmer's wife who
took a young girl into her service from the South of

England. The new comer had never heard the Yorkshire dialect spoken before, and so, as may be supposed,
she was somewhat at sea at first, and made a few
rather strange mistakes. On her arrival, for instance,
her mistress harangued her as to her duties, and after
recounting them in detail, she wound up by saying,
'An' thoo mun git a-gait i good tahm i t' moornin an'
light t' fires.' Though rather astonished, but still
thinking she quite understood this injunction, the poor
girl was seen wandering about the fields in a disconso-
late way in the early morning, as if in search of something. After coming downstairs the mistress found no
fire lighted, and on asking somewhat angrily the reason,
the girl assured her that she had searched in all directions for an old disused gate to use as kindling (for so
had she interpreted the order), but without success, and
so no fire had been made.

A similar misunderstanding is recorded of a young
south-country curate, who, on coming to a parish in
Yorkshire, and being seen by one of the villagers
shortly afterwards, was addressed by him thus: 'Ah
see you 're a-gait'; 'No,' replied the clergyman, in an
indignant tone, 'I'm the curate.'

As another example of a like blunder, I may mention
that I heard once of a lady from the South being very
greatly surprised one morning by the servant boy
coming to her with the complaint that the cook gave him
'nowt bud sauce.' The mistress having her suspicions
that the two were in the habit of 'differing,' naturally
surmised that the unfortunate lad, who evidently got
the worst of it, was complaining about what she thought
was the peculiar character of his food, rather than of the
scoldings with which 'Susan' was paying him out.

Canny Scotchmen, and especially Scotch medical

men, are to be found all the country through, York-shire not excepted. In general they do not experience much difficulty in understanding our dialect, but occasionally they make a *mauvais pas*.

A correspondent from the neighbourhood of Kirby Moorside, tells me of one which came to his knowledge. A Highland doctor was attending an old woman in the North Riding. In the course of his visit he had displayed a certain liveliness of disposition—possibly he did so with a view to cheering up the old lady's drooping spirits. Noticing this, the patient observed, by way of a slight check, 'you 're a *wick* (lively) young man.' He came from the town of Wick, and so, in astonishment, he asked her how she had found that out. She in turn could only feel embarrassed, and made no very coherent reply. What the doctor thought can only be guessed, but on relating the conversation when he returned home, he was enlightened as to the true state of the case, and so learnt that *wick* folks exist in Yorkshire as well as in the county of Caithness.

Here in Yorkshire we pronounce the *o* in such words as off, frost, lost, cost, tossed, &c., much shorter than south-country folk, who frequently draw out the *o* to *au*, making *frost*, for instance, sound like *fraust*. Another word of this kind is *cough*, which we Northerners pronounce like *doff*, with the *o* short: if it were pronounced *cauf*, as the Southerners pronounce it, our country people would think that *calf* was meant, which is always so sounded. A lady from the South of England was once talking to a husbandman at East Rounton, and happened to make the statement, 'my husband has got a cauf (cough) to-day.' Whereupon the countryman, with an interested look, took the lady aback with the enquiry, 'Is 't a bull or a wye?'

The peculiar use of the verb *to want* will be found noticed on another page. .It is a word which is apt to be misunderstood by those unfamiliar with the dialect. I heard a rather diverting illustration of this when I was travelling some few years ago from Nunburnholme to York. When stopping at one of the stations, a passenger got into the compartment where I was. While the porter was standing with his hand on the carriage door, the passenger's dog eagerly forced himself into the compartment to his master. Seeing this, the porter observed, 'He doesn't want to go, sir, does he?' by which he meant, 'He has not to go, has he?' whereupon the other, who could not have been a Yorkshireman, surely, thinking the porter meant 'he doesn't want to go, does he?' in the ordinary acceptation of the words, answered emphatically, 'Doesn't he want to go!'

It is not always an easy matter to give a perfectly truthful evasive answer to an awkward question. A good example of success in that art was given me by the wife of a North Riding clergyman not long ago. She was visiting a parishioner, one of whose ne'er-do-weel sons had lately married a lass in the neighbourhood, whose charms were not supposed to be specially attractive. On the occasion of this visit the lady naturally, though somewhat doubtfully, enquired about the new daughter-in-law. The mother did not wish to commit herself too strongly in her opinion of the young woman, though she evidently had her feelings on the subject. The lady's question was parried in the following characteristic and delightfully ingenious way: 'Noo, ah 'll tell ya, Mrs. G.; sha 's just yan o' them lasses 'at neeabody bud yan o' mah lads wad ivver a'e thowt o' marryin'.'

To the clergyman just referred to, the following truly cautious answer, such as the Yorkshireman de-

lights in, was given by an old acquaintance from a
neighbouring parish where they had lately got a new
incumbent. The man was asked how he liked the new
parson. The Yorkshireman, however, was not going
thus prematurely to commit himself; and all he would
vouchsafe to say was, ' We 've summered him, an' we 've
wintthered him, an' we 'll summer him ageean, an'
then mebbe ah 'll tell ya ! '

- A good repartee is always enjoyable, and sometimes
the Yorkshireman can give one with telling effect. It
was said of a late Rural Dean, who had on one occasion
been performing his duty of visiting the various churches
in his deanery to see if they were in proper repair and
keeping, that he arrived at a certain place where the
church was in anything but good order ; he accordingly
drew the churchwarden's attention to this, and by way
of example instanced his own church, adding that he
should come and see for himself what a model of clean-
liness and neatness it was. But the churchwarden was
not to be beaten nor in any way convinced by such an
argument, cogent though it might seem ; for he promptly
interposed with the rejoinder : 'Aye, bud Mr. A.,
there 's neeabody theer gans in ti muck 't ! '

A correspondent from Whitby tells me of a short
conversation which he remembered as having taken
place some sixty years ago, and which gives evidence
of a ready wit on the part of one of the speakers. There
was in one of the dales an old man named John D., a
devout farmer of the old school, who attended chapel
with clockwork regularity ; but John had a weakness—
he invariably went to sleep during the sermon. One
Sunday, after service (a service in which John had
been nodding more than usual) when the people were
going to their homes, one of the company said to John,

'John, ah think there wer sum folks asleep i t' chappil ti-daay !' John saw the insinuation plainly enough, but liking to think that there must have been others in the same unconscious state as himself, adds, 'Aye, whya ; mebbe if yan had been wakken, yan mud a'e seen 'em.'

I do not know what the custom in the South of England may be, but in these parts there is an extraordinary propensity for giving *by-names*, that is, nick-names, to people; so much so, that in many villages there is scarcely a person without one. Generally speaking, they are amusingly appropriate.

In the preface of a glossary of Mid-Yorkshire words, by C. C. Robinson, and published by the English Dialect Society in 1876, there is a quotation from a little publication printed at Richmond, in the North Riding, giving a list of by-names belonging to the men who were sent to do permanent duty at Richmond some time previously ; they were taken from the muster rolls of Captains Metcalf and Stewart's companies of the 'Loyal Dales Volunteers.' I will give them here verbatim.

Grain Tom, Glouremour Tom, Screamer Tom, Poddish Tom, Tarry Tom, Tish Tom, Tripy Tom, Trooper Tom (all Thomas Alderson by name), Assy Will Bill, Ayny Jack, Aygill Tom Bill, Becka Jack, Brag Tom, Bullet, Bullock Jammie, Buck Reuben, Butter Geordie, Bowlaway, Brownsa Jossy, Cis Will, Cotty Joe, Codgy, Cwoaty Jack, Curly, Dickey Tom Johnny, Docken Jammie, Daut, Freestane Jack, Gudgeon Tom, Hed Jack. Awd John, Young John, Jains Jack, Mary Jack, King Jack (all John Hird by name), Katy Tom Alick, Kit Puke Jock, Kanah Bill, Knocky Gwordie, Lollock Ann Will, Matty Jwoan Ned, Mark Jammie Joss, Moor Close Gwordie, Nettlebed Anty, Peter Tom Willie, Peed Jack, Piper Ralph, Pullan Will, Roberty Will Peg Sam, Rive Rags, Skeb Symy, Slipe, Slodder, Swinny, Spletmeat, Strudgeon Will, Tash, Tazzy Will.

An old joiner at Hutton Rudby was nick-named

Penny Nap, because he never charged less than a penny, even if he only napped the top of a nail.

In a village in the heart of the Wold country the following names occur :—

Bullock Jack, i. e. Jack who looks after the bullocks;
Sophie Jack, i. e. John P— whose wife's name is Sophie;
Bonwick Jack, i. e. John B— who came from Bonwick;
Quarton Tinner, i. e. Quarton S— who is by trade a tinner;
Zachary Ann, i. e. Ann T— whose husband's Christian name is Zacharias.

Sally George would mean Sally, the wife of George, or Betty John, Betty, the wife of John Robinson. Linkie Bill would be so called because he comes from Lincolnshire; Jinny Cracker, because she is fond of a gossip or a 'crack'; White Mary, because she is as dark as a mulatto; Tighty Thompson, because she prides herself on her smart figure; Greeat Heifer, because she is huge and ponderous; Fancy Basket, because she goes shopping with a smart-looking reticule. If Mr. Beedham has a servant called Mary, she 'gits' (i.e. is called), Beedham Mary; or if Mr. Salman has a dog named Jock, the animal will be designated Salman Jock.

In places where there are several people bearing the same name, some distinguishing mark is almost a necessity. This no doubt 'aids and abets' the habit of giving by-names; very often, however, they are given when no such quasi-necessity arises, but merely from fancy or caprice. Sometimes, again, a physical deformity or defect, or trick, will cause a man to be labelled with some appropriate by-name, which always adheres to him. Thus we find that a man who has lost one eye was nick-named ' Willy wi t' ee,' or another, who had but one arm, was always described as 'Johnny wi t' airm.'

Class by-names, as well as individual ones, are also commonly given. Thus, a tailor is called 'cabbish'; a man from a distance, an 'off chap'; a dweller in the country, a 'cuntthry hawbuck' or a 'joskin'; or a farm servant would be called by the townsman 'boily,' from the custom of having boiled milk for breakfast.

It does not appear that our dialect is specially rich in similes. On the contrary, the illustration and the thing illustrated are as a rule one and the same : 'as bad as bad can be,' 'as mucky as mucky,' 'as sad (heavy) as sad.' Such is the usual delightfully simple form the simile takes, a form which at least has the merit of being ready to hand, but which does not betoken any great originality. Nevertheless, the dialect does possess a considerable number of not inapt illustrations by means of the simile. I will here give a few such by way of example :—

1. As blake as a gowlan.
2. As bliew as a whetst'n.
3. As brant as a hoos-sahd.
4. As breet as a bullace.
5. As bug as a leather-knife.
6. As dark as a bell 'us.
7. As dark as a black coo skin.
8. As deead as a midden.
9. As deead as a scopperill.
10. As deeaf as a yat stowp.
11. As dhry as a kex.
12. As fat as mud.
13. As fond as a poke o' caff wi t' boddom end oot.
14. As fond as a yat.
15. As good as they mak 'em.
16. As hard as a grunded tooad.
17. As kittle as a moos-tthrap.
18. As lcct as a cleg.
19. As meean as muck.

20. As sackless as a goose.
21. As thick as inkle-weeavers.
22. As waak as a kittlin.
23. As wet as sump.
24. As wet as thack.
25. As yalla as a gowlan.

Most of the above will speak for themselves, or will be made plain by a reference to the glossary. On some of them a remark or two may not be out of place.

As to (4), there is an especially brilliant gloss on the skin of the wild plum or bullace which fittingly gives rise to this expression.

(5) *Bug* means self-satisfied, though why this term should be applied to a leather-knife is not apparent, an extended form of the saying is ' as bug as a lad wiv a leather-knife.'

(6) The Bell-'us is the Bell-house or belfrey of a church which is always a dark place.

(7) This I have only heard used by those from the dales.

(10) Another form for ' as deaf as a post.'

(11) The withered stem of the fools-parsley gives a good idea of utter dryness.

(14) I have only heard of this in the East Riding: the imaginary *fondness* of the *yat* is no doubt derived from the fact that it is always knocking its head against the post.

(16) That is to say, he is a tough fellow, there is no hurting him ; he will bear as much knocking about as a toad.

(17) This is applied to anything in a highly sensitive, or touch-and-go state.

(18) This is perhaps the aptest illustration of those quoted : the horsefly seems to settle more lightly than any other insect ; when it comes upon man or beast the first intimation of its having done so is its keen bite.

(21) The fabric called inkle had a very narrow web, and consequently the weavers could sit close.

(25) and (1) The colour expressed by the word *blake* is a palish rather than a deep yellow : it is often applied to butter, indeed the saying ' as blake as butter ' is as common as (1).

CHAPTER XI.

CUSTOMS AND SUPERSTITIONS.

THE system of hiring farm-servants in the whole of the East and a considerable part of the North Ridings is one which seems first to call for some remark. Until recent years, when improved arrangements have been adopted, it was not too much to say that this institution was one of the curses of the country. That system, which till a few years ago was practically a universal one, and is still largely made use of, is called the Martinmas system. The statute hirings—*statties* as they are designated locally—take place, as far as the farm-servants themselves were concerned, at the worst possible time of the year. St. Martin's Day is on November 23rd, and the days are then about at their shortest and darkest, and the roads at their dirtiest. The only thing that can be adduced in favour of such a time is that farm work is then at the slackest.

St. Martin may be considered to be the patron saint of the East Yorkshire farm-servants; but it is to be feared they lightly regarded his name.

Almost without exception Martinmas was the season for the lads and lasses to change their *spots* as they call their situations, and it was the occasion for a general holiday and merry-making all through the district. Martinmas week is a time of much social entertainment. Friends and relatives then meet at each others' houses;

parties, dances, and amusements of various kinds are got up ; and being the one great holiday of the year with the young folks, the time passes all too quickly.

Those servants who are hired under this system are bound legally to their masters for one year. When the farmer engages a servant he gives him what is variously called his *fest*, *Gods-penny*, or *arles*, which is a small sum of money varying from about two to ten shillings ; if the *fest* be returned before the appointed day the servant is freed from the engagement, but if the money is retained the agreement is then binding.

These statute hirings were, and still are, held at the same time of the year in all the principal market towns.

As I remember them when a boy, it would be hard to describe a hiring day in one of our East Riding agricultural centres ; such scenes of riot and disorder were they. Well do I recollect going through the streets of Pocklington on more than one occasion when the great festival was being held. It was *throng deed* and no mistake. In the first place, the streets were more probably than not inches deep in mud and sludge—*all iv a posh*, as we should describe it in our country speech. Farmers and their wives, farm lads and lasses by hundreds, fathers and mothers, brothers and sisters, crowded the market-place ; carriers' carts, gigs, vehicles of all descriptions poured into the town and *teemed* into the streets their living freights. Jack and Tommy, Joe and Harry, lustily greeted Polly, Sally, Jane, and Maggy ; loud and hearty were the salutations between friend and friend ; joyous and exuberant were the spirits of these stalwart specimens of humanity. Although there was an element of business in the proceedings, the young folk had come there to enjoy themselves, and enjoy themselves they did. The actual hiring of the

servants took place formerly only in the open street,
which presented an animated appearance, and might be
termed a kind of slave market. No doubt the farm lads
and lasses were free to choose, and they received certain
wages for their work ; but their build, muscle, and
general physique were minutely scanned by those who
engaged them : and well was it for them if their consti-
tution was sound and robust; for the work to which
they were called, though not disliked by those who could
stand it, was no light matter. From daylight to sunset
it was one continuous round all the year through.
Ploughing and sowing, harrowing and rolling, washing and milking, work in the hay-field and work in
the corn-field; hedging and ditching, an occasional
threshing day with its attendant hard work, *livering*
corn, *plugging* or *scaling* muck, *foddering t' beeas and sike
like*—these and countless other operations connected
with the farm kept the youths and maidens perpetually
a-gait. But after all, it was a healthy life. Early to bed
and early to rise, with plenty of good wholesome food,
preserved them in the rudest health; and if only the
place to which they engaged themselves was a good
meat spot, as it was called, that is to say, if they were well
fed, all went well. A brother clergyman, of more than
forty years' standing, once told me that in all his experience he never once had occasion to visit a sick case
in the farm-servant class. The Yorkshire *plew-lads*,
especially those in the East Riding, are as fine and well-
developed a race as one can see anywhere; an army
composed of such material might do wonders. But to
return to the market-place of Pocklington. Martinmas
Day there was a pleasure-fair day. The entertainments
provided for the young men and women were of varied
kinds. Rows of stalls lined the street, where all manner

of meats and drinks were sold which would have dis-
agreed with the constitutions of any ordinary mortals to
an alarming extent, but which were indulged in freely
and with impunity by these 'bruff' East-Ridingers.
On these occasions 'cheap Jacks' and 'quacks' carried
on a brisk trade; shooting-galleries and Punch and
Judy were attractions to not a few, and shows of fat
women, wild beasts, one-eyed and six-legged monsters,
and all manner of horrors were literally besieged by
uproarious crowds of claimants for admission, till the
places fairly reeked again. It was a splendid harvest
for the show-keepers, especially if the day was wet, and
under that condition of weather the public houses were
unfortunately also crammed almost to suffocation. It
was from this point of view a sad sight. Boys and girls,
lads and lasses, men and women were crowded together
in the parlours and passages of the inns in a state of
wild excitement, uproar, and confusion. Music, if such
it could be called, and dancing went on merrily; coarse
jests were freely indulged in; and songs of every
description were bawled out in solo and chorus, and
shouts of approval rent the air. It was like pandemo-
nium let loose. All this naturally tended to demoralise
the young people, and the results can be better imagined
than described. It was only to be expected indeed that
after a year's work and drudgery there should be some
relaxation,

'Neque semper arcum tendit Apollo';

and it was right that these hard-working farm-servants
should have their enjoyment like anyone else; the only
melancholy part about it was that it did not take a less
debasing form. Happily the worst part of the old
system is now done away with. The *statties* go on as

of yore, but they are conducted in an altogether improved
fashion. Both clergy and laity combined to get rid of
the worst phases of the institution, if possible, and rooms
are now hired in every town in which the girls are
assembled by themselves, and can be engaged by the
farmers' wives in an orderly and befitting manner ; the
Girls' Friendly Society and other kindred institutions
all help in the same good cause, and although occasional
brawls and disturbances take place, yet there is no
comparison between the state of things now and what it
was thirty years ago.

There is no class so difficult for a clergyman to deal
with as the farm-servants engaged under the Martinmas
system. They are a constantly shifting part of the
population. They like changing their 'spots,' and if
possible, bettering themselves ; and so at the twelvemonth end away they go to fresh scenes. Sometimes
they will stay on another year or more in the same
place, if they can come to terms with their employers,
but these cases are exceptions ; the rule is for them to
shift. They are at work all day, and so are tired at
night, and go to rest early. The late well-known
authoress of *Plowing and Sowing* appreciated the
difficulties of their case as much as anyone, and with
noble self-sacrifice she devoted herself some thirty years
ago or more to the work of endeavouring to raise the
moral and religious tone of the farm-servants near her
home in the East Riding. No one could be better
qualified for such a work than she was : for years she
persevered in her task ; but with all her special gifts
and qualifications, the success that she achieved could
not be said to be very encouraging, although she went
through so much. Still, after what has been said, I
feel bound to add that when these same farm lads marry,

have homes of their own, and settle down in life, they turn out generally well-conducted and decent members of society.

Although the work on the farms was hard, yet the plough lads took an interest in it, and especially in their horses. The agricultural horses in the Wold country are fine well-bred animals, and as I best re-member them—namely, twenty to thirty years ago—they used to receive every care and attention on the part of the lads whose duty it was to look after them. It was a really pretty sight to see, as I have seen times and oft, a waggon load of grain being *led* from one of the highly cultivated Wold farms down to the railway for transmission to the West Riding or elsewhere. There was the strongly-made but not ungracefully shaped pole waggon, *yoked* whereto were three or four handsome black or bay horses with well-groomed glossy coats, their manes and tails generally arranged in neatly made plaits and intertwined with ribbons of varied hue, yellow and red, blue and green. There sits the waggoner, mounted on the near-side horse, a lad, say, of twenty summers, a fine strong healthy-looking fellow as any one need wish to see ; he has the four 'in hand' and his whip-stock rests on his thigh. He is well and warmly clad, and his black wide-awake with a peacock's feather at the side, together with his red and blue variegated waistcoat add to the picturesqueness of the turn-out, As they near the bottom of a *slack*, crack goes the whip, and 'whoa-up Bonny,' 'Duke,' 'Star,' or what-ever the horses' names may be, and away they go down the end of the slope kicking up the dust or throwing up the mud, till they are pretty nearly half way up the opposite side of the rise, when the horses have to stretch their limbs for a few paces till they are at the top of the hillock, and so again on they go, making light work of their task.

The servants engaged at Martinmas are for the most part boarded and lodged at the farm-house, or with a *hind* as he is called ; that is to say, a sort of foreman among them, but living at a house other than that at which the farmer himself lives. This custom largely prevails in the East Riding, especially on the Wolds, where the farms are very large, sometimes extending to 1500 acres or more.

Besides the carnival of Martinmas, there are other lesser times of relaxation or rejoicing.

Harvest festivities, though still kept up to a considerable extent in East Yorkshire, are not held on such large or varied a scale as they were a generation ago. Means of rapid locomotion, the use of machinery, and gravitation towards the towns, have tended to do away with many interesting local customs which in former days added to country life a charm peculiarly its own.

The Mell Supper still retains its name and some of its old features amongst us at the present day, though shorn of much of its lustre. Its name is by some thought to speak for itself almost, *mell* or ' meal ' being probably the same as the Icelandic *mjöl* and Danish *mel*. The last sheaf that is gathered in, here in the North Riding, is called the mell sheaf, and the expression *We 've gotten wer mell* is the same thing as saying the harvest is finished. It may be interesting to note in passing what some of the names are which are given to the last in-gathered sheaf in Denmark. In South Jutland, for instance, it is called *enken* or *enkemanden*, the 'widow' or the 'widower'; in Vendsyssel it is named *stodder* or 'beggar,' and is driven home covered with rags; in Samsö and Funen its title is 'the old man,' and in Sealand 'the old woman.' Similarly, the last load is called in West Jutland *kvædelæs* or 'song-load,' and is driven to the farmstead with singing and rejoicing. This is very much what is done, or used to be done, here, and perhaps in almost every country in Europe.

No mell supper can take place without dancing, and formerly the advent of 'guisers' formed one of the great features of the entertainment. These 'guisers' were men with masks or blackened faces, and they were decked out in all sorts of fantastic costumes. The starting of the dancing was not always an easy matter, but by degrees, as the dancers warmed to the work and as the ale horns came to be passed round, the excitement began to grow; this was increased by the arrival of the 'guisers,' and then the clatter of the dancers' boots doing double-shuffle and various comical figures, set the entertainment going at full swing. The 'guisers' would at times come uninvited to the feast, and as a rule they were well received, but sometimes the doors would be barred against them and their entrance stoutly resisted.

About fifty years ago it was very common when the 'shearing' of the corn was finished for three large sheaves to be bound together; for these, races were run by the women amid the greatest excitement. This also was called the mell sheaf, and would contain about a bushel of corn, and in the days when wheat was at such a high price as it once was the prize was worth having.

The mell doll is rather more a thing of the past, though it is probable that there are still many old people who can recollect it. It consisted of a sheaf of corn dressed in the costume of a harvester, and gaily decked with flowers ; it was in fact a sort of rough and ready-made doll on a large scale.

I have been informed that at Kilburn, on the Hamble-ton Hills, the mell sheaf was tastefully made of various kinds of corn plaited together and covered with ribbons, flowers, &c.   When the guests were ready for the dance, the mell sheaf would be placed in the middle of the room, which was frequently a disused one, and they danced round it.   It was made like a figure and was sometimes called the mell doll.

At the time of which I speak, harvest thanksgiving services in churches were of course quite unknown ; the introduction of this custom is surely a good and sensible one, as connecting religious observances with that which is man's natural occupation—the tilling of the land ; in this matter we are but reverting to ancient usages which might perhaps be extended with advantage.

Fifty years ago seed-time had also its festival, though on a lesser scale, as well as harvest.   At the *backend*, when the early sowing had been completed, the farmer made a sort of feast for his men, the principal feature of which was a 'seed-cake,' which was given to each of them.   The cake did not get its name from anything that it contained, for it was in fact an ordinary sort of currant or plum cake, but from the occasion.   On these minor festivals the men had as much ale to drink as they liked, and right well they enjoyed themselves. This old custom has, I believe, now quite died out.

The Christmastide observances in East Yorkshire, as elsewhere, are, and still more, have been in the past, many and various.   The season is always looked upon as a time of joy even by the poorest.   On Christmas Eve the houses are decked with 'hollin' or other ever-greens, which are never burnt afterwards, but thrown

away.   The Yule clog used to be brought in and placed
upon the fire along with a piece of that from the previous year which had been carefully preserved for good
luck, in the same way as the Yuletide candle was.
The Christmas candle is always a feature in the furnishing of the feast.   It is lighted by the head of the house,
and generally stands in the centre of the table, round
which the members of the family sit to partake of the
frumety and other dainties that deck the board.   No
other candle must be lighted from it, and before the
family retire to rest the master of the house blows it
out, leaving what remains of it to stand where it is until
the following morning.   The unconsumed piece is then
carefully stowed away with other similar relics of
former years ; sometimes quite a large number of such
pieces are accumulated in the course of years : it is
considered in some localities highly unlucky to disturb
these remnants during the year.   It was further
thought unlucky not only, as I have said, to take a light
from the Yule candle, but also to give a light to any one
on Christmas Day ; so that in former times, before
matches were invented as we have them now, the question used to be asked before retiring to rest on Christmas
Eve, 'is your tunder dhry?'   In former times the Yule
candle was looked upon as almost a sacred thing.   If
by any chance it went out, it was believed that some
member of the family would die during the ensuing year,
and if anyone in snuffing it extinguished the light, that
person would, it was thought, die within the year.

The old Christmas customs hold their ground much
more firmly in the North than they do in the South of
England.   How they originated it would be rash to
surmise, but that some of them are survivals of old
heathenish customs there can, I think, be little doubt.

In the matter of the Christmas feasting there is
nothing so distinctive of it as in the making of the
frumety. He is no Yorkshireman who does not know
what *furmety* or *frumety* is. It is one of our institutions.
As regularly as Christmas comes round preparations
are made for the manufacture of this Yorkshire dish.
The name is clearly derived from *frumentum*, though
when it was introduced into the country there is, so far
as I am aware, nothing to show. The principal ingredient in this dainty, as the name implies, is grain, and
that grain is wheat. On Christmas Eve there is
scarcely a household but what makes *frumety*. If the
people have no wheat of their own they always beg
some from one of the neighbouring farmers, and with
this object in view the boys go round the villages and
outlying farmsteads on St. Thomas' Day. To make
the dish in orthodox fashion takes some time. The
usual order of proceeding is this. First of all, the wheat
is soaked in water for about a day : it is then put into a
bag, and beaten upon the floor a few times in order to
knock the *hullins* off, or the more effectual mode was
sometimes adopted of thrashing the wheat contained in
the bag with the flail ; after which the *hullins* are
separated by simply putting the whole into water, when
the outer coat of the wheat rises to the top, and the pure
corn is thus extracted. It is next put into the oven to
cree for two or three hours ; milk is then poured upon
it in a pan which is put upon the fire to boil ; sugar is
added, together with nutmeg or other spices according
to people's tastes and fancies. It is a dish which is
highly appreciated. It is eaten by the whole household
on Christmas Eve as they sit round the table with the
Yule candles burning. It is customary also to have
Yule cakes 'to' the *frumety* ; these are small round

cakes with currants, citron, and other ingredients : each person has one. There is no dish so universally partaken of throughout the whole of East Yorkshire, not excepting Yorkshire pudding, as this. It is, however, never eaten at any other season than Christmastide, and as a rule on no other day than Christmas Eve, though some families will also make it on, or keep what is left till, New Year's Eve.

The old-fashioned 'pepper cake,' the *peberkage* of Denmark, is becoming, or rather, I should say, has become, more a thing of the olden days. It is however still made in the moorland districts of the North Riding; while in the East Riding and other parts the very name is unknown. This, too, is a Yule cake ; it is a kind of gingerbread, and therefore more pungent than the Yule cakes of other districts ; hence the name. It has nothing to do with pepper, at least not at the present date, not even in Denmark ; though there, some of the dishes are doubtless what we might call 'subtleties' : but during the time of my sojourn in that hospitable country I never detected so much as a whiff of pepper in their cakes. Pepper they use certainly : perhaps they use it more than we do, for they have the saying 'Munden löber som en Peberkværn ' (the mouth, or as we should say, the tongue, runs on like a pepper-mill), or 'Munden gik paa hende som en Peberkværn ' (she chattered away at a fine rate). If our good friends the Danes liken the female tongue to a pepper-quern they must surely use that article of seasoning pretty freely in some of their concoctions, whatever they may do in their cakes ; these, I can answer for it, at all events, are free from it, and *Peberkager* are merely gingerbread cakes, just as *Pebernödder* are what we know as ginger-bread nuts.

When the pepper-cake is eaten in the moorlands of

the North Riding at Yuletide, cheese always is on the table as a concomitant, just as cheese and apple-pie go together all East Yorkshire over at all seasons.

There are many relics of old Christmastide customs which are still kept up in the district, such as the plough-stots and sword-dancers. Those connected with the sword-dancers are curious and interesting; they are described at some length in Henderson's *Northern Folk-Lore*, pp. 67–70. The vessel-cup, which is a corruption of wassail-cup, is still commonly brought round by children in certain districts at Christmas. It consists of a small figure in a box which represented the Virgin Mary, the figure being encircled with evergreens and ornamentations of various kinds.

In some places, until comparatively recently, it was commonly believed that the oxen knelt in their stalls on St. Stephen's Eve; this, of course, was supposed to be in honour of the birth of the Saviour. It was so lately as this present year (1891) that I was speaking to a native of Westerdale about old customs, when I was told that it was quite within the recollection of my informant that the people in that dale used sometimes to go out at midnight on St. Stephen's Eve to try and see the *owsen* kneel as they were tied up in their byres.

From time immemorial great importance was attached to the first foot that crossed the threshold on New Year's Day. The 'lucky bird,' as he was called, should be one of the male sex, and with dark hair. At many a house in this part of the country any other visitant than that described would on no account be allowed to be the first to enter the house on New Year's Day. In some places still it is customary for a boy or man with dark hair to call at every house on that day in order that he may be the first to cross the threshold, that so luck may follow during the year to the household. In other districts a fair man is supposed to be luckier than a dark one. Who knows but what these old traditions may have come down to us from those early times when the fair-haired invaders contended with the darker complexioned aborigines for the possession of the soil? Possibly connected with this idea is the fact which I have frequently noticed among the people of some parts of the East Riding, that they do not, as a rule, admire any one of dark complexion; 'dark-looking' and 'queer-looking' are with them convertible terms. The Norse blood of the East Ridingers may in some measure account for this; the Scandinavians are *par excellence* a fair-haired race. At the present day no hair can be fairer and no eyes bluer than those of the people of Eastern Denmark and Southern Sweden.

Many were the vestiges of ecclesiastical customs that survived till lately in this part of the country from mediaeval times. To take a single case from this parish: there was at least one old custom here that was kept up until comparatively few years ago. This was the ringing of the 'compline bell.' No one knew even what 'compline' meant, or why the bell was rung, which it always was at six in the morning, strange to say, and six in the evening, every day during Lent every year. The peculiar and confused nature of this usage can only be accounted for by the fact that the designation of the matutinal office was gradually lost in course of time, and so the titles of the two services became merged into one.

I need not speak of those customs which are common to the whole country: the keeping of the village Feast, which is held on the day formerly set apart in honour of the patron Saint of the church. Of late years these village festivals have been shorn of much of their former glory; they now frequently go by the name of 'Club Feasts,' in consequence of the benefit-clubs holding their annual social gatherings on these days. In most places on these occasions there is a service at the beginning of the day in the parish church, when some clergyman is invited to address the members of the fraternity. The religious element, however, is not so marked here as it is in the village feasts of some other countries. I was acting as chaplain at Engleberg, in Switzerland, some years ago, when the greatest village festival of the year was held. A service of a very impressive kind took place in the large church attached to the monastery there. The people flocked into it from all the country-side—men, women, and children—all gaily decked in their holiday attire; and very picturesque attire it was. They were in their places in the church before nine o'clock in the morning, when the service began. It lasted, if I rightly remember, about an hour and a half. The congregation was most attentive and devout, the singing admirable. The service ended, the people went out for the rest of the day and amused themselves in a seemly and rational manner, playing games, dancing, and so forth. It seems a pity that our Yorkshire village feasts are not more after the model of the Engleberg one. But good things are apt to degenerate, and it takes something like a revolution to restore them to their original state, if they are not exterminated altogether by the shifting tide of events.

It is remarkable how nearly all the days, great and small, that are observed throughout the district have an ecclesiastical nomenclature—sometimes distorted and corrupted, but quite unmistakeable. Events used to be spoken of as happening not upon any particular day of the month, but in some such way as the following :—'A week afoor Martinmas,' 'sumwheers aboot Thomas Day,' 'Cann'lmas,' 'A fo'tnith cum Barnaby,' Barnaby being a local fair held on the Feast of St. Barnabas; 'aboot Peter tahm,' i.e. about St. Peter's Day; 'Whiss'n Munda,' 'Paums'n Setherda,' i.e. the Saturday before Palm Sunday; 'Hallow E'en,' the vigil of All Saints' Day, and so forth.

The days of Holy Week were noted by means of the following familiar saying :—'Collop Munda, Pancake Tuesda, Frutas We'nsda, Bloody Tho'sda, Lang Frida 'll nivver be deean whahl Settherda t' eftherneean.'

It will hardly be believed when I say that some of our old folks would not know that the civil year now begins on January the 1st. I remember very well on one occasion having to enlighten an aged couple on this point, who were unable to fix New Year's Day any more definitely than by saying it was 'sumwheers aboot Kess'nmas'; but this same couple quite outdid me in their knowledge of the times and seasons of the local fairs and village feasts.

Another relic of mediaeval ecclesiastical terms survives in the saying, *Tid, Mid, Miseray, Carling, Palm, Paste-egg Day.* What *Tid* and *Mid* are, I cannot say with any degree of certitude ; some suggest that *Tid* is a corruption of Te Deum, while *Mid* may be Mid-Lent. *Miseray* is evidently a corruption of the first Latin words of the penitential Psalm appointed for use in Lent,—*Miserere mei, Deus.* *Carling Sunday* was very generally observed till quite lately ; it is the fifth Sunday in Lent. Grey peas were always eaten on that day, being fried with bacon or butter ; the Cleveland

dales-folk used to get their peas from Whitby beforehand, and I have heard them say they did not think it
was *Carling Sunday* without peas. *Palm* speaks for
itself. Palms however, or rather the substitution for
them—the hazel with catkins—are now seldom used on
Palm Sunday as they used to be. *Paste-egg Day*, also
called by another corruption, *Pace-egg Day*, is Easter
Monday; the derivation is obvious. On this and the
following day it is the custom to roll hard-boiled eggs,
coloured in various ways, and use them as playthings.
Hence Easter Monday used to be called *Troll-egg Monday*: in the neighbourhood of Pickering, and probably
in other places, it is still so called. Something of the
same kind is, or till lately was, carried on in Denmark,
where *Paaskeleg*, or, as we should translate it into
Yorkshire, *Easter laakin'*, is a term well understood,
where old and young, men, women, and bairns, meet in
the green fields near the town and play all manner of
games. I should add that in former times *Paste-egg
Day* was applied to Easter Day itself, and among the
country folk the five latter Sundays of Lent and Easter
Day were called respectively by the names just alluded
to—*Tid, Mid, Miseray, Carling, Palm, Paste-egg Day*,
no name being assigned to the first Sunday.

As already mentioned, Good Friday is sometimes
called *Lang Frida*, which corresponds with the Danish
Lang-fredag. In this part of the country it was considered unlucky or impious to turn the soil on Good
Friday with spade or plough, or in any other way.
Indeed, there is a strong feeling still surviving in some
places of Friday generally being an unlucky day; for
instance, I have heard of those who would not set a hen
on a Friday, and of others that they would not allow a
fresh servant to come upon that day. There is, too,

very commonly a disinclination to begin a piece of work on Friday; the rule generally is to do so on a Monday. The saying ' Friday flit, short sit' is well known. There was till lately a very strong tendency throughout the length and breadth of the district of which I am speaking to keep up all the old customs, to observe the days and seasons as they have been observed for generations. In no part of England, I should suppose, do they die harder than in East Yorkshire, unless it be Cornwall, perhaps. And not only is this the case with regard to the old ecclesiastical institutions, dating back to the middle ages, of which so many traces still survive ; the times and seasons connected with agricultural operations were also duly noticed—spring, summer, autumn, winter, seed-time and harvest, the new moons, May Day, Midsummer Day, with many more, have in days gone by been in some way or other specially honoured, nor are those honours yet forgotten quite.

Again, the terms employed by our country folk in speaking of the different parts of the day, are peculiar, and worthy of notice. In the first place, day and night are not used exactly in the ordinary way ; for instance, if one asks, 'Did it rain last night ? ' we may be told ' No, but it rained at two this morning,' when it was pitch dark. Night is night, and morning is morning, in the strictest sense—with this extension, that *neet* begins at *lowzin tahm*, i.e. about 5 p.m. in summer and earlier in winter. At that hour in summer-time the *plew-lad* will perhaps stop his horses, pull up his watch like a bucket from a well, and say to the girl *getherin' wickens*, 'Anne, it's neet.' She would simply say, 'Is 't ?' and set off home. Morning begins at one o'clock, and although it extends, strictly speaking, till the following noon, yet the latter part of it—that is to say, from about

nine o'clock till twelve—is always designated 'forenoon.' *T' eftherneean* (afternoon), extends from dinner
till *lowzin' tahm.*

The old idea of the sun dancing on Easter Day is one
that has extended itself to many parts of the kingdom.
It was at one time very prevalent in this district.

I was informed not long ago, by an elderly man, that
when he was in farm service fifty years back, it was the
custom on Easter morning at sun-rise for the farm lads
to get a bucket of water and place it so that the sun
was reflected in it; if the sun *glimmered*, as he expressed it, it would be wet on that day, and if it shone
bright and clear in the water it would be fine. But a
more important prognostication was always made when
the day was ended; for it was understood that if it
was fair on Easter Day there would be a fine harvest
following it, while if the morning were wet and the
afternoon fine, the 'fore-end' of the harvest would be
wet and the 'back-end' fine, and *vice versâ*. This
belief, too, was a very widespread one.

Another old Easter custom, and of a more animated
kind, was the following. From Easter Sunday noon to
Monday noon the men and lads, and from Monday
noon to Tuesday noon the women and lasses, used to
take each others' shoes and impose some fine for re-
demption. My informant, the son of a clergyman who
for many years held a living in the North Riding, says
he well remembers the excitement under this old custom when he was a boy (1838–48). A notorious
woman, a native of Welbury, used to come to that
place all the way from Sunderland yearly, and timed
her visit so as to enjoy the fun. No really modest and
timid girl durst stir out alone. Big young fellows of
eighteen, who defied the women and girls, were often

overpowered by numbers, and had their boots carried off, the laces being cut. The rector's rather dandy pupil had his coat torn right up from skirt to collar when he attempted to walk through the village on the evening of Easter Monday. At this same place it is recorded that a nurse in a farmer's service, while walk-ing on Easter Sunday afternoon with the children, was stalked, chased, seized, and robbed of her shoe by a young man in the farmer's *coo-pastur*, opposite the rectory, and that she was seen limping back with only one shoe on. A fine, cheerily given, in return for ' Please for your buckle,' settled the majority of cases. The lasses took caps, whips, or anything else they could seize. Before a shoe was taken the demand in the form just given was always made. The word 'buckle' was of course a survival from the times when buckles were in vogue ; they were not worn at the time spoken of.

In years gone by there could have been scarcely a village in North Yorkshire whose inhabitants did not connect the Eve of St. Mark's Day with death. The notion was that those who kept St. Mark's watch—that is, those who watched in the church porch at mid-night from twelve till one—would see the spirits or forms of all those in the place who were to die in the course of the year following, pass into the church one by one. By some it was thought necessary that the watch should be repeated for three successive nights, but generally the vigil was on St. Mark's *E'en* only. Many times have old people spoken to me about those whose faith in this supposed power of looking into the future was unshaken and unshakeable. I should add that if he who kept watch on St. Mark's Eve should happen to fall asleep during the hour, it was understood that he would himself die during the year from that

Q

date. I remember being told of a case of this kind by a former inhabitant of Westerdale. There was an old dame in that neighbourhood who was noted for the accuracy of her investigations in this particular; only, in her case, the watch took place always on Christmas Eve instead of that of St. Mark. On one occasion, it seems, as she was keeping her vigil she fell asleep. It was consequently acknowledged by all who knew her that she was doomed to die before the year was out; accordingly, from day to day, she was watched with no little interest, in the expectation that she would sicken and die. However, time went on and she appeared in her usual health. Six months, nine months, ten months passed, and nothing seemed to indicate that her end was at hand. But during the twelfth month a change came over her; she became ill and took to her bed. Still she lingered on till it came to the last week of the fatal time, but she continued apparently in much the same state, though she was in reality getting weaker. The last day of the year came, and she was still alive, though it was evident she was rapidly sinking, and so it went on till within two hours of the completion of the year, when she quietly breathed her last. A case of this kind would make a profound impression on the minds of the simple folk, and would more than compensate for a dozen failures. I enquired of my informant whether the old lady was generally right in her prognostications, to which I received answer, in a tone that clearly betokened unswerving faith, 'Aye, sha was reet eneeaf.'

The customs connected with marriage festivities have changed a good deal of late years. The old custom, for instance, of running races for ribbons is not so prevalent as it was when I was a boy, and as I remember it in the East Riding, when the races used to be run by the young men down the 'town street,' generally immediately after the marriage service at the church was concluded. Sometimes it used to be arranged that the races should finish at the house of the bride's father. The prize was nearly always a ribbon or ribbons, very commonly a white one as representing the bride, and coloured ones similarly the bridesmaids. Now-a-days, where the traditional custom is still kept up, scarves or handkerchiefs are frequently substituted for ribbons. It was a proud moment for the victor on these occasions, and many a man will recount with delight and elation the number of *ribbins* he has won in such contests.

In some places the old custom for the bride and bridegroom on their return from the church to be presented at the door of the bride's house with a cake on a plate is still observed. The bride takes the cake and eats a portion of it, while the bridegroom lays hold of the plate and throws it behind him. The future happiness of the young couple is supposed to depend on the breaking of the plate. Sometimes the cake is cut into small pieces and thrown by the bride over her head and the plate broken. Another 'use' is for someone to meet the newly married couple at the churchyard gate carrying a live chicken. Hé follows the bridal procession to the bride's house, making the chicken squeak, and will not go away 'till the chicken is satisfied.'

In some of the North Riding dales, and probably in other places also, the antipathy to green as a colour for any part of the bridal costume is still very strong. I was once at a farm-house in a remote district near Whitby, and, when discussing olden times and customs

with an elderly dame, was informed there were many
she knew in her younger days who would rather have
gone to the church to be married in their common every-
day costume than in a green dress. My informant
herself was evidently one of those who held the same
faith on this point as her early companions, for she
instanced a case that had come under her own observation where the bride was rash enough to be married
in green, but it was added that she shortly afterwards
contracted a severe illness ! Neither is blue much less
unlucky as a colour for the wedding dress, at least if one
may judge by the old saying anent the bride, that

'If dressed in blue
She's sure to rue.'

When the wedding party are leaving the church it
was, and still is in certain places, a custom for a handful
of coppers to be thrown to the children ; and as the
bride and bridegroom are on their way to and from
the church a salute would be fired from guns filled with
feathers : this, too, though still practised at some places,
is by no means so common as it was formerly.

In olden days, before police and detectives were much
thought about, many more offences against the law
passed undiscovered than at the present time. Private
adventure schemes, as we might word them, for the
discovery of law-breakers must have been plentiful
enough at one time ; but they have now passed out of
mind. Some, however, have survived until a comparatively recent date. One of the longest lived of
these terrors to evil-doers was the custom of resorting
to the Bible and Key for the detection of a thief. The
method was a favourite one in many parts of the
country, Yorkshire not excepted. The *modus operandi*
was this: A key was placed in a Bible, and after having

been bound round tightly with string, the Bible, with the key inside, would be hung from a nail in the wall or some convenient place.   The name of the suspected thief would then be repeated three times, and if the key turned in the Book, the person who had been named was declared the thief.   The female portion of the community sometimes had other, and to them more interesting uses for the Bible and key, I mean the finding out of their future husbands.   In these cases the Bible would be opened at Ruth i. 16, 17, and the key placed in it there, and either fixed by a piece of string and the Bible suspended by another piece of string, or the key was simply placed in it at the chapter named and then set upon the table.   The name of the wished-for husband was then mentioned, and if the wish was destined for fulfilment, the key in either case would be found turning towards the said verses.

Other means, however, of a less serious nature were resorted to by the country lasses of a generation or two ago for making the same momentous discovery as that just referred to.   There is an example told me by one who had herself made trial of it.   Twelve sage-leaves had to be gathered on a given day at noon, and put into a saucer : they were then kept in the saucer till the midnight following : at this hour the 'chamber' window was thrown open, and one by one the sage-leaves were dropped down into the road below simultaneously with each stroke of the hour on the clock.   It was believed by the young maidens that the future husband would then be seen or his step heard in the street below.

Again, another tried method, not less curious than that just recorded, was the following : The first egg of a chicken was procured : this had to be boiled or roasted.   Those interested in making the test had each of them to stand on something upon which she had never before stood ; it might be a pair of bellows or an iron baking sheet, or anything else ready to hand. The members of the company then took hold of the egg and· simultaneously cut it into portions. Thereupon each one in strict silence took her share, ate it shell and all, and walked backwards to bed. It was thought that this device enabled them to dream who their future partners in life would be.

There was another quaint old custom practised by our fanciful forelders, of which I have been told, though I have not been able to ascertain exactly what the correct usage with respect to it was : accounts vary. This custom is in connection with what was called Love Posset, or Dumb Cake. The idea was that by a due observance of the ritual connected with its manufacturé, a girl's future husband could be ascer- tained. The proper day for making Dumb Cake was the eve of St. Agnes. What all the ingredients of the cake were I know not, but one principal one was salt. I remember being told some years ago, by an old inhabitant in one of the dales, about the composition of this mystic cake. It was somewhat as follows : In the first place four people had to assist in the making of it, each taking an equal share in the work, adding small portions of its component parts, stirring the pot, and so forth. During the whole time of its manufacture and consumption a strict silence has to be observed. Even when it is being taken out of the oven each of the interested parties must assist in the work. When ·made it is placed on the table in the middle of the room, and the four persons stand at the four corners of the room. When set on the table the cake is divided into equal portions and put upon four plates or vessels.

The spirit of the future husband of one of the four would then appear and taste from the plate of his future bride, being only visible to her whose husband he was destined to be. As a preliminary to this, every door of the house had to be thrown open. The traditional hour for making the feast was midnight. My informant said that in her district this mystic repast was made on St. Mark's Eve. I cannot, how-ever, think that this was general. The orthodox time was the eve of St. Agnes. An additional observance was for each damsel to take her portion with her up-stairs, walking backwards to the bedroom; she was then to eat her share of the undainty concoction and get into bed. On carrying out strictly all the recognised forms and ceremonies she might thus hope in her dreams to behold her future husband.

Much more was I told about these functions con-nected with the Love Posset or Dumb Cake. Dreadful and unexpected things happened sometimes, especially when the feast was held on St. Mark's Eve. Possibly the spirit resented any deviation from the primitive custom of holding the rite on any other than St. Agnes' Eve; at any rate, on one occasion of which I heard tell there was evidently something not altogether pleasing to the invisible powers; for, to use the words of one whose faith in them and other like mysteries was quite unshaken, when the doors were opened on the night referred to, 'there was a soughing and a rattling, the dog's hair stood on end, and a coffin came tumbling through the door and fell at the feet of one of the party, who died in that year.' And again, on another occasion there were such unearthly noises that the whole company rushed upstairs without even giving themselves time to close the doors. On the whole, therefore, it may be as well for those who may think of resorting to the Love Posset or Dumb Cake method of determining who their partners for life are to be, to be careful not to attempt to hold festival on St. Mark's Eve or any other eve but on that of St. Agnes only.

Local peculiarities in the matter of customs and feasts exist, as might be expected, to a considerable extent. Thus, for instance, at Helmsley there is still held once a year what is called the *Vardy Dinner*. In the days before the Government appointed sanitary officers, Helmsley elected its own local committee to inspect the town once a year as regards sanitary matters. In the evening the inspectors met, supped, discussed, and gave their ' verdict.' Hence *Vardy Dinner*. The form, I am told, is still kept up, but chiefly for social purposes. The dinner is held annually, the committee having earlier in the day gone through the form of walking through the main streets, scrutinising at least the outside of dwellings as they pass. The Helmsley folk jokingly warn one another on this important day thus—' Look to your drains and chimneys.'

A custom with a somewhat similar intention used to take place at Kilburn immediately before the village feast, which there is held on the Saturday after Mid-summer Day. A man was dressed up to represent the Lord Mayor of York, and another to represent the Lady Mayoress. These two were then dragged through the village street in a cart by lads. As they went along they recited a doggerel and visited all the houses of the place, exhorting the people to tidy their gardens, trim their hedges, and make their tenements look generally respectable for the feast; in the event of these orders being disregarded a mock fine was imposed.

Some of the bee customs, or what we may call bee-lore, prevalent in the district are curious. They would be almost a study of themselves if carefully gone into. Of the habits of the bees I will say nothing; let Virgil speak about that. And as regards the customs connected with bees I will only just allude to one.

When a member of a family dies the bees must not be forgotten. Indeed, under certain circumstances connected with swarming they are thought to portend a death in the family; such for instance would be the case if they took it into their heads to swarm on the dead bough of a neighbouring tree. But when a death had actually taken place it was, and perhaps still is, no uncommon thing to put the bees into mourning. This was done by tieing a piece of black cloth or crape round the hives. But this was not all. When the funeral had taken place, and the party had returned to the house, the funeral feast began,—the *arval* as it used to be called in olden days. On these occasions the feasting was, to say the least of it, substantial. Some of the humbler classes would half ruin themselves by their lavish expenditure at these times : funeral reform had not been heard of in those days unfortunately. But what about the bees? Well! they had to be feasted also, and feasted, be it observed, in identically the same way as the house-folk had been ; that is to say, a small portion gathered from every item which went to form the entertainment indoors had to be placed in a convenient situation for the bees without ; such small portions were collected generally in a saucer or plate. Bread, cake, tea, sugar, beef, ham, mustard, salt ; even the wine was not omitted, this being steeped into the biscuits. The idea was that if the bees were not thus feasted they would all certainly die.

I remember on one occasion talking to the widow of a farmer in the neighbourhood of Egton about these bee customs, and was somewhat amazed by her telling me of the ritual they thought proper to observe at the time of her husband's death with regard to their own bees. She dilated upon the nature of the feast, and went through a long string of viands, a sort of 'bill of fare' of what they set before the bees, winding up at the last, as if she quite enjoyed the relating of it, by adding 'aye! bacca 'an pipes an' all !' ' What ! ' I ventured to observe in astonishment, 'do you mean to say that the bees ate the tobacco ? ' ' Aye,' she added, 'ah seed it mysen.' I could say no more on that point, but it would seem as if these bees must have had some nautical blood in them, for I bethought me of the strong predilection sailors have for chewing tobacco. But the pipes were not yet accounted for, and so after a pause I said, ' Well ! at all events the bees could not eat the pipes.' ' Bud,' she replied, 'they did 'owivver.' ' How in the world could they do that ? ' was my interrogation ; ' Aw,' she exclaimed, 'they teeak a steean an' mash'd 'em up intiv a poodher an' mixed it wi t' stuff an' gav it tiv em.' ' And did they eat it clean up ? ' I asked. 'Aye, hivvry bit ; ah seed it mysen.' *Ee-preeaf*, or, in other words, ocular demonstration, cannot well be got over ; and so there was nothing left for me but to express my wonder at the marvellous digestive power of the bees, and in the end to assent quietly to the fact that the bees had in some way or other made a clean sweep of the concoction. I thought possibly, after the action of the tobacco upon their systems, the bees might all have been found dead next morning, but I was assured that not one of them had been so found ; on the contrary, it was evidently thought that it was their being fed in this way alone that had preserved them from dying with their master.

The science of Folk-lore is in these days making rapid advances, though it was not till very recently that it could be classed as a science at all. No one could have read the account of the international Folk-lore Congress held in London in 1891 without being con-vinced of the probability that a great future lies in store for this deeply interesting study. Many of the old superstitious ideas which go to form the subject-matter of folk-lore may seem to many absurd and unworthy of serious thought, but out of these light materials some-thing, perhaps a great deal, connected with the early history of the human race may one day be extracted. This, the newest of sciences, is one to which any ob-servant countryman may contribute something. We con-stantly meet with traces of the superstitious feeling in all classes more or less. In his opening address last year, the president of the Folk-lore Congress alluded in playful terms to the fact of his lately meeting a young lady who, as he expressed it, 'was the very muse of folk-lore.' If she met a number of cows she remarked whether they divided on the road or all kept to one side. If she found a crow's feather in the fields, she stuck it erect in the grass and wished a wish. Old pieces of iron she carefully threw over her left shoulder. She kissed her hand to the new moon. If there were three candles alight she blew one out, not from motives of economy, but because three lighted candles in a row are unlucky. She was perturbed by winding-sheets in a candle, and so forth.

I am not aware that our Yorskhire folk are more superstitious than some others; and although curious and strange fancies do exist in the minds of many of our older people beyond doubt, they are at all events not alone in that respect. That quaint old notions of this kind are held by others outside our own county the following remarkable instance, which came under my notice only quite lately, will clearly show. A Board of Trade enquiry took place at Hull last year (1891) with reference to a collision between a Hull steamer and a Scarborough smack off Flamborough Head. It seemed that when the collision took place the crew of the smack got on board the steamer, and the abandoned vessel, which became lost in a fog, went ashore five days afterwards on the coast of Scotland more than two hundred miles from the scene of the casualty. The officer of the coast-guard at Montrose, a lieutenant in the Royal Navy, in the course of the evidence alleged that he went to the place where the smack went ashore and examined her. She was deserted, although there were no signs of any damage upon her whatever: He was therefore at a loss to know why she had been thus abandoned. He ascertained subsequently that she had sailed through some Scotch fishing-boats; the fishermen, seeing no one on board, thought she was a phantom ship; they refused to touch her in consequence, even when she was on the rocks. Another officer of the coastguard, in corroboration of this evidence, stated that it was not possible that any one could have boarded the smack before she got on to the rocks. The people of a farmhouse informed the officer about the vessel, but nobody would venture to go near her, and though he offered four shillings an hour—a pretty strong inducement with a Scotchman—to anyone who would render aid in saving the ship's stores, none would go on board. It was found impossible to get her off the rocks, and she afterwards went to pieces.

As might be expected, it is in association with death that the superstitious feeling survives most strongly. With many minds the idea of walking through a churchyard in the darkness and alone would be altogether abhorrent. The same feeling exists with regard to places that are supposed to be haunted ; nothing would induce some persons to visit such scenes. The deeply superstitious natures of our country folk in former generations caused them to live so to speak in another world almost as much as in this. False and absurd as many of their notions were, there were others that were tinged with a picturesque interest, and betokened a deep-rooted faith in the unseen world. For these one cannot but have a certain respect. It was, for instance, with the idea that nothing should be done or left undone to arrest the passage of the spirit of one just deceased in its upward flight, that no sound was uttered beyond the faintest whisper and the window of the room where the body lay, thrown open. And when the spirit had actually fled to the place of departed spirits the body was not neglected, but carefully tended and watched till it had been reverently taken to the churchyard, there to be resolved into dust. Whatever arguments there may be in favour of cremation, I am quite sure that the idea of such a thing would be most repulsive to the minds of our country folk. On the other hand, many of the old notions associated with death were no doubt absurd in the extreme. It used to be a common belief, for instance, and is so still with many old people, that a sick person cannot die if laid upon a bed composed of the feathers of pigeons or of any wild birds. I was told not long since of one Jane H—, from the neighbourhood of Westerdale, that she was lying upon a bed of that description ; that she was *in*

extremis for a week, and when it was thought she could
not die in consequence of being upon a bed of wild birds'
feathers they took her off it and laid her upon a *squab*,
where, as I was informed, she died at once ! It is also an
idea with some that there is a connection between the
lingering vitality of the dying person and the hopefulness
of the bystanders or friends that the sufferer may be
restored to health again. Thus I have heard it said
that so-and-so could not die, for they would not give
him up. This is a curious example of a belief in the
kind of mesmeric influence of the mind of another
upon the human body; at least such it would seem
to be.

Many of the superstitious observances still kept up
by some would no doubt be dropped if the observance
of them involved personal trouble or inconvenience. It
is a very easy thing to avoid walking under a ladder,
for instance ; but if the superstitious foot-passenger had
to go half a mile round in order to accomplish his end,
the chances are he would pocket his scruples and walk
straight on. Still, even at this day, there are cases to
be found where no little exertion or bodily discomfort
will be endured in order to carry out some superstitious
form or ceremony, the observance of which is calcu-
lated, no matter how absurdly, to bring about some
blessing or to ward off some danger.

I had a singular instance of this kind brought before
my notice only quite recently: it happened, I believe,
within a year or thereabouts of last summer. I was
told of it by the vicar of a remote country parish in the
neighbourhood of Whitby.

Somewhere about the time alluded to there was a
serious outbreak of measles in the village—*mezzles* as
they are called in the folk-speech. Scarcely a family

escaped.   Not far from the village a small farmer lived
with his wife and two children.   The parents felt in
considerable anxiety for their little ones, lest they should
catch the disease.   The father, however, seemed to be
satisfied in his own mind that if the children could be
put through a certain prescribed ceremony of seemingly
traditional usage they would be proof against infection
from the disease.   It will hardly be guessed what the
ceremony was.   First of all, it was absolutely necessary
that a donkey should be procured.   But unfortunately
there was not one to be had in the place.   In order to get
one, they would have to go to a village on the sea-coast,
which lay at least four miles distant.   Nothing daunted,
they accordingly made their pilgrimage to the village
referred to.   The donkey was in due course obtained,
and the whole party—father, mother and two young
children—wended their way to the beach.   One of the
children was then put upon the donkey with its face to
the tail ; three hairs were next drawn from the tail of
the animal, put into a bag, and slung round the child's
neck.   The donkey was then made to go up and down
a certain distance on the sands nine times.   This done,
the same process was repeated with the other child.
It must be added that all the time the donkey was in
motion a thistle was held over the head of the child.
Such was the function ; and when done they all returned
home as they had come.   By a singular coincidence the
children in this case escaped taking the epidemic ailment, and as a consequence the parents were the more
confirmed in their belief in the efficacy of these strange
precautionary measures.

The belief in fairies and witches would even yet
seem hardly to be clean gone ; while a generation ago
it was much stronger than is often supposed.

A correspondent from the borders of the North and West Ridings tells me of the strong belief in fairies that existed among the people of his district when he was a boy. It seems he used to talk to an old inhabitant who, as he confessed, had often 'seen the fairies.' Figures of men and women gaily clad, of full size, and in rapid confused motion, he said he had often watched in early summer mornings. He used to tell of an unbelieving horse-dealer who had stayed the night with him. At dawn the old farmer saw the fairies, as he had so often done before, and called up his guest, who, unbeliever though he declared himself to be, hurried out as he was, very lightly clad, and sat so long on a wall watching them that he caught a rheumatism that he never was cured of. Many other things did the old man relate, which unfortunately have passed out of recollection; and he into the unseen world. Now the people will not open out as their fathers used to do, though perhaps their imaginations are not inferior. By the way, a young woman, into whose house this same gentleman once went, told him that she had never *seen* fairies (though her relations often had\, but she had *smelt* them. On his asking what sort of odour he was to expect so that he might be similarly favoured, she went on to enquire if he had ever been in a very crowded 'place of worship' wherein the people had been congregated for a length of time. Such was the description; a very different one had been looked for; but it is the unexpected which happens. It was supposed that the young woman who was such an adept at scenting out the fairies was in reality trying to give an idea of the gushes of hot air one sometimes comes across on broken ground during summer time.

To talk with one who believes in the power of the wise man or witch, seems almost like conversing with one from another world. Many a time, in days gone by, have I been told stories of what the witch could do and of the dread in which she was held, stories which it was evident the narrators firmly believed in, in spite of all that one could say to the contrary; and although such people might confess that wise men and witches are just at the present moment rather scarce articles, still they seem to have a kind of lurking notion that they might easily crop up again at any time: the old ideas are hard to uproot. I shall not easily forget a certain occasion when I was speaking to an old man on some ordinary topics, when somehow or other we got upon the subject of witches. He was generally a very stolid, matter-of-fact sort of old fellow, who did not apparently take any very keen interest in anything particular; still he had, as it seemed, his fair complement of wits. On this occasion, when recounting the doings of a certain witch whom he had seen and whose name he told me, his wonted stolidity quite deserted him; I do not now remember the details of the story sufficiently well to repeat it with any degree of accuracy, but I do well recollect how his countenance, as he went on, was lit up with a degree of animation that was quite extraordinary, especially for such an old man (he was then past eighty), and for one who in general was so imperturbable: he fairly quivered again, and his eyes wore a wild appearance which I had never before seen in them. His belief in what he said was as deep rooted as anything could possibly be, and I never before realised so fully as I did then, the hold that such ideas must have had upon the men of former generations. How far those who gave themselves out to be possessed of the supposed powers of the wise man or the witch believed in them themselves, I will not pretend to say, and I do not know that I have ever been face to face with one such myself, so that I could hold an examination.

So many stories have been recorded of the performances of wise men and witches in days of old, that anything one has heard from time to time from old people touching on the subject seems merely like a repetition of what is already well known. I shall not, therefore, have much to say that has not been already said by others. Why witches were supposed to be such enemies to horse-flesh I am at a loss even to guess ; this must have made them especially unpopular in Yorkshire : certain it is that a horse-shoe was very commonly nailed upon the stable doors in order to prevent their entrance there. Mr. Henderson, in his book on Folk-lore, says he remembers a farmer telling him ' how one of his horses had more than once been ridden by the witches, and he had found it in the morning bathed in sweat, but he had nailed a horse-shoe over the stable door, and hung some broom over the rack, and the horse had not been used by the witches since ! '

On the subject of horses and witches I remember having a conversation with an old dame not many years ago. I think the conversation started about wicken-wood, which she knew about very well as a preventive against the power of the witch, though she was unable to tell me precisely, or indeed at all, what the nature of the wood was, for in the course of conversation I said to her, ' Can you tell me what they call the tree from which they get the wicken-wood ? ' ' Naw,' she said, ' Ah 's seear ah can't, bud ah knaw 'at wicken-wood 's t' stuff 'at they mak whip-stocks on for witches.' I professed

surprise that they should do such a thing now or
at any time, and added that at all events I supposed she
had never heard of any case where the fact of the whip-
stock having been made of wicken wood had been of the
slightest use for the supposed object. 'Aa, bud ah ev,'
she replied; and went on to say that a witch used to
hant (haunt) a certain 'brig' which she named. 'Did
anything ever happen at the brig?' I enquired.
'Happen! aye; an' ah 'll tell ya an' all.' 'I should
like to know what it was,' I said. 'Whya then,' she
continued, 'Yah day (it wer a good bit sen noo) sum
lads was cumin' wi carts, an' as seean as ivver they
com near-hand t' brig t' fo'st draught was stopped;
t' lads leeak'd, bud they couldn't see nowt; then they
shooted on him ti gan on, an' he tell'd 'em 'at he
couldn't: t' hosses couldn't storr; all was stopped.' To
the best of my recollection there were four or five carts
altogether, when some impassable barrier seemed to
stop the way over the bridge. But my old friend
continued her story by saying, 'Noo, yan o' t' lads had
gitten a wicken-wood whip-stock; an' when he com up
he said he would try; an' then summat leyke spak ti t'
draughts, "here's t' lad cumin' wi t' wicken-tree gad";
an' away they went; sha (the witch) couldn't stop 'em
then.' Such was the story of the power of the wicken-
tree whip-stock almost *verbatim* as it was told me, and
not a shadow of a doubt did my informant seem to
have of the literal truth of it.

Sometimes the witch was regarded as a downright
pest in a neighbourhood, and when by any chance she
disappeared from the scene, which even these mortals
did in course of years, there was often as much rejoicing
as if a savage wild beast had been slain. I have
heard of one of this sort who used to live in a small

village in the North Riding with her daughter. The mother and daughter were on anything but good terms, in fact they were incessantly quarrelling and fighting. The two, however, were very equally matched : sometimes the victory lay with the mother, sometimes with the daughter, till one day matters had got to a parlous state, and there was a regular pitched battle ; in fact, it was a life or death struggle between them. To use the words of the old man who remembered the scene and told me of it, ' eftther they 'd fowten (fought) t' main o' t' day, t' dowtther preeaved t' maastther, an' sha killed t' witch.' The news spread like wildfire, and amid the greatest excitement the whole *toon* soon assembled round the door of the house where this desperate encounter had taken place. Just at first there were, no doubt, some feelings of horror at the shocking scene that lay before them ; but ' eftther things had gotten sattled,' as my old friend expressed it, the people could do nothing but rejoice that so dangerous and hated a character had been ' putten oot o' t' rooad.'

If the witch was sometimes a pest to a neighbourhood generally, she must have been so especially to the farmer ; for not only did she ride his horses, but played sad havoc in the dairy, and worked all manner of evil against his cattle both great and small. In those imaginative days it must have cost the farmer as much trouble, one would think, to keep the witches away from his herds as the crows from his corn.

It was not so many years ago that I was told of rather an exciting encounter which took place at a farm I have frequently heard of, and the neighbourhood of which I have often visited. At the present time it happens to be occupied by a man I know very well. The struggle was between the farmer himself and a witch that was the plague and terror of the neighbourhood. I cannot give the precise date of the battle, as the school-boy does ; but I judged from what my informant said, that it took place seventy or eighty years ago; It happened that the said farmer had lost a large number of cattle. He was a very superstitious man, and the only way in which he could account for the loss of his cattle satisfactorily to his own mind was by attributing it to the work of 't' aud witch' who frequented the district. This was the more surprising, for, as I was told, 'his missis had awlus behaved well ti t' witch'; that is to say, whenever she had been to the house the mistress had given her food and treated her, as she thought, hospitably. It was plain, however, to the farmer and his wife that something had at length offended her lady-ship, and she had wreaked her vengeance upon them by destroying his beasts.

One morning after this the witch was seen by the farmer in his fold-garth. Thinking, of course, that she was there for no good purpose, he accosted her, and asked her what she was doing there ; whereupon, as we say in Yorkshire, *sha wer varry saucy.* This was too much for the farmer, so without further words he took the law into his own hands and began to *bray* her vio-lently on the back with his stick. She held her ground unflinchingly : he next dealt her a heavy blow with his fist. Upon this she seized a thorn stick which happened to be near at hand, and then the fight waxed hotter and hotter ; blow after blow was dealt in quick succession,

'Nec mora, nec requies.'

Like hail upon the housetops fell the strokes ; panting they fought—the farmer and the witch—in even contest ; swelling bruises formed upon the limbs of each, till at length the witch with fiendish force gave such a gash that blood trickled from the wound ; whereat she paused and shrieked in horrid glee, 'noo ah a'e tha.' It was enough ; she had gained her point, and she departed. The farmer was in great distress ; he knew not what to do to avert the dread consequences : he felt that his enemy had him in her power. The only thing left for him was to betake himself to the wise man. The wise man told him that the witch had wished him a bad wish, but he said that he would give him the best advice he could. It was a favourite and well-known remedy, though in this case it proved unavailing. He was without delay to go home and procure the heart of a beast, make up a fire in the house, carefully fill up all ' t' kye-hooals, nicks i' t' deears an' crivices ti keep her [the witch] oot.'· Then, according to ancient usage, he was to take the beast's heart and prick it all over with pins, and roast it upon the fire. The savoury odour, or whatever it was, would attract the witch to the house, and she would come to the door and yell like a dog. Those in the house when she thus came were neither to speak nor stir, and then she would go away. All this happened, it was asserted, as it had been foretold by the wise man : the witch came, yelled, and went ; but a day or two after the wounded man bled to death. 'Aye,' said my informant, who quite believed in the witch's power, 'sha 'd gotten ower mich ho'd on him!' Even the beast's heart and pins were powerless on this occasion : this time ' t' au'd·witch preeaved t' maastther.'

Even until quite a few years ago it was thought, and may still be so, in some places, that the witches' power was supreme. I have heard, for instance, of a mother losing her first-born son. It was remembered that so-and-so had wished the mother a bad wish. The event corroborated the half-formed idea that the evil-wisher was a witch, and the half-formed idea developed into a deep-rooted belief. In this case I was told that the mother's adversary had wished a bad wish, and it had 'fallen on t' ·bairn,' which soon died.

Scarcely less strange than such ideas as those just alluded to, was the extraordinary faith in the efficacy of many fanciful remedies for all manner of diseases : they would of themselves fill a volume.

One of the strangest cases that ever I heard of was one that was brought to my notice at a friend's house near Yarm. The lady of the house told me that only a short time previously she had been calling to see a poor woman, one of whose children had the 'thrush.' The mother firmly believed that if one born after the death of his father were to blow three times down the child's throat the disease would beyond doubt depart ; indeed, so implicit was her faith in the virtue of the remedy that my friend told me that had she seemed to doubt the power of the means used, the mother would have felt quite hurt.

This reminds me of a cure for the whooping-cough (these, by the way, might be recounted by the dozen), which was resorted to in a place I know very well. It is as follows : Catch a frog, and put it into a jug of water ; make the patient cough into the jug ; this *smits* the frog, and the patient is cured. 'Did it do any good ? ' was asked in a certain case. 'Yes,' was the answer, 'the frog took it, and coughed as natteral as a Christian.' Another singular cure for the same malady is for the child to be passed nine times over the back and under the belly of a donkey. Mr. W. Henderson, in his *Folk-lore of the Northern Counties*, gives an instance of this having taken place at Middlesbrough, which operation was actually witnessed by a friend of his.

But there are charms for animals as well as for human beings. The Vicar of a parish near Yarm one day noticed in his kitchen a number of little sprigs of hazel, with catkins upon them, stuck into various objects round the fire-place. On asking the senior servant why she had made the decoration, she said it was Jane (the junior maid), who had gathered them and stuck them about because they were good for the sheep at lambing time !

The cures for warts are many and various. It is remarkable to find what strange methods were sometimes resorted to. Here is one which seems to be rather out of the beaten track of medical remedies. A common black slug is caught, and rubbed several times over the wart. The slug is then fixed tightly to a thorn on a hedge or elsewhere, and then left to die and wither away. It is supposed that simultaneously with this withering away of the creature the wart will also consume away and disappear. Only it is essential that the patient shall not again look at the slug, otherwise the healing power would be arrested in its operation.

I was told of another remedy, by a farmer whose sister's warts had been supposed to have been removed by the following means. It was the night of a new moon ; indeed it was necessary that so it should be for the efficacy of the means used. The young woman had on no account to look at the moon, but some one had to go out and observe in which quarter of the heavens she was, and then come and lead the patient out into the garden, whereupon she had to stoop down and rub the warts all over with the soil without attempting to look at the quarter where the moon lay, and return to the house at once. I was assured that in this case the operation was a complete success !

It is believed by many that these excrescences may be brought on by washing the hands in water in which an egg has been boiled.   An old lady, a native of one of the dales, once told me that she was always very careful to throw away water in which eggs had been boiled for fear of its being used for washing purposes.

There is a widespread belief that if the cock crows in the house, or if the fowls enter it, visitors may be expected.   I remember very well going to a farm house in Cleveland once, and being told by the farmer that they had been looking for a visitor because the cock had been crowing on the doorstead.   I wonder what the Irish peasantry have to say to this; their string of callers must be incessant.

Happily hens do not often crow, but when such a portentous event does actually take place, the unlucky bird is generally immediately killed, as its existence is supposed to bring nothing but misfortune upon the household ; à propos of this there is the old saying,

'A crowing hen, and a whistling maid
Both bring bad luck';

another form of which runs thus :—

'A whistling maid and a crowing hen
Are fit for neither gods nor men.'

When leaving a house for a journey it is deemed unlucky that at the time of departure there should be thruff-oppen deears, that is to say that both front and back doors should be open at the same time : if the mistress of the house be leaving home by the front door, for instance, the servant maid will instantly run to the back door if it be open, and shut it.   And after the journey has been begun it is thought to be unlucky if the first person met be of the female sex.   Under these circumstances it is a man who brings a prosperous journey.

CHAPTER XII.

IT is generally admitted, and no doubt with truth, that the English Bible has done more to preserve our language from decay than anything else. If we want to see what pure and forcible English is, we shall find it in the pages of the Authorised Version : there is a musical flow and rhythm about it, and as regards certain passages, if we take them as specimens of our language only, they cannot be surpassed for beauty. I will not take upon myself to select examples, but as instances of this let me give Mr. Ruskin's list. Indeed, perhaps I may be allowed to quote in passing what he himself says about his own Bible in his *Outlines of Scenes and Thoughts in my Past Life.* He remarks :—'I have just opened my oldest (in use) Bible ; a small, closely, and very neatly printed volume it is, printed in Edinburgh by Sir D. Hunter, Blaine, and J. Bruce in 1816. Yellow now with age, and flexible, but not unclean, with much use, except that the lowest corners of the pages at 1 Kings viii. and Deuteronomy xxxii. are worn somewhat thin and dark, the learning of these two chapters having cost me much pains. My mother's list of the chapters with which, thus learned, she established my soul in life has just fallen out of it. I will take what indulgence the incurious reader can give me for printing the list thus accidently occurrent. Exodus xv. xx, 2 Samuel i from seventeenth verse to the end, 1 Kings viii, Psalms xxiii, xxxii, xc, xci, ciii, cxii, cxix, cxxxix, Proverbs ii, iii, viii–xii, Isaiah lviii, S. Matthew v, vi, vii, Acts xxvi, 1 Corinthians xiii-xv, S. James iv, Revelation v, vi.'

Far be it from me to question the desirability of a Revised Version ; it is a *fait accompli*. That there are faulty translations and blemishes in the Authorised Version none will deny. These we should be at pains to amend at all costs. One great object of the late Revision was of course to give the exact meaning of every word of the original in language thoroughly understood at the present time. In accomplishing this, certain words supposed to be obsolete had to give way to their more modern equivalents ; in some cases the choice of the right word had to be exercised with the greatest care and judgment ; different words to express the same thing would naturally present themselves to the minds of the translators ; those of Scandinavian origin, for example, vied for the ascendency with others that were Romanesque.

But between these two component sources of our language there is no doubt from which the choice should be made as supplying words most easily intelligible to our ordinary country folk, at least as regards those who inhabit this north-eastern side of the country, where the talk of the people is mainly made up of words of Norse origin.

If the English Bible has done so much to conserve what is best in the English tongue, we should indeed be careful how we lay hands upon it, even to make a single alteration. No doubt every alteration made by the last Revisers was carefully weighed. There is, however, just one point which perhaps has been a little overlooked: I mean the fact that many words and phrases supposed to be obsolete are still in common use by a large number of our people. Because such words do not ordinarily appear in modern literature, it does not follow that they are not spoken, and consequently well understood.

The American Committee would have gone further in the direction referred to than the English Revisers. This may be gathered from the list of readings preferred by them and recorded at their desire in the form of an appendix at the end of the volume. This appendix is deserving of every respect, however much we may differ from the conclusions arrived at. I will not attempt to do more than make one or two remarks as far as some of their recommendations bear upon our dialect.

In St. Matt. viii. 4, St. Matt. xxvii. 65, and St. Mark i. 44, for instance, they recommend to change 'go thy way' to simply 'go.' Now, in our dialect, 'come thy ways' and 'go thy ways' are the forms always in use in the imperative mood ; it would surely be better therefore to retain the old form. At St. Luke ix. 12, they suggest to substitute 'provisions' for 'victuals'; it is here worthy of remark that in the dialect neither of these expressions would be used, but the word 'meat,' which is so frequently found in the Authorised Version in the same sense. There seems no reason why it should not be adopted in this passage.

Again, in xxiii. 23 of the same Gospel, neither 'instant' nor 'urgent' would be understood by many of our people : it might be a little difficult to know what to give as an alternative ; 'hasty' would be a familiar word, and would perhaps convey the sense most nearly.

The change from 'evil' to 'ill' in St. John viii. 20 is a good one, *ill* being a word very generally used, while *evil* is never heard. 'Dark sayings' seems preferable to 'proverbs' in St. John xvi. 25, but probably 'hidden

sayings' would be more intelligible than either. As
regards Rom. viii. 13, 'kill' or 'put to death' would
bring home the meaning of the passage with greater
clearness than 'mortify,' which in the dialect is only
used in a very restricted sense. Neither 'heresies' nor
'factions' would have any meaning for our older people ;
the passage—1 Cor. xi. 19—would have to be expressed
differently. Such words as 'edification' and 'exhorta-
tion' (1 Cor. xiv. 3) might as well be written in Greek,
but 'comfort' would be understood fully. The Americans
do well to suggest 'lay hold on' for 'apprehend' in
Phil. iii. 12. 'Figure' would be no better than 'par-
able' in Heb. ix. 9 ; some such expression as 'way of
speaking' might be preferable to either. Why 'existing'
should be substituted for 'being' (Phil. ii. 6) I know
not : it would, moreover, not be contained in the vocabulary of our folk-speech.

It may be seen, even from these few examples, in
what direction change or no change was needed in a
re-translation of the Bible which would be 'understanded
of the people' in East Yorkshire as far as might be. As
has been elsewhere observed, it is remarkable how few
words, comparatively, of Latin derivation are used in the
dialect, and therefore all such words, whether written
or spoken, are better avoided if we would be readily
and clearly understood.

Nevertheless, as a whole, the language of the Bible is
better understood than that of the Prayer Book, which
presents great difficulty to many of the older country folk,
containing as it does such a large number of words of
Latin origin. But even with regard to the Bible, much of
it was unintelligible to the country folk of a generation
ago. As an instance of this I will mention what came
within my experience some years since. I was desirous of

testing upon this point an old man whom I knew very well: he was quite up to the average in intelligence, but he had had very little schooling. For the purpose in view I took in a haphazard way a few words from the Bible, and after repeating each slowly and distinctly twice over at least, and giving him plenty of time to think, I asked him to tell me in his own words what he thought each word meant. The words chosen, being all of Latin derivation, were these :—*fragment, expound, impediment, admonish, doctrine, dominion, disperse, confidence, consolation, contrite, esteem, descend, perpetual.* For only one of these, *perpetual,* could he give me a correct equivalent ; but the moment I explained them as follows, the meaning was perfectly understood :—*fragment* (a small piece of anything), *expound* (to tell the meaning of), *impediment* (a stoppage), *admonish* (warn), *doctrine* (teaching), *dominion* (rule), *disperse* (scatter), *confidence* (trust), *consolation* (comfort), *contrite* (sorrowful), *esteem* (worth), *descend* (go down). This may serve to show how many passages in the Bible—and in sermons, for a matter of that—must have been unintelligible formerly to a certain portion at least of an ordinary country congregation. I may remark, in passing, that although generally not used in every-day speech, there are some words of Latin derivation which occur very frequently in the dialect, and are preferred to their Anglian equivalents. Of such, *to expect* is a fair example of what I mean. This word is used in the sense of '*to understand*' or '*to have heard,*' e.g., if I were to say ' I hear so and so is ill,' the reply would probably be ' I expect so ; '—that is to say, ' I have heard so,' or ' I understand so.'

But though there is such a considerable number of words in the Authorised Version unintelligible to many of our older people, yet there are others which would be

better understood by them than by many a Londoner even.
I do not mean to imply that the Londoner would fail in
all probability to understand the words, but he would
use others in preference, whereas the Yorkshireman
would employ them rather than others of like meaning
and more ordinary usage. As examples of what is
meant let me quote the following :—*Afore, ailed, back-
side, bid, brake, bray, clout, drave, fain, folk, frame,
gat, gather, gatherings, gotten, haft, handled, hungered,
light* (verb), *mindful, naught, overmuch, quick* (Yorksh.
wick), *rank, shaked, spake, sware, wrought, yesternight,
yet.* The equivalents of these, commonly in use, are
apparent ; but I will add them : they are, *Before,
mattered, back, invite, broke, beat, cloth, drove, gladly,
people, give promise of, got, collect, collections, got*
(participle), *handle, treated, became hungry, alight* or
settle, careful, nothing, too much, alive, thick or *luxuriant,
shook, spoke, swore, worked* or *laboured, last night, still.*

It may be noted that the dialectical use of the word
backside is applied to the back parts of things and places
only, and especially to the back premises or yard of a
house. *Bray* is in common use in the sense of beating
generally, and especially flogging. The good old word
fain, though dying out, is still employed by elderly
people. *Quick* is an every-day word with us under the
form *wick*. *Yet* is invariably used instead of *still*, and in
this sense it is very frequently found in the Bible. The
phrase ' Does it rain yet ' would mean, not ' has it
begun to rain ? ' but ' is it still raining ? ' The perfects
spake and *sware* drop the final *e* in folk-speech, and
shaked is pronounced *shakk'd.*

These and many other words and expressions in the
Bible, supposed to be obsolete or nearly so, are still in
daily use in what are called our dialects : but in many

of such cases the line which separates dialect and literary language is by no means easy to be traced. The two streams seem at times to meet. Are we to say, for instance, that our common Yorkshire word *hodden* is a vulgarism because *held* has taken its place, although *hodden* or *holden* occurs certainly ten times in the Authorised Version? *Chamber* is used in 1 Kings xvii. 23 in just the same sense as in the dialect, apparently, signifying as it does an upstairs sleeping apartment as distinguished from the 'house.'

There are some interesting remarks made by Professor Max Müller on this point in his *Lectures on the Science of Language.* He says, quoting Booker's *Scripture and Prayer-book Glossary*: 'The number of words or senses of words which have become obsolete since 1611 amount to 388, or nearly one-fifteenth part of the whole number of words used in the Bible.' With all deference to so high an authority, I venture to think that this proportion is somewhat greater than is warranted by fact—if, that is, we admit that words in constant use by our country folk are not to be reckoned as obsolete.

A comparison of the language of Wycliffe's New Testament, which dates from about the year 1380, with that of our Authorised Version and with our Yorkshire dialect, would be a study worth pursuing with some care. Wycliffe was born at Hipswell near Richmond, and therefore his language might be expected to have a Northern tinge, and such clearly is the case. The following passages, taken from Purvey's *Revision of Wycliffe's New Testament*, contain words and forms in constant use at this day in the North Riding dialect which have dropped out of the literary language. The words in question are printed in italics :—(1) 'The keperis weren *afeerd*,' St. Matt. xxviii. 4. (2) 'Clensid;

with *besyms* and maad faire,' St. Matt. x. 44. (3) 'And
he took seuene looues . . . and *brak*,' St. Matt. xv. 36.
(4) '*Moun* comprehende with alle seyntis which is the
breede,' &c., Eph. iii. 18. (5) 'He concitide to fille his
wombe of the *coddis* that the hoggis eeten,' St. Luke xv.
16. (6) 'Whether God has not maad the wisdom of
this world *fonned*,' 1 Cor. i. 20. (7) 'Joseph *lappide*
it in a clene sendel,' St. Matt. xxvii. 59. (8) 'And
thei token up . . . seuene *lepis*,' St. Mark viii. 8. (9)
'Ye spake *myche*,' St. Matt. vi. 7. (10) 'For who that
trowith that he be *ought* when he is *nought*,' Gal. vi. 3.
(11) '*Mayster* Moises seide if *ony* man is deed,' &c.,
St. Matt. xxii. 27. (12) 'For what *partinge* of righteous-
nes,' 2 Cor. vi. 14. (13) 'It schal not *rewe* Him,'
Heb. vii. 21. (14) 'That he schulde *ridile* as whete,'
St. Luke xxii. 31. (15) 'For it was founded on a *sad*
stone,' St. Luke vi. 48. (16) 'The erthe openyde his
mouth and *soop* up the flood,' Rev. xiii. 16. (17) 'Y
stie to my fadir,' St. John xx. 17. (18) 'But Barnabas
took . . . and *telde* to him,' Acts ix. 27. (19) 'And to
brast the myddil,' Acts i. 18. (20) '*Twey* men metten
Him,' St. Matt. viii. 28.

In order to make the connection between these
fourteenth-century words and the modern Yorkshire
forms of them perfectly plain, I will give them in order
as below:—

14*th Century.*	*Modern Yorkshire.*	*Standard English.*
Afeerd.	Afeeard.	Afraid.
Besyms.	Bizzum*or*Bezzum.	Broom.
Brak.	Brak.	Broke.
Brast.	Brast.	Burst.
Breede.	Breed.	Breadth.
Coddis.	Cods.	Pods *or* Husks.
Fonned.	Fond.	Foolish.

S

14th Century.	Modern Yorkshire.	Standard English.
Lappide.	Lapt.	Wrapped or Folded.
Lepis.	Leeps.	Baskets.
Mayster.	Maaster.	Master.
Moun.	Mun (?)	Be able.
Myche.	Mich.	Much.
Nought.	Nowt.	Nothing & Naught.
Ony.	Onny.	Any.
Ought.	Owt.	Anything & Aught.
Partinge.	Parting.	Division.
Rewe.	Rewe.	Repent & Rue.
Ridile.	Ruddle.	Sift.
Sad.	Sad.	Heavy.
Soop.	Sup.	Drink or Swallow.
Stie.	Stee (a ladder).	Go up.
Telde.	Tell'd.	Told.
Twey.	Tweea.	Two.

It may be noted that *leeps* in the dialect is now only used for the peculiarly shaped fishermen's baskets for catching eels, &c.

The verb *stie* is not used, but only the noun *stee*—that by which one steps up.

The usage of *sad* has become restricted, and is now applied mainly to bread or food that is heavy.

On the whole, then, we may observe that as far as our Yorkshire folk of the old school are concerned—and there are still a considerable number of them surviving—we need not be anxious to modernise in any degree the stately and melodious language of the Authorised Version; on the contrary, the only change advantageous to our people would rather be a reverting to older and still purer English by rooting out words of southern growth which have never flourished in our northerly air.

Happily, no one has yet thought of making a revised

version of Shakespeare. We are content to read him as he wrote. It is true the English Bible and Shakespeare are not altogether parallel cases, the one being a translation and the other in the original; still, the two, simply as specimens of English, date from nearly the same time, and so, from a linguistic point of view, they are not wholly unlike.

It is not for a moment to be supposed that our older, unlettered country folk would understand very much of the language of Shakespeare; nevertheless there are many words and expressions to be found in Shakespeare's plays which, although they may be said to have passed out of use as standard English, are still to be heard in the folk-speech of Yorkshire. I must content myself with a very few examples on this point, and leave it to those who may feel an interest in the subject to make other like discoveries for themselves.

The word *parlous* is more generally used than it was some years ago: whether it would now be reckoned as standard English or not I am not authority enough to determine: certain it is that it forms one of the very commonest components of our dialectic vocabulary; *parlous* roads, *parlous* weather, *a parlous tahm*, &c., may be constantly heard, though we should hardly say 'a parlous knock,' as Shakespeare does in *Romeo and Juliet*.

Quick, meaning alive, is retained in our folk-speech under the form *wick*; the transition from one to the other is so slight that we may take the two words as one. We have an example of this, so frequent in the Bible, in the following quotation from Shakespeare :—

'Thou 'rt quick, but yet I 'll bury thee.'
Timon of Athens, iv. 3.

We do not reckon *obliged* in the sense of forced as part of our vocabulary; instead we make use of the equivalent just mentioned or of *tied*; it is in this sense, too, that Shakespeare wrote the word in *The Taming of the Shrew*, where this passage occurs, 'And I am tied to be obedient.'

As in Psalm xxv. we have the old use of *learn* in the sense of teach : so too in Shakespeare the same is to be found ; thus, 'You must not learn me how to remember any extraordinary pleasure,' *As You Like It*, i. 2. I need not remind a Yorkshireman that we generally employ this word under the form *larn*, the now prevailing *teach* of standard English being seldom heard.

Again, we not unfrequently use the indefinite article before the plural noun *many*; for instance, we say *Ah seed a many on 'em*, or *There was a many*. Here, too, we are supported by Shakespeare, as in the following passages :—' A many fools,' *Merchant of Venice*, iii. 5 ; 'A care-crazed mother to a many sons,' *Richard III*, iii. 7.

It may now sound vulgar to say *for to come* or *for to do*, though I confess I scarcely know why it should ; at all events, it is an almost universal form still found in our dialect ; and for this we have Shakespearian, to say nothing of Biblical, authority, as in *Hamlet*, iii. 1, where the phrase 'for to prevent' occurs. In Yorkshire speech *fond* is commonly used in the sense of foolish, which is also repeatedly found in the great dramatist's writings.

The separation of the two parts of *towards*, or perhaps we should rather say the addition of *wards* to nouns as a suffix indicating direction, is of frequent occurrence in our folk-talk : and this is the case after *from* as well as after *to* : thus we should say *ti Newton-wards* or *fra Newton-wards*. Illustrations of the former may be gathered from two of Shakespeare's plays, namely, 'Unto

Paris-wards,' 1 *Henry VI*, iii. 3; and again, 'And tapers burned to bed-ward,' *Coriolanus*, i. 6.

The prepositional use of *against*, with regard to time or event, is another case in point. For example, it is good Yorkshire to say *Thoo mun be riddy agaan ah cum ;* and in *Romeo and Juliet* we read 'against thou shall awake'; also similar usages are to be found in *Hamlet*.

Furthermore, we have the company of the immortal poet in our use of such words as *afeard, awkward* (contrary), *barm, barn, beteem* (pour out : though in this word the prefix is omitted), *cess, chuff* (coarse), *daff* (to befool ; the present form being *daft*, and only used as an adjective), *deny* (to refuse), *eyne* (eyes ; present form *een*), *sneaped* (checked), *urchin* (hedgehog).

To *sowle* is used in much the same sense still as in the passage in *Coriolanus*, iv. 5, 'He'll go, he says, and sowle the porter of Rome gates by the ears.'

As a term of endearment, there is no commoner word in the dialect than *hunny* : it is always used without an accompanying noun, thus : 'aye, hunny,' 'cum thi waays hunny,' &c. I am not aware that it is used in Shakespeare except in agreement with another word, though in that connection we find it several times, as the following examples will show :—'O honey nurse, what news?' *Romeo and Juliet*, ii. 5; 'My good sweet honey Lord,' 1 *Henry IV*, i. 2; 'And now, my honey love,' *Taming of the Shrew*, iv. 3; 'My fair, sweet, honey monarch,' *Love's Labour's Lost*, v. 2.

One of the most marked grammatical features in the dialect is the want of the possessive case, which I have elsewhere alluded to : perhaps the best example of this peculiarity to be found in Shakespeare is when the Fool says, in *Lear*, i. 4, 'The hedge-sparrow fed the cuckoo so long, that it's had it head bit off by it young.'

Again, the Yorkshireman would understand better than some others the force of the passage, 'The heart I bear shall never sag with doubt nor shake with fear,' *Macbeth*, v. 3. To *sag* implies, in our dialectical speech, a sinking or depression, as when a rope hangs loosely: it is one of our very commonest words.

It is noticed in another chapter that *beginning* is a word seldom heard in our folk-speech, *first-end* or *fore-end* being generally substituted : agreeing with this usage is that in the passage which runs thus, 'Where I have liv'd at honest freedom ; paid more pious debts to heaven, than in all the fore-end of my time,' *Cymbeline*, iii. 3.

To *crack* of a thing, in Yorkshire, means to boast of it : and we find it used in the same sense by Shakespeare in the passage 'And Ethiopes of their sweet complexion crack,' *Love's Labour's Lost*, iv. 3 ; and again, 'What cracker is this same that deafs our ears ?'—*King John*, ii. 1.

It does not appear that *to jump with* is found in Shakespeare in exactly the same sense as that in which it is used in Yorkshire, viz. *to fall in with* a person, to meet one by chance, though in a sense not widely different from this it is found, viz. in *Othello*, i. 3; also in *The Merchant of Venice*, ii. 9, 'I will not jump with common spirits,' the expression here meaning to agree with.

Some remarks on *thill-horse* or *shill-horse* bearing on the subject we are now considering will be found in the Glossary following.

It may not generally be known what a *kex* is : but that Shakespeare knew the word and the thing may be gathered from the quotation, 'Nothing teems but hateful docks, rough thistles, kecksies, burs,' *Henry V*, v. 2. A *kex* is the fools-parsley, the stalk of which, when dead, becomes so dry as to be used as a simile to denote utter dryness.

Though *geck* is not used in the folk-speech, *gicken*, which has the same root, is not uncommon ; a *geck* means a fool, and to *gicken* signifies to laugh like a fool. Thus we read : 'And made the most notorious geck and gull that e'er invention played on,' *Twelfth Night,* v. 1. For further remarks on this word, see Glossary.

Many more examples similar to those above-mentioned might be quoted. But let these, with previous remarks, suffice to show that there are elements in our dialect worthy of something better than scorn or ridicule. I do not claim for it the dignity of a literary language ; though more, much more, might be done towards perpetuating and elevating it than has yet been attempted : we sorely need, as I said, a Yorkshire Burns to uplift the good old speech of a hardy, independent, practical, and hearty race of men, possessed not only of human sympathies, which though not perhaps appearing on the surface, are none the less real and true, but imbued also with deep religious feeling.

Still, though not claiming for our speech the stateliness of a literary language, yet I do claim for it a history. The old traditional tongue of the East Yorkshire folk might be traced through many generations, resisting in its essence and main features the penetrating influences of the Norman Conquest, defying alike monarch, court, and statesmen, having little or nothing to say to Latin or French importations which have so strongly im-pressed their indelible mark on the Queen's English, holding its own, so to say, against all comers, and to this day retaining in clearly marked lines the unmistake-able lineaments of its Norse birth.

Well may every true Yorkshireman have an affection

for the unwritten mother-tongue of his fore-elders and do what he can to preserve this connection with the past, which, though it has withstood so many opposing influences in bygone times, is in these latter days in danger of being blotted out of its very existence by the advancing tide of education.

GLOSSARY.

ABBREVIATIONS.

adj., adjective.
adv., adverb.
A.S., Anglo-Saxon.
conj., conjunction.
D. or Dial., Dialect.
Dan., Danish.
E.R., East Riding.
esp., especially.
ex., example.
Fr., French.
Gael., Gaelic.
Germ., German.
Icel., Icelandic.
Interj., Interjection.
Jutl. D., Jutlandic Dialect.
lit., literal or literally.
N., Norse or Norwegian.
n., noun.
N.R., North Riding.
num., numeral or number.
O. Fr., Old French.

O. N., Old Norse.
part., participle or participial.
perf. or pf., perfect.
pl., plural.
pr., pronunciation or pronounce.
prep., preposition.
pron., pronoun.
rel., relative.
sing., singular.
Std. Eng., Standard English.
v., verb.
Wel., Welsh.

C. after a word signifies that it is in common use in some place or district in the North or East Riding.
F. signifies similarly that the word is in fairly common use.
R. that it is but rarely used.
O. that it is obsolete.

A.

A, num. adj. C. One. Vide **Yah.**

Aa! interj. C. An interjection expressing admiration, surprise, and other emotions. It is more generally followed by another word than used singly. The pronunciation of this word, as well as of the *a* generally, is peculiar and characteristic ; the sound corresponds very nearly with the *a* in *air*, only in this interjection it is more drawn out.

    Ex.—*Aa! bud them 's bonnie 'uns. —Aa! noo sha was sair putten aboot.*

Aback, adv. C. Behind.

    Ex.—*It popp'd oot aback o' t' stee.*

Aback o' beyont, adv. F. A very long way off; somewhere unknown through its distance.

    Ex.—*Ah wadn't mahnd if they was all aback o' beyont,* i.e. I wish they were anywhere.

Abear, v. C. (pr. abeear). To bear, endure.
> Ex.—*Ah can't abeear stooryin'.*
Abide is also used in the same sense and with about equal frequency.

Ablins, aiblins, adv. C. (pr. aablins). Perhaps, possibly.
> Ex.—*He 'll aablins mannish.*

Aboon, prep. C. Above; applied either to position or quantity.
> Ex.—*It leeaks bad aboon heead. — There 'll be aboon a scoore.*

Abrede, adv. C. Vide **Brede**.

Acoorn, n. C. (pr. accron, and yakkron). An acorn. Vide **Yakkron**.

Acoz, conj. C. Because.

Addle, v. C. To earn, to save money by little and little; also, in a general sense, to gain.
> Ex.—*He 's addled a deal o' brass. — Ah 's addlin' nowt. — He addles a good wage.*

Addlins, n. C. Earnings, savings, wages.
> Ex.—*Them 's all mah addlins. — Hard addlins an' nut mich when deean.*

Aether, conj. C. Either; there is another form—owther—of this word.
> Ex.—*He gav aether on us yan.*

Afear'd, part. C. Afraid.
> Ex.—*Ah 's sadly afear'd on 't.*

Afore, prep. C. (pr. afoor). Before. Dan. För (before).
> Ex.—*He 'll mebbe cum afoor neet.*

Again, prep. C. (pr. agaan). Against, i. e. near to.
> Ex.—*Oor spot ligs agaan Helmsla.*

Agate, agait, C. (pr. agaat and ageeat). Engaged in doing; astir; going. Dan. At gaa (to go, move, work).
> Ex.—*Thoo mun git agate i good tahm. — Ah 's kept agate; i. e. I am kept on the move.—They 've gitten ageeat wi pleewin.*

Agate, part. C. Set going; let loose, as a horse into a pasture.
> Ex.—*He set 'em all agate.*

Agee, adv. R. (The *g* is pr. soft.) On one side, not straight.

Ah, pron. C. I. This pr. is universal; in certain connections short *e* or *i* is used instead, but never *I* with the pr. as in Std. Eng. In the Jutl. dialect A = I. This pr. is usual in the whole of North Jutland; in other districts *æ* is the ordinary pr.
> Ex.—(1) *Ah is. —* (2) *Ah mun cum. —* (3) *Mun ah cum?* (4) *Mun ě cum?*
In (3) the *ah* is emphatic, and signifies 'must *I* come' as

distinguished from some one else; (4) is the ordinary expression for 'must I come?'

Ahint, adv. and prep. C. (pr. ahinnt). Behind.

Ex.—*It's nut mich ahint t' uther.*

Aiger, n. F. The tidal wave; the 'bore' of the South of England.

Ex.—*Wahr aiger* (the common warning when the wave is approaching).

Aim, v. C. (pr. aam and yam). To intend, suppose, expect; to be under the impression that; to lead in the direction of.

Ex.—*Ah aamed ti git all on 't sahded afoor noo.—Wa yam ti start i t' morn.—Ah nivver aamed at t' lass wad a'e sattled.—Yon rooad yams ti Whidby.*

Airm, n. C. (the *r* in this word is silent; the peculiar pr. is perhaps best indicated by aa'm). Arm.

Airn, n. R. Iron; seldom used now, but with some old people the word is still familiar. Dan. Jern (iron).

Airt, n. R. Quarter of the heavens; point of the compass.

Ex.—*T' wind's gotten intiv a cau'd airt.*

Ak, n. C. (pr. yak). The oak. Dan. En Eg (an oak).

Akwerd, akwert, adj. F. On the back; usually applied to a sheep laid on its back.

Ex.—*Ah fund yan o' Simpson yows laad akwert.*

In Cleveland *rigged* is the usual word.

Al, n. C. (pr. yal). Ale. Vide **Yal**.

All-fare, adv. R. For good and all.

Ex.—*He's gone for all-fare.*

All-out, adj. R. Altogether, quite, entirely.

Ally, ally-taw, n. C. A playing marble as distinguished from *steeanies* and *potties*—stone or baked clay marbles.

Al-hoos, n. F. (pr. yal-oos). An ale-house, a public house.

Almous, n. F. (pr. awmous). Alms; money given in charity.

Ex.—*What awmous a'e ya gotten?* Dan. Almisse.

Along of, prep. C. In consequence of, through, owing to.

Ex.—*It warn't along o' me; it war along of him.*

Amaist, adv. C. (pr. ommeeast and ommost). Almost.

Ex.—*Ah wer ommost flayed ti deead.*

Amang, prep. C. Among: frequently shortened to *'mang*.

Ex.—*Ah put doon mi brass 'mang t' rest on 'em.*

Amell, prep. R. Between, among. The form *mellem* is, or was till lately, used at Staithes, where the fishermen are said to divide the fish, *mellem yan anoother*. Dan. Mellem (between).

Ex.—*Amell tweea steeals.*

An' all, conj. and adv. C. (1) As well, also, besides. (2) Indeed, truly. This is an abbreviation of ' and all.'

Ex.—*Tak them wi ya an' all.*—Q. 'Did you enjoy yourself?' A. '*Ah did an' all*,' i.e. I did indeed.

Ance, adj. C. (pr. yance). Once.

Ancle-bands, n. R. Sandals for shoes. Dan. Ankel-baand (ancle-band).

Ane, num. adj. C. (pr. yan and ane). One. Vide **Yah**.
> Ex.—*T' ane t' ither.*

Anenst, prep. C. Against, by the side of, near to; also used in the sense of opposite to. It is almost always preceded by *ower*.
> Ex.—*Yon 's him stannin' ower anenst t' plantin.—Ah seed him set ower anenst us.*

Angry, adj. C. (pr. ang-ry not ang-gry). Inflamed (of a sore or wound), and consequently painful

Ananthers, Anthers, conj. O. In case, lest, peradventure; possibly a corruption from N. Fr. *aventure*. The form *ananthers case* was frequently used near Northallerton some years ago; but I believe the word in any form is now obsolete, or very nearly so; though *anthers* was current a few years ago at East Acklam.
> Ex.—*Thoo mun stop here ananthers he cums.*

Anparsy, n. R. Boys in repeating their alphabet would say x y z anparsy; they did not know what it meant, but pointed in their spelling-books to the character, and this character was also termed parsy-and.

Any, adv. C. (pr. onny and any). At all.
> Ex.—*Sha dizn't mend onny*, i. e. She does not improve in health.—*It didn't rain onny.*

A-quart, ower-quart, prep. R. (pr. a-quahrt). Across, athwart. The latter form is perhaps the most frequent, and is used of motion across. Vide **Over-quart**.
> Ex.—*T' beeos ran a-quart t' staggarth.*—A-quart is also used of people at variance.
> Ex.—*Jim an me 's gitten a-quart.*

Arf, arfish, adj. F. Afraid.
> Ex.—*Ah felt a bit arfish.—Rooads is seea slaap ah 's arf o' travellin'.*

Ark, n. O. A large chest or bin with divisions inside, formerly used for keeping dressed corn in.

Arles, n. F. Money given to a servant on being hired by a master; it is thus the pledge of a contract: the sum given generally varies from 2s. to 5s. Also called Fest or God's-penny.

Arr, n. R. A scar left by a wound—also occasionally used as a verb. Dan. Ar (a scar).
> Ex.—*He 's gitten an arr ov his back.*

Arran-web, n. R. A cob-web. Fr. Une Araignée (a spider).

Arridge, n. C. The edge of a squared piece of timber, &c.

Arse, arse-end, n. C. The lower part or end of anything.

O.N. Ars. Jutl. D. Ast. The frequent use of this word to the exclusion of others of like meaning is remarkable. Ex.—A Rector's wife asks, 'Are you going to carry the wheat to-day?' '*Lead? naay!*' says the farm man, '*t' shaff arses is as wet as sump.'—Stop, mun; t' cart arse has tumml'd out.* Atkinson (*Clevel. Gloss.* p. 10) gives the following example :—*Pick thae stooks doon an' let t' arse-ends o' t' shaffs lig i' t' sun a bit.*

Arsy-varsy, adv. R. Upside down.

Arval, n. O. A funeral feast. Dan. Arve-öl (a funeral feast ; literally, Heir-ale).

Ask, adj. C. Vide **Hask.**

Ask, esk, n. C. The newt. Gael. Esc (the newt).

Ass. n. C. Ashes, as distinguished from cinders ; the latter being applied generally to coke. Dan. Aske (ashes). Ex.—*Put a bit o' ass uppo t' trod, it 's sae slaap.*

Ass-coup, n. R. A wooden box or sort of pail for carrying ashes.

Assel-tree, n. C. An axle-tree.

Ass-hooal, ass-pit, n. C. The hole or pit where ashes fall or are thrown. Dan. Aske-hul (ash-hole).

Assil-tooth, n. C. A double tooth or grinder. Dan. En axel Tand (a double tooth). Ex.—*T' lahtle lass is sadly plagued wi yan ov her assil teeth.*

Ass-manner, ass-muck, n. C. Manure from an ash-pit.

Ass-midden, n. C. An ash-heap. Dan. Aske-mödding (ash-heap).

At, rel. pron. C. Who, which, that. This is probably not a corruption of *that* but the O.N. *at.* Ex.—*Them at* (equivalent to 'those who '). *There 's nowt at ah knaws on.*

At, conj. C. That. Dan. At (that), e. g. Jeg veed at, &c. (I know that, &c.). Ex.—*Ah deean't knaw 'at ivver ah seed him.*

At, prep. C. To ; also used in a peculiar sense of urging a request, and especially of persistent urging. Ex.—*What hez sha deean at t' bairn ?—He wer awlus at ma aboot it,* i. e. he was constantly making a request about it.

At-after, adv. O. After, afterwards.

Athout, prep. and conj. C. (pr. athoot). Without, unless. Other forms of the equivalent for *without* are *wioot, widoot, wivoot, bedoot,* the last being seldom heard except in the North Riding. With this qualification the various forms of this word are used very indiscriminately, often by the same individuals. *Without* in the sense of 'unless' is invariable.

Ex.—*Wa sa n't be able ti lead ti-morn athoot wa git a bit o' wind.*

Atter, Atteril, n. F. Matter of a poisonous nature, as from an ulcer; that which causes irritation or itching to the skin : a child with a scabbed face is said to be *iv a atteril.* Dan. Edder (matter, pus).

Ex.—*Ah feels all iv a atteril.—Mi mooth 's all iv a atteril.*

Attercop, n. R. A spider. Dan. Edderkop (a spider).

Aught, ought, n. C. (pr. between *owt* and *ote*). Anything— a word in universal use.

Ex.—*A'e ya seed owt of oor Dick?*

Auntersome, adj. O. Adventurous, bold, rash. *Auntre* is used by Chaucer in the same sense. *Venturesome* (pr. ventthersum) has now taken the place of *auntersome* and is very common, *bold* and *rash* being seldom heard.

Awebund, part. F. (pr. Awe bun'). Subservient, submissive, obedient.

Ex.—*Ah nivver was awebun' tiv him.*

The primary meaning of this word is overawed, but it is now seldom so used.

Awhile, conj. C. (pr. awhahl). While, until.

Ex.—*He ligged i bed awhahl dinner tahm.*

Sometimes the initial letter of this word is omitted, but generally it is heard.

Awkward, adj. C. (pr. okkard). Contentious, obstinate, bad-tempered.

Ex.—*He wer varry okkard aboot it.—Ah doot t' meer 's boun ti be okkard.*

Awm, n. F. The elm.

Awns, n. C. The beards of corn. Dan. Avne (husks).

Ax, v. C. To ask, invite. *Ax'd* is commonly used in reference to banns of marriage, *ax'd oot* signifying that the publication has been made for the third time. Although *ax'd* is often used with regard to an invitation to a funeral, *bidden* is the more general word on such occasions.

A-warrant, v. C. (pr. a-wand). To certify. This word is only used in the future tense in the phrase *Ah 'll a-wa'nd ya,* and is equivalent to ' you may take my word for it ' ; it is generally used in a tone of encouragement, e.g. in reply to a boy asking doubtfully, ' *Di ya think ah can mannish 't?* ' '*Aye, ah 'll a-wa'nd it.*'

Aye, marry, adv. F. An intensified affirmation equivalent to the slang expression *yes ! rather*; it would be more correct to write it *aye Marie,* being a corruption of ' yes !

by Mary.' *Marry* is sometimes added to emphasize the adverb of negation, *nay*, *marry*, but it is more frequent in the affirmative form.

B.

Back-bearaway, n. F. (pr. back-beearaway). The common bat.

Back-cast, n. F. (pr. back-kest). A loss; especially a loss of strength or health, a loss of ground, a relapse, a failure. *Throwback* is frequently used instead of *backcast* in the sense of a relapse.

Backen, v. C. To retard, delay.

> Ex.—*T' maaster hesn't com'd ; wa mun backen t' dinner a bit.*

Back-end, n. C. (1) The latter part of the year from after harvest. (2) The latter part of other periods of time. (3) (in plural) Tail-corn. Vide **Hinderends**. Dan. Bagende (hind part).

> Ex.—*We 'd nobbut a dowly tahm t' last back-end.—Ah 'll cum t' backend o' t' week.—Ah wants sum back-ends for t' chickens.*

Backendish, adj. F. Rough and wintry; generally applied to the weather.

Backening, n. C. A relapse.

> Ex.—Q. ' How is Jane to-day ? ' A. ' *Sha 's neea bether ; woss if owt ; sha 's had sum sad backenings.*'

This word is synonymous with *back-cast*.

Back-side, n. C. (pr. back-sahd). (1) The back yard and premises of a dwelling-house. (2) The lower or under side of anything.

> Ex.—*Wa 've gitten wer back-sahds fettled up, an' they leeak weel noo* ; i. e. We have had the back premises of our row of houses repaired, and they now look tidy.

Backerly, adj. and adv. F. Late, backward ; after the usual time. Jutl. D. Bagerlig (late).

> Ex.—*Them ooats is a bit backerly.*

This word is not heard so much in the East as in the North Riding.

Bad, adj. C. (1) Difficult. In this sense the word is universally used, besides in the ordinary sense of worthless. Hard to please, difficult to be done, hard to beat, difficult to find, &c., are never heard in the dialect, but instead, *bad to please*, *bad to do*, *bad to beat*, *bad to find*, &c. (2) Sick, poorly. The adverbial form (*badly*) in this sense is very common.

Ex.—Q. 'Why isn't your sister here (school) to-day ?'
A. '*Sha 's bad.'—Ah 's badly.'*
Badness, n. C. Mischievous evil, or active wickedness.
> Ex.—*There 's neea badness aboot her.—It 's nowt bud badness on him.*

Bain, adj. C. Good, easy, near, straight; applied only to a road, path, &c. There is a good deal of confusion between *bain* and *gain;* indeed the two are frequently used indiscriminately, but often the old and correct distinction of meaning is observed, as it ought to be. *Bain* is properly ' good' or 'easy '; so that of two *t' bainest rooad* is the road in the best condition and so the easiest one to travel on, whereas *t' gainest rooad* is simply the nearest in point of distance. *Bainer* and *bainest* are more frequently heard than *bain*. Dan. En Bane (a pathway); At bane (to lead). Icel. Beinn (straight).

Bairn, barn, n. C. (pr. ba'an : it is seldom that the *r* is heard, even slightly, though it is difficult to give an exact indication of the pronunciation of this word). (1) A child. (2) A term of familiarity used by elderly people to those younger than themselves, esp. in such phrases as *Aye, bairn; bless ya, bairn.* (3) Used jestingly, reproachfully, or in admiration to an adult as well as to a child, e. g. after some brag, or outrageously absurd statement, has been made. O.N. and Dan. Barn.
> Ex.—(1) *Cum thi ways, mah ba'an.* — (2) *Aw! bless ya, ba'an, t' wo'lld 's to'nn'd arsy-varsy sen ah wer a lad.*—(3) *Thoo is a bonny ba'an, Dick, ti deea leyke that.*

The form *Barn* is commoner than *Bairn* in parts of the Wold country.
Bairn-lakings, n. R. (pr. ba'an laakins). Toys, playthings.
Bairnish, adj. C. Childish.
> Ex.—*It 's nobbut bairnish deed.*

Bakstan, n. F. A stone for baking cakes upon ; but in more recent years an iron plate is used instead. A frying-pan. Dan. Bage sten (bake-stone).
Balk, n. C. (pr. bawk). (1) A beam. (2) A strip of land, whether in a field or by the side of a road. Sometimes the balk gives its name to the road itself. Dan. En Bjælke (a beam), En Balk (a ridge of land between furrows).
Ball, n. C. The palm (of the hand), the sole (of the foot).
> Ex.—*It catched ma i' t' ball o' my han'.*

Bam, v. R. To take in by playing a trick upon one.
> Ex.—*He bam'd ma.*

There is the slang word bam-foozled, or bam-boozled, which has a similar meaning.

Bam, n. C. A take in, a trick, or practical joke; 'all non-sense,' as it was once described to me.

Ex.—*It's nowt bud a bam.* — *It's all a bam.*

Band, n. C. String, twine. A rope is called a band if used for binding, otherwise it is also called a line; the ligature of a sheaf of corn or the straw rope used in thatching is called a band. Dan. Baand (rope or string).

Bandmakker, n. C. The maker of bands (generally a lad) for tying the sheaves in the harvest field. The trio engaged in this part of the work were the *bandmakker*, the *takker up* (generally a woman), and the *binndther*. Dan. Baandmager (ribbon-maker).

Bannock, n. F. A kind of cake. Also used as a verb. To *bannock i' bed* means to lie in a lazy fashion.

Ex.— *Sha wad sit up hauf o' t' neet, an' bannock i' bed hauf o' t' daay.*

Barfhame, barfam, barfan, n. C. (pr. barfam; barfan being probably a corruption). A horse-collar. There are a great variety of spellings of this word, and the derivation seems most uncertain. I have given the preference to the first-named form, for there is probably a connection between the last part of the word and the hames: vide **Hames**. The *bumble-* or *bass-barfam* was specially used for young colts and fillies when first yoked, and was usually borrowed, there being but few in a village. A *horse-collar* in some parts of Yorkshire is the bridle with blinkers, *head-stall* applies to a halter only.

Bargh, barugh, n. C. (pr. barf). A hill; generally an isolated one, and of no great height. The use of the word is chiefly confined to particular hills, and is not applied as a generic term. There is an analogy between the pronunciation of this word and that of *though, through, plough*, &c., which are pronounced *thoff, thruff, pleeaf,* &c.

Barguest, n. F. An apparition, described as most like a donkey, or big black dog with very large eyes. The word is now frequently used as a term of reproach or abuse, e. g. *thoo barguest,* the original sense being lost or forgotten. The latter part of this word is connected with Germ. Geist, the first syllable being Germ. Bahr, or Dan. Baare (a bier).

Barm, n. C. Yeast. Dan. Bærme (yeast).

Bass, n. C. Matting; sometimes also applied to material made of straw, &c. A joiner's basket is termed a *bass*, and a hassock is sometimes called a *knee-bass*. Dan. Bast (the inner bark of a tree).

Bassak, Bazzak, v. F. To strike either things or persons, to

T

beat; the corresponding noun Bassaking—a beating—is in frequent use. Dan. Et Bask (a blow, a flogging); at baske (to slap, to beat).

Ex.—*Ah bassak'd 'em in wi a mell.*—*T' grund's that hard they want a vast o' bassakin' doon.*

Bat, n. C. (1) A blow or stroke. (2) A state or condition. (3) In plural it is equivalent to a flogging.

Ex.—(1) *He gav him sikan a bat ower t' back.*—(2) *Ah 's aboot at t' last bat.*—(3) *Noo thoo 'll git thi bats inoo if thoo deean't behave thisen.*

Bath, v. C. (pr. as bath, and never as bathe). To foment with hot water. To wash children all over. Dan. At bade (to bathe, foment).

Ex.—*T' doctther tell'd ma ti bath it weel.*

Batten, n. C. Two sheaves of straw bound together; a bundle of straw.

Batter, n. C. A leaning or inclination inwards, as generally applied to a wall, to counteract the tendency in what is behind it to push it forward.

Ex.—*T' wall wants a bit mair batter back.*

Battin, n. C. A spar of wood, generally 7 inches wide, 2½ inches thick, and of any length ('deals' being somewhat wider and thicker).

Batt'l-door, n. C. Part of the apparatus, still to be seen, for mangling clothes; the other appendage being the *roller* or *rolling-pin.* The *batt'l-deear*, as it is called, is a piece of wood, flat at one side or both, about 2 feet long, and in shape something like a cricket bat. The use of it involved harder work than the mangle, and it is probably on this account mainly that it has given place to the modern mangle, though in some farmhouses the battel-door and rolling-pin are occasionally used still. The battel-door was also called a bittle.

Baubosking, part. R. It is difficult to give the precise meaning of this word, and I do not remember to have heard it used but by a single individual; that it is a word of some interest I have little doubt. It would seem to have reference to the straying away of cattle or sheep from the pasture assigned to them. If, as seems certain, much of the pasture of cattle in the old days lay in the *boscus* (the 'sylva pasturalis' of Doomsday), the idea conveyed in the example given below, of straying away from the pasture to which the animals are 'hoofed,' into the woods, is quite intelligible: the expression made use of before me was a figurative one, and the speaker merely meant to say that he was a man who seldom left his own home for the sake of visiting new places. His words were these : *Ah deean't gan bauboskin' aboot leyke sum on 'em; ah sticks ti t' heeaf.*

Beal, Beel, v. C. (pr. beeal). (1) To bellow, to roar (used of an animal). (2) To shout, to cry, or in other ways to raise the voice above the usual pitch.

Jutl. D. At bjæle (to bellow).

Ex.—*What 's ta beealin at?* i. e. What are you crying for ?

Beeast, n. C. A beast of the ox kind. (The *t* final is seldom heard in the singular number, and never in the plural.)

Ex.—*They 're gran' beeas is them.*

Beastlings, Bisslings, n. C. (pr. beeaslins). The first and second milkings drawn from a cow after calving. From this milk beastlings pudding is commonly made, which is considered a great delicacy—it is called *beeaslin' puddin'*. The milk is also used sometimes in making bread.

Jutl. D. Bjæst (the first milk after a calf is born).

Beck, n. C. A stream of running water, a brook. Dan. En Bæk (a brook). This word is a prefix to several other words the meaning of which is obvious, e.g. *Becksteead, Beckside, Becksteeans,* &c.

Bedfast, adj. C. Confined to one's bed by sickness, either permanently or temporarily.

Ex.—*Sha 's been bedfast sen Tho'sda.*

Bed-happings or **Happings,** n. C. Bedclothes of whatever kind.

Bed-piece, n. C. That part of the framework of a cart into which the arms of the axle are laid.

Bed-stock, n. C. The bedstead proper, i. e. the wooden framework of the bed only. Dan. Senge-stok (bed-stock).

Bedoot, beoot, prep. and conj. C. Without, unless.

Ex.—*Ah 'll gan yam bedoot tha.*

Beeld, bield, or **beild,** n. C. A shelter from weather, especially rough weather; a shed. The word *building* is always pr. *beelding* in E. Yorkshire. There seems therefore to be a connection between *beeld* and building, the object of a building being to afford shelter from weather. O. Swedish Bylja (to build).

Ex.—*T' au'd esh-tree maks t' best bit o' beeld of owt i t' pairk.*

Beelding, n. C. (pr. beeldin'). A building. The form and pr. of this word is universal throughout the district. The derivation seems in all probability the same as that of *beeld*, vide sup.

Bee-skep, n. R. A beehive made of rushes or straw.

Bee-sucken, adj. R. This word is applied to a tree that is

T 2

diseased, as shown by a gummy substance issuing through the bark. It was once described to me as 'like honey coming out of a tree.' Under these circumstances the tree is said to be *bee-sucken*.

Beggar-staff, n. R. A state of beggary ; a hopeless state of insolvency, as when a man has to be sold up ' dish, pan, and doubler,' as the saying is. Dan. Tigger-stav (beggar-staff).

    Ex.—*He'll seean cum ti t' beggar-staff.*

Begging-poke, n. R. A bag carried by a beggar. This bag was not only used by professional beggars, but often by poor and honest folk who in hard times used to visit the houses of those well-to-do, and beg from them the necessaries of life. The bag was frequently made of ' harden,' but more often than not consisted of a pillow-slip.

Beholden, part. C. (pr. beho'dden). Under obligation, indebted.

Belantered, part. R. Belated, benighted.

Belder, v. C. To bellow as a bull ; to cry aloud, to roar. Dan. At buldre (to roar).

    Ex.—*Noo, what's ta belderin at?*

Belike, adv. F. (pr. beleyke). Probably.

    Ex.—*Belike it may fair up.*

Belk, v. C. To belch. Used also substantively.

Belker, n. F. Anything large of its kind.

    Ex.—*It war a reg'lar belker.*

Bell-house, n. F. (pr. bellhus or bell'us). A church tower, belfry. This word applies to that part of the lower story of a tower which opens into the nave of a church as well as to the part containing the bells.

    Ex.—*T' childer awlus used ti sit i' t' bell'us.—As dark as a bell'us.*

Belly-wark, n. C. The stomach-ache. Dan. Bælg (belly), værk (ache).

Belong, belang, v. C. To own, to form part of. When used in the sense of ' to own,' the owner is made the appendage of the article rather than *vice versa*.

    Ex.—*Wheea belangs t' stick? — Yon swath field belangs John Smith farm.*

Belt, p. part. of Build. C.

Bensil, n. F. A blow with the fist or a stick : also used as a verb.

    Ex.—*Give him a good bensil.*

Bent, n. C. A species of wiry grass or rush that grows commonly on the moorland hills.

Berry, berry-tree, n. C. The gooseberry, *par excellence*. The other fruits of the berry kind take a prefix, as *corr'nberries, strawberries, blackberries,* &c.

Ex.—*There 's a vast o' berries ti year; oor trees is that ragg'd whahl they 're fit ti brek.*—Q. *Wheer's t' lass?* A. *Pullin' berries.* (This in the dialect can only mean 'picking gooseberries.')

Besom, n. C. (pr. bizzum). A broom. The simile *as fond as a besom,* is commonly used for a very foolish person.

Bessy-babs, n. F. One given to silly talk, or one fond of childish things ; also used of a female fantastically dressed.

Ex.—*Sha 's a poor bessy-babs.*

Best, adj. C. The right ; as applied to hand or foot. *Better* is also used in the same sense. There is, again, a verbal use of this word in the sense of to get the best of.

Ex.—*My best hand. — T' best feeat.*

Bet, part. C. Beaten. Also perf. tense of To beat.

Ex.—*Ah wer fair bet. — We bet 'em at creckit.*

Better, adv. C. Well, after an ailment ; generally preceded by *quite* (pr. quiet).

Ex.—Q. *How are you to-day?* A. *Ah 's nut betther yit ; bud ah 's a deal betther 'an what ah a'e been. — Ah feels quiet betther.*

Better, adj. C. More, longer in time.

Ex.—*Betther'an a scoore. — Betther'an a twelvemunth. — Betther 'an a fo'tnith.*

Bettermy, adj. C. Of a higher class in the social scale.

Ex.—*They 're bettermy folks.— Sha 's quiet a bettermy body.*

Beuf, n. C. (pr. beuf, and more commonly beeaf). A bough of a tree. The form *bew* is also common.

Beyont, prep. C. Beyond.

Bid, v. C. To invite to a feast, as at a wedding or funeral. Dan. At byde (to invite). The corresponding noun—*bidding*—is also commonly used.

Bide, v. C. (pr. bahd). (1) To wait, remain. (2) To bear, to endure or suffer. (3) To dwell. Dan. At bie (to wait).

Ex.—*It 's bad ti bahd. — Sha bahds at Malton.*

Big, v. O. To build ; whence *biggin,* a building. Dan. Bygge (to build), Bygning (a building). Although obsolete generally, the word is still found in many local names, as Newbiggin, Biggin-houses, &c.

Bigg, n. C. Barley having four rows of ears on each stalk. Dan. Byg (barley).

Bike, n. C. The nest of the wild bee.

Ex.—*Ah 's funnd yan o' them bee-bikes.*

Billy-biter, n. C. The common blue tit.

Billy-boy, n. C. A keel rigged for sea, with bulwarks, gaff, boom, and bowsprit, and carrying fore and aft sail.

Ex.—*Sha leeaks leyke yan o' them billy-boys.*

Bind, v. C. (pr. binnd). To bind, to tie sheaves of corn with ' bands.'

Ex.—*T' maasther wants ya ti cum an' binnd for 'em.*

Binder, n. C. (pr. binndther). The tier up of sheaves of corn.

Bink, n. C. A bench or long seat without a back, whether of wood or stone. The stone bink is commonly placed near the cottage door. Dan. En Bænk (a bench).

Birk, n. C. The birch-tree. Dan. En Birk (a birch-tree).

Bisen, n. F. (pr. bahzen). An unusual sight or spectacle of a personal kind. Also used as a term of reproach.

Ex.—*Thoo mucky bahzen.*

Bisshel, n. C. Bushel. I do not remember to have heard this form or pronunciation of the word except in Cleveland.

Bitings, n. F. A name given to certain fields in the Wold country ; grazing land. Icel. Beit (pasturage).

Bittle, n. C. Vide Batt'l-door.

Biv, Byv, prep. C. By. The *v* is here added for euphony.

Ex.—*Nut byv o lang waay.*

Blackberries, n. C. Black currants ; Brambles, or Bummel-kites being the terms usually applied to the common wild blackberry generally so called.

Bladdry, adj. C. (pr. bladdhry). Very muddy or dirty. The corresponding noun, *Bladther*, is also in common use. As regards muddiness there are practically three degrees of comparison of it in ordinary use, viz. *mucky, bladdry,* and *all iv a posh.*

Ex.—*T' rooads is bladdhry.*

Blae, adj. F. (pr. blae and bleea). Blue, especially as regards the appearance of one blue with cold.

Ex.—*He 's blae wi' cau'd.*

It would seem that this word is a corruption of the Norse *blaa* ; while *bliew*, which is common in the dialect, is another form of *blue*.

Blaeberry, n. F. The common bilberry. Dan. Blaabær (bilberry).

Blair, v. C. To bellow as a bull ; to cry as a child.

Ex.—*Whist, wi ya ; what 's ta blairin aboot ?*

Blake, adj. C. A pale yellow colour, like that of the best quality of butter or the finest cream. Dan. Bleg. In Modern Danish the word means simply pale or pallid, without any idea of yellowness. In Yorks. Dial. it is frequently used as a participle, e. g. *T' butther 's gitten nicely blaked.* The simile *as blake as a gowlan* is in common use.

Blane, v. F. (pr. bleean). To bleach. Dan. At blegne (to grow pale), blegning (bleaching).

Blash, v. C. To splash with water, whether by treading in or spilling it. Jutl. D. Blasfuld (so full that the vessel runs over).

Blash, n. C. (1) soft mud, thick muddy water ; also used of intoxicating or other drink of poor quality. (2) Nonsense, foolish talk. Dan. En Plask (a splash), plask regn (heavy shower).

Ex.—*Ah can't sup sike blash.*

Blashy, adj. C. (1) Wet, as regards weather, roads, &c. (2) Weak, watery, as applied to drinks.

Ex.—*It's a blashy tahm been.—Ah thinks this tea's nobbut blashy.*

Blather, v. F. (pr. bladther). To talk rapidly and inconsiderately; to talk nonsense. Jutl. D. Bladder (much talk, also applied to persons who chatter a great deal).

Ex.—*His chafts hing lowse: he's allos blathering and talking.—Cleveland Glossary.*

Bleb, n. C. A drop of liquid, a bubble, a blister (most common in the latter sense). Jutl. D. En Blæb (a cow-dropping).

Bleck, n. C. The black grease used for cart wheels, or oil that has become blackened by friction. Dan. Blæk (ink).

Ex.—*Thoo mucky bairn; thoo's gitten thi feeace daub'd ower wi bleck.*

Blendcorn, n. C. (pr. blen'corn). A mixture of corn (wheat and rye) used for making cakes and bread. Dan. Blandkorn (mixed corn).

Blendings, n. C. A mixture of peas and beans. Dan. En Blanding (a mixing), Blandings-korn (mixed corn). Jutl. D. Blanding (blend-corn).

Blether-heead, n. F. A senseless, stupid fellow.

Ex.—*Thoo greeat bletherheead, ger oot o' t' rooad.*

Bloss, n. F. An ugly sight, a fright, a spectacle. Jutl. D. Blostre (to be red and swollen by drink or sickness).

Ex.—*Thoo diz leeak a bonny bloss i' that au'd goon.—What a bloss sha leeaks!*

Blotch, v. C. To blot; hence *blotch-paper* or *blotching-paper*, the common terms for blotting-paper. Jutl. D. En Blak (a blot in a book); also Blakpapir (blotting-paper).

Blow, n. C. (pr. blaw). Blossom.

Ex.—*There's a good leeak on o' blaw ti-year.*

Blustery, adj. C. Windy, squally, rough. A word very frequently used by people when they meet on a squally day and a remark is passed on the state of the weather.

Ex.—*Noo, Bill, it's a bit blustthery.—It's varry blustthery.*

Blutherment, n. F. Soft mud, or other slimy substance. Dan. Pludder (slime).

Boddums, n. C. Low-lying fields, or low ground generally.
Ex.—*He's doon i' l' boddums.*
This word is the same as *bottoms*, which may be a corruption of *bottons* (O. N. botn), but the word is by no means confined to hilly districts. Vide **Botton.**

Boggle, n. R. A spectre, a hobgoblin. Wel. Bwgan (a bugbear). 'Boggle about stack' is a game which boys used to play about the *staggarths*—a sort of unblinded 'Blind man's buff.'

Boggle, v. C. To jib (of a horse).

Bolk, bolken, v. F. (pr. bawk or booak). To vomit, to retch. The latter form seems to be the commoner.
Ex.—*Sha booaken'd hard.*

Boll, n. C. The trunk of a tree. Dan. En Bul (a trunk of a tree).

Bonny, adj. C. (1) Good-looking, pretty, fine, beautiful. (2) Well-pleasing. (3) An intensive as applied to number, size, &c. (4) Used ironically.
Ex.—(1) *T' bairn leeaks bonny eneeaf.*—(2) *Gie ma ho'd o' t' band, theer 's a bonny lass.*—(3) *There 's a bonny lot on 'em.*—(4) *Aw! Polly thoo 's brokken t' pankin'; noo there 'll be a bonny ti-deea aboot it.*

Book or bouk, n. C. Size—a corruption of *bulk*.
Ex.—*Ah 've knawn it ivver sen ah wer t' book o' mah leg.*

Borrill, n. C. The gadfly.

Bot, n. R. An iron implement used for marking sheep.

Botchet, n. R. A drink made from honey; mead. The liquid honey is first allowed to drop from the comb, which, with whatever honey adheres to it, is put into water and washed till all the remaining honey is extracted from it; the comb is next removed and the washings are allowed to ferment; it is then prepared for bottling. The drink is intoxicating to a high degree, and is very liable to produce headache, even though not drunk in any large quantity.

Bottle, n. F. A bundle (of straw, hay, &c.). This word was in everyday use some years ago, but is now not so commonly heard. There is but little difference between a *bottle* and a *batten*, except that the former has a single and the latter a double binding. Other names for a bundle of straw are *loggin* and *boddin*, which have one or two bands indiscriminately: indeed *batten, boddin, bottle*, and *loggin* all have much the same meaning, and it is a matter of some difficulty to define the distinctions. The following seems to me the explanation of the various terms :—*Boddin* is a general term, being another form of *bodd'n*, which is a corruption of *burden*, and means a bundle of straw tied up for carrying ; but curiously enough *bodd'n* is specially and almost exclusively applied to the bundles carried by gleaners in sheets. *Bottle* has a general signification, and means a tied bundle of straw, but is more commonly used in some parts than others ; being most frequently heard in the East Riding. *Batten* or *batt'n* is a bundle of 'drawn' straw for thatching, &c., is consequently longer than a *bottle*, and is generally tied with two bands. *Loggin* has the same meaning as *batten*.

Botton, n. R. The lowest part of a valley. O. N. Botn (found in place-names).

Bottry, n. C. The common elder ; this word may also be written bur-tree; indeed *bottry* is the local pr. of the same. In Jutl. D. Burretree is the burdoch.

Bound, part. C. (pr. bun', approximately). Compelled, whether morally or physically.

Ex.—*Ah 'll be boun' for 't.*

Boun, adj. C. (pr. bun, approximately). Ready, going, or on the point of doing anything. O. N. Buinn (made ready). There are few words more common, and at the same time more characteristic of the dialect, than this ; it is distinct from the preceding word, though pronounced the same, only that in this word the emphasis is always, by the sense, less than in the preceding one, and thus may be distinguished from it.

Ex.—*Ah doot t' au'd meer 's boun ti dee; sha diz leeak badly.—Sha 's boun ti git wed.*

Bowdykite, n. R. A corpulent person ; but now only used as a term of reproof in the case of a mischievous child—a forward child.

Ex.—*Thoo bowdykite; cum oot o' t' rooad.*

Brade, v. R. To spread a report. Dan. At brede (to spread).

Ex.—*Sha brades it aboot 'at,* &c.

Brae, n. R. (pr. breea). The brink of a river. O. N. Bra (the brow of the face).

Ex.—*Breea full* (of a stream bank full).

Braid, v. C. (pr. breead or braad). To resemble a person, to take after.

Ex.—*Sha breeads of her moother.*

Braid-band, n. C. (pr. breead-band). A sheaf of corn laid open on a band : it is often so placed in order to dry.

Bramble, n. C. (pr. bramm'l). The fruit of the bramble, or blackberry ; also used as a verb, in the sense of to gather brambles. Dan. Brambær (blackberry).

Brandery, n. C. A wooden frame used in making wells.

Brant, Brat, adj. C. Steep; generally applied to a hill side or road up a steep hill, such as the road down to the North Landing at Flamborough. The word *brat*, which is the Danish form, is still retained in place-names, e. g. Nunburnholme Brat, which is a very steep wooded hillside. The word also is used with a secondary meaning, in the sense of pompous, or stiff in manner. Dan. Brat (steep) ; Swedish Brant (steep).

Ex.—*Aye! but it 's a bit brant; it 's t' rooad t' bait lasses gans ti gether flithers.*

Brash, n. C. Rubbish, refuse.

Brashy, adj. C. Rubbishy ; esp. applied to anything of smaller quality than usual, e. g. sticks for kindling are *brashy* when broken into small bits and half rotten.

Brass, n. C. Impudence, impertinence.

Ex.—*Deean't gie ma neean o' yer brass.*

Brass, n. C. Money, whether gold, silver, or copper.

Ex.—*He 's addled a deal o' brass.—T' brass 'll tak a deal o' getherin.*

Brassend, adj. C. Impudent, without any sense of shame (pr. Brazz'n'd).

Ex.—*Sha 's a brazz'n'd un.*

Brassic, n. C. (pr. brazzic). Wild mustard or charlock, also called Ketlock.

Ex.—*Wa a'e been pullin' brazzics.*

Brat, n. R. A child's pinafore. Welsh Brat (a piece of cloth). This word, so common in parts of the West Riding, is seldom heard in East Yorksh.; *slip* or *pinny* being used instead.

Bratty, bratted, adj. C. Clotty, lumpy, curdled ; applied to cream which does not melt when taken from the bowl, or to milk which is turning sour.

Braunging, adj. F. Coarse in feature.

Ex.—*Sha 's a bold braungin'-leeakin woman.*

Brave, adj. C. Goodly. Dan. Brav (worthy, goodly) ; en brav mand.

Bray, v. C. (pr. braay). To beat violently; to flog.

Ex.—*Ger oot o' t' hus, or ah 'll braay tha.*

Brazzil, n. C. This word, so far as I know, only occurs in the two following phrases, ' as hard as a brazzil,' which is an expression of very frequent occurrence to denote any kind of unusual hardness : if, e.g., the bread is overbaked it is said to be baked 'as hard as a brazil' ; or if the housewife cannot break her Bath brick easily she exclaims ' it 's as hard as a brazzil.' The other expression is ' as fond as a brazzil ' ; here the word *brazzil* probably means a low impudent girl, in which sense it is sometimes used still.

Bread-loaf, n. C. (pr. breead-leeaf). A loaf of bread, whether whole or cut from, as distinguished from cakes, which are so commonly used.

Bread-meal, n. C. Flour from which brown bread is made.

Brede, n. C. Breadth, extent; with the prefix *a* the word signifies in breadth, or thickness. Dan. Bredde (breadth).

Ex.—*T' wall 's nobbut a brick a-brede.—T' brede o' t' beck.—T' brede o' t' trod.—There was a greeat brede o' watther oot at tahms.*

Breeacus, n. C. Breakfast : the form *breecus* is also often used.

Ex.—*Ann, git t' childer ther breeacusses.*

Breear, n. C. The briar.

Ex.—*T' lad 's as sharp as a breear.*

Breek, v. C. To break. This work is also pr. brek, but never break as in Std. Eng.

Bride-door, n. O. The door of the house from which the bride goes to the church on the wedding morning. In the olden days the bride-door was the scene of the wedding festivities, and especially of the races run by the young men of the place, connected with which were many peculiar customs.

Brief, n. C. A begging letter or petition carried by one who has undergone some pecuniary or other misfortune, e. g. the loss of a cow or horse, and who solicits help from those living in the neighbourhood. Dan. En Brev (a letter).

Brigg, n. C. A bridge of all sorts, not excepting that of the violin. Dan. En Bro (a bridge).

Ex.—*Hez t' brigg brok?* said on the occasion of an accident to a fiddle.

Briggs, n. C. A small frame consisting of two pieces of 'wood with cross bars, placed as occasion may require across the cream bowl in a dairy, on which the sile rests.

Brim, adj. F. Exposed, as regards situation; bleak, as on rising ground or the edge of a cliff where the full force of the wind is felt. Dan. En Bryn (a brow of a hill).

Ex.—*Oor hus stan's varry brim.*

Broach, n. C. (pr. brauch). The spire of a church.

Ex.—*You 'll be Bainton brauch.*

Brock, n. R. (1) The badger. (2) C. The cuckoo-spit insect. Dan. En Brok (a badger).

Ex. 2.—*Ah sweeats like a brock*

Brog, n. F. A short piece of a small branch of a tree, esp.

the oak ; such a piece as might be used for a clumsy walking-stick. This word is connected with *break*, and is sometimes used as a verb.

Ex.—*A brog of oak.—He's broggin 'em off.*

Brown-leemers, n. C. Ripe nuts ; nuts brown with ripeness and which consequently slip easily from the hull. This word is not applied to any particular kind of nut, but merely to their state of ripeness generally.

Bruff, adj. C. Florid or fresh-complexioned ; also applied to one of exuberant spirits combined with a certain roughness of manner.

Ex. —*He's a bruff-leeakin' chap.*

Brumm'l-nosed, adj. F. Having a red nose and one thicker than usual, like that of a drunkard.

Brusten, C. (pr. brussen). The past part. of *brust* (burst), which is applied as a prefix in a variety of ways, as *brusten up, brusten oot.*

Buer, n. F. (pr. booer). The common gnat ; another form of the word was *buver.*

Bugh, n. C. (generally pr. bew, but frequently beeaf is the form used). A bough.

Ex.—*T' stee whemm'ld, an' t' beeaf brak, an' ah tumm'ld soss inti t' beck.*

Bullace, n. C. The wild plum. This is sometimes confused with the sloe or blackthorn, the fruit of which is smaller and more oval shaped.

Ex.—*As breet as a bullace.*

Bull-fronts, bull-faces, n. C. The coarse rough hair-grass ; so called from its resemblance to the tufty hair on a bull's forehead.

Bulls, n. C. The long beams in a harrow, which are made of ash, as distinguished from the cross beams or slots, which are generally made of oak : a harrow has four or five bulls. Jutl. D. Buller (beams of a harrow in which the teeth are inserted). In Jutland a one-horse harrow has three ' buller ' each with five teeth.

Bull-seg, n. C. A bull castrated when it is full grown or nearly so.

Bull-spink, n. C. The chaffinch.

Bullstane, n. C. (pr. bullst'n, the *t* being scarcely heard). A stone for sharpening a scythe, or other edged tools ; generally about 14 inches long, rounded, and slightly tapering towards the ends.

Bull-stang, or **Horse-teng**, n. F. The dragon-fly.

Bumble-kites, n. C. (pr. bumm'l-keytes). Common blackberries. The derivation of this word is not clear ; the following seems a probable explanation—*Bumble* means to hum, and sometimes to roll about as loose stones upon a road ; *kite* being the stomach, *bumblekites* would be so called from the fact that they do not lie easily on the stomach, especially when eaten, as they often are, in an unripe state.

> Ex.—*Oor Bess hez been getherin bumml-keytes.*

Bunch, v. C. To kick with the foot or knee. This word must not be confounded with *punch*, which is a blow from the arm ; it is also to be observed that the word is never applied to animals kicking.

> Ex.—‘ *Pleeas 'm, will ya tell Jane to give ower,*’ said a child to the Rector's wife in a Sunday School. ‘ *What does she do ?*’ ‘ *Sha bunches an sha nips.*’—*He was fit ti bunch t' deear doon.*

Bunch, n. F. Eight gleans or handfulls of gleaned wheat bound together is called a bunch.

> Ex.—*Spreead oot t' bunch arses an' then they weean't whemm'l ower* (spoken to a lad setting up bunches in the harvest field).

Burden, n. C. (pr. bodd'n). A bundle of gleanings carried by women on the head : the *boda'n* is always tied in a sheet. Vide **Bottle.**

Busk, n. F. A bush, esp. a low bush. Dan. Busk (bush).

> Ex.—*Ah ho't mysen sadly i yan o' them whin-busks.*

By-name, n. C. A nick-name. Dan. Binavn (nick-name, also surname).

By now, C. By this time.

> Ex.—*It 'll be fit by now.*—*He 'll be there by now.*

Byre, Coo-byre, n. C. A cow-house. Dan. En Buur (a cage).

C.

Cadge, v. C. To collect and convey articles or goods from one place to another, especially corn to the mill. To beg, or live partly by begging or picking up a livelihood anyhow.

Cadger, n. C. One who cadges ; esp. one who collects corn and conveys it to the mill for grinding.

Cael, n. F. Vide **Kale.**

Caff, n. C. Chaff.

Caff-hearted, adj. F. Weak or faint-hearted.

> Ex.—*They 're nobbut caff-hearted uns; they seean gav ower.*

Caingy, adj. C. Fretful, peevish, discontented : a term generally applied to children.

> Ex.—*Thoo caingy lahtle thing: whist, wi ya!*

Cake, v. C. To cackle as a goose, or as a hen when she wants to sit. Dan. At kvække (to cackle).

Call, v. C. To make use of abusive language towards a person; to call a person names to his face; to scold. This word is never used in the ordinary sense of summoning anyone to you; in that case *call of* or *call on* would be the term invariably employed. When one person calls another, and words run high, the pronoun *thou* is used, great emphasis being laid on that word; hence to *thoo* anyone is sometimes the equivalent for calling him names, though in ordinary parlance it is used as a mark of intimacy and friendship.

> Ex.—*Sha called ma shamfull.*—*They were calling yan another like all that.*

Call, n. C. Occasion, necessity.

> Ex.—*He'd neea call ti saay that.*

Call of, call on. Vide **Call**.

Calling, calleting, pres. part. of *Callett*, v. C. (pr. căllin'). To gossip, to spread false reports, to act the talebearer. Generally used in the participial form.

> Ex.—*Sha's nobbut a plain 'un; sha's awlus callin' aboot.*

Calven-cow, n. C. (pr. cauven-coo). A cow which has lately calved. Dan. At kalve (to calve).

Cam, n. C. An earthen ridge; esp. in form of a hedge-bank, which is also called a cam-side. O. N. Kambr; Dan. Kam (a comb, the top of a ridge of hills).

> Ex.—*He's fettlin up t' cam sides.*—*Git them cams cleaned.*

Cam, v. C. To form a cam.

> Ex.—*Thoo's camm'd it ower high.*

Cambril, or **Caum'ril**, n. C. (generally pr. caum'ril). A notched piece of wood used by butchers on which to hang a slaughtered animal by the hind legs.

Canny, adj. C. (1) Knowing, intelligent, skilful. (2) Cautious, careful. (3) Advantageous, convenient. (4) Considerable, as to size, number, &c. *Cannyish* is a modification of *canny*.

> Ex.—*He's a canny soort ov a chap.*—(2) *Thoo'll a'e ti be a bit canny wiv him.*—(3) *It's a canny spot.*—(4) *There'll be a canny bit on 't left.*—Great Ayton is commonly called Canny Yatton.

Cannily, adv. F. Knowingly, carefully, cautiously.

> Ex.—*He mannished cannily eneeaf.*

Cansh, n. F. Vide **Kansh**.

Canty, adj. R. Lively. Jutl. D. Kanter (lively).

> Ex.—*Sha's a canty au'd lass.*

Cap, v. C. To surpass, exceed, excel; to astonish; to put a finishing touch upon. This word is of universal occurrence.

> Ex.—*It caps owt*, i. e. it exceeds everything; it is

astonishing.—*Ah wer fair capp'd ti see 'em.—Ah muck'd it weel t' last backend, an' that capp'd it.—That last bottle capp'd ma* (spoken to a doctor).

Capper, n. C. Super-excellent of its kind.

Ex.—*Noo, sitha ; them 's cappers.*

Carl, n. R. An opprobrious epithet, generally applied to one of weak intellect. Dan. En Karl (a man).

Ex.—*Thoo greeat carl.*

Carlings, n. R. Peas which are prepared in a special manner and eaten on the · Sunday before Palm Sunday, which used to be called Carling Sunday. The custom seems to be more kept up in the West than in the East side of the county, where it has nearly died out.

Carr, n. C. Low marshy land containing the remains of ancient forest trees ; flat land under the plough, of peaty and moist quality as distinguished from *ings*, which are almost always pasture : generally used in the pl. Dan. Kjar (a bog or fen).

Carryings on, n. C. Disorderly proceedings.

Ex.—*Sike carryings on as you nivver heeard tell on.*

Cassen. The ordinary past part. of cast. Vide **Kest.**

Cassons or **Cazzons,** n. C. The dried dung of animals, which is used for fuel sometimes, clay being occasionally mixed with it.   .

Cat-collop, n. F. Cat's-meat.

Cat-haws, n. C. Hawthorn-berries.

Cats and eyes, n. C. Vide **Kitty-keis.**

Cat-whins, n. F. (pr. catchin). The dog-rose.

Causer, Caus'ay, n. C. (pr. cawzer). A paved footpath. A narrow footway paved with cobble-stones or flags, either by the side of a road or across an open country ; a corruption of causeway.—The *causer* must be distinguished from the *ramper*, which is the sloping side of a raised footway.

Ex.—*Ah went thruff t' toon a-top o' t' cawzer.*

Cess, n. C. A rate or tax levied on a parish for any purpose. This word is merely an abbreviation of 'assessment.' It is sometimes used in the sense of force ; e. g. *Lie cess on* was often shouted to persistent blockers at cricket, meaning 'Hit harder.'

Ex.—*We awlus pays wer cess.*

Cess-getherer, n. C. The collector of cess.

Chaff, Chaffs, n. F. The jaw ; most commonly used with reference to the pig ; e. g. *Pig-chaffs.*

Challenge, v. C. (pr. almost in one syllable). To recognise.

Ex.—*He varry seean challeng'd ma.— Sha 's good ti challenge.*

This word is a hunting term. A hound that picks up a scent either in cover or at a check, and gives tongue in rather a short cry is said to challenge.

Chamber, n. C. (pr. chaamer). A room not on the ground floor, whether in a house, stable, or other building, as e. g. an apple-chamber in some out-building. Dan. Kammer (chamber). For further observations on this word vide **House**.

Change, v. C. To turn sour, esp. of milk ; to show signs of decomposition.

Channelly, adv. F. Grandly.

Chatt, n. C. A fir-apple ; a fir-cone.

Chavel, v. C. To chew, to masticate slowly, esp. of chewing the cud ; to nibble at, to gnaw.

    Ex.—*T' dog 's chavvel'd t' raake-shaft sadly.*

Chiffs, n. F. Bran.

Childer, n. C. An old pl. of child, still in common use.

    Ex.—*T' childer 's all gone ti skeeal.*

Chimpings, n. R. Oatmeal grits of rough quality.

Chip up, v. C. To trip up.

    Ex.—*Ah chip'd up ower t' deear-st'n.*

Choops, n. C. Hips, the fruit of the dog-rose.

Chow, v. C. To chew.

Chuff, adj. F. Fresh-complexioned, healthy-looking.

    Ex.—*Sha 's a chuff-leeakin' body.*

Chunter, v. C. To complain, murmur ; also to speak in a low tone, as if muttering to oneself.

    Ex.—*He 's awlus chunterin at ma, an' ah keeps drollin' him on.*

Churlish, adj. F. (pr. chollous). Ill-natured, rough, cold in manner (as applied to persons) ; rough, cold, cheerless (of weather, esp. of wind). Dan. En Karl (a man not of gentle birth).

    Ex.—*T' wind 's varry chollous.*

Clag, v. C. To stick to, as thick mud to the boots. Dan. Klag (clay).

    Ex.—*T' muck clags ti yan's beeats despertly.*

Claggy, adj. C. Sticky, very commonly applied to the roads, esp. at the breaking up of a frost.

    Ex.—*It 's claggy deed for t' hosses plewin'.*

Clam or **clem**, v. C. To pinch ; to suffer hunger or thirst. Dan. At klemme (to pinch).

    Ex.—*Mah insahd 's fair clemm'd.*

Clame, v. C. To cover over, esp. with a sticky substance ; to smear ; to cause to adhere, as a notice on a wall. O. N. Kleima (to smear).

    Ex.—*Thoo mucky ba'a'n, what 's ta been deein claamin*

thisen all ower wi that messment.—They 're claam'd up, i. c. fastened by sticking. *Sha claam'd t' firesteead fra top ti boddom wi' whitenin.*

Clammy, adj. F. Parched with thirst.

Clap, v. C. To give a blow, generally a short and light one; but the word is sometimes applied to a blow of greater force : to pat, as e. g. in the case of a dog; indeed this is a common word for the 'stroking' of an animal, where the motions of the hand are not always alike, sometimes being strokes properly so called, when the hand is drawn more or less horizontally, and sometimes vertical short blows or pats. The word is also used in the sense of an ailment (esp. a cold) settling upon a particular part of the body. The other uses of this word are various and difficult to define, but the above are ordinary ones. Dan. At klappe (to clap the hands); En Klap (a pat, a caress).

Ex.—*That dog o' yours weean't let ma clap him.—T' cau'd clap'd on tiv his chest.—Clap yoursen doon;* i. c. sit down.

Clart, v. C. To smear, to make dirty; also fig. to flatter.

Ex.—*Deean't clart thysen all ower wi muck.*

Clarty, adj. C. Sticky; also dirty, when the stickiness of the thing spoken of is liable to make dirty by touch or otherwise.

Ex.—*T' storm 's owered, an' it's despert clarty noo.*

Clawt, v. C. To scratch with the nails; also formerly used for performing ordinary acts of manual labour.

Clash, v. C. To move about or work under the influence of excitement, to shut with force, to throw down with violence, to flurry, to excite; also used as a noun. Dan. At klaske (to smack).

Ex.—*Sha gans clashin aboot t' hoos.—Sha can't bahd ti be clash'd.*

Cleeas, n. C. Clothes. *Cled* is also commonly used for clothed. Dan. Klæder (clothes).

Ex.—*Them cleeas wants weshin.*

Clean, v. F. To tidy or dress oneself, either with or without the act of washing.

Ex.—Q. Where 's Anne? A. *Cleeanin hersel.*

Cleg, n. C. The horse-fly. Dan. En Klæge (a horse-fly). Icel. Klegg.

Ex.—*Is 't clegs 'at 's plaagin t' gallowa?*

Cletch, n. C. A brood of young birds, esp. chickens, ducks, &c.; a setting of eggs. *Cletching* is also used, but less commonly. Dan. At klække (to hatch).

Ex.—*Pleeas will ya sell ma a cletchin o' your eggs?*

Clever, adj. C. Well-made, good of its kind ; of a tool—that which does its work well.

    Ex.—*It taks a clever knife ti cut it.*

Click, v. C. To snatch ; to inflict a sudden blow, generally accidentally.

    Ex.—*Noo, mi lad, be sharp, click ho'd.—T' hoss threw up it heead an' click'd ma ower t' shoodther.*

Click-net, n. C. A net for catching salmon as they jump : it is held over the water, and so is distinguished from the sweep-net which is drawn through the water.

Clip, v. C. To cut short off, as wool from a sheep, in which sense this word is generally used. Dan. At klippe (to clip).

    Ex.—*That grass wants clippin.*

Clippin' tahm, n. C. The season for sheep-shearing.

Clock, n. C. A beetle (of various kinds).

    Ex.—*We 've getten a vast o' them clocks iv oor hoos.*

Clog, n. C. A log of wood: vide **Yule-clog**. Dan. En Klods (a log).

    Ex.—Q. What is that wood for? A. *Them 's clogs for t' stack boddums.*

Closed, part. C. Closed up. Oppressed with a cold, esp. in the chest, and when there is consequently a difficulty in breathing; the condition of what is termed a 'surfeit of cold.' The word *closed* is occasionally used singly, but in nine cases out of ten the expression is *closed up.*

    Ex.—*Ah 's full o' cold; ah 's fair closed up.*

Clot, n. C. A clod of earth.

Clout, n. C. (pr. cloot). A piece of cloth used for any purpose, or a torn piece ; a rag. Vide **House-clout**. Sometimes applied to a table-cloth. Dan. En Klud (a rag).

Clout, n. C. A sharp or heavy blow, generally when inflicted on the person ; also used as a verb.

    Ex.—*He catch'd him a bonny clout ower t' heead.—Ah 'll cloot thi lug for tha.*

Clubster, n. C. The stoat. So called probably from the character of the animal's tail.

Cludder v. F. (pr. cludther). To collect or mass together, to congregate.

    Ex.—*Ah seed 'em cludtherin up.*

Clum, adj. C. Sodden, heavy (esp. of land difficult to work), clayey. Dan. Klam (clammy).

    Ex.—*T' land 's that clum, it tews t' hosses weeantly.*

Clunter, v. C. (pr. cluntther). To tread heavily ; to make a clattering noise with the feet. Dan. At klunte (to jog, to stump along).

Clunter, Cluntering, n. C. Confusion ; sometimes also used of a confused noise, esp. with the feet in walking.
> Ex.—*They made a despert clunterin' wi' ther feet i t' yard last neet.—Noo, mahnd, if they decan't com doon wi a clunter.*

Coat, n. F. (pr. cooat). A gown, a dress.
> Ex.—*Sha 'd a new silk cooat on.*

Cobble, cobble-steean, n. C. A smooth stone about the size of one's fist, or larger, such as is used for common paving. *To cobble* is commonly used of throwing stones generally.
> Ex.—*Thoo young raggil, give ower cobblin them geslins, or ah 'll wahrm tha.*

Cobble-tree, n. C. The piece of wood which connects the two swingle-trees to the plough-beam ; it is, in fact, a large swingle-tree, and is sometimes called the ' maistther swingle-tree.' It is of course only requisite when two horses plough abreast. Dan. At koble (to unite).

Cobby, adj. C. Cheerful, lively ; well (in health).
> Ex.—*As cobby as a lop.—Ah feels as cobby as owt.*

Coble, n. C. (pr. cōble). A fishing-boat of peculiar build, and in ordinary use on the Yorkshire coast.

Cockrose, n. C. The common scarlet poppy, called also *cuprose* ; but *cockrose* is by far the commoner name.

Cod, n. C. A bag, hence a pod or shell of peas, beans, and the like, called a pea-cod, bean-cod, &c. Jutl. D. Koje (a pea-shell).

Codlings, n. R. A game of the cricket type, the bat being a stout straight hazel stick, the ball a piece of wood or stick 2½ inches long, and the wicket a round hole about an inch deep and 4 inches across.

Coif, n. R. A cap. O. Fr. Coif.
> Ex.—*Ah mun a'e mi mucky feeace weshed an' a cleean coif on.*

Collar, n. C. A halter for securing a horse in a stable : the collar used to be made of hemp, but is now commonly of leather. Vide **Head-stall**. Sometimes the word is applied to the blinkered bridle of a cart-horse.

Collop, n. C. A slice of meat of any kind, but generally applied to bacon. The spleen of a pig was generally called cat-collop, because it would be fried for the cat.

Collop Monday, n. C. The Monday before Ash Wednesday, on which day collops of bacon and eggs are eaten, according to an old custom.

Come again, v. C. To appear as the ghost of one dead. Dan. En Gjenganger (an apparition).

Come by, v. C. (In prn. the *m* of the *come* is scarcely audible, the sound of the two words approximating to cu' bahy.) This expression is never used but in the imperative mood, and is equivalent to 'get out of the road,' 'make way,' &c. It is of very frequent occurrence, much more so than any equivalent ; and is perhaps most commonly heard when addressed to children and animals.

Ex. *Cu'bahy wi yer.*

Come-to, n. C. (pr. cum-teea). A place or abode.

Ex.—*He 'll want it for a cum-teea,* he will require it as a place to stay at.

Comfra, n. R. Home, place of abode (old settlement).

Ex.—*Wheer 's his comfra ?*

Company, n. C. (pr. cump'ny). A gathering together of people, with an object ; e. g. at church, at a concert, entertainment, &c. It is noteworthy how general the use of this word is, in preference to all others of a like meaning ; e. g. the word 'congregation' is seldom used in the way it usually is, but *company* takes its place.

Ex.—*We 'd a good cump'ny at chetch last neet.*

Conceit, v. F. (pr. consate). To suppose, to be of opinion.

Ex.—*He consated 'at it wer t' uther man.*

Conny, adj. C. The precise meaning of this very common word is not altogether apparent. I am inclined to think that the primary meaning is 'pretty' or 'comely' in appearance, 'neat' and 'tidy'; but there is also the sense of 'small' which the word has, and which, in fact, is its ordinary signification : e. g. *a conny bit* is a small piece ; it is also added to the word *lahtle* much in the same way in which we add *tiny* in ordinary English to the same word, except that *conny* generally comes after *lahtle.* There seems to be a connection between this and the Dan. word *kjøn,* handsome, or comely. *En kjøn sum* means a handsome sum (of money). It is difficult to see how the sense of smallness is arrived at, except perhaps through the idea of neatness.

Ex.—*Sha 's a lahtle conny body.* — Q. Will you have any more pudding ? A. *Just a conny bit.*

Consumpted, part. C. Suffering from consumption.

Ex.—*Mah wo'd, bud he diz look a bad look ! ah doot he 's consumpted.*

Continuy, v. C. (The con- is pr. distinctly, though without emphasis.) To continue.

Ex.—*Ah doot he weean't continuy lang* (i. e. live long).

Contrary, v. C. (pr. contrāry). To contradict.

Ex.—*He didn't leyke ti be contraried.*

Coom, n. C. Dust, particles of refuse : most frequently applied to saw-dust, called *saw-coom,* and the refuse of malt, which is called *malt-cums.* O. N. Kam (a speck of dust).

Coo-tie, n. C. Vide **Tie.**

Cots, n. F. Tangled masses; esp. of wool on a sheep— i. e. wool matted together; hence the adj. *cotty.*
Them 's nobbut cotty 'uns.

Cotter, v. C. (pr. cotther). To become entangled or twisted together.
Ex. *They 're all cotthered tigither.*

Cotty, adj. C. Vide **Cots.**

Coul, n. C. (pr. as 'coal' approximately). A swelling on the body, esp. when caused by a blow. Dan. Koll (a knoll or round hill-top).
Ex.—*It 's risen a girt coul atop o' mah heead.*

Coul, v. C. (pr. as preceding word). To scrape towards one, to rake together.
Ex.—*He 's coulin muck off t' rooads.*

Coul-rake, n. C. A scraper for removing the mud, &c., from roads, or ashes from a fireplace, &c.
Ex.— *Git t' ass oot aback o' t' hood wi t' coul-rake.*

Counting, n. C. (pr. coontin'). Arithmetic. Similarly *counter* is the equivalent for arithmetician.
Ex.—Q. How is your boy getting on at school? A. *He 's gitten inti coontin'.*

Cow-clags, n. F. (pr. coo-clag). Dirt adhering to the buttocks of cattle. Vide **Clag.**

Cow-gate, n. C. Pasturage for a cow; lit. cow-walk or way. Dan. En Kogang (pasturage for cows).

Cow-pasture, n. C. (pr. coo-pastthur). A pasture-field that is never mown : it is generally for convenience close to the farmhouse.

Cowstripling, n. R. The cowslip.

Crab, v. C. To speak disparagingly of; to give a bad name to : also in passive sense, to be provoked.
Ex.—*He crab'd mah 'oss,* i. e. He gave my horse a bad name. — *He was crab'd when he heeard tell on 't.*

Crack, v. C. To brag, to talk boastfully.
Ex.—*It 's nowt ti crack on.*

Crack, n. C. (1) A short space of time; a moment. (2) A chat; in pl. news.
Ex.—*Ah 'll be back iv a crack.* — *We 're like to hev a crack tigither.* — *What cracks ?* i. e. What news?

Cradle, n. R. Three long teeth or prongs attached to a scythe and having a like curve with it. It was very commonly used some thirty years ago for mowing oats, unless the crop was very heavy, when a 'bow' was used instead.

Crake, n. C. (pr. crecak). Any bird of the crow tribe ; generally applied to the rook. Dan. En Krage (a crow).
Ex.—Q. *Wheer 's Tom ?* A. *He 's flaying creeaks.*

Cramble, v. C. (pr. cramm'l). To walk haltingly, as when disabled by rheumatism or other infirmity ; to hobble.
　　Ex.—*Ah 's hard set ti cramm'l aboot.*
Cramble, n. R. A crooked bough of a tree. Sometimes also used for lengths of oak in small branches, or for a roughly made walking-stick.
　　Ex.—*Ah stood mah au'd yak cramml agaan t' yat.*
Crambly, adv. (strictly), but used as an adj. C. (pr. crammly). Not firm on the legs ; tottery.
　　Ex.—*Ah 's nobbut varry crammly. — Willie 's a crammly au'd man gotten.*
Cranch, v. C. To grind anything with the teeth, by which the sound of the grinding is heard.
Craps, n. C. Pieces of skin left after 'rendering' fat into lard. *Craps* are thought a delicacy, and are eaten generally at breakfast or tea.
Crashes, n. F. Water-cresses.
Creckits, n. F. Cricket. *Laakin at creckits* was formerly the general expression for playing at cricket. The final *s* is now generally omitted.
Cree, v. C. To soak in order to soften. To simmer before a fire.
Creel, n. C. A frame on legs, upon which pigs are placed after they have been slaughtered.
Creeper, n. R. A small globular-shaped piece of lead with long hooks (four in number) fixed into it and attached to a line. It is used by eel-fishers for drawing up night-lines from the bottom of a river to the bank.
Cricket, n. F. A low stool with four legs, generally with a hole in the centre for lifting it. Swedish D. Krakk (a stool).
Croodle, v. C. To crouch down and contract oneself into as small a space as possible.
　　Ex.—*When they seed ma, they all croodled doon.*
Crook, n. C. (pr. creeak, sometimes crewk). (1) A hinge or hook on which gates and doors are hung. (2) A disease in sheep.
　　Ex.—*T' lads 'as rahv'd t' yat off t' creeaks.*
Crouse, Cruse, adj. C. Feeling pride in anything, elated with, lively, happy ; in good spirits. Dan. At kruse (lit. to curl) ; at kruse for en (to make a great fuss about one).
　　Ex.—*Sha wer varry cruse on her new dhriss.—Thoo need na be sae cruse, mun. — Thoo 's ower cruse.*
Crowdy, n. F. Oatmeal porridge, made either with milk or water.
Crow-prate, n. R. A rookery.
Crown, n. C. (pr. croon). The centre or middle of a road or causey.
　　Ex.—*Gan i' t' croon o' t' rooad.*

Cruds, n. C.   Curds.
Cuddy, n. C.   (1) The hedge-sparrow.   (2) A donkey.
Cuddy-handed, adj. F.   Left-handed.
Cum, n. F. (the same word as *combe*, but pr. rather shorter). Long and deep-lying meadow or grazing land.   Wel. Cwm (a hollow).
Currant-berry, n. C. (pr. corr'n-berry).   The red currant.
Cush-pet, n. C.   A term of endearment addressed to a cow : the common call for a cow being *cush-cush*.
   Ex.—*Cush-pet; reet tha.*

D.

Daffle, v. C.   To be confused.   Also used in an active sense, To grow weak and imbecile.
   Ex.—*It 's oft varry dafflin when yan 's putten oot o' t' way.*
Daft, adj. C.   Dull, stupid, foolish.
   Ex.—*What 's ta stannin' leeakin seea daft for ? Tak ho'd o' t' hoss heead.*
Daggle, deggle, v. F.   Vide **Degg**.
Dale, n. C.   The common name for a valley both in the Wold district of the East Riding and in Cleveland ; e. g. Deep-dale, Cobdale, Thixendale, &c.   Icel. Dalr (a valley).
Dale-end, n. C.   The point where a dale opens out into wider country.
Dale-head, n. C.   The point where a dale begins to form in the hills.
Dap, adj. R.   Full-fledged, as young birds in a nest.
   Ex.—*If nobbut ah 'd ga'en ti skeeal a bit, afoor ah wer dap, ah sud a'e been yan o' them Parliment men noo.*
Dap, v. F.   To move lightly, with short and quick steps ; to trip along.
Dar, v. C.   To dare.
   Ex.—*He didn't dar ti gan.*
Dark, v. C.   To listen unperceived ; to stand unnoticed : also used of a dog scenting, when not in motion.
   Ex.—*What 's ta darkin at ?* said to one caught listening.
Daub, v. C.   To smear ; to cause to adhere.
   Ex.—*Steeath'd an' daubed. — Thoo mucky bairn ; what 's ta been daubin' thysen ower wi ?*
Daul'd oot, part. F.   Wearied, or tired out.
   Ex.—*Ah 's fair daul'd oot.*
Daytal, adj. C.   By the day.   This word is used in such connections as *Daytalman*, i. e. a man who works by the day ; *daytal-work*, i. e. work done by a day labourer.   Dan. Dagetal (number of days), I dagetal (day by day), Dagetals Arbejde (work by the day).

Dead, n. C. (pr. deead). Death.

Ex.—*Ah 's ommast flaay'd ti deead.*

Deaf, adj. F. (pr. deeaf). Without fruit, barren, empty, blighted. This word is commonly used with regard to trees, and fruit, such as nuts, when there is no kernel; also applied to land which does not grow good crops. Dan. En döv Nöd (a nut without a kernel). Icel. Daufr (without savour).

Deary, adj. C. Small, undersized; generally followed by *lahtle*.

Ex.—*It 's nobbut a deary lahtle thing.*

Deave, v. R. (pr. deeave). To deafen. Dan. At döve (to deafen).

Ex.—*It 's fit ti deeave yan.*

Deed, n. C. Doings. This word is of very frequent occurrence, and is used in either a bad or a good sense: e. g. *Throng deed* (busy work); *queer deed* (questionable transactions); *dowly deed* (a badtime of it, as when a person has a sick household); *poor deed* (a thin attendance, as at a meeting, &c.); *great deed, sad deed*, &c., &c. Sometimes also the word is used without any qualifying adjective, and in the form of a question, as when a man comes home from a fair, and the wife asks him, 'Well, what sort of *deed* was there?' In short, it is only by a close acquaintance with the dialect that the right application of the word can be ensured. Dan. Daad (deed).

Ex.—*Sike deed as nivver was.* — *There 'll be bonny deed inoo if they deean't mahnd.*

Degg, v. C. To sprinkle with water. Other forms of this word are *daggle* and *deggle*. Dan. At dugge (to bedew); also, though rarely, at dygge.

Ex.—*Fetch a sup o walther ti degg them cleeas wi.*

Delf-rack, n. F. Shelves and bars attached to the dresser in kitchens, on and behind which plates and dishes are arranged, often up to the ceiling.

Deny, v. F. To decline, to refuse.

Ex.—*He denied going*, i. e. he refused to go. — *He nivver denied ma nowt 'at ah ax'd him.*

Desperate, adv. C. (pr. despe't or desprit). This is one of the commonest intensives—equivalent to 'very.'

Ex.—*Ah 's despe't dhry.*

Dess, n. C. A portion, and generally a clearly defined and regular portion, of any piled up mass. The most common use of the word is that of a rectangular block of hay cut out of a haystack, generally about 2½ feet square. Jutl. D. At dese Törv (to pile peats).

Ex.—*We 're middlin' off for haay; wa 've nobbut ta'en three desses oot o' t' new stack.*

This word is also sometimes used as a verb, viz. *to dess up*, meaning to pile up neatly.

Devil-screeamer, n. F. The common swift.

Dib, v. C. To dip. Also used as a noun.

Ex.—*Ah gal a bonny dib i' t' dyke yisttherda* (said by one who had accidentally tumbled into a river).

Didder, v. C. (pr. didther). To shiver. This word has much the same meaning as *dodder* : vide inf.

Differ, v. C. To wrangle, to quarrel.

Ex.—*T' weyfe an' him varry seean started ti differ.*

Differing, n. C. A wrangling or quarrel.

Ex.—*There was part differins amang 'em. — They 'd sad differin bouts.*

Dike, n. C. A ditch ; a long bank of earth ; a river. This word has a wide signification, being used for a small ditch as well as for a wide river ; it is also used figuratively, as *Ah 's all doon t' dyke*, which signifies 'I am unwell.' Jutl. D. Et Dige, (1) a wall. (2) a ditch.

Dill, v. C. To lessen or take away pain ; to deaden pain temporarily.

Ding, deng, v. C. To throw or thrust violently, to throw down, to strike, to wrench off. Dan. At dænge (to heap blows on a person) ; Icel. Dengja (to beat).

Ex.—*Ah 'll ding tha on ti t' fleear. — He ding'd t' decar off t' creeaks.*

Dingle, v. C. To tingle. Dan. At dingle (to swing to and fro).

Ex.—*Mah ears dingles like a bell.*

Docken, n. C. The common dock.

Ex.—*Ah deean't care a docken for 't.*

Dodded, adj. C. Hornless (cattle).

Dodder, v. C. (pr. dodther). To shake or tremble as with cold or fear.

Dodderums, n. F. (pr. dodthrums). A shaking or trembling.

Ex.—*Ah 's all i t' ditherums dodthrums.*

Doddery, adj. C. (pr. dodthry). Shaky.

Doddings, n. C. The clippings of matted and dirty wool cut from the hind quarters of sheep.

Doff, v. F. To take off clothes.

Ex.—*Doff them au'd cleeas.*

Dog-choops, n. C. The fruit of the dog-rose.

Dog-loups, n. F. The vacant spaces between two houses.

Dollop, n. F. A large quantity, either of things or persons ; a lot.

Ex.—*It did ma a dollop o' good.*

Dolly, n. C. A tub for washing, made like a low barrel, and furnished with a dolly-stick or rod with a handle, and terminating at the lower end with four prongs fitted into a flat piece of wood, which gives it almost the appearance of a stool. The dolly is generally used for washing heavy articles in order to economise labour. Also used as a verb.

Ex.—*Be shahp, lass, an' git them cleeas dollied.*

Don, adj. F. Clever, skilful ; esp. in manual labour. Dan. At danne (to shape, mould).

Ex.—*Sha 's a don hand at it, is t' au'd woman.*

Don, v. F. To put on clothes.

Ex.—*Don thi bonnet, bairn.*

Donky, donk, adj. C. Damp. This word is another form of 'dank.' Jutl. D. At dynke (to sprinkle things with water).

Ex.—*T' haay 's quiet donky tonnd;* i. e. the hay has turned quite damp.

Donnot, n. F. A good-for-nothing person ; a do-nought.

Ex.—*He 's a donnot at it.*

Door-cheek, n. C. The side-post of a doorway.

Door-sill, n. C. The threshold of a door. Jutl. D. Dörsil (threshold), syld (foundation-stones of a house).

Door-stead, n. C. (The pr. of this word is deear-steead, the first part of the word being so pronounced in all connections.) The whole framework of a door.

Door-stone, n. C. (pr. deear-stan, the *t* in *stan* being very slightly sounded). The large stone at the entrance of an outer doorway.

Doubler, dubler, n. R. A large dish, such as pies are made in, or for putting meat on. This old word is wellnigh obsolete, it being now hardly ever, if ever, heard, except in the expression *Sold up, dish, pan ana doubler,* or *dish and doubler,* implying a state of utter bankruptcy.

Ex.—*Au'd Joe 's selled up, dish an' dubler at last.*

Doubt, v. C. (pr. doot). To be pretty sure of a thing, when the event implied or expressed involves unpleasant or more serious consequences. The equivalent *fear,* or *afraid,* is never used in the ordinary sense in which it is spoken ; e. g. we should never say in the dialect, 'I am afraid' (it 's going to rain, &c.), but *I doubt,* &c.

Ex.—*Ah doot sha 's boun' ti be badly.*

Of words in commonest use this is one of the few that are of French importation.

Doven, v. R. (pr. döven). To slumber, to doze. Dan. At dovne (to be lazy, to decline—used of pain dying away). This word is heard more in the East than in the North Riding.

Dow, v. R. To improve in health. I do not remember to have heard this word except in the expression *He nowther* *dees nor dows*, i. e. 'He neither dies nor grows better.' It is used in a somewhat similar sense in West Jutland, e. g. Det duer ikke til noget (it is good for nothing).

Dowly, adj. C. (pr. between dōly and dowly). Sorrowful, dull, low-spirited, melancholy, gloomy, poorly, depressing. This expressive and much-used word is applied to persons, things, places, and conditions in any of the above senses. Dan. Daarlig; Jutl. D. Dōle (poor, worthless).

> Ex.—*Oor Bess has been badly a lang whahl; sha's had a dowly tahm.—It's a dowly hay-tahm been; ah doot it'll a'e gitten spoilt.—It's a weeant dowly spot.—Ah feels varry dowly widoot her.*

Down, v. C. To knock or throw down.

> Ex.—*He doon'd him wiv his neeaf.*

Downwards, adv. F. (pr. doonwards). This word, as applied to the wind, signifies westerly, though I have only heard it used so in a part of the East Riding.

> Ex.—*T' wind's gotten doonwards.*

Dowp, n. R. The carrion crow.

Dozzend, adj. R. Withered, shrunk.

> Ex.—*Them apples is sadly dozzened.*

Draff, n. F. Refuse, rubbish, brewer's grains. Jutl. D. Drav (grains).

Drape, n. C. (pr. dreeap). A cow not in milk. This word may spring from the same source as the Dan. Draabe (drop).

Draught, n. C. A team of horses, together with cart, waggon, &c. Sometimes it seems to be used for the cart or waggon only, as in the phrase, *Ah rade iv a draught* (meaning a cart); but whether in such an expression the horses are included, it is hard to decide.

Drawn - straw, n. C. Straw sorted or pulled through the hands until rough pieces are separated from it, and thus fairly straight and clean thatching straw is the result.

> Ex.—Q. Why have you two men at work tying up straw? A. *Yan on em's dthrawin.*

Dream-holes, n. O. The holes in a church tower to allow the sound of bells to escape freely; also applied to holes in towers for the admission of light and air, and possibly for keeping a look-out therefrom.

Dree, adj. C. (pr. dhree). Long and troublesome, tedious. Dan. Drōi (large, heavy), et drōit arbeide (a tough piece of work).

> Ex.—*It's a dree job cutting these beeans; they're all ankled tigither seea.*

Dreep, v. F. (pr. dhreeap). To drop slowly; to cause to drop slowly. Dan. At draabe (to cause to drop).

Ex.—*If 'ah tumml'd inti t' dyke an' gat ool ageean, ah su'd natthrally want ti be dhreeap'd.*

Dress, v. C. It is difficult to determine the usages of this word as differing from those of standard English ; perhaps the commonest uses are (1) to tidy, the word *up* being added generally ; and (2) to chastise or flog. Also used as a noun (dressing).

Ex.—*When his faather coms yam he 'll varry seean dhriss him up.*

Drinkings, drinking tahm, n. C. A short meal in the middle of an afternoon during *hay-tahm* or harvest, consisting generally of bread-and-cheese and beer.

Drite, drate, v. F. To utter an indistinct sound; to speak thickly ; to lack clearness in tone ; to drawl in speaking. Jutl. D. Trate (to play the fool).

Drity, adj. F. Indistinct in tone or utterance, whether as regards the human voice or a musical instrument, &⬛; slow in speaking.

Ex.—*It 's nut drity* (said of the tone of an old violin which was of excellent quality and responded readily to the slightest variations of bowing).

Droll on, v. F. To draw on by feigned argument, and so to satisfy one who can ill endure the existing state of things. A mother frequently puts off a troublesome child in this way.

Ex.—*He dizn't want it, bud ah keeps drollin' him on.*

Droppy, adj. C. Very rainy ; i.e. when the rain is of long continuance.

Droughty, adj. C. (pr. dthrooty). Dry, parching. This word is seldom used except with the post-positive *tahm* ; a *dthrooty-tahm* is not so much a season of dryness caused by lack of rain, as that caused (often very rapidly) by winds, especially in March, which seem at once to dry up the land and make it hard. The word *drought* is but little used.

Ex.—*We 've had a desprit dhrooty tahm.*

Droup, v. F. (pr. dhroop). To drench.

Ex.—*Drouping wet.—Ah wer drouped wi wet.*

Duds, n. R. Clothes, rags.

Ex.—*Ah doff'd my duds.—Ah off wi my duds an' jump'd inti t' walther.*

Dundy-cow, n. C. The ladybird.

Durdum, n. F. (pr. doddom, and durrum). Noisy or riotous proceedings ; confused disturbance, as with children at play ; a drunken brawl, &c. Wel. Dwrdd (a stir).

Ex.—*What a durrum t' baa'ns is makkin.*

Dwine, v. F. (pr. dwahin). To waste away, to wither. Jutl. D. At dvine (to pine away).

E.

Eam, n. O. An uncle. Germ. Oheim (uncle—poetical).
Earand, n. C. (pr. earan). An errand. Dan. En Ærende (an errand).
Earn, v. F. (pr. yearn ; or perhaps more nearly as yen). To cause milk to curdle.
Earning, earning-skin, n. F. (pr. yearning or yenning). That which is used for curdling milk. Rennet.
Easings, n. C. (pr. easins). The eaves of any building, particularly of thatched houses. Jutl. D. Ovs (eaves).
Een, n. R. Eyes (the old plural). The singular *ee* is also used. Dan. Öie (eye), pl. öine.
　　Ex.—*He 's gotten tweea black een.—Bang her amang her een.*
E'en, n. R. Evening ; seldom heard except when used for the eve of a Holy Day, as *Kess'mass E'en, St. Mark's E'en,* &c.
Een-holes, n. R. The eye-sockets. Dan. Et öje hul (eye-socket).
Efter, prep. C. (pr. eftther). After. Dan. Efter (after). This word is also used in a verbal sense, e. g. *Ah efther him* (I went after him).
　　Ex.—*It 's a bit eftther t' tahm.*
Efter-clecking, n. F. A brood of chickens, goslings, &c., hatched after the first brood of the season. This word is also applied to the brood in the pl. number.
　　Ex.—*Them fahve geslins is eftther-cleckins.*
Efternoon, n. C. (pr. efttherneean). Afternoon. Morning, as distinguished from afternoon, is always termed forenoon. *Morning*, when used in the dialect, means early morning, and forenoon the interval between breakfast and dinnertime.
Eldin, n. C. Fuel, or kindling of any kind, generally wood or ' turves.' This word is not so common as it was a few years ago, and when used now the word *fire* is sometimes prefixed, which is quite redundant. Dan. Ild (fire). Jutl. D. Ilding (firewood).
　　Ex.—*Noo, Bobby, gan an' late some eldin.*
Eller, n. F. The alder-tree. Dan. En El (an alder), pl. eller. There is a house near Newton-on-Ouse called Ellers, hence derived.
Elsin, n. C. A shoemaker's awl. I have heard this word called *nelsin*, which is of course a corruption of *an elsin*.

End-deck, n. F. The tail-board of a cart, more commonly called end-door.

End nor side, F. Synonymous with 'nothing'; esp. in the expression 'to make nothing of.'
Ex.—*They meead nowther end nor sahd on 't.*

Endways, to get, R. This expression is sometimes used to denote success—to do well.
Ex.—*Aye, ah heerd he 'd gitten endways.*

Entry, n. C. The space, greater or smaller, immediately within the entrance of a house.

Esh, n. C. The ash-tree. Dan. En Esk (an ash-tree).

Even down, adj. F. Straight down, perpendicular.

Expect, v. C. To suppose, to understand (from hearsay). There are few words of Latin derivation so commonly used as this.
Ex.—*Ah expect seea.—Ah expect there 's boun ti be a stir i t' toon.*

F.

Fadge, v. C. To make way by a motion between a walk and a trot. The word is applied to man or horse or other animal. Vide **Fidge-Fadge,** also used as a noun.
Ex.—*Ah 's just fadged on wi t' au'd meer.—Sha kept him at a fadge* (spoken of a man and woman when the woman walked quicker than the man could).

Faff, v. R. To blow in puffs.

Fain, adj. and adv. R. Glad, gladly. Although this word is more classical and poetical than dialectical in its use, yet I here insert it because, although it has fallen into disuse among the more educated classes as a spoken word, it is still heard occasionally with the older country folk. It is matter for regret that such a good old word should be so nearly extinct.
Ex.—*Sha 's fain ti be wiv her muther ageean.—Ah 'd fain a'e gitten yam ageean.*

Fair, adv. C. Entirely, wholly, altogether. Also used adjectively, in the sense of easy, in a few phrases, such as *fair ti see, fair ti tell,* &c.
Ex.—*Ah wer fair capp'd ti see 'em.—Ah 's fair bet wi 't.— T' maistther wer fair ranty when he seed what t' lad had deean.*

Fair up, v. C. To become fair weather again.
Ex.—*Ah think it 'll fair up inoo.*

Fairlings, adv. C. (pr. fairlins). Fairly, clearly.
Ex.—*Ah can't ken whau it is fairlins.*

Fairy-butter, n. C. A fungus growing on dead trees, &c.

Falter, v. F. (pr. fawter). To knock the awns off the barley-grains by means of the faltering-iron, an instrument made for that purpose. The faltering-iron has gone out of use, 'humblers' being used instead.

Fan', fand, fun', fund, pf. tense of *finnd,* C. The *d* final is seldom heard, the forms *fan'* and *fun'* being about equally common. Dan. Fandt, p. part of finde (to find).

Ex.—*They varry seean fan' it oot.—A'e ya fun' it yet?*

Fantickle, n. C. (pr. fahnticle and fanticle). A freckle.

Far, adj. C. Further, more distant. Dan. Fjermer (far, or 'off' horse); N. Fjerr; Icel. Fjarr.

Ex.—Q. 'Where's your husband?' A. *He's plewin yonder i t' far clooas.*

Farantly, adj. R. (pr. fareantly). Well-behaved, orderly.

Fare, v. F. To go on, to approach, to draw near, to succeed. Dan. At fare (to go).

Ex.—*Sha fares o' cau'vin.*

Far-end, n. C. The end, as opposed to the beginning of anything. The words *beginning* and *end* are not used, but instead, *start* and *finish,* as of a piece of work; *fore-end* and *back-end,* or *far-end,* as of a man's life or other period of time; *first-end* and *last-end,* as of a book, or other matter.

Farness, n. F. Distance.

Ex.—*It's sum farness.*

Far-side, n. C. The right-hand side of a horse; the left being called the *nar-side. Far-side* is used in other ways, e.g. the far-side of a field, road, &c. Dan. Frahaands Hest (the right-hand side of a horse); Jutl. D. Fier Hest (off-horse).

Fash, v. C. To create worry and anxiety (generally about small matters) either to oneself or others. Dan. D. Fasse (to exert oneself to do anything).

Ex.—*Shq's a werrity body; sha oft fashes hersen when there's ni 'casion.*

Fast, adj. C. At a standstill, esp. in work, from any cause.

Ex.—*Ah's nivver fast for a job.—Whyah, mun, he'll lend ya t' galloway hard eneeaf; he weean't see ya fast, howivver.*

Fat-dabs, n. F. A term for a fat, awkward person or child.

Ex.—*Sha's a fat-dabs.*

Fat-rascal, n. C. A tea-cake made with currants, butter, &c. Very common in the Whitby district, but not known in the East Riding.

Faugh, n. C. (pr. fawf). Fallow-land, used also as a verb. Jutl. D. Falg (fallow-land), falge (to fallow).

Ex.—*Wa mun start wi t' fawf i t' morn.—It'll be ti fawf ti-year.*

Feck, n. O. The largest part of anything; might. There may be a connection between this word and Danish fik, the past tense of faa (to get). The adjectives *feckful* (strong), and *feckless* (feeble), seem also to have died out.

Ex.—*T' feck on 't 's deean.*

Fele, v. F. To hide away: commonly used in the participial form, *felt*. In playing the game of hide-and-seek, the cry ' felto' was generally raised by the one who had hidden; the same word is also applied to the game itself. Dan. At fjæle (to hide).

Ex.—*They fun' it felt awaay i t' Bahble.—He had it felten undher t' mat. —They 'd felt t' tweea kags o' gin amang t' whins.*

Fellon, n. C. A disease common with cattle, esp. cows : it arises in the first instance from cold.

Felly, v. F. To break up fallow land : this is done by means of dragging, plowing, and harrowing. Dan. At fælge (to break up fallow).

. **Felt, felten**, F. part. of fele. Hidden. Vide **Fele**.

Feltrix, n. C. A disease common with horses, in the course of which lumps filled with watery matter appear underneath the belly. A continuance of cold and wet weather is supposed to induce the disease, as also the habit of allowing the animals to lie out of doors too late in the year.

Fend, v. C. To provide for; to look after; to manage. Jutl. D. At fænte (to catch, to seek with care and toil).

Ex.—*He 'll varry seean a'e ti fend for hissen.*

Fend, n. C. Ability and readiness to act for oneself, manage- · ment. There are few words more expressive in our dialect than this : its meaning will perhaps be best understood by saying that one who has no *fend* about him is a poor helpless creature. The word is often applied to sick people who cannot do anything for themselves.

Ex.—*Sha 's neea fend aboot her, na mair 'an nowt.*

Fendable, adj. C. Contriving, capable.

Ex.—*Sha's a very fendable lass.*

Fest, v. F. To bind by an agreement. Dan. At fæste (to . secure), fæste sig bort (hire oneself).

Fest, fest-penny, n. C. Earnest-money paid by a master to a servant on engaging him. Called also *Arles*, or *God's-penny*. The sum thus paid generally varies from a shilling to half-a-crown, but sometimes more than this is paid. The word is only applied with regard to servants hired under the Martinmas system. Dan. Fæstepenge (earnest-money). This word is used for the fine paid on taking over a leasehold farm.

Ex.—*Ah's ta'en t' fest.* — *Ah weean't tak t' fest back; ah'll gan.*

Fet, v. C. To last out; to keep one supplied with. Dan. At föde (to nourish, supply with food).

Ex.—*Them cauls 'll fet ma whahl t' backend.* — *A'e ya what 'll fet ya a twelvemonth?*

Fetch, v. C. To give (a blow).

Ex.—*He fetch'd ma a big clout ower t' heead.*

Fettle, v. C. To prepare, put into order, get ready, arrange, repair; frequently the adv. *up* is added to the verb, the sense being the same.

Ex.—*Fettle an' gan.* — *Wa mun fettle up wer hoos afoor t' backend.* — *You far sahd o' t' clooas is varry sumpy; ah doot werstuff weean't be i' ower good fettle for leading.* — *Ah wasn't i' varry good fettle yisttherda.*

Few, n. C. A number, amount. The application of this word is peculiar, being used as an adjective in the ordinary sense, and as a substantive, in which latter case it is preceded by a qualifying adjective, generally *good*; but others, such as *middlinish, gay, poorish,* &c., are not uncommon qualifications. Dan. Faa (few).

Ex.—Q. 'Are there many mushrooms in that field?' A. *Aye! there's a middlin' few on 'em* (equivalent to a pretty good number). — *Ah see'd a good few bo'ds amang t' tonnups yisttherda.* — *There was a good few at chetch last Sunda.*

Fezzon, v. R. To lay hold of greedily or fiercely; to eat with avidity. This word was in commoner use a few years ago. It is followed by *on* or *in.* *Fezzon* has the same root as *fest.*

Ex.—*He's fezzonin' intiv it* (i. e. He is eating greedily).

Fick, v. C. (pr. fick or feek). To move the feet with a somewhat rapid motion, as an animal does when under restraint in a recumbent posture; to struggle with the feet in order to get free. The motion implied by *ficking* is quite distinct from kicking, although a kick may be inadvertently given during the ficking. The word *fick* is rarely used except when some kind of restraint and consequent struggle accompanies the action.

Jutl. D. At fike [or fige] (to hurry). This word is always connected with quick movement: hence the ironical Jutlandic phrase *fik et saa* (make haste); or again, *han gor saa figelig.* The Jutl. pr. of the word is almost identical with our own.

Ex.—*T' bairn ficked aboot i' bed despertly.* — *What's t' au'd coo fickin leyke that ti deea?*

Fick, n. C. A short quick motion of the feet, whether of man

x

or beast, when subjected to restraint, esp. when lying on the ground.

Ex.—*T' ratten just ga'e three ficks an' then it deed.*

Fire-eldin, n. C. Vide **Eldin.**

Fire-fanged, part. R. Burnt (in cooking) ; overdone by the fire. Dan. At fænge (to catch fire), befænge (to infect). This latter signification comes very close to that of *fanged* in our word.

Fire-pote, n. R. A poker. Wel. Pwttio (to push, poke).

Fire-stead, n. C. (pr. fire-steead). The fireplace.

Fit. adj. C. Ready, inclined to, prepared.

Ex.—*Ah 's fit for off* (i. e. I am ready to go). — *Are ya fit?* (said by a schoolmaster to pupil learning a lesson by heart). — *They were fit ti mo'ther ma.*

Flacker, v. C. To flutter : also to throb with pain ; to flicker as a candle. Dan. At flagre (to flutter).

Ex.—*T' cock flackered ower t' wall.* — *Mah feeat flackers sadly.* — *What maks yon cann'l flacker seea?*

Flag, n. C. A flake ; esp. of snow. Dan. En Flage (a flake).

Ex.—*It snew i girt flags.*

Flan, v. F. To spread out at the top.

Jutl. D. At flanre (to expand towards the top).

Flappy, adj. C. Wild, 'harum-scarum'; also light and frivolous.

Ex.—*Sha 's a flappy body.*

Flaup, n. F. Silly talk. Dan. Flab (chaps) ; also colloquially, Hold flab (none of your jaw).

Flay, v. C. To frighten, to scare. Hence the adj. *flaysome* (frightful), which however is not very commonly used. O. N. Flæja (to frighten).

Ex.—Q. 'Why isn't your brother at school?' A. *Pleeas Sir! he 's flaain creeaks.* — *T' lahtle lass wer flaay'd ti gan wiv hersen.*

Flay-boggle, n. F. A hobgoblin : that which frightens ; esp. at night.

Flay-crow, flay-creeak, n. F. A scarecrow.

Flee, n. C. A fly. Dan. At flyve (to fly). In the Danish pr. a distinct *w* is heard which is lost in the Yorkshire pr.

Ex.—*T' flees plagues t' hosses weeantly.*

Flee-by-sky, n. F. (pr. fleebisky, the accent being on the first and third syllables). A passionate female ; a giddy, flighty girl.

Ex.—*Sha 's a reglar fleebisky.*

Fleece, v. C. To make thin, generally applied to persons who have lost flesh through illness ; to get out of condition.

Ex.—*Mah wo'd, bud it 's fleeced him!*

Fleece, n. F. Bodily condition; esp. as regards fatness.

Ex.—*He 's a good fleece.* — *It 's ta'en his fleece frev him.*

Fleeing-ask, n. R. The dragon-fly.

Flesh-fly, n. C. The common blue-bottle fly.

Flesh-meat, n. C. Butcher's meat as distinguished from swine's flesh.

Flick, n. C. A flitch (of bacon). Icel. Flikki (a flitch).

Flig, v. F. To fly. Dan. At flygte (to flee).

Ex.—*T' cock fligg'd ower t' wall an' flaayed t' lahtle lass.*

Fligged, adj. F. Fledged.

Ex.—*Are they fligg'd yit?*

Fliggers, n. C. Young birds fully fledged, those newly hatched being termed *bare gollies*, and those in the intermediate stage *penners*.

Flipe, n. C. The brim of a hat or cap. Dan. En Flip (the extreme part of a thing).

Flit, v. C. To move to a new home, with all household furniture and other goods and chattels. Dan. At flytte (to remove, shift), flytte ind (take possession), flytte til (go to live with).

Ex.—*When are ya boun ti flit?* — *We 've nobbut just flitted ti wer new hoos.* — *They 're throng flittin'.*

Flite, v. C. To scold; to come to high words.

Ex.—*Sha started ti flite.* — *A fliting bout.*

Flite, n. C. A flow of quarrelsome words.

Ex.—*They 're awlus on wi ther flites.*

Flither, n. C. The common limpet.

Ex.—*Them 's t' lasses getherin flithers.*

Flittermouse, n. R. The common bat. Dan. En Flaggermus (a bat).

Flitting, n. C. A removal to a new home.

Ex.—*Wer things isn't fairly reeted yit, we 've nobbut just gitten wer flittin' owered.*

Flobbed up, part. C. Swollen or puffed up.

Ex.—*His airm wer all flobbed up.*

Flowtered, part. C. In a state of trepidation; nervous, excited, from any cause. The word is generally used in the participial form from the verb *flowter*; the substantive *flowter* is also used in the same sense.

Ex.—*Ah felt flowtered all i' bits.*

Fluke, n. C. (pr. fleeak). A maggot.

Ex.—*They 're as full o' fleeaks as ivvir they can ho'd.*

Fod, n. C. A bound bundle of newly thrashed straw. This word is pr. as faud, but rather shorter, and is probably an abbreviation of *fold*, i. e. an armful—that which can be enfolded by the arms.

Fodderum, n. C. A building or part of a building for storing fodder: it is generally in close proximity to where the cattle are kept, e. g. between two cow-houses, from which the 'hecks' or racks could be easily filled, I do not remember to have heard this word in the E.R., but it is very commonly used in the southern and other parts of the N. Riding. Dan. Et Foderrum (a place for keeping fodder).

Fog, n. C. Meadow-grass after the hay has been in-gathered: the aftermath. This curious word seems to bear no trace of Scandinavian origin; it is probably an old British word: conf. Wel. Ffwgws (dry leaves).

Ex.—*T' fogs leeaks middlin' weel ti-year.* — *It'll mak a good fog will you.*

Foisty, adj. C. Musty, mouldy; esp. when accompanied by a smell of dampness, as in the case of hay heated in a stack, &c.

Fold-garth, fold-yard, n. C. (pr. fo'dgarth). The farm-yard, that is, the inner yard surrounded by the farm buildings.

Folk, n. C. (pr. fau'k and fooak). People. I insert this word in the glossary; for although it is frequently found in the best standard English authors, yet it can scarcely be said at the present time to be a word that would be used exactly in an ordinary way, whereas it is throughout this East Yorkshire district the word universally used for *people.* It is used both with and without the plural termination *s,* more often with than not, though being a noun of multitude this is clearly redundant. Dan. Folk (people).

Ex.—*Folks 'll say owt.* — *A vast o' folk.—A deal o' folks.* — *Sum folks says seea.* — *Bettermy folk.*

Fond, adj. C. Foolish, wanting in common sense, silly. Dan. En Fjante (a silly person).

Ex.—*Ah nivver heeard tell o' sikan a fond tthrick.*

Fond-heead, n. C. A silly fellow.

Ex.—*Thoo fondheead thoo.*

Fondness, n. C. Foolishness, silliness, nonsense.

Ex.—*He 's good ti nowt bud talkin' fondness.*

Fond-plufe, n. O. This was formerly the name given to the practice of dragging a plough from place to place on or about the Feast of the Epiphany. The young men who took part in it used to collect money, which they spent in merry-making in the evening; some of the party were disguised and dressed in fantastic costumes.

Fondy, n. C. A simpleton, one half-witted. Dan. En Fjante.

Footings, n. C. The lowest rough foundation on which masonry is built up.

For, prepositional in its force, though placed after instead of before its connection. C. (pr. foor and forr). To, towards.

In this sense, which is of the commonest, it is only used in such expressions as *Wheer are ya foor?* or *Wheer 's ta foor?* meaning 'Where are you going to?'—the verb being understood. It is also used satirically when a person accidentally makes a *mauvais pas*.

Ex.—*What a numb baa'n thoo is! wheer 's ta foor?*

For-anenst, R. In front of. I have only heard of this word being used at the present time in a part of the Wold district.

Forboden, part. R. Forbidden.

Forced, part. C. (pr. foorced). Obliged. This word, though Std. Eng., is here inserted because it is universally used in the dialect in this sense, to the exclusion of all others, as *obliged, compelled,* &c.

Ex.—*Ah 's be foorced ti gan.* — *They 're foorced to fend for thersells.*

Fore-elders, n. C. Forefathers. Dan. Forældre (parents), Forfædre (ancestors).

Fore-end, n. C. (pr. foorend or forrend, with rather a strong stress on the last syllable). The beginning. Jutl. D. For-ende (the fore-part of anything).

Ex.—*Wa started t' foorend o' t' last week.*

Forkin'-robin, n. C. The earwig. This designation of the earwig is not universal: I used to hear it very frequently in the E. R., but not in the southern part of the N. R., where *twitchbell* is the word generally used.

Ex.—*There was a vast o' clocks an' worrms an' forkin'-robins.*

Forks, n. F. (pr. forrks). The main perpendicular beams which fork out at the top to support the roof in the old timber houses ; they hold the 'ribs' to which the 'spars' are attached ; across these again are the 'latts,' and so the whole frame work is held together.

Fortherly, furtherly, adj. F. (pr. fo'therly). Forward, or early of its kind, or for the season.

Ex.—*Them 's mair fo'therly na t' uthers.* — *It's a fo'therly taatie.*

Forwoden, adj. F. In a state of dirt, disorder, and waste ; generally applied to such a state of destruction as is caused by vermin. Dan. At forőde (to waste, consume).

Ex.—*Oor apple chaim'er is fair forwoden wi' rattens an' meyce.*

Foulmart, n. F. (pr. foomart). The polecat. Wel. Ffwlbart (the polecat). These animals were common fifty years ago, when 4*d.* apiece, or some such sum, was given for one by the village constable. They are still to be seen, but only here and there, and that occasionally.

Fout, n. C. A fool, a stupid lout.

Ex.—*Thoo 's a fout.*

Fowt, n. C. (pr. the same way as owt). A spoiled child.

Ex.—*Sha 's nobbut a lahtle fowt.*

Fra, frav, frev, prep. C. From. *Fra* is generally used before a consonant, *frav* and *frev* before a vowel. Dan. Fra (from).

Fra by, prep. R. Beyond, compared with, in proportion to.

Framation, n. F. Skill in action or management, readiness and aptitude in work, esp. in beginning it.

Ex.—*There 's neea framation aboot him.*

Frame, v. C. To give promise in the performance of work of any kind, whether in man or beast; to make an attempt or beginning in any undertaking. This expressive word is one of the commonest: it occurs in Judges xii. 6, though in a slightly different sense from the above. In the dialect it is rarely followed by *to* as in the passage alluded to. Dan. At fremme (to advance, to take in hand).

Ex.—*Cum, fraame. — T' lad nobbut com'd yisttherda, bud ah think he fraames middlin'.*

Fratch, v. C. To be quarrelsome, especially as to trifles; a word commonly said to children who are fretful and quarrelsome with one another.

Ex.—*Let him be; thoo 's awlus fratchin'.*

Fraunge, v. C. To go on a spree. Also used as a noun.

Ex.—*He taks off, fraunging aboot.—He's had a fraunge.*

Fresh, adj. C. The worse for liquor; drunk.

Fret, n. F. A shower of misty rain from the sea; generally called a *sea-fret.*

Fresh-wood, n. C. The threshold of a doorway. This word may be a corruption of *threshold.*

Fridge, v. C. To rub against, so as to cause irritation; esp. of the skin, as when the clothes rub against any place inclined to soreness; to wear away by rubbing; to fray out.

Ex.—*Mah feet 's sair, an' t' beeats fridges 'em.*

Frightened, part. C. (pr. freeten'd). This word is frequently used in a weaker sense than in Std. Eng., being equivalent to 'apprehensive,' or even 'shy.'

Ex.—*Ah's freeten'd 'at we 'r boun ti a'e some raan.—Noo, you mun reach to; you maun't be freeten'd.*

Frowsy, adj. F. Cross and forbidding-looking; ill-tempered.

Fruggan, n. O. A long iron rake for scraping ashes out of an oven of the old-fashioned kind.

Frutas, Fruttish, n. R. A dish consisting of an egg, flour, sugar and currants, beaten together and fried. It was only eaten on Ash Wednesday; consequently that day was often called Fruttish or Frutas Wednesday.

Fullock, n. C. Rapid motion, impetus, force.

Ex.—*It kom wi sikan a fullock.*

This word is sometimes used as a verb, e. g. a common saying with boys playing marbles is, *Knuckle doon, neea fullocking,* i. e. no false impetus from the wrist.

Full up, adj. C. Quite full.

Ex.—*We 're full up.*

'Full' or 'quite full' are never used to express complete fulness.

Fulth, n. R. Fill, fullness.

Ex.—*He 's had his fulth on 't.*

Furmety or **Frumety,** n. C. A dish consisting of wheat, milk, sugar, and spices, always eaten on Christmas Eve, and sometimes on New Year's Eve also. The word is usually pr. frumety. Lat. Frumentum.

Ex.—*Wa mun a'e wer bit o' frumety, howivver.*

Furtherly, adj. F. Vide **Fortherly.**

Fustilugs, n. R. A term of abuse.

Ex.—*Thoo 's a fustilugs.*

Fuzzack, n. F. A donkey.

Fuzz-ball, n. C. The large common ground fungus found in fields.

G.

Gab, n. C. Idle talk. Dan. Gab (mouth).

Ex.—*There 's ower mich gab aboot him.*

Gad, n. O. A long whip, formerly used for driving horses and oxen. The word is also applied to a fishing-rod, which was called a fishing-gad. Jutl. D. Gaj (a long whip), fiske-gaj (fishing-rod). Icel. Gaddr.

Gag-bit, n. C. A strong bit used for breaking in or restraining 'miraklous' horses.

Gah, v. C. To go. This form of the word is common enough, although *gan* is more usual, taking the whole district through : *gah* (pr. not quite so open as ordinary *ah*) is comparatively seldom heard in the E. Riding. Dan. At gaae (to go).

Ex.—*Wheer 's ta gahin' ?*

Gain, adj. C. (pr. gaan). Short, near by reason of straightness, esp. of a way or a road. Conveniently near, also quick in doing.

Ex.—*This rooad 'll be t' gainest. — Ah knaw it 'll be t' gainest cut.*

Gain-hand, adj. C. Conveniently near, easy of access.

Ex.—*It 's a varry gain-hand spot. — We 're gain-hand for t' scheeal.*

Gains, n. F. (pr. gaans).   Advantage.
>   Ex.—*It 's neea girl gaans ti gan that rooad.*

Gair, geir, gairing, n. F.   A triangular piece of land at the corner of a field, which cannot be ploughed.   Icel. Geiri (a goar, or triangular strip).

Gaits, n. F.   Small sheaves, of oats generally and clover sometimes, set up singly, and tied at the 'throat' instead of at the middle.
>   Q. 'What are you going to do to-day?'   A. *We 're gahing ti binnd t' gaits.*

Also called *gaitings* or *yaitings.*

Gallic-handed, adj. F.   Left-handed.   Dan. Gal; galt (wrong); e.g. Klokken gaar galt (the clock is wrong).   In Danish *gal* would be applied as we apply it in such a phrase as 'the wrong hat.'

Galloway, n. C. (pr. Gallowa).   An under-sized horse, or an over-sized pony; probably so-called from the district from which the breed was imported into England.

Gallowses, n. C. (pr. gallases).   Braces for attaching to trowsers.

Gally-bauk, n. C.   A pivotted iron balk or beam attached to the larger or main-beam or rann'l-bauk which stretches across the fireplace in houses; from the gally-bauk pots can hang off or on the fire at pleasure.
    The word *gally* is merely a corruption of *gallows*; it may be noted that in Jutl. D. *galli* is similarly a corruption of *galge.*

Galore, n. F.   A quantity, esp. a large quantity; sometimes the word is used in pl.
>   Ex.—*Galores o' stuff.*

Gam, n. C.   Fun, sport, ridicule.   Dan. Gammen (mirth).
>   Ex.—*Noo, give ower; thoo maun 't mak sik gam o' t' au'd man.*

Gamashes, also abbreviated to **Mashes**, n. R.   Gaiters.   This word is applied both to the long and short gaiters; the latter covering the foot only, the former more or less of the leg also.   They were generally made of stout cloth. Under the heading 'Gamacha' of the *Glossarium Manuale* of Du Cange, we read of this curious word ' pedulis lanei species, quæ etiam superiorem pedis partem tegit; Gallis *Gamache*, Occitanis *Garamacho, Gamacho*, vox uti videtur deducta a *compagus* vel *gampagus.*'   In our dialect the word is distinctly pronounced *gamahshes* : this is probably one of the words we have got through the French.   Dan. Kamascher (gaiters).

Gammer, v. C.   To idle about; to be disinclined for work.

Gang, gan, v. C.   To go.   (The latter form is almost always used.) Dan. At gange (to go), En Ganger (a goer, poetic). The word is also, though less commonly, used as a noun, in the sense of a way, generally a by-way. As a verb, *gan* is the general form in which the verb is used. In the pres. participle, *gahin*' is commonly used as well as *gannin*', esp. in N. Riding.

Ex.—*Cu' mi lad, be sharp, sneck t' yat, gan thi ways yam, an' fettle t' gallowa.—Ah doot ah 's gannin' fast* (i. e. I am afraid I am failing rapidly).—*Sha 's nut gahin' yit.* Atkinson, in his *Cleveland Glossary*, gives as an example of this word, *Are you ganging or riding?*—*ganging* being here used for walking, as opposed to riding. In Danish it is also used in this sense.

Gang, n. F. A set or course, e. g. a course of thatch on the roof of a house.

Gantree, n. C. A wooden stand for barrels to rest upon. Gantree-tiles are the large horse-shoe drain tiles.

Gar, v. R. To make, to cause. Dan. At gjöre (to do, to make).

Ex.—*It gars ma greet,* i. e. it makes me weep.

Garfits, n. R. Entrails.

Garn, gairn, n. C. (pr. gaa'n, the vowel-sound being the same as the *a* in *air*). Yarn, woollen thread.

Garsel, n. F. (pr. garsil). Dead sticks from a wood or hedge; undergrowth of woods, rubbish. Dan. Gjærdsel (dead hedge-wood).

Garth, n. C. An enclosure, generally of small dimensions — as e. g. round a church or farm-house. The word is used as a suffix in *staggarth, fold-garth,* &c. It is also commonly applied to a small paddock near a farm-house. Dan. En Gaard (a yard, enclosure near a house).

Gate, n. C. A way, road, street. This is a very common termination to the names of streets in many of our old towns and villages, e.g. Goodramgate in York, Baxter-gate in Whitby, Nether-gate in Nafferton. Cf. Cow-gate. It is also in the plural a common adverbial suffix, e.g. *allgates, onygates.* It has, moreover, the secondary meaning, in the singular, of manner. Dan.: En Gade (a street).

Ex.—*Ah can't mannish neea-gates.—He 'll cum ti t' beggar-staff at that gate.*

Gaum, v. F. To understand, to pay attention to. Norse Gaum (attention), giva Gaum etter (pay attention to); also gau, an obsolete word (clever).

Gaumish, adj. F. Quick-witted, intelligent.

Ex.—*He 's a gaumish chap.*

Gauve, v. C. To stare vacantly. This word is equivalent to

gaup, which is used also commonly, especially of women ;
hence *gaupy* (one who stares vacantly).

Ex.—*What's he gauvin' at?—What a greeat gauvin' chap
ah is* (said by one who slipped, through not looking
where he was going).

Gauvy, n. C. A half-witted person.

Ex.—*He's a girl gauvy.*

Gavelock, n. C. (pr. gaavlock). A crow-bar of any size ; a
bar of iron. O. N. Gaflok (a dart).

Gawk, gowk, n. F. The cuckoo. Dan. Gjög (cuckoo). At
Kilvington the young cuckoo and its foster-mother are still
called *t' gowk an' titling.*

Gay, adj. C. This word is generally used in the sense of
considerable, as regards size, number, &c., though its
primary meaning is also retained in its ordinary sense.
The diminutive *gayish* is also in common use.

Ex.—*A gay few*, i. e. a considerable number.—*A gayish
nag that leeaks 'at thoo's astthrahd.—A gay bou'k.*

Gayly, adv. R. In good health, quite well.

Ex.—*Ah's gayly.*

Gear, gears, gearing, n. C. Apparatus, machinery, furnishings ; esp. harness.

Ex.—*T' hoss gans weel iv all gears.*

Gee, v. C. (pr. *g* soft). The word of command given to a horse
to turn it to the right hand.

Gen, v. C. To grin, to show the teeth, to cry as a child. This
word may also be written girn, though always pr. gen.

Ex.—*Cum, laddie, gen* (said by a man to a dog which
had been taught to show its teeth as if laughing).

Genning, ginning, adj. C. Besides the ordinary meaning of
this word as the participle of *gen*, there is the secondary
meaning of fault-finding, or discontented.

Ex.—*Sha's a ginnin' au'd woman.*

Gep, v. C. To try to gain knowledge secretly.

Ex.—*They wer geppin' ti git it if they could.—He gans
geppin' aboot.*

Gesling, n. C. A gosling. This is not a mispronunciation
of gosling, but the old form of the word. Dan. En
Gjæsling (a gosling).

Gess, gerse, n. C. (pr. *g* hard). Grass.

Get, v. C. (pr. git). This word, used though it is in the
ordinary sense, is also found in many dialectical variations.
Perhaps the commonest peculiarity of use is in the sense
'is called' ; e. g. *Sha wer kessen'd Mary, bud sha awlus gits
Polly.* Again, in the sense of to reach, visit, or call at
a place ; e. g. *Ah want ti gan ti York, bud ah doot ah san't
git wahl Settherda.* Such expressions as *git a-gate, git t'*

length of, speak for themselves. As an auxiliary verb it is very common ; e.g. *Wa s'all git deean inoo.* The word is also used substantively for *a breed*, e.g. *What git is 't?* In the past tense there is also a common use of the word by sailors on the east coast ; when a man is drowned at sea a Flamborough fisherman would say, *The sea gat him.*

Getherer, n. C. (1) A collector : thus, Cess-getherer, the rate or tax collector. (2) One who gathers the corn in the harvest fields into bundles for binding. (3) A large, light, four-pronged fork, often with a bow attached, for gathering the swathes of oats into gaits or sheaves.

Getten, gitten, gotten, part. C. These are all common forms of the past participle of *get*, the two last being the commonest.

Gew-gow, n. C. (pr. with *g* hard, *gow* nearly rhyming with *how*, but with a little of the *a*-sound before the *o*). Jew-trumps, or Jew's-harp.

Gib, n. F. (pr. *g* hard). A band or hook, as in a stick.

Gib-stick, n. C. (pr. *g* hard.) A stick with a hook at one end. A nutting-hook is called a nut-stick.

Gicken, gecken, v. F. To laugh like a fool. Dan. En Gjæk (a fool, a jester).

Ex.—*Leeaksta hoo he gickens.*

Cf. 'The geck and scorn o' the other's villany.'—*Cymbeline*, v. 4. The word may be connected with *giggle*.

Gilder, gilderd, n. C. (pr. gildthert). A snare of horse-hair for catching birds. Dan. Gilder or Gildre (a trap).

Gilefat, n. F. The tub in which ale is put in order to ferment ; when it ' works ' well, it is said to be a *good gahlfat*.

Gill, n. C. (pr. *g* soft). A half-pint.

Ex.—*Ah 'll tak a gill o' yal.*

Gill, n. C. (pr. *g* hard). A narrow rocky valley. Icel. Gil (a dale).

Gilt, n. C. A young female pig. Jutl. D. En Gylte (a sow when she is for the first time with young).

Gimmer, n. C. A female lamb from the time of birth to that of weaning. Jutl. D. En Gimmer (a ewe-lamb). Icel. Gymbr.

Gimmer-hog, n. C. A ewe-lamb from weaning-time to first shearing.

Ginner, adv. R. Rather ; more willingly.

Ex.—*Ah 'd ginner gan.*

Gissy-gissy, n. The call of the tender of swine in summoning them to him. Dan. En Gris (a pig).

Girt, adj. C. Great. There are two distinct forms of this word, viz. *greeat* and *girt*; the former is commonest in the East, the latter in the North Riding. The pr. of *girt*

in the southern part of the N. R. is peculiar and difficult
to acquire, the vowel-sound being nearly extinguished by
the consonantal; so much so that the word might almost
be correctly written *grt.* In this district it is difficult to say
whether the *i* precedes or follows the *r*, so closely are the
two letters blended together in this word.

Gitten, p. part. of get, C.

    Ex.—*Then thoo 's gitten back.*

Give ower, v. C. Leave off. It is remarkable what a
strong preference is given to this expression over all its
equivalents; *leave off* or *stop* is seldom if ever heard,
especially as a command.

    Ex.—*Give ower wi t' bairn; noo ah 's telling o' ya.*

Gizzenen, n. C. The gizzard.

Glazzen, v. C. To glaze; hence *glazzener,* a glazier.

Glent, n. F. A glimpse, a look in passing; also and more
common as a verb—to glance off after impact.

    Ex.—*Ah flang t' steean at t' yat stoop an' it glented off an'
went thruff t' windher.*

Gliff, n. F. A glimpse. Dan. At glippe (to blink, wink).

    Ex.—*Ah just catch'd a gliff on him.*

Gloar, gloor, v. C. To stare hard. Dan. At glo (to stare, gaze).

    Ex.—*What 's ta gloorin' at ?—Thoo gloors hard.*

Glor-fat, n. and adj. F. (pr. glorr, slightly rolling the *r*).
Soft fat, exceedingly fat.

    Ex.—*It 's glorr-fat ivvry bit on 't.*

Glut, n. C. A wooden wedge for splitting timber. ·

Goalin, n. F. (pr. goälin). A narrow passage. This word,
which I have only heard of in the Wold country, is
probably a derivative or diminutive of *gole* (a flood-gate,
a hollow between two hills, a throat, a narrow vale):
cf. Loan, lonnin, which has the same termination as the
diminutive.

Gob, n. F. The mouth. Dan. Gab (mouth).

    Ex.—*Ho'd thi gob thoo au'd feeal.*

Gobstring, n. C. A string fastened to a bridle; a makeshift
bridle.

Godspenny, n. C. Vide **Arles.** Jutl. D. Gudspenge, Fæstepenge (earnest-money).

Goffen. v. F. To laugh idiotically; an E. R. word.

    Ex.—*Noo then, Goffeny, what 's tha goffenin' at ?*

Goke, n. C. (pr. gauk). The heart or central portion of anything, as the core of an apple, or the centre of a haystack, or the hard part of a boil, &c.

    Ex.—*Ah can't git t' gauk on 't oot.*

Goldie, n. C. The yellow-hammer; also commonly called
a gold-spink.

Gollin, golly, n. C. A newly hatched bird.

Ex.—*They 're lahtle bare gollins.*

The prefix 'bare' is generally used before this word.

Good, v. C. To flatter (oneself).

Ex.—*Ah gooded mysen 'at he 'd com ti see ma.*

Good, adj. C. There are various peculiar uses of this word : (1) Easy; e. g. *good ti tell,* i. e. easy of recognition. (2) Well; e. g. *Yan mud as good lap up,* i. e. One might as well finish ; *Them 's as good made 'uns as need be,* i. e. Those are as well made &c. (3) Considerable, e. g. *a good few,* i. e. a considerable number. In Danish there is a similar usage to (2), e. g. Dette maleri er godt udført, i. e. That picture is well done ; Saa godt som aldrig, i. e. as good as never ; or all but never.

Goodstuff, n. C. Sweetmeat.

Ex.—Q. 'What will you do with this halfpenny if I give it to you ?'—A. *Wear 't i' goodstuff.*

Gote, n. C. A narrow passage or opening from a road or street to the water side. This word is very common in Whitby and other places on the coast. I connect this interesting word with the Danish Gade, a road or way, which in the Danish dialects is written Gäde, the vowel-sound of which is identical with that of the Yorkshire word *Gote.*

Gotherly, adj. R. Kind-hearted.

Goupen, n. R. The hollow or 'ball' of the hand, a handful, esp. when both hands are placed together. Icel. Goupn.

Ex.—*They gat gold by goupens* (De fik Guld i gjöbninger Jutl. D.).

Gowk, n. C. The cuckoo. Vide **Gawk.**

Gowland, n. C. (pr. gowlan'). The corn-marigold, also applied to the yellow water-lily, called *watergowland.* Dan. Gul (yellow).

Ex.—*He leeaks as yalla as a gowlan'.*

Graft, n. C. (pr. graff). The depth of a spade in digging ; also applied to that which is dug up by a single turn of the spade. Dan. At gröfte (to dig a trench).

Ex.—*A spade graff deep.*

Grain, v. C. To groan, to grumble, to complain.

Ex.—*Oor Bet 's awlus graanin' aboot summat.*

Graining, n. F. The point in the trunk of a tree where the branches begin to spread out. Dan. En Gren (a branch). Icel. Grein (a branch).

Graith, v. F. To clothe or furnish with anything ; also to fit or adapt. Also used as a noun for any kind of furnishing or provision, *graithing* being another form of the same word when used as a noun.

Ex.—*He 's fettled an' graith'd.*

Grave v. C. To dig. Dan. At grave (to dig).
Ex.—*Ah 's gitten t' garth graved ower, an' it 's a back wahkin job been an' all.*

Greet, v. R. To shed tears, to weep. Dan. At græde (to weep).
Ex.—*Noo then honey, thoo munna greet.*
This old word is wellnigh obsolete, but it is known by many old people.

Griff, n. R. A deep narrow valley. Robinson gives this word in his *Whitby Glossary*: it is probably confined to the northern part of the county, at least I do not remember to have ever heard it in the E. Riding. The word may be connected with *grip*. Swedish Grift (a grave).

Griming, n. C. (pr. grahmin). A light sprinkling. It is rather singular that a word suggestive of blackness should always be applied to a light sprinkling of snow.
Ex.—*Just a grahmin' o' snaw.·*

Grip, n. C. A small trench or narrow ditch very common in clay districts, where, before the days of draining, narrow rig and furrow were in vogue, and when cross trenches or grips were cut at intervals to carry off the furrow water to the side ditches of a field.
Ex.—'Where's your father?' *Grippin' at Robert Garnet's.*

Gripe, n. C. (pr. greyp). A three- or four-pronged fork for digging purposes; a short-handled muck-fork. Dan. Et Greb (a grasp), at gribe (to grip).
Ex.—*If thoo can't lowzen it wi' yer hand, tak t' gripe til 't.*

Grizeley, adj. R. (pr. grahzly). Extremely ugly.

Grob, n. C. A derisive term for a puny, undersized, insignificant-looking person.
Ex.—*Sha 's a lahtle grob.*

Grossy, adj. C. Of large, ful and rapid growth. Fr. Gros.
Ex.—*Wo'zzels is varry grossy ti-year.*

Grue, adj. R. Grim, severe-looking; dark. Dan. At gruc (to shudder at); gruelig (horrid).
Ex.—*He leeaks as grue as thunner.*

Gruff, adj. F. Sulky, sullen.

Grund, n. C. (pr. grunnd; *u* as in pull). Ground. Dan. Grund (ground).

Grun'stan, n. C. (pr. *t* scarcely heard). A grindstone.
Ex.—*Thoo mun tak t' au'd lae ti t' grun'stan.*

Guider, n. C. (pr. gahdther). A tendon or sinew

Gulls, n. R. Oatmeal porridge, hasty-pudding.

Gyme-hole, n. R. (pr. gahmhooal). The hole caused in the bank of a stream or river by the water washing a circular sweep in it. Possibly this word may have the same root as *gimlet*. I only know of one instance of its use ; but my authority is such a reliable one that I have no hesitation in inserting the word. Since writing the above, another case of this word has come before my notice on the banks of the Ouse below York, where there is a spot called the ' Gyme pownds.'

Gypsey, n. C. (pr. *g* hard). Streams that break out at certain points in the chalk-formation in the E. R. are called *gypseys* ; these frequently may be seen after a long continuance of rain. Icel. Geysir (a hot spring).

H.

Hacker, v. F.   To hesitate in speech, to stammer.
  Ex.—*He hackered an' stammered.*
Hackle, n. C. The natural covering of any animal, the human skin ; a good hackle implies good-looking, well-cared-for ; a good ' coat ' is the common equivalent.
  Ex.—*He 's got a good hackle ov his back.*
Haddock, n. R.   A shock of corn consisting of eight sheaves. In some districts a haddock was distinguished from a stook by the latter having two additional sheaves placed on the top of the other eight, as an extra precaution against injury from rain.
Hag, n. R.   A hedge, or a low, bushy wood. This word is now not used except in field or other names. Dan. En Hegn or Hæk (a fence, a hedge).
Hag-berry, n. F.   The bird-cherry.   Dan. Hæg (bird-cherry).
Haggle, v. F.   To hail. This word is most frequently in use in the E. R., where hailstones are in some places called haggle-steeans.   Dan. At hagle (to hail).
  Ex.—*It haggled heavy t' last neet.*
Hag-snar, n. R.   A stump of a tree.
  At Linton-on-Ouse there are two contiguous fields called *T' hag* and *Snahry clooas*. A hundred years ago this part of the township was wood, as the names imply, *Snahry clooas* having had in it many snars or stumps of trees which have been felled.
Hagworm, n. C.   A snake : the word is used generically rather than specifically. Robinson, in his *Whitby Glossary*, gives the Cleveland usage of the word as synonymous with viper. Dan. En Hugorm (a viper).
Hake, v. R.   To follow with enquiries, to annoy, to pester ; to hurry on.
  Ex.—*Hake 'em away*, i. e. urge them on almost faster than they are able to go.

Hale, v. R. To pour water from a vessel. Dan. At hædle ud (to empty).

    Ex.—*Hale it oot.*

Hales, n. F. The handles of a plough; the left-hand one being called the Steer-tree : also used for the handles of a wheelbarrow.

Half-rocked, adj. F. Lacking in intellect, not very sharp, silly. The idea implied by the word is not properly nursed, only half-rocked in the cradle.

Hallock, v. C. To wander idly from place to place without any definite aim ; to 'loaf.'

    Ex.—*He gans hallockin' aboot frev hoos ti hoos.*

Hames, n. C. (pr. hceams). The moveable fittings attached to a barfam or horse-collar, to which the traces are fixed by a hook.

Ham-skackle, v. R. To tie the head of an animal to one of its legs to hinder easy motion.

Hanch at, v. C. To make a grab at with intent to bite ; almost always used of the dog. Possibly this word was originally a coursing term.

    Ex.—*That dog o' yours hanched at ma when ah tried ti clap him.*

Hand-clout, n. C. (pr. han'-cloot). A towel, sometimes also called a hand-towel.

Handle, v. C. In passive voice this word is used in the sense of to be afflicted with sickness.

    Ex.—*He 's very queerly hannl'd.*

Hand-running, adv. C. (pr. han'-runnin'). One after another in regular succession.

    Ex.—*We 've had three deeaths i' t' toon three tahms han'-runnin'.*

Handsel, v. F. (pr. hansel). To use for the first time. Dan. Handsel (earnest-money).

    Ex.—*Ah handsel'd mah new dhriss last Sunda.*

Handstaff, n. C. (pr. han'-staff). The handle of a flail, at the end of which is the *cap* to which the *swipple* is attached.

    Ex.—*It 's as good a han'-staff as onny i t' toon.*

Hand-turn, n. C. (pr. hanto'n). A stroke of work.

    Ex.—*Ah a'en't deean a han'to'n this backend.*

Hangedly, adv. C. Unwillingly, sulkily ; in a hang-head way : from which idea the word possibly has its derivation.

Hank, n. C. A hitch or loop of a band or rope. Dan. Hank (the ear of a pot). Norse Hank (a ring), Swedish (string for tieing).

Hank, v. C. To tie a horse to a gate &c. by the bridle.

    Ex.—*To hank a band,* i. e. to fasten or secure a band.

Hankle, v. C. To be in a state of entanglement or in a confused mass; to be mixed up with; to unite with: generally used passively.

Ex.—*It 's a dree job ; they 're all seea hankled tigither.* (The reference is to the cutting of a field of beans much overgrown with rubbish.)—*Ah is vexed at oor Tom 's gitten hankled in wi sike a rafflin lot.*

Hap, v. C. To cover over, to put on clothes, esp. of a heavy kind ; to throw earth over anything ; to bury.

Ex.—*Hap ma.—Thoo mun hap thysen weel; it 's varry cau'd.—Then you 've gitten poor au'd Willie happed up at last.*

Happen, v. C. To meet with, to fall out ; hence the sense in which it is often used, viz. 'possibly,' 'perhaps'; this is an elliptical form of 'it may happen.' The word is often used in the sense of 'if by chance,' 'if it happen that,' 'perhaps.'

Ex.—*Ah 's happen'd a bad accident.—Q. Is 't boun ti fair up, thinks ta? A. Happen it mud eftther a bit.— Ah 'll waat happen sha cums.*

Happing, n. C. A covering of any kind—very commonly applied to bed-clothes.

Ex.—*A'e ya happins eneeaf ?*

Hard, adv. C. Surely—only used in this sense in connection with *enough.*

Ex.—*Aye ! that 's him hard eneeaf.*

Harden, v. C. (1) To encourage, to incite, to egg on. (2) To clear up gradually after long or heavy rain.

Ex.—*He 's awlus hardenin 'em on intiv a mischeef.—He hardened hissen up at last,* i.e. he took courage.—*It 'll a'e ti harden oot afoor wa git onny matters o' sun.*

Harding, n. C. (pr. hard'n). Coarse linen for kitchen purposes, wrappers, &c.

Ex.—*Wheer 's my au'd hard'n appron ?*

Hardlings, adv. C. (pr. hardlins). Hardly, scarcely

Ex.—*Ah 's hardlins fit yit.*

Hard-set, adj. C. With difficulty able.

Ex.—*Ah lay he 'll be hard-set ti a'e deean afoor neet.— Ah 's hard-set ti walk.*

Hark yer, or **Hear yer**, **Hear yer**, v. C. Hear you ; sometimes also repeated, as 'just fancy that' is said.

Harrygaud, n. F. One given to riotous and noisy behaviour ; also a great eater.

Ex.—*Whau 's them harrygauds 'at gans shootin' an' beealin an' gaapin i t' toon ?*

Hartree, n. C. The tail-piece of a gate.

Harv, v. C. A call to a horse to go to the left hand.

Hask, hasky, adj. C. (pr. ask, asky). Dry, rough, harsh. This word is very commonly applied to a dry cold wind, such as one gets in March ; also to bread which is dry and coarse ; but it may be applied in many other ways. Dan. Harsk (rusty, rancid).

Ex.—*T' grass is bad ti cut, it 's varry ask at t' boddum. —T' breead 's that asky ah can't eeat it.*

Haunt, n. C. (pr. hant). A habit or custom.

Haunted, part. C. (pr. hanted). Accustomed.

Ex. —*Ah s'all nivver git hanted ti t' job.—Hanted ti t' spot.*

Hauvy-gauvy, n. F. A stupid lout.

Haver, n. F. (pr. havver). Oats. The word is now seldom heard except in connection with cake, haver-cake being thin cake made of oatmeal, called also *haver meal.* Dan. Havre (oat) ; Havre-mel (oatmeal).

Ex.—*Havver-cake.—Havver-sack.*

Hawbuck, n. C. A vulgar, mean, ignorant fellow.

Hay-bauks, n. C. Loose poles in a cowhouse, arranged for holding hay for the use of the cattle.

Hazel, n. C. (pr. hezzle). To chastise with a stick.

Hazeling, n. C. (pr. hezzlin). A flogging : *heshing* or *eshing* has a similar meaning, the derivation from the hazel or the ground-ash being obvious.

Hazzled, adj. R. Speckled with red and white—applied to beasts so coloured.

Head-rigg, n. C. The headland of a field, where they turn when ploughing, and which is itself finally ploughed horizontally to the rest of the field.

Head-stall, n. C. A halter.

Heart-grown, adj. R. Strongly attached to.

Ex.--*They were despertly heart-grown on it.*

Heave, v. C. To throw corn from one place to another so as to expose it to a current of wind in order to roughly winnow it.

Heck, n. C. A rack for fodder. Dan. En Hæk (a rack), also called Foderhæk. There is another application of this word, or rather another word of the same form, signifying the inner door of a house opening towards the outer door. It is also used of the double doors on the floor of a granary through which the sacks of corn are hauled up ; in this sense it is sometimes pronounced hetch.

Ex.—*It blaws cau'd ; steck t' heck.*

Heckling, n. C. A scolding.

Ex.—*He gav him a good heckling.*

Heeall, yal, adj. C. Whole.

Ex.—*Ah 've deean t' heeal on 't.—Ah tell'd him t' yal ti deea.*

Heeze, v. R. To breathe thickly or hoarsely ; hence *heazy* (wheezy). Dan. Hæs (hoarse).

Heft, v. F. To supply with a handle ; most frequent in passive – to be supplied with a handle ; hence, to be fitted with, or simply to be supplied with.

Ex.—*He 's weel hefted wi brass,* i. e. he is well off.

Heft, n. C. (1) A handle. (2) An excuse, a pretence. Dan. En Hefte (a hilt or handle of a sword).

Ex.—*It 's all heft,* i. e. it 's a mere excuse.

Helm, n. C. (sometimes pr. hellum and sometimes helm). A shed (generally roughly built) in the fields or elsewhere for cattle ; a hovel. Dan. Hjælm (a kind of open shed on four posts, for corn, the cover of which rises and falls as occasion requires). Icel. Hjalmr.

Helter, n. C. A halter ; hence *heltering*—a term applied to the first lesson in ' breaking ' a young colt or filly, when a long halter shank or cart rope is attached, and when it often takes half a dozen or more men and lads to drag the animal forward *nolens volens.*

Hemmel, n. R. A wooden bar or hand-rail. Dan. En Hammel (a splinter-bar). Jutl. D. Hamlestok (the beam fastened by a bolt to a waggon pole, to which the two swingle-trees are secured).

Hempy, adj. R. Mischievous.

Henbauk, n. C. The beam on which fowls roost ; hence a hen-roost, sometimes termed *bauk* for shortness ; also used figuratively for bed.

Ex.—*Ah's boun ti flig up ti t' bauks,* i. e. I am going to bed.

Hen-bird, n. C. The domestic fowl. Cocks and hens are generally designated *male bo'ds* and *hen bo'ds.*

Heronsew, n. C. The heron. O. Fr. Heronçeau (the heron).

Heshing, eshing, n. C. Vide **Hazeling.**

Hesp, n. C. The fastening of gates, doors, windows, &c. ; but esp. of gates, that being also called a *sneck.* Dan. En Hasp (a bolt or fastening of a door).

Hetch, n. F. The loose back-board of a cart ; an E. R. word. Vide **Heck.**

Hig, n. (1) C., (2) F. (1) Offence taken. (2) A sudden shower ~ of rain.

Ex.—(1) *Sha 's ta'en t' hig.* This is a very common expression when a person previously on good terms passes an acquaintance without speaking.)—(2) *March higs.*

High-larnd, adj. C. Highly learned ; i. e. highly educated, well-read. *High-up* is similarly used for one in a high position in society.

Hind, n. C. A higher class agricultural labourer; i. e. one who has a house on the farm rent-free, and who acts as manager of a farm or part of a large farm under the farmer or owner of the property. The hind is in quite a different position from a bailiff in this, that the hind always works with his own hands of necessity, which the bailiff does not. Again, the hind is to be distinguished from the foreman, who is simply *primus inter pares*, whereas the hind is in a somewhat higher position, inasmuch as he has more control and responsibility than a foreman, besides, as a rule, having higher wages. A farmer who rents two farms generally puts a hind into one of the houses and lives himself in the other. (This word is frequently pr. hine.)

Hinderends, n. C. Tail-corn; i. e. corn which is light and poorer in quality than the rest, and so is blown by the winnowing-machine along with the chaff. Such corn is generally used as food for chickens.

Hing, v. C. To hang; to cling to, esp. as an ailment.
Ex.—*It hings for rain*; i. e. it threatens or looks likely to rain. — *Sha hings an' trails aboot.*

Hing-by, n. R. A hanger on. Dan. Hæng paa (dependent).

Hipe, v. C. To push with the horns (said of cattle); also used metaphorically—to attack or assail with accusations as to character or conduct.
Ex.—*They 're awlus hiping at ma.*

Hiper, n. C. A mimic.

Hirple, v. R. (pr. hopple). To stick up the back, as cattle under a hedge in cold weather.

Hirsel, v. R. To move restlessly.

Hissen, pron. C. Himself. *His-sel* is also very common, but not so frequently heard in the E. R. as *His-sen.*
Ex.—*He 'll a'e ti gan wiv hissen.*

Hitch, v. C. To hop.
Ex.—*Ah 'll hitch tha ti yon yat* (a boy's challenge).

Hitch, strahd, an' loup, n. C. Hop, step, and jump. A slight variation of this, the orthodox form, is *Hitch, strahd, jamie, strahd, loup,* the *jamie* being a crossing of the legs after the *hitch.*

Hoarst, adj. C. Hoarse.
Ex.— *Ah 's that hoarst ah can hardlins talk.*
The old dialectical word, now obsolete, for the throat was *hause,* with which *hoarst* is connected.

Ho'd, v. C. To hold. This word, with the corresponding noun, is used in a great many connections, but all more or less with the sense of holding or retaining : e. g. *Tak ho'd* is 'take hold '; *Ho'd thi noise* is ' keep quiet'; *a ho'd* is ' a holding of land '; *ti ho'd fair* is ' to continue fine weather '; *ti ho'd talk* or *pross* 'to have a gossiping talk,' the Dan. equivalent to this use being At holde Snak.

Hog or **Hogget**, n. C. A young sheep from the time of its being weaned to that of first shearing. Hogs are of two kinds, wether-hogs and gimmer-hogs, so called according to sex ; after shearing they are all called shearlings.

Hoit, v. F. To play the fool ; hence the noun, one who plays the fool.

Ex.—*He 's a hoit.*

Holl, n. R. A hollow in land.

Hollin, n. C. The holly.

Holm, n. C. (as a place-name) (pr. home or howm ; in Dan. the *l* is sounded). Land which at times is or has been liable to be surrounded or partly surrounded by water. Dan. Holm (an islet).

Honey, n. C. (pr. hunny, i. e. with the *u*-sound as in *put*). A word addressed continually to children, and often, too, by the old to grown-up people, as a term of endearment ; it corresponds to ' dear ' in Std. Eng., that word being never so used in the dialect. The derivation is obvious.

Ex.— *Cum thi waays, hunny.*

This word is frequently found in Shakespeare in a similar sense.

Hoodend, n. C. The ends or corners of the large open fire and chimney place such as was always to be found in old houses, and which may still be seen occasionally. In the *hoodend* there was space for seats, and in the evenings generally was to be seen *t' au'd man* at one side, and *t' au'd lass* at the other ; these were comfortable corners. At the present time, when houses are differently designed, the *hoodend*, properly so-called, is done away with, but the name is retained, and I have frequently heard it applied to the hobs of an ordinary iron fire-grate—a poor substitute for the *hoodend* of older days. The *hoodend* evidently gets its name from the fact of the fireplace and chimney being built somewhat like a hood in shape, the part in question forming the end of the hood, so to speak. It was formerly, and is still often called simply the hood.

Hoof, Hofe, n. R. (pr. heeaf). The abode whether of man or beast, esp. sheep ; when sheep were assigned a pasture on the Moors, they were said to be ' hoofed ' to it.

Hooind, part. F. Harassed, fatigued. I have only heard of this word being used in the E. R.

Hoomer, n. R. The grayling.

Hopper, n. C. The basket containing the seed-corn, and hung by a strap across the shoulder of the sower—called also a *seed-lip.*

Hoos-lek, n. C. The houseleek, commonly planted on the ridge of thatched houses. When bruised with cream it is supposed to be good for scalds or burns.

Hopple, v. C. To tie the legs of an animal so as to retard free motion, that with which the legs are tied being called a *hopple.* This word is also used in the sense of to limp, which of course would be the natural result of tieing the legs; but the word is used when the legs are free, though the motion is of a limping character. It is another form of *hobble.*

> Ex.—*He gans hopplin' aboot.*

Horse-gogs, n. C. A yellow plum which hangs on the tree till nearly Christmas. They were very common near Raskelfe. Atkinson applies the word to a highly astringent blue plum which grows abundantly in the Cleveland district.

Hotter, v. R. (pr. hotther). To shake up, to throw into a state of confusion, to romp or play, especially with an animal inclined to be playful. The word is also used as a noun, a *hotter* being equivalent to a shaking-up; e. g. a dog-hotter would mean a game of romps with a dog, such as a child would indulge in.

> Ex.—*They were all hotthered tigither.*

Hound, v. R. To incite others, to some unworthy purpose (as a rule). The usual term is to *harden.*

> Ex.—*Jack was au'd eneeaf ti knaw better, bud he nobbut hoonded t' others on* (said of lads maltreating a donkey).

House, n. C. The use of this word is quite peculiar: it does not signify the entire house in the ordinary sense of the word, but only the daily room in which the occupants sit; this single room, however small it may be, is called *t' hoos,* the upper rooms being called *cham'rs,* i. e. chambers. Dan. Et hus (a house).

> Ex.—*Sha 's nut i' bed, sha 's i' t' hoos.*

Housefast, adj. C. Confined to the house through illness or some infirmity.

Housen, n. R. (pr. hoosen). Houses. An old plural. I have occasionally heard this old form used even recently on the moors in Cleveland.

> Ex.—*Aback o' t' hoosen.*

Hout, interj. F. An expression denoting incredulity on hearing some statement, and corresponding to 'nonsense' 'surely not,' &c.

Hover, v. C. (pr. hower or 'ower). To hang over : it is however generally used in the sense of to wait, to stop, to take time.

> Ex.—*Hower whahl they come up.* — *Thoo mun 'ower a bit.*

Howsomever, conj. R. (pr. hoosumivver). Howsoever.

Howze, Ouse, v. C. To bale out water from a vessel or receptacle. Dan. At öse (to bale), öse en baad (bale a boat).

> Ex.—*A'e ya owz'd t' watther oot on 't?*

Hubbleshoo, n. R. A great commotion among people.

Huffil, hoffil, n. C. A finger-stall, or finger-poke. O. N. Hufa (a hood).

Hug, v. C. To carry. This word is used to express every kind of carrying, whether e. g. carrying out for burial, or holding any light article, like a stick ; it is never used in the ordinary sense, to embrace.

> Ex.—*Hug it.* — *Sha 'll nivver cum oot na mair whahl sha 's hug g'doot.* — *Wheea hugs t' kei?* (who carries the key ?)

Huggan, Ooven, n. F. The hip.

Huke, n. R. The hip. This word is another form of *yuk* (a hook). Dan. At huke (to hook).

Hull, Hullin, n. C. The shell or outer covering of peas, nuts, &c. Also used as a verb. Dan. At hæle (to conceal).

> Ex.— *Thoo mun braay it weel ti git t' hullins off.*

Hummel, v. C. To break off the awns of barley after thrashing. The past part. (hummel'd) signifies hornless, being applied generally to a cow without horns, such an animal being termed *a hummel'd coo.*

Hunger, v. C. (The *g* is pr. as in singer.) To suffer from hunger ; to starve.

> Ex.—*Ah 's ommost hungered ti deead.* — *Ah 's that hungered whahl ah can hardlins bahd.* — *T' pigs is beealin seea, ah lay you 've been hungerin' 'em.*

Hurne, n. O. A corner by the side of the *hoodend* in old houses, in which ' fire-eldin' was kept. Jutl. D. Hjörne (a corner).

Hussocks, n. C. Tufts of coarse grass growing in pastures, esp. in moist ground.

Hut, n. F. A ridge of clay in the bed of a river. This word, to which *clay* is generally prefixed, is well known in places on the banks of the Ouse.

I.

I, prep. C. (pr. *i*-short). In. Before a vowel *v* is generally added for euphony. Dan. I (in).

Ex.—*It brak i two iv 'er han's.*

Ice shoggle, or **shoglin,** n. C. Icicle. Jutl. D. En Egle (an icicle).

If in case, if so be that, conj. C. Common redundancies for ' if.'

If no more, C. If not more.

Ex.—*There 'll be a scoore on 'em if no mair.*

Ill, adj. C. Bad. This word is commonly used in the dialect in the same way as in the old proverb, ' It is an ill wind that blows nobody any good.' Dan. Ild (ill).

Ex.—*Sparrow-feathers dizn't mak an ill bed when weel cleeaned an' ruddled. — There was ill deed amang 'em.*

Illify, v. C. To speak evil of people behind their backs ; to take away a person's character. Dan. Ilde (ill).

Ex.—*Sha diz nowt bud illify ma. — They 're awlus illifyin' yan anoother.*

Ill thriven, adj. F. Feebly or imperfectly developed ; having the appearance of illness. The prefix *ill* is here, as in other instances, used in the sense of *badly*.

Ill-turn, n. C. Mischief, harm, an injury.

Imp, n. F. An added ring of straw or other material inserted at the base of a beehive to increase its size. Dan. En Ympe (a graft).

Ings, n. C. Grass-land near water, generally low-lying. The singular number of the word is never used ; a double plural *ingses* is frequently heard. Dan. En Eng (a meadow near water). In West Jutland the low-lying fields or grazing-land close to the sea are called *Enge*.

Ex.—*T' watther 's gitten all ower t' ingses. — T' beeas was i' t' ings last neet*

Ingate, n. F. A way in, an entrance.

Ingle, n. R. Fire ; hence *ingle neuk*, the fireside corner, called also *ingle-neeakin*.

Inkleweavers, n. F. Weavers of inkle, i. e. a narrow fabric something like tape, and formerly used somewhat as tape. The word is also used as an opprobrious epithet, and is applied collectively to those who cause trouble.

Ex.—*They 're all inkleweavers tigither is that lot.*

Inow, adv. C. (pr. inoo). Shortly, soon, presently. The derivation of this very common expression is not clear, and its meaning rather variable according to circumstances, being sometimes almost equivalent to ' at once,' and sometimes to ' after some little time.' When in Denmark, I have been much struck by the identical pronunciation of the Danish *endnu* (yet, as yet, even now), and the Yorkshire *inoo* : the following sentence, *Du maa ei komme endnu* (you must not come yet, i. e. at once), when pronounced quickly, sounds exactly the same as *Thoo maunt com inoo.* In this connection *yit* would be used in the dialect ; still, the sentence as it stands would be quite understood, except that *ei* for *not* is dissimilar.

Insense, v. C. (the accent is on the second syllable). To inform, to enlighten a person, to instruct or explain.

Ex.—*Ah 'll seean insense tha inti t' yal ti deea* (' York Minster Screen.')—*He 'll gie tha t' brass hard eneeaf nobbut he 's reetly insensed.*
This word is found in Shakespeare apparently with a similar meaning. Vide p. 89.

Intak, n. F. Land enclosed from a common, road, &c., generally a small piece. Dan. At indtage (to take in).

Inti, intil, intul, intiv, prep. C. Into. It is impossible to give a fixed rule as to the uses of the different forms of this word ; *inti* however is used before a consonant, and *intiv* before a vowel ; *intil* and *intul*, though not so frequent, are still very common, esp. at the end of a sentence and before ' it.'

Ex.—*There 's neea spot ti put t' gallowa intul.* —*Noo, lads, ram awaay intul 't.*

Intiv, prep. C. Vide **Inti.**

Iv, prep. C. Vide **I.**

J.

Jack, n. C. Half a gill; i. e. a quarter pint.

Jag, n. C. A light load, as much as will fill the body of a cart without being piled up.

Jannock, adj. C. Even, level ; hence, fair, just and right—the sense in which the word is generally used. Dan. Jævn (even, equal).

Ex.—*Jannock* (a common quasi-interjection when two parties are bargaining).—*It isn't jannock.*

Jaup, v. C. To shake violently water or other liquid in a vessel.

Ex.—*Deean't jaup it aboot.*

Jealous, adj. C. Apprehensive, afraid lest.

Ex.—*Ah wer jealous sha wer boun'.ti be awk'ard.—Ah 's jealous he weean't cum.*

Jenny-owlet, n. C. (pr. jinny-ullot). The screech-owl.

Jimmer, n. F. The hinge of a door; also applied to small hinges. A Holderness word.

Ex.—*T' deear beeals oot on t' jimmer,* i. e. the door creaks on the hinge.

Job, v. C.   To trade in.
   Ex.—Q. *What diz he deea?*   A. *He jobs a few hens or owl.*
Jodder, n. F. (pr. jodther).   A state of shaking or quivering.
Atkinson gives an amusing example of the use of this
word, viz. ' Well, how did you like your ride on the rail-
way, Mrs. B?' (A very stout unhealthy fat woman.)
*Wheea, sae badly, ah'll nivver gan i yan o' thae nasty vans
nae mair. Ah trimml'd an' dither'd whahl I wur all iv a
jother.*
Joggle-stiok, n. C.   The movable stick in a cart, with which
the body of the cart is secured to the shafts, the stick
being removed when the cart has to be tilted.
Joskin, n. F.   A country lad.   I have only heard of this word
being used in the E. R.
Joul, v. C. (pr. jowl or jaul).   To jolt, to shake.
   Ex.—*They gat thersens sadly jauled wi t' rahd.*

K.

Kale, Kail, Cael, n. F. (pr. keeal).   Porridge, broth; hence
kale-pot, F.   Dan. Kaal, Kaal-potte.   Wel. Caulen (cole-
wort), Cawl (broth).   Lat. Caulis.   Gr. καυλός (a cabbage).
Kame, n. C. (pr. keeam).   A comb; also used as a verb, of
which the p.p. is *kem't.*   Dan. At kjæmme, p.p. kjæmmet
(combed).
   Ex.—*Git thi hair kem't.*
Kansh, n. F.   (1) A hard ridge of gravel or rock in the bed
of a river, dangerous to navigation.   (2) A rough channel
cut on a road to carry off the surface water sideways into
the ditch.
Kave, v. C. (pr. keeave).   To rake the ' pulls ' and ' caff' from
corn in thrashing; also to paw the ground impatiently,
as a horse in good condition does.   Norse Kava (to
scrape with the hands); Swedish Kafva; Icel. Kafa.
Keck, v. F.   To make the effect produced by something
between a cough and a choke; also used as a noun.
Keckenhearted, adj. C.   Over particular in the matter of
food, dainty, loathing the sight of food.
   Ex.—*They 're varry keckenhearted 'uns.*
Kedge, v. C.   To fill; generally applied to eating and drinking.   Hence a *kedge,* one who eats greedily; also *kedging,*
food of any kind.
   Ex.—*They 're kedgin' ther insahds wi mull'd yal an'
whistlejacket.—He 's ower-kedg'd hissen.*
Keek, v. R. (pr. keeak).   To raise perpendicularly; to tilt up
a cart, or partially so, in order that it may be the more
readily loaded.

Keld, n. O. (pr. kel). A spring of water. This word is now only to be found in place-names. Dan. Kilde; Jutl. D. Kel (a spring).

Kelk, n. C. (1) A heavy blow or thump. (2) The common fœtid parsley of the hedgerows.

Ex.—*He gav him sikan a kelk ower 't shoodthers.*

Kelter, n. C. Condition, state, case; esp. when applied to an animal, e. g. a horse. This word has also sometimes the meaning of *money*.

Ex.—*He's a bit o' good keltther aboot him.*

Kelterment, n. C. Things of no real value, odds and ends, rubbish.

Ex.—*Ah nivver seed sike kelterment; they're good ti nowt.*

Ken, v. C. To know, to recognise, to be acquainted with. The use of this word is not so general as it used to be. Dan. At kjende (to know).

Ex.—*Ah can't ken ya, bairn.—Di ya ken whau yon man is?—Yan wadn't ken t' hoos noo* (said after a house had been re-furnished).

Kenning, n. C. Knowledge, recognition. Dan. Kjending (acquaintance).

Ex.—*Ah 've neea kennin' for him*, i. e. I do not recognise him.

This word is also the common pr. for churning; e. g. *a kennin o' butther* is a churning of butter.

Kenspack, adj. F. Easy to be distinguished or recognised. This is no doubt the right form of this old word, though *kensmak* may be sometimes used. Jutl. D. Kjendespag (one who easily distinguishes).

Ex.—*That 's maist kensmak'd o' t' two*, i. e. that is the better likeness of the two.

Kep. v. C. To catch anything that is thrown or tossed, as a ball, brick, &c. Icel. Kippa (to catch hold of).

Ex.—*Kep it.—Noo! canst ta kep?*

Kern, n. C. (pr. ken, approximately). A churn; also commonly used as a verb for the act of churning or being churned.

Kern, n. R. The form which this word generally takes is *kerning*, and may be equivalent to *kerneling*: e. g. *a good kerning time* is a good time for the grain to set after the blooming; and when it has well set it is said to be *weel coornea*.

Kess'mas, **Kess'nmas**, n. C. Christmas.

Kess'n, v. C. To christen; hence *Kess'nd name* (Christian name).

Kest, v. C. To cast, to throw off—the past part being *kess'n*. This word is commonly applied to throwing off any ailment, e. g. a severe cold.

Ex.—*T' lahtle lass has had t' kincough a fo'tnith, an' sha
, hesn't kess'n 't yit.—Wa maun't kest wer flannin skets
yit; it's ower cau'd bi hauf.*

Ket, n. C. Carrion, tainted meat ; also used as an adj. in
the sense of ' high.' Dan. Kjöd (flesh meat).

Ex.—*Ah can't eeat sike ket.*

Ket-man, n. F. One who deals in dead animals, a knacker.

Ex.—*T au'd hoss is fit for nowt bud t' ket-man.*

Ketlock, n. C. The common charlock ; also called *brassic*,
esp. in the East Riding.

Ex.—*They 're pullin ketlocks yonder, see ya.*

Kevel, n. R. A large hammer used in quarrying.

Kex, n. F. The dry seed-stem of the fools-parsley, cow-
parsnip, &c.

Ex.—*As dhry as a kex.*

Kid, n. R. A bundle. It is noteworthy that this word is
only retained in connection with ' whins ' or thorns ; e. g.
A kid o' whins.

The form *kidding* is also in use in Holderness, and
signifies strengthening the bank of a river, &c., by laying
bundles of thorns along the weak places. Wel. Cidysen
(a faggot).

Kindling, n. C. (pr. kinlin). Material for lighting a fire,
generally wood.

Kink, v. C. To laugh so as to gasp for breath.

Ex.—*He fair kinked ageean wi laughin'.*

Kink, n. C. A twist in a rope ; also used participially in
. the sense of twisted. The word s commonly applied, too,
to a violent fit of coughing. Dan. Kink (a nautical term
for a twist on a rope).

Ex.—*A kink o' laughter.—T' raupe's gotten kinked.*

Kink-cough, n. C. (pr. kin'-cough). The whooping-cough.
Jutl. D. Kink-hoste (whooping-cough).

Kirk, n. R. A church. This word is now seldom heard
except in place-names, *chetch* having pretty generally
supplanted it. Dan. Kirke (church).

Kirkgarth, n. F. A churchyard. Dan. Kirkgaard (churchyard).

Kirk-warner, n. F. A churchwarden ; now generally called
chetch-warner.

Kist, n. C. A chest, in its various senses. Dan. Kiste (a
chest), Ligkiste (a coffin).

Kit, n. F. A small pail for milking, and having a perpendicular handle. Sometimes the kit was carried on the head.
The word is also used for a small kind of tub of similar
shape, e. g. a *sau't-kit*, a kit for keeping salt in.

Kite, n. C. The belly ; hence the adj. *kity.*

Kitling n. C. (pr. kitlin). A kitten. Dan. Killing (kitten).
Kittle, kitling, adj. C. Easily put in motion, ticklish, excitable Dan. Kilden (ticklish).
    Ex.—*As kittle as a moos-trap.—A kitling cough.*
Kittle, v. C. To tickle, to excite. Dan. At kildre (to tickle).
Kitty-keis, n. F. The seeds of the ash-tree ; called also *cats and eyes.*
Knack, v. C. To talk affectedly, to talk in a mincing manner.
    Ex.—*Ah deean't ken their knick-knackin talk.—He spoils hissen sadly wi knackin.*
Knag, n. F. A stubble rake. Dan. En Knag (a wooden peg to hang anything upon).
Knap, v. C. To give a short but quick blow, esp. with a stick ; to knock ; also to crack anything into pieces which is brittle, as a grain of corn between the teeth, a stone, &c. Also used correspondingly as a noun.
    Ex.—*Keep them fingers oot o' t' tthreeacle or they 'll git knapp'd inoo.*
Knap, n. C. A rogue, a knave.
Knar, n. F. A knot or small piece of hard wood for playing the game of 'knar and spell,' called more commonly in the North Riding 'dab and spell,' *dab* being the short blow or *knap* requisite to raise the *knar,* and *spell* being properly not the 'trap' but the act of playing. From Dan. Spil (play).
Knep, v. C. To nibble, to bite off. Dan. Knibe (to pinch). Vide **Nip.**
    Ex.—*T' au'd coo 's been kneppin t' young shuts off ageean.*
Knodden, part. of Knead. Jutl. D. Knæde (to knead).
Knoll, v. F. To toll a bell, esp. a church bell ; e. g. at a funeral. Dan. Knald (a report).
    Ex.—*Wheea 's t' bell knollin' for ?*
Kye, n. F. Cows. Whether this be an old plural of cow or not is uncertain ; there is however a seeming analogy between the Yorkshire Koo—Kye and the Danish Ko—Köer. Icel. Kyr.

L.

Labber, v. R. To splash about in water or mud. Dan. At labe (to lap).
    Ex.—*He labbered aboot i' t' watther.*
Laboursome, adj. F. Laborious and fatiguing.
Lae, n. C. (pr. lay and leea). A scythe ; hence *Leea-sand,* i. e. sand of a biting kind for sharpening a scythe. Dan. En Le (a scythe). This word is most common in the E. R. at the present time. Another form of the word was *lye—*

this was used in the Northallerton district, and may be
so still, *My au'd lye* being there a common expression ;
lae, however, was a much commoner form.

Lafter, n. C. A 'sitting' of eggs, i. e. the whole number on
which a hen sits at one time. Sometimes also the word
is applied jestingly to a large family of children. When
the hen has laid the last egg before sitting she is said to
have 'laid her lafter'; hence some have called that egg
only the lafter, but generally it is applied to the entire
number.

Ex.—*Ah aims she 's ligged her lafter* (Atk., *Cl. Gloss.*).

Lag, n. C. One of the wooden divisions of a cask or tub.

Lagged, part. F. Tired, exhausted.

Ex.—*Ah feels ommaist lagged ti' deead.*

Lahtle, adj. C. Little. Vide **Lile**. O. N. Litill.

Lair, n. F. A barn ; mostly used in the E. R. Dan. En
Lade (a barn).

Ex.—*It 's liggin ov oor lair fleear.*

Lake, v. C. (pr. laak). To play. Dan. At lege (to play).
Icel. Leikr (a game). This word is commonly added
as a suffix to a specific game, e. g. *ball-laakin, creckit-
laakin*, &c.

Ex.—*Will ta com an' laak a bit, Jack?*

Lame, v. C. To hurt ; to damage ; to render any member
of the body incapable of performing its functions properly.

Ex.—*Ah 've laamed my han' sadly.—Ah 's weeanily
laam'd i' my shoodher wi t' rheumatics.*

Land, n. C. (pr. lan). The space between two adjacent furrows in a ploughed field.

Land, v. C. (1) To reach one's destination. (2) To succeed.

Ex.—(1) *Ah had ti put t' au'd meer intiv a muck lather,
bud it 's owered, an' ah 's landed* (said by one who had
driven hard to catch a train).—(2) *Dust ta think thoo 'll
land?*

Lang, adj. C. Long. Dan. Læng (long).

Ex.—*Deean't be ower lang.*

Lang-length, adv. C. (pr. lang-lenth). At full length.

Ex.—*Ah see'd him stthritch'd lang-lenth upo' t' grunnd.*

Langsettle, n. C. A long wooden seat with high back and
an arm at each end ; used to be common in public-houses,
and may still be seen pretty frequently. A. S. Setl.

Ex.—*Ah seed him set i' t' langsettle ower aneust us.*

Langsome, adj. R. Long and tedious. Jutl. D. Langsom (slow).

Lantered, part. R. Belated, delayed instarting, esp. on a
journey. Dan. Lænte (to linger).

Lantern light, n. C. (pr. lantron leet). The horn of a lantern
through which the light shines.

Lanty, n. F. Late one, slow-coach ; generally addressed to one who keeps others waiting.

Ex.—*Noo! lanty.*

Lapband, n. F. Hoop-iron.

Lapcock, n. C. The first form of collected hay after spreading, consisting in twisting a ' fold ' of hay in the arms and laying it lightly on the ground. In a wet ' hay time ' this was commonly done in certain districts, and is so still occasionally ; in this state, by a *façon de parler*, the hay is said to be ' off the ground.'

Ex.—*Wa mun a'e wer haay inti lapcock.*

Lap, v. C. To wrap ; generally followed by *up*, but by no means always so; when so followed it has also the meanings to finish, to give up, to stop work, &c.

Ex.—*T' stuff were lapp'd iv a bit o' paaper. — It wer lapp'd roond wi band. — Ah think Willie 's varry seean lapp'd up wi t' job. — It 's aboot tahm ti lap up.*

Larkheel'd, adj. C. Having receding heels, the opposite of duck-heeled ; said of persons.

Ex.—*Sha 's a reg'lar larkheel'd 'un yon.*

Lasty, adj. C. Durable, esp. of wearing apparel, or indeed of any fabric or material.

Ex.—*It 's a bit o' good lasty stuff.*

Lathe, n. R. A barn ; sometimes the word was used for the ends of a barn only. Another form of *lair*. Dan. Lade (barn).

Lat, n. C. A lath.

Late, v. C. To seek. Dan. At lede (to seek).

Ex.—*Q. Wheer 's that lad ov 'oors? A. Ah deean't knaw; ah laay he 's laatin bo'd-nests.*

Later, n. F. A seeker.

Ex.—When something had been lost, boys, as they begin to search, will sometimes say to one another, *Lossers, laters; findders, keepers*; i. e. You who have lost and you who seek, let it be understood that those who find what you have lost will keep it.

Latty, adj. C. Thin, like a *lat*.

Ex.—*Mr. A. 's a tall latty man.*

Lax, n. C. Diarrhœa. or complaints of a similar nature.

Lay, v. C. To half cut a hedge. Vide **Lig.**

Lead, v. C. (1) To convey goods on a cart ; to carry, cart, haul. (2) To navigate a vessel through a short bend in a river. Vide **Rack.**

Ex.—(1) *Wa start leadin' ti-morn.— Matty's gitten his haay led, then. — T' parson 's on leadin'. — (2) They're leading t' rack.*

Lead-eater, n. R. India-rubber. In former years this was the term always applied to this article.

Leafs, n. C. The thick lines of fat along a pig's carcase.

Learn, v. C. (pr. larn). To teach.

Ex.—*He nivver larnt ma nowt.*

Lease, v. R. To pick out, to gather by picking; hence *leasing*, i. e. the separating of two kinds of corn in the sheaf.

Leathe-wake, adj. F. (pr. lceath-wek). Pliant or supple in limb. Jutl. D. Lede-myg (joint-supple). This word is applied generally to flexibility of limb shortly after death, or in the case of a stiff joint when it begins to show signs of returning suppleness.

Ex.—*It's quiet leeath-wek yit* (said on picking up a dead bird).

Leavelang, adj. C. (pr. leeavelang). Oblong.

Leave loose, v. C. (pr. leeav lowse). Let go, e. g. of a rope, chain, &c. 'Leave hold' is also in use.

Ex.—*Leeav lowse han's* (said by a child walking hand in hand with another).

Leck, v. C. To leak; also to cause to drop or sprinkle. To *leck on* means to add more water, &c. Dan. Lække (to leak). Icel. Lek. The substantive also retains this form, which has been evidently handed down unchanged through many generations.

Lee, n. C. The watery discharge from a wound. This is also the pronunciation of *lie* (a falsehood) and the corresponding verb. Dan. Lud (lye); Icel. Lang.

Leef, lief, adv. C. Willingly; also common in the comparative, *leefer.*

. Ex.—*Ah 'd as leef gan as stop.*

Leets, n. C. The lungs.

Leetsome, adj. F. Vide **Lightsome.**

Lenny, n. C. The linnet.

Lesty-day, interj. R. An exclamation, equivalent to 'alas!' I suspect this word is wellnigh obsolete : a correspondent who lived for many years near Northallerton tells·me he never heard but one person use the expression.

Let on, v. F. To divulge, to tell a secret.

Ex.—*Jack knew all t' tahm, bud he nivver let on aboot it.*

Leve, v. C. To raise by leverage.

Ex.—*Wa mun leve it up.*

Liberty, n. C. The area of territorial rights; often applied to a parish or township, sometimes also to a manor or even small freeholds.

Ex.—*Sha 's gitten inti Bo'nby liberty.*

Lie on, v. C. To apply force to.

Ex.—*He didn't lie on a deal. — Lie mair on* (said of hitting out at cricket).

Lig, v. C. To lie, to lie down in sleep, to be situate ; also in a transitive sense, to lay down, esp. to half cut a hedge. Dan. At ligge (to lie).

Ex.—*Wheer does sha lig?* i. e. sleep.—*Lig doon.—It ligs ower agaan Uskill* (Ulleskelf).— *Thoo maun't lig it doon.* — *Whau's that liggin yon hedge?*

Light, v. C. (pr. leet). (1) To alight, to settle upon. (2) To fall in with, to meet.

Ex.—Q. *Wheer did them bo'ds leet?* — A. *They let iv oor coo-pastur.* — *Ah let on him at t' toon-end.* — *A'e ya letten on a job yit?*

Light, in that, C. (pr. I that leet). Like that.

Ex.—*Thoo maun't deea it i' that leet.* — *Just i' that leet, si-tha* (suiting the action to the word).

Light on, v. C. (pr. leet on). To fare.

Ex.—*Hoo sal wa leet on this tahm, thinks ta?* — *Your Dick 's letten on middlin', ah expect.*

Lightsome, adj. F. (pr. leetsom). Light, cheerful, bright.

Ex.—*Ah feels a bit leetsomer.*

Like, adj. used adverbially, C. (pr. leyke). Likely, highly probable, in duty bound; to be expected. Dan. Lige (like). Cf. Jeg var lige ved at tumle (*ah war like ti tumm'l*).

Ex.—*He's leyke ti knaw.* — *Ah 's leyke ti gan,* i. e. It is to be expected I should go. — *Thoo 's leyke ti cum,* i. e. you must come.

Like all that, C. Like anything.

Ex.—*He ran leyke all that.* — *T' bairn ruored leyke all that.*

Lile, adj. C. (pr. lahl and leel). Little. I am inclined to think that *lahl* is the commoner pr., although *leel* more nearly approaches the Danish *lille* from which this comes, the Danish sound of the word being as nearly as possible *leell.* *Leel* is a pr. seldom if ever heard in the E. R. The usual equivalent is *lahtle*, which is heard all the district through more or less, though the form *laitle* is also used.

Lillilow, n. R. A flame, a blaze, the light as from a candle. Dan. Lue (a flame). It is possible this word may be a combination of *ild* and *lue*.

Lilting, adj. F. Lively, frolicsome.

Ex.—*They were liltin' aboot* (i. e. jumping about).

Limmers, n. F. Shafts of a cart, &c. O. N. Lim (the branch of a tree).

Lin, n. C. (pr. line or lahn). Flax. Dan. Liin (linen); linned klud (linen clout).

Ling, n. C. Heather : hence *ling watther*, i. e. water from off the moors, easily distinguished by its yellowish brown colour. Dan. Lyng (heather).

z

Ling-nail, lin-nail, n. C.   The lynch-pin of a wheel.   Dan.
Lund-pind (lynch-pin).

Lingy, adj. C. (pr. linjy).   Active, supple of limb ; said of
men, esp. if somewhat tall.
> Ex.—*Mr. A 's as lingv as a lad. — A lingy chap.*

Lisk, n. C.   The groin.   Dan. Lyske (groin).

Lite, v. F.   To rely upon, to wait for.   Dan. At lide paa (to
depend upon).
> Ex.—*Ah lited ov him, an he lited o' me. — Ah 've lited ov
> him ivver sae lang.*

Lithe, v. C.   To thicken anything boiled with flour, linseed,
&c. ; hence *lithing,* that which thickens anything boiled.

Liver, v. C.   To deliver.   Dan. Levere (to deliver).
> Ex.—*He 's throng liverin' cauls.*

Live upright, v. F.   To live in independent circumstances.

Loan, Loaning, n. C. (pr. looan, loanin, lonnin, lounin).   A
lane, a by-road, a road.   Icel. Leyningr (a hollow way'.
> Ex.—*Ah see'd him gannin' doon' t' looanin.—T' coos is i'
> t' looans noo, an' oor Fred 's tentin on 'em.*

Loggin, n. C.   A bundle (of straw).

Long-strucken, part. C.   Having legs long in proportion to
the size of the animal, esp. a horse ; this is seen when, in
running, the hind feet strike the ground in advance of the
previous tread of the forefoot.

Look a bad look, C.   To look very ill.
> Ex.—*Poor Jamie leeaks a bad leeak.*

Loose end, n. C.   The phrase, to be 'at a loose end,' signifies to have ' gone to the bad ' or verging towards it.
> Ex.—*Ah doot at sum on 'em 's nobbut at a loose end.*

Loosing, part. R.   Going about idly from place to place.

Loo' ya ! interjectionally used, C.   Look ye !

Lop, n. C.   A flea.   Dan. En Loppe (a flea).
> Ex.—*Ah 'll be back i' t' crackin of a lop.*

Loss, v. C.   To lose.
> Ex.—*Thoo 'll a'e ti mahnd an' nut loss it.*

Lound, adj. C. (pr. lown').   Calm, still, free from wind,
sheltered.   Dan. Lun (sheltered).
> Ex.—*It 's varry loun' this eftherneean. — T' wind 's loun'.*

Loup, v. C. (pr. neither lope nor lowp but between the two).
To leap, jump.   Dan. Löbe (to run).
> Ex.—*T' beeos is loupin aboot weeantly.*
This word is also used as a noun.

Low, n. C.   A flame, blaze, glow.   Dan. Lue (a flame).
> Ex.—*It brak intiv a low just as ah gat theer* (said in de-
> scribing the outbreak of a fire). — *T' low o' t' cann'l. —
> T' low 's catched it.*

Lowance, n. C.   The allowance of ale drunk at hay and harvest time; this is brought into the field in large stone jars and drunk at about 4 p.m. during a half-hour's pause from labour. Sometimes this refreshment is called 'drinkings,' but the more familiar term is *lowance* (sometimes pr. launce).

Lowse, v. C. (pr. lozc, nearly). To loose, to unfasten; also to terminate. Dan. At löse (to loose).

Ex.—*Hez t' chetch lowzed yit?* i. e. has the congregation broken up yet?

Lowzin tahm, n. C. The time for unyoking the horses after a day's work, preparatory to taking them home, generally about 5 p.m.

Luby, n. R. Cloth clothes; generally used for better or Sunday clothes. Dan. Lu (nap of cloth).

Ex.—*Git that theer luby off.*

Lug, n. C. The ear; the handle of a jug, &c.

Ex.—*What fahin lugs t' dog 's gitten.*

Luke, v. C. To pull up weeds from fields of corn. This is commonly done by gangs of women and children in the Wold country. Dan. At luge (to weed); Icel. Lok (a weed).

Ex.—*There 's a deeal on 'em lukin i' yon field seem'nly.* Weeds of any kind pulled up by the hand are said to be *han' luked.*

Lungeous, adj. F. Revengeful.

Ex.—*They 're a varry lungeous thing is an elephant.*

M.

Mad, adj. C. Very angry.

Ex.—*He was mad, noo.*

Maddle, v. C. To confuse, esp. by noise; to become bewildered.

Ex.—*T' noise o' t' organ maddles ma.*

Mafted, adj. C. Oppressed with heat, stifled.

Ex.—*Ah wer that mafted, ah wer fit ti soond awaay.*

Main, adj. and adv. C. (1) The chief part, the largest portion, the majority. (2) Very, especially.

Ex.—(1) *T' main on 'em gans tiv oor pump.*—(2) *Ah 's main glad ti see tha.*

Mainswear, v. R. To take a false oath. Dan. Mened (a false oath).

Mair, adj. C. More. The superlative is Maist or Meeast. Dan. Mere (more).

Ex.—*Ah knaw na mair 'an nowt (or na nowt).*—'*Mair heeast warse speed.'*

Mak, v. F. To pet, to make much of, to coax: always followed by *on.* Also the common pr. of *make.*

Z 2

Ex.—*You maun't shoot* (shout) *at her, you mun mak on her*
(said to a sportsman when borrowing a timid pointer).

Mak oot, v. C. To make progress, prosper, succeed ; generally used in a qualified sense, in which case it is
commonly accompanied by *badly*.

Ex.—*Au'd Neddy maks badly oot wi' t' job.* — *Sha maks
badly oot*, i. e. makes slow progress towards recovery.

Maks and mandthers, n. C. Sorts and kinds, shapes and
sizes ; lit. makes and manners. Vide **Manders.**

Mak-shift, n. C. A rough and ready substitute. A makeshift. This word is not peculiar to the dialect, but I give
it, as a similar expression is used in Danish, Et Mage-
skifte, meaning an exchange.

Malack, n. F. (pr. maalack, the accent being on the first syllable). A spree, a disturbance. An E. R. word.

Ex.—*There wer sike maalacks as ah nivver-seed.*

Manders, n. C. (pr. mandthers). Varieties, different kinds.

Ex.—*They were all maks an' manders.*
This word is generally used in connection with *maks*,
and is a corruption of *manners*.

Mannish, v. C. To manage ; hence *mannishment*, which is
used esp. for manure for land.

Ex.—*Oor tonnops 'as had plenty o' good mannishment.*

Marrish, n. O. A marsh. We have this word in the place-
name Marishes, and it has the same meaning as *Marsk*,
the Danish for a marsh.

Marrow, n. C. One of a pair, or one to match another ;
generally followed by *to*.

Ex.—*We had two, bud we 've lost t' marrow tiv it.*

Marry, interj. F. This word is only used in cases of decided
assent or dissent, and is equivalent to 'yes, indeed.' It
is by no means so commonly used as formerly. It is of
the nature of an oath, being no doubt a corruption of *by
Marie*. The same use of the word is found in the South-
West Jutland dialect.

Ex.—*Aye, marry ; they will that.* — *Naay, marry ; nivver.*

Mash, mask, v. C. To make, or draw out the strength of
tea by pouring water upon it. Dan. At Mæske (to mash
—in brewing).

Ex.—*T' tea isn't quiet mash'd yit.*

**Mashelson, mashelshon, mashelton, mashelgem, mashlin,
maslin, meslin,** n. F. Wheat and rye mixed together,
and often grown together for the purpose of making
brown bread : this, however, is not so commonly used
as formerly. Sometimes the word is used figuratively in
the sense of 'neither one thing nor another.'

Ex.—*They can mak nowt bud mashelshon on 't* (said of

ignorant persons who try to speak in a refined manner).

Mask, n. F. The face, without any idea of disguise. The hunter's term for the fox's head or face.

> Ex.—*Sha 'll tak' thi mask for tha,* i. e. she will photograph you.

Matter, v. C. To care for, value, take account of.

> Ex.—*Ah deean't matter him mich.*

Matters, n. C. Quantity, account. Very commonly used in such phrases as *neea matters, onny matters,* &c.

> Ex.—*Ah can't tak neea greeat matters o' meeat.*

Maumy, adj. C. Possessing a woolly ripeness, soft. Dan. Moden (pr. moen), ripe. Jutl. D. Mo.

> Ex.—*It 's soft an' maumy leyke.*

Maun't, v. C. An abbreviation of may not, and mun not, i. e. must not.

Mawk, n. C. A maggot. Also used as a verb. Dan. Maddike (maggot); Jutl. D. Majek; Norse Makk; Icel. Madhkr.

> Ex.—*They 'll mawk leyke sheep.*

Meadow-drake, n. F. The corn-crake.

Meal, n. C. Flour of various kinds that is not dressed; e. g. oat meal, barley meal, bread meal, which latter is wheat flour from which brown bread is made.

Mean, adj. C. (pr. meean). This word is not only used in the ordinary sense, but also to express worthlessness of character or conduct. Dan. En Men (a hurt, defect, harm.)

> Ex.—*It 's a varry meean tthrick,* i. e. a piece of badness.
> —*He coms yam as meean as muck.*

Meat, n. C. (pr. meeat.) Food.

> Ex.—*It 's nobbut a middlin meeat spot,* i. e. it 's not a very first-rate house for getting well fed at.

Meat, v. C. (pr. mecat). To provide with food. This is a good instance of the common habit of verbalizing substantives in the dialect.

> Ex.—*He meeats hissen, an' ah weshes him,* i. e. he finds his own food, and I wash for him.

Meeastther, maastther, n. C. Master.

Meg, n. R. A halfpenny. I have only heard this word used in the phrase *Ah a'e n't a meg.*

Mell, v. C. To meddle; always followed by *on* instead of *with.*

> Ex.—*Thoo maun't mell on 'em.*

Mell, n. C. A wooden mallet.

Mellsheaf, n. C. The last sheaf of corn in the harvest-field.

> Ex.—*We 've gotten t' mell,* i. e. the harvest is ended.

Mell-supper, n. C. The harvest supper given by the farmer

to those he has employed for the ingathering of the corn :
a harvest home. Dan. Mel (meal) ; Icel. Mjöl.

Mend, v. C. To improve, to grow better— esp. in health.
>Ex.—Q. How is your husband ? A. *He 's mending nicely.*

Mends, n. C. Improvement ; also used much in the same way as 'prospect of improvement ' in Std. Eng.
>Ex.—*Ah doot there 's neea mends for her.*

Mense, n. C. Decency, becoming conduct, good appearance.
Dan. En Menneske (a human being).
>Ex.—' *There 's nowther sense nor mense i sike a peeace*' ('York Minster Screen').—*Wheer a'e ya been? Thoo 's ta'en all t' mense off'n thi cleeas. . .*

Menseful, adj. C. Decent, becoming, neat, orderly ; also adverbially, *mensefully.*
>Ex.—*A menseful funeral.—Thoo deean't leeak menseful i them things.*

Met, n. C. Two bushels measure, or five stone weight.
Originally no doubt this was a measure only, but now the word is applied to things bought by weight, e. g. coals, as well as those by measure. A *met-poke* was the name given to a narrow bag holding two bushels.

Meuse, v. R. To study, to contemplate. This word, which is now wellnigh obsolete, was very common fifty years ago.
>Ex.— *Cum here ti meuse mi hand* (said by a servant maid as she picked up the ace of trumps).

Mew, perf. of mow. C.

Mew-burnt, adj. C. (pr. mew-bo'nt). Heated or burnt in the stack.

Mew up, v. F. To pile up, to store, to stack.

Mich, adj. C. (pr. mitch). Much.
>Ex.—*Nut mich.*

Mickle, adj. R. Much. O. N. Mikill ; O. Dan. Mögel (much).

Midden, n. C. A manure-heap, a heap of rubbish or muck.
Dan. Mödding (a manure-heap).

Middle-band, n. C. The band which connects the swipple of a flail with the handstaff, allowing it free play.

Mig, n. C. The drainings of a manure-heap, cow-house, stable, &c. ; any kind of liquid manure. Dan. Mög (manure).

Milk-can, n. C. Milk-pail. Dan. Malke-kande (a milk-pail or jug).

Milled in, part. R. Shrunk, withered.
>Ex.—*He 's milled in a good bit.*

Milner, n. C. (sometimes pr. minler). A miller. O. N. Mylnari ; Dan. En Möller (a miller).

Mind, v. C. (pr. mahnd). To remember.
Ex.—*Ah mahnd yance,* i. e. I remember once—a very common preface to a story.

Mindful, adj. C. Careful. So too the verb 'to mind' is almost always used rather than to 'take care,' and 'to observe.'
Ex.—*Thoo 'll a'e ti be mahndful gannin' thruff t' yat.*

Mint, n. C. To intend, to aim, to make a pretence at doing; to mimic.
Ex.—*They didn't deea it, bud they minted at it.*

Miraculous, adj. C. (pr. miraklous). Lively, precocious, cleverly mischievous. This word is applied to children, and sometimes to animals.
Ex.—*He 's a miraklous young jockey.—There 's neea badness aboot him, bud he 's a bit miraklous.*
I have not heard the word in the East Riding, but it is very common in the south part of the North Riding. A horse full of play, or frisky on being brought out of the stable, would be said to be *miraklous.*

Misken, v. F. (in pr. the accent is on the second syllable). To mistake anyone's identity. Dan. At miskjende (to misjudge).

Mistal, n. F. (pr. mistle and mis'l). A cow-house.

Mistetched, part. C. Fallen into bad habits. This expression is most commonly applied to a horse that has acquired some bad habit through ill-usage or otherwise.
Ex.—*Sha's gotten quiet mistetched.*

Moit, n. F. A small piece or particle.
Ex.—*He's nobbut just a moit o' bread.*

Moozy-faced, mouzy, adj. C. (pr. something between moozy and mouzy). Downy-faced, a face having on it the first symptoms of a beard. This word is also applied to the moon when it looks thick and hazy.

Mostlings, adv. C. (pr. mostlins and meeastlins). For the most part, generally.
Ex.—*Ah meeastlins gans.*

Moudiwarp, n. C. (pr. moodiwahrp). The common mole. This word is frequently shortened to *moudi.* Dan. En Muldvarp (a mole).

Mounge, v. F. To munch, to chew.

Muck, n. C. Dirt, manure. Dan. Mög ; Jutl. D. Mog (manure).

Muck, v. C. To spread manure on the land. Jutl. D. Moge (to muck).
Ex.—*Hez Sammy gitten his swath garth mucked ower yit?*

Muck out, v. C. To rid of dirt or muck.
Ex.—*Noo, be sharp an' git t' pig-sty muck'd oot.*

Mucky, adj. C.   Dirty; also used opprobriously for foul, mean.   Jutl. D. Moget (foul, mean).

> Ex.—*Thoo mucky beggar, ger out o' t' rooad!—There was sike mucky deed as ah nivver seed.*

Mud, v. (auxiliary) C. (pr. as would).   Might.

> Ex.—*Yan mud as weel gan.*

Multure, n. R.   The portion of corn taken by the miller as pay for grinding.   Formerly when corn was sent to the mill for grinding, the miller was never paid in money but only in kind.   More than a due share was called *double mooter* (pr. mootther).   Lat. Molitura (a grinding), hence Fr. Mouture.

Multure, v. F.   To take pay in kind for grinding corn.

> Ex.—*Ha'e ya mootther'd oor corn?—Wa mostlins mootthers oor bit o' stuff.*

Mump, n. C.   A blow on the face with the fist; also used as a verb in a similar sense.

> Ex.—*He gav him a mump ower t' mooth.*

Mun, v. (auxiliary).   Must.

> Ex.—*Mun I tak ho'd* (the *I* here is pronounced as *y* at the end of a word).—*Yan mun deea as weel as yan can.*

Mun, n. C.   Man (in vocative case only).

> Ex.—*Tak ho'd, mun.—Ah 've ta'en it, mun.*

This form, though very common, is seldom used except under a certain amount of excitement on the part of the speaker, or when emphasis is required.

Mush, n. C.   Dusty refuse, anything decayed into small fragments, e. g. rotten wood; sometimes used as a verb in a similar sense.

Mushy, adj. C.   In a state of decay; dusty from decay.

My song, by songs, interj. R.   A corruption of the old French oath (La Sangue).

> Ex.—*Mah song! bud ah will smack tha.—By songs! bud he 's deean it this tahm.*

Muz-web, **mus-web**, n. C.   Cob-web: in Cleveland *muz-web* is generally applied to gossamer, but not so in the south of the N. R.   Fr. Mouche.

N.

Na, conj. C. (pr. nă).   (1) No.   (2) Than.   This word is possibly a shortened pronunciation of *no* or *nor*, though more probably it is an inversion of the letters in *'an*, which is itself an abbreviation of *than*; it is used only, but very commonly, in certain phrases.

> Ex.—Q. 'Do you remember it?'—A. *Na mair na nowt.*

The expression *na mair 'an nowt* is also common. The form *na* is never used as the simple negative.

Naay, adv. C. Pr. of *nay*. Vide **Neea**.

Nab, n. F. An abrupt and generally rocky point whether on the coast or inland ; e.g. Wo' Nab (Wold Nab), a steep projection on the west side of the wolds between Acklam and Leavening. Jutl. D. Nabe (a point, lit. a bill).

Nacks, n. R. An old-fashioned game that used to be played a generation ago. Nine holes were made on the ground, and the principle of the game was something like bagatelle.

Naether, conj. C. (The pr. nowther is also in pretty frequent use). Neither.

Naff, n. C. The nave or central block of a wheel. Dan. Et Nav (a nave).

Naff-head, n. R. (pr. naff-heead). A blockhead.

Ex.—*Thoo greeat naff-heead ; what 's ta deeain ?*

Nafle, Naffle, v. F. (pr. naafle and naffle). To idle under pretence of working ; to 'potter' and get nothing done.

Ex.—*He gans naaflin' aboot.*

Nakt, adj. C. (pr. naakt). Naked, bare. This word is always pronounced as one syllable, and is commonly applied to any object that looks unfurnished or bare.

Ex.—*T' chetch steeple leeaks varry naakt.*

Nanpie, n. R. (pr. nan-pie, i. e. almost as two words). The magpie.

Ex.—*Nan-pie rack* (a place-name).

Nap, v. F. To prowl ; to go about with dishonest intentions.

Ex.—*Ah see'd him nappin' aboot.*

Narside, n. C. The near side, i.e. the left hand side of a horse, or that nearest to him who directs the animal. It is remarkable that this pr. of the word only survives in this phrase. Dan. Nær (near) ; nærhaands hest (the left-hand horse in a pair).

Nasty, adj. C. Ill-natured, petulant, impatient.

Ex.—*When ah ax'd him he wer varry nasty aboot it.*

Natter, v. C. To complain about trifles, to be constantly fretful. Dan. At gnadre (to grumble).

Ex.—*Sha 's awlus natterin aboot nowt.*

Nattery, adj. C. (pr. natthry). Given to complain about trifles, petulant.

Naup, n. C. (1) A sharp blow on the head, either with the fist or a stick. (2) The top part of a pig's head, the lower part being called the *chaff* or *chap*. Dan. Et Knubs (a blow on the head).

Naup, v. F. To give a sharp blow on the head ; hence a *naupin*—a beating.

Naw, adv. C.　Vide **Neea**.

Nazzled, nazzed, nizzled, adj. F.　Somewhat the worse for liquor, unsteady.

> Ex.—*Ah seed him nizzled wi drink.—They gan nizzlin aboot.*

Neaf, n. C. (pr. neeaf).　The fist.　Dan. En Næve (a fist).

> Ex.—*He up wiv his neeaf an' knocked him ower.*

Neaf-ful, n. F. (pr. neeav-ful).　A handful.　Dan. En Nævefuld (a handful); begge Næver fulde (both fists, i.e. hands, full).

> Ex.—'*An' rahv'd off t' hair by neeavesful frev her heead*' ('York Minster Screen.')

Nears, n. C.　The kidneys.

Near, adj. C.　Close-fisted, stingy, extra careful.　Dan. Nöje (exact); Jutl D. Nyw, e.g. Han er saa nyw (he is so very parsimonious).

Near-hand, adv. C.　(1) Near.　(2) Nearly.　It is quite remarkable how universal the use of this word is in the dialect instead of *near*, which is never used without the suffix *hand*.　In the sense of 'nearly,' though common, it is not by any means so general—*ommost, varry near*, &c. being frequently used also.

> Ex.—*He nivver coms near-hand ma noo.—Tho maun't gan near-hand t' dog or he 'll mebbe hanch at tha.—It cost near-hand fahve pund.*

Neat, n.　Vide **Nowterer**.

Neavil, v. F. (pr. nevvil).　To strike with the fist: hence *neavilling*—a pummelling Dan. Næve (the fist); Jutl. D. At nefle (to pull one's hair with the fist—a punishment for schoolboys).

> Ex.—*He nevilled him weel.*

Neb, n. C.　The bill of a bird; also sometimes used for the human nose.　Dan. Næb (bill); in Icel. (nose).

Nebbs, n. C.　The handles on a scythe shaft.　Dan. Næb (nose).

Neea, adv. C.　No.　With regard to the simple negative particle there are three varieties in the dialect: (1) *Naay* (nay); this, though common, is never used singly, and is by no means such a strong form of the negative as the other two; it is generally followed by such words as *bud, noo*, &c., e.g. *Naay! bud thoo weean't gan, wilt tha?—Naay! noo, honey, sha weean't ho't tha.—Naay! ah deean't knaw.* (2) *Naw.* (3) *Neea.* The two latter are the ordinary forms; *neea* being perhaps somewhat the commoner in the E. R. It is worthy of note that in Danish there are two distinct forms of the negative in common use, viz. (1) *Næ* (though not written thus), pronounced almost as our *nay*; and (2) *Nei*, the latter implying a more decided negation than the former.

Neest, adj. F. Next. Dan. Næst (next); e.g. hvad næs ? (what next ?)

Neet, n. C. Night : this begins on an average throughout the year at about 5 p.m., or *lowzin tahm.* The word *evening* is hardly ever used.

Neuk, n. C. A corner of anything. Norse Nokke (a small iron hook).

Nibble, n. C. A nipple.

Nice, adj. C. (pr. neyce). (1) Over particular, shy. (2) Large, considerable.

Ex.—*Noo, deean't be neyce; help yoursells* (commonly said by a hostess at table).—*A neyce few.*

Nicking on, v. R. An old-fashioned rough-and-ready method of scoring at cricket, viz. cutting a notch on a hazel stick for every run made, a larger notch being cut at every ten.

Niff-naff, n. F. A trifle.

Nim, v. C. To move quickly ; to walk with a quick, short, light step ; also to catch up quickly. Dan. Nem (quick in apprehension, adroit, handy).

Ex.—*He can nim awaay at a bonny speed.*

Nip, v. C. To run or walk quickly ; generally used in such expressions as *nip off,* i.e. run away ; *nip across,* i.e. step quickly across, &c.

Ex.—*They can nip awaay.*

Nither, nidder, v. C. To shiver with cold, to be chilled.

Ex.—*Nitherin lambs.*

Nivver, adj. C. Never.

Ex.—*Nivver heed.*

Nobbut, adv. C. Only ; lit. not but.

Ex.—*They 're nobbut just cum'd.*

Nogg, n. R. The angle of a stream. Jutl. D. Nokke (small hooks in the wings of the distaff).

Nominy, n. F. (pr. nomminy). A doggerel rhyme, a jingle. I connect this word with Lat. Nomine, and group it with other ecclesiastical words that have been handed down from mediæval times ; it is an example among many which shows how a word may degenerate.

Ex.—*A'e ya t' nomminy off ?* i. e. do you know the rhyme by heart ?

Noo, adv. and interj. C. Now ; well ! This word when used as an interj, is the commonest form of salutation between man and man ; it corresponds with ' How do you do ?' Sometimes *then* is added.

Ex.—*Noo ! Bill.* (Bill) *Noo !—Noo then ; wheer 's ta forr ?* i. e. Well ! where are you going to ?

Noos an' thans, adv. F. Occasionally.

Nor, conj. Than. Vide **Na.**

Noration, n. F. A disturbance, a stir, a row, &c. This word is often applied to the play of children.

Nought, n. C. Nothing. This, which is one of the commonest words in the dialect, is at the same time one of the most difficult to describe the pronunciation of accurately, lying as it does between *note* and *nowt*. There is no vowel-sound corresponding to it in Std. Eng.

Ex.—*Ah knaw nowt aboot it.*

Nowt, nowts, n. R. Cattle, esp. horned cattle. Vide **Nowterer.** The old word *nowt fair* is still so-called here and there.

Nowther, conj. R. Vide **Naether.**

Nowterer, n. R. One who tends cattle. This old word is wellnigh obsolete ; it is, however—or was till lately—in use in the neighbourhood of Millington Pastures, a tract of unenclosed land in the East Riding at the edge of the Wolds : in the Pastures at certain times of the year a large number of cattle have *gaits* or freedom to stray at large. The man who looks after these cattle or *nowts* is called *T' nowttherer.* Few, if any, of the people know the meaning of the word, but from time immemorial this has been the designation of the herdsman.

Ex.—Q. *Canst ta tell ma wheer t' beeos is ?*—A. *Naw, bud mebbe t' nowttherer can tell ya.*

Numb, adj. C. Helpless, clumsy, awkward, dull ; lacking in handiness, stupid.

Ex.—*Aw dear, aw dear! what a numb lahtle lad thoo is !—They weean't a'e ti be varry numb-heeaded uns for that job.*

Nut, adv. C. Not. This form of the word is universal ; the *u* is pr. somewhat shorter than in most cases where it occurs.

Ex.—*Nut yan.—Ah 's nut boun' ti gan.*

O.

Off-man, n. F. One from a distance, a stranger.

Offen, prep. C. (pr. off'n). From off, off. This form of the word is very generally used, the simple equivalent *off* being rarely heard as a preposition.

Ex.—*He 's rahv'd t' reeaf offen t' hoos. Tak t' top offen t' pot; it gallops weeantly.*

Oftens, adv. C. (pr. off'ns). Often.

Ex.—*Ah off'ns thinks aboot it.*

Ommost, Ommaist, adv. C. (sometimes pr. ommeeast). Almost.

Ex.—*It wer ommost fit to burst.*

On, adv. C. Here: e. g. *He 'll be on eftther a bit.* There is also a use of this word equivalent to 'engaged in ' or 'at work': e.g. *They 're on kluin' yonder. — Smith 's on leading.* Sometimes *wi* (with) is added.

O'n, prep. C. Of. This usage is equivalent to *o'*, the *n* being added before a vowel for euphony.
Ex.—*Sum o'n 'em.*

Once over, adv. C. At one time, once, for a time.
Ex.—*It started ti raan yance ower.—Jim lived at yon spot yance ower.*

Onny bit like, owt like, C. Fairly well, tolerable; generally used with reference to health or the weather, but in other connections also.
Ex.—*Wa s'all be leadin' ti-moorn if it be onny bit leyke. —Ah 's nobbut badly yit, bud ah 'll gan if ah be owt leyke.*

Oot o' coorse, adv. C. Extraordinarily, greatly ; also used as an adj.
Ex.—*Ah wer oot o' coorse pleeased.*

Oppen, v. C. To open.
Ex.— *Mud sha oppen t' box.*

Othergates, adv. R. Otherwise.

Othersome, adj. C. (pr. uthersum). Others (the antithesis to *some*).
Ex.—*Sum 'll mebbe deea t' job, an' othersum weean't.*

Ought, n. C. (vowel-sound pr. as in nought). Anything.
Ex.—*A'e ya seed owt o'n him.*

Out, outing, n. C. (pr. oot). Absence from home on pleasure, an excursion.
Ex.—*He 's had a lang ootin.—Sha mun ev a neyce oot.*

Oot o' fettle, C. Out of repair, unfit for use, unwell.
Ex.—*Ah feels all oot o' fettle ti-daay.*

Oot o' t' rooad, C. In an inconvenient situation, out of the way, out of sight ; hence, destroyed, killed.
Ex.—*It puts her oot o' t' rooad an' tews her sadly.—Wa 've gitten t' poor au'd dog putten oot o' t' rooad.*

Ouse, v. C. Vide **Howze.**

Outs, adv. R. At all.
Ex.— *Was he outs nasty ?* i. e. was he at all angry ?

Over, to have it, C. To discuss any matter.
Ex.—*Him an' me 's had it ower tigither.*

Overquart, prep. R. (pr. owerquahrt). Across, athwart.
Ex.--*He ran owerquart t' clooas.*

Oversail, n. C. The top course of masonry in a wall or building of any kind.

Overwelt, weltover, n. F. (pr. owerwelt). A fall or slip on to the back, and continuing in that posture, esp. of a sheep. Jutl. D. Awvælt or ovælt (a throw on the back).

Ex.—*Yan o' t' yows is owerwelted yondher.*

Owe, v. C. (pr. ow and aw, approximately). To own. This word is only used interrogatively, in such expressions as *Wheea's owes it? Wheea's awes t' box?* &c. Some would express the first of these *wheea's owe t'?* This, however, is incorrect, and cannot be analysed satisfactorily. The full rendering of *Wheea's owe's it?* is *Wheea is (t' (who) owes it?* i. e. Who is (it who) owns it? The difficulty here is that *it* and *who* being omitted, the phrase does not sound grammatical, for as it stands it reads Who is owns it? It must be regarded as an elliptical expression. Icel. Eiga (to own); Dan. Eie (to own).

Ower, v. C. To be over with, to come to an end, to cease.

Ex.—*Ah doot it 'll varry seean be owered wi poor au'd Tommy.—T' raan 's owered.*

Ower, prep. and adv. C. (1) Over. (2) Too. As adv. *ower* is invariably used in place of *too*. It is observable that the Danish pr. of *over* is always *ower*, as in Yorksh.

Ex.—*Thoo mun gan ower t' brig.—There's ower monny o'n 'em.—T' maastther weean't be ower weel suited.*

Ower anenst, prep. C. Near to, opposite to.

Ex.—*He wer set ower anenst us.*

Owerhand, owerance, n. C. The mastery, the upper hand.

Owergait, n. R. A gap in a hedge, or a stepping-place across a brook.

Owerset, v. C. To overdo, to overtax one's strength; also to overturn.

Ex.—*Deean't owerset yoursen wi t' job.—Ah doot sha 's owersetten hersen wi t' weshin.*

Overwelted, part. C. Vide **Overwelt.**

Owse, n. R. An ox; pl. *Owsen.* Jutl. D. En Ows (an ox).

Owther, conj. R. Either. Besides this form of the word there is the commoner one, *aether*; the ordinary pr. of the word is not heard in the dialect.

Oxter, n. C. The armpit. Dan. Axel (the shoulder), Axel-hule (the armpit).

P

Pack-rag Day, n. R. The day after Martinmas Day, when farm-servants change their places. The name speaks for itself.

Paddle, v. C. To walk, esp. slowly or with some difficulty.

Ex.—*Ah can just paddle doon ti t' shop.*

Pafty, adj. F. Uppish.

Ex.—*Ah can deea nowt wiv him, he's ower prood an pafly by hau'f.*

Pain oneself, v. F. To give outward signs of pain.

Ex.—*He pains hissen a deal; he diz nowt bud pleean.*

Pairtner, n. C. Partner, esp. a husband or wife.

Ex.—*T' au'd woman's a good pairtner.*

Pan, v. C. To fit into, to make to fit, to agree with; used esp. of things that are crooked which are intended to fit on to each other. It is also sometimes used of persons much in the same sense as to *frame*.

Ex.—*It nobbut pans badly.—He pans weel,* i. e. he gives good promise of learning.

Pankin, n. C. (1) A large earthenware vessel of various shapes, but always of considerable size. This word, which looks like a diminutive in form, is in reality the same word as *pancheon.* (2) A rage, a violent passion.

Ex.—*He was iv a pankin, noo.*

Pannel, n. C. A riding pad.

Par, v. R. To dirty.

Ex.—*See ya noo! t' bairn's par'd deearst'n.*

Parlous, adj. C. Perilous. This word is used in a variety of senses, but it generally carries with it the idea of some kind of badness, or danger, or difficulty. It is also frequently used adverbially as an intensive, and much in the same way as 'desperate,' 'fearful,' &c. The Danish word corresponding to this is farlig, which is used in almost identically the same sense and way as *parlous,* e. g. En farlig Hoben Penge (*a parlous lot o' brass*); farlig stor (*parlous big*).

Ex.—*He's a parlous chap,* i. e. He is a queer character; perhaps a drunkard, a rowdy, &c.—*It's a parlous tahm been,* i. e. It has been a season of unusually bad or unfavourable weather.—*T' hoos hez gitten intiv a parlous state,* i. e. The house has got into thoroughly bad repair, or into a condition of great dirt and untidiness.

Part, adj. C. (pr. part and pairt). A considerable number, a large quantity of anything; many, more than usual.

Ex.—*There's part apples ti year.—There's pairt folks astir i t' toon this eftherneean.—We've had part changes i wer nighbours.—He'd hed pairt dhrink.*

Pash, v. F. To break in pieces, to smash.

Ex.—*They pash'd it all i bits.*

Pash, n. Vide **Posh.**

Past, part., used as a prep. and adj. C. Beyond, incapable of.

Ex.—*It's past owt,* i. e. It's beyond everything.—*He's past deeain' owt wi,* i. e. It is impossible to do anything with him.—*Ah 's that full o' paan while it 's ommost past bahdin*, i. e. I have so much pain I can hardly bear it.

Pawky, adj. C. Impudent, uppish, impertinent.

Ex.—Q. 'Was she disobedient?' A. *Aye, an' sha wer varry pawky an' all.*

Paze, v. C. To force by leverage.

Ex.—*We can mebbe paze it off.*

Connected with this word are *pawse* and *poose* (to strike with force).

Pea-hulls, n. C. The shells of peas.

Peen, adj. C. (pr. peean). Thin. Dan. Pæn (dainty, slight).

Ex.—*Ho'd it by t' peean end.*

This word is seldom used except when applied to the thin end or handle of an implement, tool, &c.

Peerching, adj. C. (pr. peechin'). Piercing, biting; used only of a cold wind.

Peff, v. C. To breathe hard ; also used as a noun in the sense of breath. Hence also the adj. *peffing* and *beffing*. These words are connected with *puff*.

Ex.—*He 's short o' peff.—He 's gotten a nasty peffin' cough.*

Pelt, n. C. The skin of an animal ; sometimes also used derisively of the human skin in a figurative sense. Dan. Pels (the hide of an animal).

Ex.—*They 're thick i t' pelt is yon lot*, i. e. they are idle.

Pettle, v. C. To pet, to nurse, to fondle.

Ex.—*T' bairn 's badly ; sha wants a deal o' pettlin.*

Pick, n. C. Pitch. Dan. Beg ; Jutl. D. Pik (pitch).

Ex.—*T' neet 's as black as pick.*

Pick, v. C. (1) To pitch, to throw, to cause to fall. (2) To gather up and throw, esp. applied to forking the sheaves off a stack for thrashing.

Ex.—*That feeal Jack picked oor lahtle Annie doon inti t' muck, an' theer sha ligged whahl t' muther com an' picked her up.—Sha 's pickin' atop o' t' stack.*

Pick at, v. C. To make small attacks on a person by word ; to find fault, generally about trifles.

Ex.—*T' au'd man 's varry natthery ; he 's awlus' pickin' at ma.*

Pick-fork, n. C. A pitch-fork ; sometimes also called *langfork*.

Pie, v. F. To spy about with curiosity.

Ex.—*He 's awlus piein' aboot t' toon.*

Pie, n. C. A heap of any root crop, but esp. potatoes. It is covered first with straw and then padded down with a coating of earth: by this means the crop is safely preserved from frost through the winter. The pie is about four feet high, generally conical, and, for larger crops, long-shaped like the roof of a house. The word is also commonly used as a verb

Ex.—*T' bull loup'd reet inti Nanny Nicholson taatie-pie.— Wa a'e gotten t' biggest part o' wer tonnops pied.*

Piece, for a, adv. C. For a time.

Ex.—*Ah stayed wiv him for a piece.—He wer theer for a neyce piece.*

Piggin, n. F. A small tub or pail with a vertical handle which when empty was carried under the arm : it was used for milking into, the milk being poured from it into the larger tub or skeel.

Pig-swarth, n. C. (pr. pig-swath). The rind of bacon.

Ex.—*Ho'd thi noise; here 's a bit a pig-swath for tha.*

Pike, n. C. A very large haycock, usually about as much as would make a good cartload. This is the universal application of the word throughout the East Riding and the southern part of the North Riding : in Cleveland, however, it is applied to a circular stack or collection of corn. The custom of pikeing hay is by no means so common as it was twenty years ago.

Pile, n. F. (pr. pahl). A blade (of grass), sometimes also used of the coat of an animal.

Pillow-slip, n. C. A pillow-case.

Pimpish, adj. F. Dainty in the matter of food, taking it in small quantities.

Fin, n. F. The middle place when three horses go in single file.

Ex.—*We 'll put him i t' pin.*

Pinchery, n. F. A state of extreme carefulness approaching to miserliness.

Pinder, n. F. (sometimes pr. pidner). The man who has charge of a pinfold.

Pinfold, n. C. A pound or place for detaining straying cattle.

Pinshow, n. R. A child's peep-show : a plaything common formerly among children at school, the show being generally made of a sort of paper box with flowers, &c., inside, a pin being demanded for a peep.

Pisle, v. C. (pr. pahzle). To walk about in a lazy manner. With regard to this word, Atkinson quotes the Swedish D. word *pisla*, to walk heavily, with which it would seem to be connected.

Ex.—*He gans pahzlin aboot.*

Pissimire, Passimire, n. C. The common ant.

A a

Place. placing, n. C. (pr. pleeace). Service.

> Ex.—Q. 'Where 's Anne now?' A. *Sha 's gone ti Stowsla ti pleeace,* i.e. She has gone into service at Stokesley.

Plain, v. C. (pr. pleean and plaan). To complain.

> Ex.—*He gans tiv his maasther ti pleean on him.—Sha 's awlus pleeanin is oor Anne.*

Plain, adj. C. (pr. plaan). This word refers not only to outward appearance, but also to morals.

> Ex.—*Sha 's nobbut a plaan 'un.*

Plash, v. C. To splash. Dan. At plaske (to splash).

Plate, v. C. To clench or bend back the end of a nail when driven, and so to flatten the end of it. Dan. Plat (flat).

Please, v. F. (pr. pleease). To give an equivalent or make a return for a kindness received, or something of a like nature.

> Ex.—*My muther says mud sha hev a dhrop o' brandy an' sha 'll pleease ya for 't.*

Pleeaf, pleugh, n. C. A plough. The two forms of this word are about equally common, the pr. of the latter is not *ploo* but *pleew.* Dan. En Plov (a plough).

Pleugh-stots, n. C. Plough lads, properly twelve in number, who traverse the district in which they live on Plough-Monday; formerly a plough used to be dragged about with them, the lads representing the *stots* or oxen, as the word signifies. In former years the rounds lasted for a fortnight or three weeks, but now the time is shortened, and the numbers who take part in the performance are also reduced. The performers are fantastically dressed, a leading feature being the wearing of white skirts trimmed with ribbons outside their other garments : two of the number act as king and queen. The chief part of the acting consists in sword dances, for which reason they are frequently called *swurd dancers.* They are always accompanied with music of some kind. Vide Stot.

Pload, v. R. To walk with some difficulty through boggy or muddy places; to wade through water. Jutl. D. Pladder (thick muddy water).

Plosh, v. C. To splash ; hence *ploshy,* i.e. splashy, as when one walks through melting snow. Dan Plaske (to splash).

Ploughing-day, n. C. The day on which neighbouring farmers assist a new tenant of a farm in ploughing his land for him.

Plug, v. C. To load a cart with manure.

> Ex.—Q. 'What is Tom doing?' A. *Pluggin' muck.*

Plugger, n. C. Anything large of its kind.
  Ex.—*It wer a plugger.*
Pluke, n. C. A spot or pimple.
Plumb, adj. C. Perpendicular ; also used for the steepest part of a hill.
  Ex.—*Wa mun 'ev it plum, howivver.—They seean gat ti t' plum o' t' hill.*
Pluther, n. F. Sludge, and dirt in a semi-liquid state. There are various forms of this word, *bladther* and *plother* having precisely the same meaning. In South Jutland *pladder* is used in the same sense. and these may all be connected with the Danish word *pladre* (to mix up), *pladder* or *pluther* being always a mixture of soil or dirt of some kind and water. Jutl. D. Pladder (sludge).
Poat, v. F. (pr. paut and pooat). To move quietly with the foot or with a stick, &c. ; hence it is used of one who looks inquisitively into things. From this word *pooatler* is derived.
  Ex.—*He cums pautin aboot.*
Pock-arr, n. C. The mark caused by the small-pox ; hence *pock-arr'd*, i. e. marked with the small-pox. Jutl. D. Pok-arret (marked with the small-pox).
Poke, n. C. (pr. pooak). A sack or bag, esp. a corn-sack. Dan. En Pose (a bag) ; Jutl. D. En Poge (a bag) ; Fr. Poche (pocket).
Pooatler, n. F. A long stick, held about eighteen inches from the top, such as drovers use ; it is something like an alpenstock. Vide **Poat.**
Poose, v. F. To strike, as at a cricket ball.
  Ex.—*He poos'd her oot o' t' clooas.*
Porringer, n. R. A mug bellied like a pitcher, and made of coarse ware ; formerly it was commonly used by children at meal-times. No doubt this word is derived from porridge.
Posh, n. C. A dirty mess, mud, sludge.
  Ex.—*T' rooads is all iv a posh.*
Posh, poss, v. F. To dash violently with water.
  Ex.—*Poss them things weel.*
Poshing-stick, possing-stick, n. C. A stick with feet at the end of it, used for washing heavy articles in a peggy-tub, or other vessel.
Posskit, n. R. A tub in which heavy clothes, &c., are washed by means of a possing-stick.
Post-and-pan, adj. R. A name applied to old timber-framed houses. *Pan* refers to the fitting of the timbers. Vide **Pan.**
Pot-sitten, part. O. Burnt or overdone by excessive cooking or seething. Dan. Syde (to seethe).

A a 2

Prickle, v. C. To prick.

> Ex.—*Ah 've prickled my han's despretly* (said by one when ' shearing ' among thistles).

Prick-o'-back-urchin, n. C. (pr. pricky-back-otch'n). The hedge-hog.

> Ex.—*Ah seed yan o' them pricky-back otch'ns a bit sen.*

Proffer, v. C. To make an offer. The word *offer* is seldom used in this sense.

> Ex.—*Ah proffered him a rahd, bud he wadn't cum wi ma.* —*He proffered ma fahve pund for t' dog.*

Pross, v. F. To gossip, to talk in a familiar manner ; also used as a noun. Jutl. D. At praase (to froth, as beer ; to raise the dust).

> Ex.—*He did pross.—There 's ower mich prossin' aboot him.—Ah ho'ded a bit o' pross wiv her.*

Providance, n. C. (pr. providance). Supply of food for an entertainment.

> Ex.—*We s'all a'e ti mak providance for 'em.*

Puddings, n. C. Entrails.

Pulls, n. C. Heads of corn which have not been completely threshed ; broken heads of corn.

Pull, v. C. To pick ; esp. fruit.

> Ex.—*Sha 's pullin' berries,* i.e. She is picking goose-berries.

Pum, v. C. To beat with the fists.

> Ex.—*Ah pummed him weel.*

Purlings, pirlings, n. C. Ribs for carrying the spars of the roof of a house.

Put aboot, v. C. To disturb in mind, to excite, to cause in-convenience and annoyance.

> Ex.—*Ah can't bahd it ; it puts ma aboot sadly.—Sha wer despertly putten aboot wiv him.*

Put off, put away, v. C. To put to death.

> Ex.—*T' au'd dog 's that bad, ah think we mun put him off.—We 've gitten t' poor thing putten away.*

Putten, part. C. Put.

> Ex.—*Wheer 's ta putten them things ?*

Putting in, part. C. The act of clearing the thickest of the hay with a fork or the handle of a rake out of the way of the rakers who are to follow, by which means it is made into windrow, either for the men to form large cocks from, or for the horses to ' sweep ' into pike if the hay be fully dried. The work of *putting in* is frequently done by women.

> Ex.—*Run an' tell yer muther ti cum an' put in a bit ; it leeaks as thoff it wer boun ti raan.*

Q

Quality, n. C. Gentry.

Ex.—' *An' ah 'mang t' rest o' quality put doon,*
For ivvry lahtlę helps, thoo knaws, a croon.'
—York Minster Screen.

Quart, v. F. (pr. quahrt). To cross transversely, esp. in ploughing a field a second time and in a different line to the first ploughing.

Ex.—*Noo, lads, we mun quahrt t' fauf.*

Quick, adj. C. Vide **Wick.**

Quiet, adv. C. Quite, entirely.

Quite better. C. (pr. quiet better). Quite well again. Vide **Better.**

R.

Rack, n. C. This word is commonly applied to a bend in a river, generally of no great length, which deviates almost at right angles from its general course; thus when a vessel is sailing with a fair wind up a river and comes to a rack, she cannot proceed through it under sail, but has then to be navigated by towing or other means; this is called *leading* the rack. There are numerous racks along the Ouse, e. g. *Cuddy Shaw Rack, Nanpie Rack, Poppleton Rack, Crabtree Rack,* &c.

Raddle, v. C. To beat soundly with a stick, &c.

Raddling, n. C. A sound beating.

Ex.—*He gav him a good raddlin'.*

Raffle, v. C. To lead a loose, dissolute sort of life; to become dissipated.

Raffle-pack, n. F. A good-for-nothing fellow.

Raffling, adj. C. Riotous, disorderly, loose (in mode of life).

Ex.—*Ah deean't want ti gan wi' that rafflin' lot.*

Ragabash, n. C. A disreputable character; the lowest of the low.

Rageous, adj. F. Savage, furious.

Ex.—*That dog o' yours is rageous.*

Ragg'd, part. C. Covered, or laden with fruit.

Ex.—*T' berry trees is weel ragg'd ti-year.—They 're ragg'd as thick as they can hing.*

Raggel, n. C. (pr. raggil). A rascal, a blackguard. Jutl. D. En Rægl (a rag).

' *An' theer ah fan' t' oad raggil ti be seear,*
Stthritch'd ov his back deead dhrunk o' t' parlour fleear.'
—York Minster Screen.

Raitch, n. C. The white mark or star on a horse's face.

Raited, part. C. Influenced or damaged by exposure to the weather ; frequently said of *line* or flax when so exposed and steeped, by which means the *shivs* are more easily detached. Dan. Rōde (putrefaction).

Rakapelt, n. C. A man of dissolute habits.

Ram, v. C. To work with vigour. Dan. At ramme (to hit, strike).

> Ex.—*Noo, lads; ram away, an' wa s'all seean a'e deean.*

Ram, adj. C. Stinking, offensive in smell. Dan. Ram (sharp, acrid in taste) ; En ram Smag (an offensive taste). Icel. Rammr.

Ramble, v. C. (pr. ramm'l). This word, which is in very common use, has a different meaning in the dialect from what it has in Std. Eng. It is seldom, if ever, used in the simple sense of wandering abroad, but generally in a bad and more restricted sense, esp. of children getting into mischief, e. g. by climbing to a place where they ought not ; it is also applied to young fellows idling about a village, without any idea of roaming away from it.

> Ex. – *Cum off that stee this minute; thoo 's awlus ram'lin aboot an' gettin' intiv a mischeef.—Them lads o' Frank's is awlus ram'lin aboot t' toon.*

Rammack, v. F. This word is equivalent to *Rannack*, of which it is another form.

Ramp, v. C. To make a series of inclined drops on the upper part of a wall, when built on sloping ground, by which means the coping of the wall is kept horizontal.

> Ex.—*Wa mun ramp it doon a bit mair.*

This word is also used as a substantive.

Ramper, n. C. The sloping side of a raised footway, whether paved or not ; sometimes also applied to a similar slope at the coping of a wall.

Randle-balk, n. F. (pr. rann'l-bauk). A beam or bar across the upper part of a fire-place, from which are hung the *reckons*. The old *randle-balks* were always of wood, and so should they always be, as the name implies.

Rannack, v. C. To be noisy, wild, and boisterous. A word frequently applied to children.

> Ex.—*Them bairns o' Betty Robison's is awlus rannackin' aboot t' stthreet.*

Also used as a substantive in the sense of a person of dissolute habits.

Ranty, adj. C. Heated with passion, excited, angry.

> Ex.—*Mah wo'd, bud he was ranty!*

Rap off, v. C. To throw off quickly, esp. of speech.

> Ex.—*Ah thowt nowt aboot it; ah just rapp'd it off.*

Rash, v. C. To air or dry thoroughly, esp. of clothes before the fire. This word is mainly used in the E. R.

Rasps, n. C. Raspberries.

Ex.—*Berries, corr'n-berries, an' rasps*, i. e. Gooseberries, currants, and raspberries.

Ratten, n. C. A rat. Dan. En Rotte (a rat).

Rattener, n. C. A rat-catcher.

Raum, v. C. (pr. raum and reeam). To raise the voice unduly, to shout. Dan. At raabe (to shout).

Ex.—*What 's ta raumin' oot leyke that ti-deea ?*

Rax, v. C. To stretch to the full, esp. the limbs ; to strain the joints.

Ex.—*They rax thersens oot.*

Rax, n. R. A strain.

Razzle, v. C. To cook meat hastily over the fire, leaving the outside scorched and the inside half done. Jutl. D. At ræse (to smoke, to burn ; esp. fish). Norse Ræsa.

Reach, v. C. To hand or pass a thing on to another.

Reach to, v. C. To help oneself at table.

Ex.—*Noo, deean't be ower neyce ; reach tul an' git agait,* i. e. help yourself and begin.

Rear, v. C. To raise to a more or less upright position. Although this word is similarly used in Std. Eng., I insert it here because in the dialect it is preferred to the word *raise* in cases where the latter would always be used ordinarily.

Ex.—*Ah can't rear mysen i bed,* i. e. I can't sit up in bed.—*Cum here ; ah can't rear this stee wi mysen.*

Rear, adj. C. Half cooked (of meat), underdone. It is noteworthy that this old word is commonly used in the same sense in the United States.

Reckling, n. C. · The smallest or poorest in a number of animals ; e. g. in a flock of sheep or a litter of pigs. Icel. Reklingr (an outcast).

Reck'n, n. C. The iron bar suspended from the *randle-bauk,* on which the pots are hung.

Reck'n-crook, n. C. The hook at the end of a *reck'n-bauk,* for holding the pots.

Reek, v. C. To smoke ; also used as a noun. Dan. Rög (smoke).

Ex.—*Oor chimler reeks sadly.—T' hoos is full o' reek.*

Reesty, adj. C. Rancid ; esp. of bacon.

Reet, v. C. (1) To set in order, to straighten, to put to rights. (2) To comb the hair. Dan. Rede (order) ; at rede Haaret (to comb the hair).

Ex.—*Reet tha*—said to a cow preparatory to being milked, and in order that its legs might be easily tied.—*Wa a'en't gitten reeted yit.*

Rein, n. F. (pr. as rain). The ends or edges of fields which are overgrown with brushwood and cannot be ploughed. Icel. Rein (a strip of land).

Ex.—*T' field's nowt bud reins an' gairs.*

Reist, v. C. To be restive.

Remmon, v. C. To remove from one place to another, to set aside. This word has not the same meaning as *flit*, which is invariably used for the act of removing, with furniture, &c., to a new abode. Dan. At römme (to decamp) ; at römme en Plado (to vacate a seat).

Ex.—*Wa mun remmon it.*

Render, v. C. To liquefy by means of heat, esp. in cooking ; e. g. fat from which lard is obtained.

Renky, adj. C. Tall and somewhat thin. Dan. Rank (tall) ; En rank ung Mand (an upright young man).

Rezzel, n. C. (pr. rezzil). A weazel.

Rickle, n. C. A small heap of *peats* set up to dry. A diminutive of *rook*.

Ride, v. C. To travel in a vehicle of any kind. This word is used commonly for riding on horseback, but its extended usage is peculiar.

Ex.—*Did'st ta rahd wi t' traan ?—He rade in t' cart wi ma. —Wilt ta rahd ?* i. e. Shall I give you a lift in my conveyance ? said to one overtaken on a road.

Riding, ridding, n. C. An open space in a wood, esp. a road through a wood ; properly a clearance in a wood made by felling trees. This word is very commonly applied, esp. in the E. Riding, to a road through a wood, and it is pr. riding rather than ridding, though the latter is more correct. Dan. En Rydning (a clearing) ; Rydnings land (clearing-land). There are fields at Linton-on-Ouse called 'The Ruddings,' which formerly, no doubt, were clearings from the forest.

Rife, adj. F. Ready, inclined for.

Ex.—*He 's rife for a fight.*

Rigg, n. C. The back, either of man or beast ; also the ridge of anything, as of a hill, the roof of a building, lands in a ploughing field, &c. ; the rows in which turnips grow. Dan. Ryg (back).

Ex.—*Them tonnop riggs is ower near-hand yan anuther.*

Rigged, Rig-welted, part. C. Laid on the back, as a sheep which cannot raise itself from that position. I have never heard *welted* used simply in this sense. Dan. At vælte (to upset, to overturn).

Ex.—*Sitha ; ther 's tweea o' t' au'd yows rigg'd yonder. —Ah seed yan o' t' gimmers rig-welted.*

Rigging, n. C. The wooden framework of the roof of a house. Dan. En Rygning (a ridge).

Rigging-tree, n. C. The top and main spar of the roof of a house running along the ridge. Dan. Rygtræ (the main spar in a roof).

Right, adj. C. (pr. reet). True. This equivalent is almost universally used.

Ex.—*What ah 's tellin o' ya 's reet.*

Right on end, adv. C. (pr. reet'n end). Straight away, straight, perpendicularly.

Right up. v. C. To put into order ; to make orderly, either of persons or things.

Ex.—*He wants reetin up sadly.*

Ring-shaken, part. F. This word is applied to wood that is diseased, and which has the appearance almost as if struck by lightning ; it is not so common in the oak or ash, being most frequently seen in the sweet chestnut.

Ripple, v. F. To cut corn, esp. beans, with a long-handled sickle. By this process the strokes were short and quick, and the sheaf was gathered into the left arm. In this way the work was more quickly done than by the ordinary process : the operation is not so common as formerly. Norse .Ripla (to scratch).

Rive, v. C. (pr. rahve). To tear in two ; to tear, to pull, to split, esp. when considerable force is requisite Dan. At rive (to tear).

Ex.—*T' pig 's fit ti rahve t' yat off t' creeaks.—Sha ommost rahv'd t' hair frev her heead.—Ah 'll naether splet nor rahve,* i. e. I'll neither split the difference, nor give back anything. The past participle of this verb is *rovven.*

Roar, v. C. (pr. roor). To weep bitterly, as a child.

Ex.—*Thoo maun't roor i that leet.—T' lahtle lad starts ti roor at nowt ommost.*

Roke, n. C. (pr. rauk). A fog ; esp. a mist or fog off the sea. Norse Rok (pr. raak), the foam of the sea driving before the storm. Jutl. D. Raag (a drizzling rain driven by a fresh wind).

Roky, adj. C. Misty, foggy.

Ex.—*It 's varry rauky.*

Rook, n. F. A small heap or cock of clover or other crop twisted at the top, and set up to dry in a wet time. There is little or no difference between this and a *gait* or *gaiting*. Also commonly used of a pile of turves.

Rook, v. C. To pile or set up in a heap ; commonly used with reference to clover and other crops. Also, and most frequently, spoken of turves heaped up after having been previously dried in pairs, as a final preparation before being carted away. Jutl. D. Röge (a heap of turves).

Roupy, adj. C. (pr. roopy). Hoarse; not clear in speech, from the effects of cold.

Ex.—*Ah 's that roupy whahl ah can hardlins talk.*

Rout, n. C. A long round of visits or calls.

Ex.—*Ah 've had a reg'lar rout ti-day.*

Also used as a verb.

Row, v. C. (pr. between ro and rou). To work hard, esp. if the work be of a rough nature.

Ex.—*Ah 've been rowin' amang t' tonnops.*

Rown, n. C. (pr. raun). The roe or spawn of fish. Dan. Rogn; Jutl. D. Rawn (spawn of fish).

Rowty, adj. C. Thick or luxuriant in growth.

Roy, v. C. To lead a fast life; to live extravagantly.

Ex.—*They 're royin awaay; they 'll seean d'e deean,* i. e. they will soon come to the end of their money.

Royously, adv. Extravagantly (in living).

Ex.—*They 're living royously awaay.*

Ruckle, v. R. To spread out sheaves of 'line' to dry, a ruckle being the same as a small sheaf tied or 'lanked' at the top.

Rud, n. C. Red ochre, used for colouring floors, &c. Dan. Röd (red).

Rud-stake, n. C. A perpendicular post in a beast's stall, on which is an iron moveable ring to which the beast is tied by a chain.

Rug, v. F. To pull violently, to tear. This word is commonly used in connection with *rive*. Dan. At rykke (to pull, to jerk); Rykke en i haaret (pull one by the hair).

Ex.—*He 's been ruggin an' rahvin at it.*

Rumbustical, adj. C. Noisy, fond of rough play.

Runnel, n. F. A rill; a tiny stream. I have only heard this word in the north part of the N.R.

Runty, adj. C. Short and thick-set; applied either to people or animals.

Ex.—*Sha can deea ommost owt; sha's a stoot runty lass.*

Rust, n. C. Rest. This pr., with many of our old folk, is very common; the pr. is approximate to *roost* though not so long. Also used as a verb. Dan. Rast (rest); Icel. Röst.

Ex.—*Ah can't get a bit o' rust neeaways.—Sha nobbut rusts badly.*

Ruttle, v. C. To breathe with a rattling noise, as when suffering from a bronchial affection or like a person *in extremis*.

S.

Sackless, adj. F. Idiotic, simple-minded.

Ex.—*He 's nobbut a poor sackless bairn.*

Sad, adj. C. Heavy, as applied to articles of food ; esp. bread, cake, &c. Sometimes applied to soil or land that does not 'work' well.

Ex.—*He weean't bring t' barm ; t' breead 's as sad as sad ageean.*

Sadly begone, part. C. Deceived, taken in, disappointed ; esp. when outward signs of the deception &c. are visible.

Safe, adj. C. (pr. seeaf). Certain, sure.

Ex.—*He 's seeaf ti com.—It 's seeaf ti raan.*

Sag, v. C. To hang like a chain suspended at each end, which naturally sinks towards the middle ; to sink down.

Said, part. C. Persuaded by argument.

Saim, n. C. (pr. saam and seeam). Lard. Wel. Saim (grease).

Ex.—*Ah 'd nowt bud a bit o' saam ti mi breead.*

Sair, adj. C. Sore. Dan. Saar (sore).

Sair, sairly, adv. C. Sorely, greatly.

Ex.—*Ah wer putten aboot sair.*

Sam, v. C. To collect together. This word is used in a variety of ways, sometimes e. g. in gathering of corn or other farm produce, or in the house in tidying or 'siding' up things that are scattered about. Dan. At samle (to collect).

Ex.—*Noo ah mun away an' git them things sam'd up.*

Sammer, n. F. Anything large of its kind.

Ex.—*Sitha ! you 's a sammer.*

Sark, n. F. A shirt, of any kind. Dan. En Særk (a smock, a shift).

Sarra, v. R. To serve, esp. as regards supplying animals with food. This old word has about died out and given place to *sarve*.

Sarve, v. C. (This pr. is universal ; also *sarvent, sarvent, lass*, &c.). To serve, to feed.

Ex.—*Ah 'll gan an' sarve t' pigs.*

Sattle, v. C. To settle, esp. in a new place, whether of men or beasts ; also to fall in price.

Ex.—*Wa 've gotten t' new pig, an' it 's sattled as neyce as can be.—Barley sattled a bit t' last Settherda.*

Sauce, n. C. Impudence in word ; used also as a verb.

Ex.—*Sha sauced her missis*, i. e. she was impudent, insolent, towards her.—*T' lad gav him nowt bud sauce.*

Sau't, n. F. Salt.

Sau't-kit, n. F. A small tub in which salt is sometimes kept at farm-houses. Vide **Kit**.

Sauve, n. C. Salve, ointment ; also used as a verb.

Saw, saw, interj. R. For shame !

Ex.—*Saw, saw, lads ! ah 'll tell t' maasther o' ya.*

Saw-cum, Saw-coom, n. C. Saw-dust.

Saw-horse, n. C. An extemporised frame for sawing, raised on tressels, instead of a saw-pit.

Scale, v. C. To spread, to scatter; esp. used of the spring spreading of manure, lime, &c, with a sort of toothed hoe. Dan. At skille (to separate).

Ex.—Q. 'Where is your mother?' A. *Scaalin at Robert Smith's* (without mention of the thing scaled).—*Thoo mun scaal it weel.*

Scallibrat, n. C. A noisy, screaming child; also used as a verb in the sense of using loud and vituperative language.

Ex.—*Ah scallibrats 'em i t' stthreet.*

Scaup, n. F. The head; a pr. of scalp. The word is generally used in anger, when two people are quarrelling.

Ex.—*Ah 'll brek thi scaup if thoo deean't mahnd.*

Scopperill, n. C. A teetotum; generally made of a button or part of a button, having a hole pierced in the centre.

Sconce, n. F. A ruse, a deception.

Ex.—*It wer all a sconce on 'em.*

It would seem as if this word were derived from the O. Fr. *esconer* (to hide), as conveying with it the idea of a hidden motive or meaning.

Scow, v. C. To place bark on the top of a pile of oak to dry, the smaller pieces being put at the bottom and the larger ones above.

Scraffle, v. R. To move with difficulty, as through a crowd; to work one's way along. Dan. At skravle (to walk in a tottering manner, as old or infirm people do).

Scran, n. F. Victuals; meal-time being sometimes called *scran-time.*

Scrat, v. C. To scratch; also, to save money with difficulty and by hard toil. Dan. Kratte (to scratch).

Ex.—*Wa manished ti git wer rent scratted up.—See ya! there 's t' hens scrattin undther t' berry trees.*

Scraumy, adj. C. Straggly, untidy in shape, ungainly; often applied to plants, shrubs, &c.

Ex.—*It 's a greeat scraumy thing is yon.*

Screed, n. C. An edge or border of any material; e. g. a *cap-screed.*

Screeve, v. F. To mark wood or other substance by scratching the surface; the instrument with which the mark is made is called a *screeving-iron.*

Scrogs, n. F. Stunted shrubs; the hazel for instance.

Scroggy, adj. F. This word is applied to trees that are badly grown and so become bushy and stunted.

Scruffle, v. C. To apply the horse-hoe for working between the turnip-rows. Dan. At skrælle (to pare); skrællc Plov (paring plough).

Ex.—*Hez oor Jack gitten them tonnops scruffled?*

Scruffler, n. C. A horse hoe for weeding between turnip-rows.

Scuff, n. C. The back of the neck; also as a verb—to strike, shake, &c. on the back of the neck.
Ex.—*Ah 'll scuff him weel.*

Scug, v. R. To hide; hence *scuggery* (hiding).

Scunchins, scrunchins, n. R. Remnants of food, broken meat, remains of a feast.
Ex.—*Ah a'en't monny scunchins left.*

Sea-fret, n. F. Vide **Fret.**

Seckaree, n. F. The long smock formerly worn by labourers; also, and usually, now applied to the short smock which does not come below the waist. A Holderness word.

Seea, sae, adv. C. So. The pr. of this word is twofold, viz. *seea* and *si* (short), thus we say *an' seea,* and *ivver si monny.* It is preferable to adhere to the form *seea* in writing.

Seear, adj. C. Sure; the corresponding adverbial being *for seear.*
Ex.—*Ah 's seear ah a'en't.—Aye, for seear.*

Seed, v. pf. t. C. Saw.
Ex.—*Ah seed 'em nobbut a bit sen.*

Seed-lip, n. C. A long-shaped basket suspended from the shoulder, from which seed-corn is taken by the sower. A. S. Leáp (a basket); Dan. En Sæde-löv (a seed-basket made of straw).

Seeing-glass, n. C. A looking-glass.

Seemlings, adv. F. (pr. seemlins). Apparently, seemingly.

Seeve, n. C. (pr. seeav). The common rush, which grows in moist ground; formerly used in making rushlight candles. Dan. Et Siv (a rush).

Segs, n. C. Rushes, sedges; this latter being another form of the word.

Seize the heart, v. C. To take to heart.
Ex.—*It 's seized her heart sadly,* i. e. she has taken it greatly to heart.

Sen, adv. C. Since. Dan. Siden (since).
Ex.—*Ah tell'd him a bit sen.*

Sessions, n. R. A disturbance; a *to-do,* such, for instance, as many people quarrelling, or a number of cattle fighting one another.
Ex.—*Noo there 'll be a bonny sessions aboot it.—There was a bonny sessions amang 'em.*

Set, v. C. (1) To accompany a person on a journey or part of a journey. (2) To fix a rent for a holding.
Ex.—*Ah 'll set tha a piece o' waay yam.—Thoo mun set*

her ti t' to'n, an then sha can gan wiv hersen.—He set him t' spot at fo'tty pund.

Set on knees, v. C. To kneel.

Ex.—*Ah seed him set ov his knees peerin' thruff t' smout hooal.*

Setten on, part. C. Short, stunted.

Ex.—*He 's setten on.*

Setten up, part. C. Highly pleased, elated.

Ex.—*T' lahtle lass is weeantly setten up wi startin scheeal.*

Set-pot, n. R. A large boiler fixed by masonry in its place. These were formerly common, but are at present seldom seen.

Settle, n. C. Vide **Lang-settle.**

Shackle, n. C. The wrist.

Ex.—*Ah 've ho'tten t' gahdhers o' mi shackle sadly.*

Shade, n. C. A shed. This pr. is universal.

Shaffle, v. C. To shufflle (in its various senses).

Ex.—*They want ti shafflle thersens oot on 't.*

Shaft, n. C. The handle of anything, e. g. a rake, fork, &c. Dan. Et Skaft (a handle).

Shak, v. C. To shake.

Ex.—*It shak'd it heead.*

Shak-bag, n. C. One who is not to be trusted; a term often applied to one who has deceived another.

Ex.—*Ah calls him nowt bud a shak-bag.*

Shak-fork, n. F. A wooden fork used for shaking grain out of straw in a barn.

Shape, v. R. (pr. shap). To give promise of; to make an attempt, as by a beginner; equivalent to *frame.*

Ex.—*T' lad shaps weel.*

Sharp, v. C. To turn up the ends of horse-shoes to prevent slipping in frosty weather.

Ex.—*T' rooads is that slaap wa mun a'e t' meer sharp'd.*

Sharp, adj. C. Quick; also used adverbially.

Ex.—*Be sharp !* the invariable expression for 'make haste !' 'be quick !'

Shaum, v. F. To warm one's legs by sitting near the fire. This word may be derived from the French *jambe.*

Ex.—*He 's set shaumin' ower t' fire.*

Shear, v. F. To cut corn with the sickle. Now that machinery is so much used, this word is seldom heard, except when speaking of bygone days. Dan. At skjære (to cut with a knife or other instrument); Leen skjærer godt (the scythe cuts well).

Shearling, n. C. A sheep of the first year from the time of shearing.

Shelvings, n. C. The moveable four-sided framework of

two rails put on an ordinary cart when *leading* hay or corn.

Ex.— *Tak t' shelvins off o' t' cart.*

Shibbin, shubb'n, shoven, n. C. That which binds or ties a shoe, a shoe-lace.

Ex.—*Sitha ! thi shubb'n 's lowse.*

Shift, v. C. Besides the ordinary meaning of changing places, another very common one is to change clothes.

Ex.— Q. *Wilt tha gan wi ma ?* A. *Aye, if thoo 'll stop a bit whahl ah shift mysel.*

Shifty, adj. C. Untrustworthy.

Shill, shilly, adj. C. This word is commonly applied to a high wind. Some think it is merely another pronunciation of chill; its meaning, however, is clearly ' noisy,' ' shrill,' &c.

Shill, v. C. To separate, to put asunder ; to curdle milk.

Shill-horse, sill-horse, n. C. A shaft-horse.

' Thou hast got more hair on thy chin than Dobbin my thill-horse has on his tail.'—*Merchant of Venice,* ii. 2.

Thill seems to have given place to *shill* or *sill* in the dialect, though I am inclined to think the two words are distinct. Dan. At skille (to separate).

Shillockers, n. F. Ivory needles with a knob at one end and a kind of hook at the other, something like a large crochet needle ; they are used for doing a species of worsted work.

Shills, sills, n. C. The shafts of a cart, &c. Also called *thills* and *limmers*.

Shim, v. F. To give a glancing cut. Dan. At skimte (to catch but a glimpse of anything). Icel. Skimi (a glimpse).

Shim-hoe, n. C. A Dutch-hoe, so called because of the glancing way in which it cuts.

Shin, v. C. To trump at whist after playing false. To *shin aboon shin* is to overtrump.

Shinnop, n. C. Hockey (a game).

Ship-starnel or **shipster,** n. C. The common starling.

Shirl, v. C. (pr. sholl). To slide ; to glide, esp. on ice.

Ex.—*They 're shollin' yonder uppo t' pownd.*

Shiv, n. C. (pr. as in give). A broken particle of line-stalk, husk of corn, &c. Dan. En Skjæve (a particle).

Shive, n. C. (pr. shahve). A slice, a thin piece cut off anything. Dan. En Skive (a slice).

Ex.—*Wilt ta gie ma a shahve o' breead.*

Shog, v. C. To jog; to shake or jolt in motion ; to proceed at a slow pace in driving, something between a walk and a *fadge*.

Shoglin, n. C. Vide **Ice-shoggle.**

Shool, n. R. A shovel.

Shool, v. F. To seek to obtain a trifling advantage from another ; to sponge upon.

Shoon, n. F. The plural of shoe. (At the present time this form of the word is thought not so ' refined' as shoes.)

Shoot, v. C. (The *oo* is pr. as *u* in put). To break into ear (of corn). Dan. Skyde (to push) ; Skyde Knopper (to put forth buds).

Shot, adj. C. (sometimes pr. shot, and sometimes shut). Rid, free.

> Ex.—*Ah thowt wa'd gitten shut o' ya.—Ah can't git shot on 'em.*

Shout, v. C. (pr. shoot). To call, but not necessarily in tones of more than ordinary loudness.

> Ex.—*Thoo maun't shoot on him whahl ah 's riddy ti gan.*

Showd, n. F. A shallow place in a river, across which vessels have to be navigated with caution. The word is used of points on the Ouse where such places occur ; particular names being sometimes given to them : e. g. *man showd, woman showd.*

Shudder, v. C. (pr. shoodther, the *oo* being rather short). To shake ; used both in an active and neuter sense.

> Ex.—*He cam up an' shoodthered ma.—T'au'd helm fair shoodthered ageean; it wer ommost fit ti whemm'l ower.*

Shut, v. C. (pr. as put). To shoot with a gun. Also the word *shutters* is commonly used for a shooting-party in the same way as *weddiners* would be for a wedding-party.

Shy, adj. C. Bitter and piercing, of the wind.

Side, v. C. To remove, esp. out of sight ; to bury.

> Ex.—*Noo ! you 've gotten au'd Willie Barker sahded.*

Side-line, side-long, v. F. (pr. sahd-lahn, sahd-lang). To tie the fore and hind leg of a sheep together, and sometimes also the head, to prevent it from straying.

Side up, v. C. (pr. sahd up.) To put into order, to make tidy, to remove things that are lying about.

> Ex.—*Be sharp, Jane, an' git them things sahded up.*

Sidelings, adv. F. (pr. sahdlins). By the side of, near to, alongside of. .

> Ex.—*He went somewheers sahdlins o' Lon'on.*

Sideway, adv. C. Aside, out of the way.

> Ex.—*Ah put it sahdewaay.*

Sie, v. F. To stretch ; also to fall in drops. Dan. At si (to filter).

> Ex.—*He 's siein' hissen out,* i. e. he is stretching himself,

Sike, adj. C. Such.

> Ex.—*There nivver was sike deed afoor.—Ah nivver seed sike apples.*

Sike-an, sikan, adj. C. Such. This and the foregoing word are sometimes confounded. They may be distinguished thus : *sike* is always used when followed by a word without the article before it, or when followed by *a* or *an* with a noun simply, but when an adjective intervenes then *sikan* is used. E. g. Such apples = *sike apples* ; such an apple = *sike an* (not *sike-an*) *apple* ; such great apples = *sike greeat apples* ; such a great apple = *sikan a greeat apple*. Dan. Sikken (such a, what a).

Sike-like, adj. C. (pr. seyke-leyke). Suchlike, so forth.
Ex.—Q. 'What had you to do ?' A. *Deea ? Whya ! Ah had ti muck oot t' pigs, an' fodther t' hosses, and leeak eftther t' beeos, an' seyke-leyke.*

Sile, n. C. (pr. sahl). A strainer ; generally applied to a milk strainer. A wooden or tin vessel with a hole at the bottom across which fine gauze or canvas is stretched N. Sil (a strainer).

Sile, v. C. To strain by means of a sile. N. Sila (to strain).
Ex.—*Thoo sahl t' milk an' ah 'll sahd t' childer.*

Sile-briggs, n. C. Two pieces of wood united by two cross pieces and placed across the milk-bowl for the *sile* to rest upon when the milk is poured through it from the pail.

Sills. Vide **Shills.**

Silly, adj. C. In a poor state of health.
Ex.—Q. ' How is your wife ? ' A. *Sha 's nobbut silly, an' hez been of a good bit.*

Sind, singe, v. F. To wash out, to rinse, as e.g. a dirty pail.

Sing, v. C. To purr.
Ex.—*Oor cat sings weeantly ti-neet.*

Sipe, v. C. To drain away gradually ;, to sink away, as water into the ground.

Siss, v. C. To hiss ; commonly used to express the sound made by water dropping on a fire, &c.
Ex.—*It 's tahd ti be raanin hard, t' fire sisses seea.*

Sit fast, set fast, n. C. The central part of a wound, boil, &c.

Sitha. sutha, interj. C. Calls to attract attention. *Sutha* is sometimes used in the form of a question, being then equivalent to ' saw thou ? ' *Sitha* is the same as ' see thou ! '

Sittings, n. C. Statute hirings : these are held at the market towns throughout the district annually at Martinmas. Sometimes they are called *statties.*
Ex.—*We 're off for Pockli'ton sittins.*

Skare on, v. F. To splice two pieces of wood together in such a way that the thickness at the juncture is not greater than the rest : oars are commonly spliced thus. Jutl. D. At skarre ved (to join two pieces together).

Skeef, n. R. The front wheel of a plough, used formerly instead of the coulter for cutting the ground.

Skeel, n. F. A large wooden pail into which the milk was put at milking time and carried home on the head. A *piggin* was used for milking into, and the milk was poured from the *piggin* into the *skeel*. Tin cans have now almost universally taken the place of wooden pails: still the word *skeel* is very familiar to old people. The derivation of this word appears to be uncertain. There would seem to be a connection between it and the Danish *Skaal*, but this word applies to a bowl. of crockery or cup. The O. N. word Skiola (a milking-pail) seems a more probable derivation, the root of the word being the same in each case.

Skeg, n. F. A glance (of the eye); also a squint, a cast. Dan. Skjæv (oblique); se skjævt til (look askance at).
Ex.—*A skeg o' t' ee.*

Skeggle, v. F. To sway from side to side, as a horse sometimes does.

Skel-beast, n. F. The partition which separates the cows in a cow-shed. Dan. At skille (to separate).

Skell up, v. C. (pr. skell and skeyl). To tilt, esp. a cart when the body is sloped to the ground while the shafts remain in a horizontal position. O. N. Skæla (to turn aside).

Skelp, v. C. To beat with the palm of the hand; also to ride or walk quickly.
Ex.—*Whisht! or ah 'll skelp tha.—He skelp'd off yam.*

Skelping, adj. C. Very large; generally preceded by *greeat*.
Ex.—*Sha 's a greeat skelpin meer.*

Skep, n. C. A basket; esp. a garden basket with an arched handle across it. It was formerly used as a measure, and is so still in Denmark, where a *Skjœppe* equals half a *tönde*. This purely Danish word, so commonly used in East Yorkshire, seems to be unknown in Westmoreland.

Skill, v. R. To distinguish, to make out. Dan. D. At skelle (to discriminate between).
Ex.—*It 's bad ti skill*, i. e. It is difficult to distinguish.

Skillet, **skellit**, n. R. A small pot for the fire, with a long handle, generally made of tin.

Skime, v. F. (pr. skahm). To squint, to look scowlingly. Dan. At skimte (to see faintly); skimte efter (to gaze after).
Ex.—*He skahms oot ov his een.—He skahms wi yah ee.*

Skimmer, v. F. To shimmer, to glisten. Dan. At skimte frem (to glimmer forth).

Skirl, v. C.   To scream ; hence *skirling*, a screaming. Dan. At skralde (to peal forth).

Ex.—*He skirls leyke a pig iv a yat.*

Skirting, part. F.   Under-cutting a haystack three feet or so upwards from the ground.   After due settlement from ' sweating,' a stack (always called ' she ') would be 'pulled,' ' skirted,' and ' topped out.'

Skirts, pair of, n. C. (pr. ske'ts).   This is the common equivalent for a petticoat.

Skrike, v. C   To screech.   Dan. At skrige (to screech).

Ex.—*Ah fair skrik'd oot i paan.*

Slack, n. C.   The hollow part of an undulation in the ground.   A *slack* scarcely amounts to what would be called a valley : a good specimen, among many, of a *slack*, is on the road from Driffield to Nafferton, which always goes by the name of *The Slack.*   Also used as an adj., in the sense of depressed, easy, light, &c.   Dan. Slak (slack—a nautical term).

Ex.—*It wer a varry slack market yisttherda.—Wa s'all 'ev a slack tahm inoo.*

Slafter, n. F.   Slaughter.   There is also a similar verbal form.

Slain, n. F. (pr. slaan or sleean).   The bluish-black blight on wheat ; hence also the adj. *slainy*, with corresponding meaning.

Ex.—*There 's a vast o' slaany ears amang t' coorn.*

Slair, v. F.   To idle away one's time.

Slaister, v. C.   To idle, or do work in a slip-shod manner ; hence *slaisterer* and *slaistering*, also in common use.

Ex.—*He 's a slaisterin' soort ov a man.*

Slake, v. F.   To lick.

Ex.—*Sitha ! he 's slaakin' t' treeacle off.*

Slap, v. C.   To spill water.   Jutl. D. Slap (to lap) ; slap-tid (slack water).

Ex.—*Thoo maun't slap it.*

Slape, adj. C.   Slippery, smooth ; also used figuratively for an untrustworthy person.   O. N. Sleipr (slippery).

Ex.—*T' rooads is varry slaape.—Sha 's a nasty slaape soort ov a woman.*

Slappy, adj. C.   Soft and wet, puddly, esp. under foot ; but sometimes also applied to the cause, viz. rainy weather.

Ex.—*T' trod 's varry slappy.—It 's a slappy tahm been.*

Slaps, slap, n. C.   Rinsings, dirty water, pig-wash, &c.

Ex.—*Ah gi'es 'em a bit o' slap i t' mornin's.*

Slash, v. C.   To trim hedges with a *slasher*, or long straight blade with a handle.

Sleck, v. C.   To apply liquid to a fire with a view of putting

B b 2

it out; also used frequently as a noun, in the sense of any draught that allays thirst well. Dan. At slukke (to quench).
> Ex.—*T' lahm wants sleckin' a bit mair.*—*Aa! ah was dhry, bud t' yal maks a good sleck.*

Slidder, v. C. (pr. slidther). To slide.
> Ex.—*Sha went slidtherin doon t' ramper.*—*Ah thowt sha wer nivver boun ti stop slidtherin.*

Sliddery, adj. F. (pr. slidthery). Slippery, equivalent to *slape.*

Slight, adj. R. Smooth, glossy. Dan. Slet (level).

Slip, n. C. A case for a pillow.

Slipe, v. C. To remove any substance rapidly from the surface of anything.
> Ex.—*We sliped off a bit o' t' shaff.*

Sloke, n. F. Scum; also refuse or loose straw that attaches itself to *line*, which is removed prior to *ruckling*, and which brings with it a portion of the *line* itself, this being twisted at the top of the sheaf when placed upright on the ground.

Slope, v. C. (pr. slowp). (1) To leave a place in debt. (2) To make a noise in drinking, to gulp; also used as a noun in the sense of a gulp.
> Ex.—(2) *Hoo thoo diz slowp.*—*He supped it at yah slowp.*

Slough, n. C. (pr. sluff). The outer skin, esp. of fruit; e.g. the gooseberry. This word is never applied to a skin which cannot be easily taken or cast off. Sometimes the act of taking the heads and tails off gooseberries preparatory to preserving was called *sluffing berries*, though strictly speaking the *sluff* is only the skin of the fruit.
> Ex.—*Thoo maun't eat them berry sluffs.*

Slowdy, n. and adj. C. One who goes with his clothes in a very untidy and dirty state.
> Ex.—*Sha 's a big slowdy.*

Slubbard, n. R. A basin for drinking milk out of.

Sluddery, adj. C. (pr. sludthery). Dirty and untidy Dan. Slud (rain and snow mixed).
> Ex.—*Sha 's a sludthery sooart ov a woman.*

Slushing, adj. C. This word is commonly applied to a situation where there is much rough work to be done; a *slushing-pleeace* or a *slushing-spot* are common expressions for such places.

Slythe, n. R. An oppressive smell, foul air; sometimes also applied to cold or chilliness.
> Ex.—*We 'll leet t' fire to be rid o' t' slythe.*

Smally, adj. F. Puny, slight, thin.

Smiddy, n. C. A blacksmith's shop. Dan. En Smedic (a smithy).

Smiddy-cum, n. C. The sweepings of a blacksmith's shop.
Smit, n. C. Contagion or infection; also used as a verb.
Dan. Smitte (contagion or infection).
   Ex.—*It 's that 'at taks smit ti folks* (said of the particles
   of skin in a case of scarlet fever).
Smit, Smitch, n. C. A particle of soot which falls from
smoke. Dan. Hver Smit og Smule (every particle).
Smitting, adj. C. Contagious or infectious.
   Ex.—*Ah doot all t' bairns 'll tak t' mezzles; they 're varry
   smitting.*
Smittle, n. and v. C. This word is used in the same sense
as *smit.*
Smock, n. R. A chemise. This word is now commonly
applied to the short fustian or other kind of jacket tied by
a band with button round the waist and worn outside the
other garments.
Smoor, v. C. To smother; this word is generally followed
by *up.*
   Ex.—*Thoo maun't smoor 'em up.*
Smout, v. R. (pr. smoot). To hide the face through shyness,
like a child. Dan. At smutte (to steal away).
Smout-hole, n. C. (pr. smoot-hooal). An opening at the
bottom of a fence wall, used for letting hares or sheep
pass through; also in the E. R., a hole in a hedge through
which the snow drifts. Dan. En Smutte (a secret
entrance); Smut-sti (a by-way); Smut-vei, &c.
Smout-stone, n. C. A large stone for stopping up a
smout-hole.
Smouty-faced, adj. R. (pr. smooty-feeaced). Bashful, shy.
Smudge, v. C. To smear, to soil, esp. in writing, painting, &c.
Dan. At smudse (to soil).
Snaffle, snavvle, v. C. To speak through the nose. Dan.
At snôle (to muffle).
Snag, v. C. To cut off the branches from a felled tree; also
commonly used as a noun for a branch cut off.
Snape, v. C. (pr. snaap and sneeap). To check. This
word is of wide application, and refers to things as well
as people, e.g. plants that are killed or checked by frost.
Dan. D. At snævve (to check).
   Ex.—*Them lads is awlus in a mischeef, an' they 're bad ti
   snaape an' all.—T' frost has snaaped wer taaties sadly.*
Snarly, adj. F. Gusty and biting (of the weather). I have
never heard this word applied simply to chilly weather,
but only when accompanied by wind, and esp. squally or
gusty wind. It is happily expressive of what it describes.
Dan. At snerre (to snarl); snerret (bitter—from too long
boiling).

Sneck, v. C. A latch or fastening of a door or gate ; also commonly used as a verb.

Ex.—*Is t' sneck brokken ?—Sneck t' yat.*

Snevit, n. F. A blow (of the nose). This word, which is used in the E. R., is connected with *snifter* and with the Std. Eng. *sniff.* Dan. At snive (to sniff) ; Icel. Snippa.

Snickle, v. C. A wire snare for catching game or any animals ; also commonly used as a verb, and sometimes under the form *sniggle.*

Snifter, n. F. A snuff, a scent, a smell of short duration ; also used as a verb

Ex.— *Give him a snifter on 't.— What's ta snifterin at?*

Snig, v. C. To draw timber along the ground from where it has been felled, horses being always used for the purpose. The idea conveyed by this word is that of moving slowly and bit by bit. Dan. At snige (to slink or steal away).

Snig cut, n. F. A short cut. The primary meaning of this expression is a secret way, that by which one can get away unobserved ; hence, a short cut generally.

Snite, v. C. To blow the nose ; either with or without applying a handkerchief. Dan. At snyde (to blow the nose) ; snyd din næse corresponds to *snite thi nooaz* in our dialect, as commonly addressed to a child.

Snitter, v. F. To laugh in a subdued and derisive manner.

Ex.—*What's ta stannin' theer snitterin' an' laffin' at.*

Snocksnarls, n. C. The twistings or entanglements of thread, string, rope, &c. Dan. At snære (to bind up tight, to tangle) : obsolete.

Snod, adj. F. Smooth, neat-looking.

Ex.—*It leeaks neyce an' snod at t' top.*

Snow-flag, n. C. A snowflake. Dan. En Sneflage (a snowflake).

Snubbits, n. F. Two pieces of wood let into the back part of the body of a cart on which it rests when tilted up.

Soamy, adj. C. Close, warm, oppressive (of the weather).

Sock, n. C. The ploughshare.

Sodgy, adj. R. Bulky, fat, large-sized.

Soft, adj. C. (1) Of weak intellect, half-witted. (2) Applied to the weather when it is very rainy.

Ex.—*Whya ! ah think t' poor bairn 's a bit soft.— We 've had a soft tahm on 't.*

Soles, n. C. (pr. saules) Four pieces of oak wood running along the length of the framework of the body of a cart, the two outside ones being thicker than the other two

This is probably another form of *syles*, used in other parts for the main rafters of a house.

Soonest, adj. C. (pr. soonest and seeanest). This word is commonly used as an adj. in the sense of shortest and quickest, as applied to a road or distance.

Ex.—*If thoo gans by t' trod it 'll be a deal t' soonest.*

Sort, n. F. (pr. soort). Many people or things ; a gàthering of people more or less.

Ex.—*' Frev iv'ry pairt a soort o' chaps did thrang.'*—' York Minster Screen.'

Soss, v. C. To fall with a splash : sometimes, however, the word is used abverbially, some other word being employed for the act of falling ; e. g. it is said *he soss'd inti t' beck* or *he tumml'd soss inti t' beck.* Also used as a noun. This word is further used commonly to express to drink with a noise, to lap like a cat or dog.

Ex.—*See ya ! t' dog 's sossin all t' cat milk.—It fell wi a soss.*

Soughing, n. C (pr. so'in or soo'in). The noise made by the wind or anything similar to it ; a sighing.

Ex.—*Ah 's gitten sikan a so'in i mah heead.*

Sound, v. C. (pr. soond). To faint, to swoon. Also used as a noun.

Ex.—*Sha ommaist soonded reet awaay.—He fell intiv a soond.*

Soup, v. C. (pr. between sope and sowp). To soak with water.

Ex.—*Ah 's ommaist soup'd thruff. — T' things is soupin' wet.*

Sowl, v. C. To rinse or wash with water, generally accompanied with a decided amount of exertion ; also to chastise. The corresponding noun is *sowling.*

Ex.—*Ah sowled them drisses weel.—Give them things a good sowlin', they 're varry mucky.*

Spade-graft, **spade-graff**, n. C. The depth of a spade as made by digging.

Spane, v. C. (pr. speean). To wean, esp. lambs. O. N. Speni (the breast).

Spang, v. R. To throw forward with force or vigour ; to throw forward the legs ; hence, to *walk quickly* (an old use). Dan. At spanke (to walk upright). I do not remember to have ever heard this word used in the sense of to walk quickly, and it is probably now obsolete, though its disappearance is regretable, being very expressive in such a phrase as *spang thi gaits*, i. e. put your best leg foremost. It is, however, still in use in such a phrase as *he spang'd him doon*, i. e. he threw him violently to the ground.

Span-new, adj. F. An expression frequently used instead of *brand-new.*

Sparrow-feathers, n. C. This term is commonly applied to the chaff of oats when used for beds instead of feathers.

Spattle, n. F. Spittle.

Speak, v. R. To address, to accost.

Speeak, n. C. The spoke of a wheel; *speeakwood* being the wood from which spokes are made.

Spelder, v. F. To spell, as a child in reading.

Spelk, n. F. A thin piece of wood used in thatching, a *stack-prod,* a *splint.* The *spelks* for thatching houses are generally made of hazel or willow, split down the middle and pointed at each end; they are then bent like a staple and pushed in to hold the thatch. Dan. At spjælke (to bind up by spelks).

Spell, n. C. A thin piece of wood for lighting candles, &c., a *spill.* It is a common thing to see a bundle of wooden spills hung up by the side of the fireplace in cottages. Icel. Spilda (a slice).

Spice, n. C. Gingerbread, whether a solid cake, nuts, or thin and chippy; but a *spice-keeak* would be a rich plum cake, and *spice-bread* would be cake of the bread and currant type.

Spit, n. C. A long and thin spade for draining. Dan. Spid (a spit), Spids (a point). There is also an intermediate tool of the same kind between a *spit* and a *spade,* which is called a *mule.*

Spittle, n. C. A small kind of spade; also used as a verb.
Ex.—*He 's spittlin' yon trod.*

Splauder, v. F. To spread out, to expand, to display, to make a display.

Splaudy, adj. F. Having a tendency to spread out, wide-spreading.

Splaws, n. R. The part of a pen which expands under pressure, the nibs.

Sponge, n. C. To swell or rise by, or as by, leaven. To cause bread to rise; to rise, to swell, as a dead body frequently does. Atkinson gives another use of this word as a noun, viz. a portion of leavened dough reserved to *raise* or lighten the next batch with.
Ex.—*T' breead nobbut sponges badly ti-daay.*

Sprent, v. R. To spurt out as any liquid does when struck, &c. This word is seldom heard now; but formerly it was very commonly used by school-boys when speaking of a pen that spurted.
Ex.—*Pleeas sir! mah pen sprents badly.*

Spring, v. C. A word commonly applied to a cow near calving time, when parts of the body undergo change.
Ex.—*Sha springs for cauvin'.*

Sprunt, n. R. A steep hill, or road up a hill.

Spurrings, n. R. The publication of banns of marriage in church. This word, so common formerly, is now seldom heard, although there is no single word which so well expresses the act as this. Dan. At spörge (to ask).
Ex.—*Pleeas sir! will ya put up mah spurrins i t' mornin?—A'e they gitten t' spurrins put up yit?*

Squab, n. F. A roughly made couch or long-settle with cushions; frequently seen in cottages. It differs however from the ordinary long-settle, in that it has one arm instead of two.

Stack-bar, n. C. A Hurdle.

Stack-garth, n. C. (pr. staggarth). The enclosure on a farmstead in which the stacks are made. Dan. En Stak (a stack); en Gaard (a yard).
Ex.—*Wa 've gotten a good staggarth full o' coorn.*

Stack-prod, n. C. A stick commonly used in thatching, to which the thatch bands are tied.

Staddle, n. R. A frame of posts and cross-beams on which a stack is built. These are not so common in the North as in the South of England; in Yorkshire at least the stacks are for the most part built upon the ground. Dan. Stade (a station). This word has also another and commoner application, viz. a mark, or stain, or spot left upon anything, esp. on clothes after washing; e.g. inferior 'blue' is sometimes said to go *staddled* upon the linen.

Stag, n. F. A gelding of over a year old. This word is not so much used in the south of the North Riding as in some other parts, e. g. Cleveland. The derivation is the same as *steg.*

Stagnated, part. C. Greatly surprised, astonished. Though other parts of the verb are also heard, the participle is by far the most general.
Ex.—*Ah wer fair stagnated.—It stagnates yan ti hear tell on 't.*

Staithe, n. F. (pr. steeath, but in pl. the *th* is dropped). A landing-place. Icel. Stödh (a harbour).

Stakker, v. C. To stagger.

Stall, v. C. To fill to the full, to satiate, to weary out.
Ex.—*Ah 's fair stall'd oot.*

Stand, v. C. To be responsible, to make responsible, esp. in monetary transactions.
Ex.—*Ah s'all a'e ti stan' tul 't.—It stood him ti fahve pund.*

Stand for, v. C. To act as sponsor.

Ex.—*We s'all be varry pleeas'd if you 'll stan' for oor bairn.*

In Denmark the custom at a Baptism is for the sponsors to stand up at a certain part of the service while the rest of the congregation sit.

Standing, n. C. (pr. *d* silent). A stall for a horse or beast in a stable, cow-house, &c.

Stand-ups, n. R. Godparents on the occasion of a public baptism. (I have not heard of this word except in Cleveland.)

Stang, n. F. A long pole. This word is only used in the expression 'riding the stang.' Dan. En Stang (a pole or bar).

Stang, to ride the, v. F. A rough-and-ready way of shaming a husband who ill-treats his wife. The custom, which is still kept up here and there, is as follows : A cart with a long pole in it, on which is placed a representative of the offender in straw, &c., is drawn up and down the village by lads or men, a horn being blown the while, accompanied by loud shouting and jeering. At length the cart is pulled up opposite the offender's house, where a long 'nominy' or doggerel is recited recounting the man's offences. This is repeated for three successive nights, and at the end of the third occasion, amid wild excitement, the effigy is burnt in the street, accompanied by a bonfire.

Starken, v. C. To become stiff or rigid; also to tighten, esp. a rope.

Start, v. C. To begin. This word, which is found commonly in Std. Eng., is used in the dialect universally to the exclusion of all others of like meaning : 'begin' or 'commence' are never heard ; *it started ti rain, he starts ti roor, they've started harvest, wa sa'n't start whahl t' mornin'*, &c., &c., are the invariable forms of expression.

Starve, v. C. This verb is generally heard in the passive voice, in the sense of to suffer from cold, or to be cold. It is however sometimes used in the active voice, in the sense of to make cold. In the active voice it sometimes is also used in the ordinary sense of 'to cause hunger,' but it is never so used in the passive. Thus e. g. *He starves t' bairns* would properly mean, he lets his children suffer cold; but it might also mean, he does not sufficiently feed his children. Whereas *ah's starved* could only mean 'I am very cold.'

Staup, v. F. To walk with heavy and clumsy tread. The derivation of this word seems to be from the Danish

stolpe or *stolpre* (to stagger or totter), the latter form being only used colloquially.
Ex.—*He gans staupin aboot.*

Stawter, v. R. To stumble.

Stead, n. C. (pr. stcead). This word is obsolete as used alone, but is very common as a suffix, and signifies a fixed place ; we find it most commonly in such connections as *door-stead*, *fire-stead*, *midden-stead*, &c. Dan. Et Sted (a place).

Steck, v. C. (pr. steck and steek). To shut, to fasten, esp. a door, gate, &c.
Ex.— *Steck t' yat.—Steck t' deear.—Steck thi een.*

Stee, n. C. (pr. stee, but sometimes not with quite such a closed sound as indicated by this spelling of the word). A ladder ; a series of steps upwards, even when there are but two or three, as in a stile. Dan. At stige (to mount) ; en Stige (a ladder). In Jutl. D. this word is pr. stie.
Ex.—*Wilt tha set ma ti t' stee ?* i. e. Will you accompany me to the stile ?

Steean, n. C. A stone. The form *stane* is also used, though not so commonly, and *stein* very rarely. Dan. En Sten (a stone).

Steer-tree, n. C. The left-hand *hale* or handle of a plough.

Steg, n. F. A gander. Icel. Steggi (a gander).

Stegly, adj. F. Unsteady, lively. The root of this word is probably connected with stagger. Icel. Stakra (to stagger).

Stell, n. C. A large open drain.

Stevn, stevven, n. R. A loud shout, a roar. Also used as a verb. Dan. At stævne (to summon, to cite).
Ex.—*He gav oot sikan a stevn.—It stevvons and stoors* (*Whitby Glossary*), i. e. It blows hard and comes down like dust.

Stickle-haired, adj. C. Bristling as to the hair ; commonly applied to the hair of a horse. Dan. Stikkel-haaret (bristly-haired).

Stiddy, n. C. An anvil. Icel. Stedhi (an anvil). Jutl. D. Stede (an anvil).

Stife, stify, adj. F. Close and suffocating as to air ; also strong tasted, but in this sense probably the word is obsolete.

Stingy, adj. F. (pr. *g* soft). Fretful, irritable, esp. of a child.
Ex.—*T' bairn 's that stingy ah can't deea nowt wiv her.*

Stinted, part. F. A stinted pasture is a pasture limited to carry so many sheep : if, e. g., it would carry two hundred sheep, A. would be said to have fifty stints, B. thirty, and so on, dates being fixed for stocking and clearing. I have only heard of this word being used in the West of the North Riding.

Stirk, n. C. A heifer, or bullock of more than a year old.

Stirrings, n. C. Any show or unusual excitement.

Ex.—*We 're gahin ti Allerton ti see t' stirrins.*

Stitching, n. R. This term is used of the method by which the thatch was secured to the woodwork in old timber houses. If properly done it kept the thatch in its place a remarkably long time. The stitching was always formed of twisted straw, which was firmly tied on to the spars.

Stob, n. C. (1) A piece of wood of various lengths, pointed at the end, e. g. a thorn spike ; also a hazel or other kind of bough, one, two, or three feet long, used for thatching, marking out ground, &c. (2) Also commonly applied to the stump of a tree. In the dialect this word is closely connected with the Std. Eng. stab ; indeed stab is used in the dialect in the same way as a prick or puncture would be in Std. Eng. The primary idea in the word seems to be that which projects in a more or less pointed form. (1) Icel. Stafr, Dan. Stav (a staff or stake). (2) Icel. Stubbi, Dan. Stub (the stump of a tree).

Ex.—*Aw deear ! ah 've gi'en mi han' sikan a stub.— Mak us a few stobs, Bill, wilt ta?*

Stock, n. C. A post, esp. the post or framework of a bed-stead, i. e. the fixed part of it. Dan. Stok (a stick).

Stooden, p. part. of Stand, C.

Ex.—*Ah 've stooden theer monny a tahm.*

Stook, n. C. A number of sheaves of corn (generally a dozen) placed upright in two rows against one another in the harvest field in order to dry. Also commonly used as a verb. The manner of *stooking* varies in different localities ; sometimes two head-sheaves are placed on the top of the *stook* to afford additional protection from wet.

Storm, n. C. A continuance of frosty or snowy weather ; there being no idea necessarily of wind contained in this word.

Ex.—*Wa can deea nowt wi 't whahl t' storm ho'ds.—Ah doot we 're boun ti hev a lang storm.*

Stot, n. R. A bullock of more than a year old. Icel. Stutr (a bull) ; Dan. Stud (a bullock over four years old); Norse Stud (a bull). Vide **Plough-stot.**

Stothe, v. F. (pr. steeathe). To place or fix wooden bars or posts vertically on the main timbers in building old-fashioned houses. To these bars laths are nailed preparatory to plastering, this latter being called *daubing*; the term *daubing* is still used in connection with *stothing*, the houses built in this way being said to be *steeath'd and daub'd.*

Stoup, n. F. A measure for ale, a drinking-cup.

Stoup, n. C. (pr. between stope and stowp). An upright post, esp. a gate post. Dan. En Stolpe (a post); e.g. Stolpeseng (a four-post bedstead).

Ex.— *T' au'd yat-stoup 's gitten varry whemmly.*

Stour, v. C. To blow violently in dust-like clouds, whether in snow or rain, &c. Dan. At styrre (to disturb), rarely used in the simple form, but common in the compound forstyrre.

Ex.—*It fair teeam'd doon; it stour'd, an' it reek'd an' it drazzled* (a description of a storm).

Stoven, n. F. The stump of a tree, as e. g. in a hedge ; esp. one from which young shoots grow. Dan. At stævne (to lop), et Stævnetræ (a pollard).

Ex.—*Tak that au'd stoven oot.*

Stower, n. C. A strong piece of wood of various lengths ; a stake, a rail, a pole, the long pole used on barges ; the middle bars of a cattle-rack. Dan. En Staver (a stake). The Danish pr. of this word exactly corresponds with the Yorkshire.

. **Stra**, n. F. (pr. stthrah). Straw. This form of the word is found in the E. R. Icel. Stra (straw).

Straighten, v. C. (pr. stthreighten, almost as in heighten). To put in order, to make tidy ; also to correct or punish.

Ex.—*Noo ! be sharp, an' git stthreightened up.—If thoo deean't give ower this minute, ah 'll tell thi faether, an' he 'll varry seean stthreighten tha.*

Straightforward, adj. C. Bold.

Strand, n. C. The sea-coast, the beach. Dan. Strand (the sea-shore).

Strength, n. F. (pr. stren'th). Right, title, proof.

Ex.—*Let him shew his stren'th for 't,* i. e. the grounds of his claim (to a right of pasturage).

Strengthy, adj. F. (pr. stren'thy). Forcible, strong.

Strick, v. R. To separate flax by handfuls preparatory to its being beaten by ' scutchers.'

Strickle, n. C. A tool for sharpening a scythe, being a four-sided piece of oak narrowed towards one end, with a circular handle, of a piece with the rest, at the other. The sides of the *strickle* are smeared with grease upon which fine gritty sand is sprinkled freely ; nothing gives a better edge to a scythe than this. Other kinds of *strickles* are manufactured, sometimes with two and sometimes with four sides, these are called emery *strickles* ; but they are very inferior to the old-fashioned sort. Dan. At stryge (to rub) ; en stryge-spaan (a *strickle*).

Strick-stick, n. R. A round stick for throwing off the superficial excess in measuring corn, also called a *strickle*. Now that corn is sold by weight the *strick-stick* is seldom required. When the measuring had to be done with care, the *strick-stick* was rolled over the surface of the measureful of corn so that the amount might be adjusted with the greater accuracy.

Stridewallops, n. R. A tall long-legged lass.

Strike, v. C. (pr. stthreyke, approx.) To kick like a horse, i. e. with a back stroke. 'Kick' is never heard in the dialect, *bunch* or *strike* being exclusively used.

> Ex.—*Cu' by, or else t' hoss 'll mebbe strike tha.*

Strip, v. C. To draw the last drainings of milk from a cow, after milking in the ordinary way. The *strippings* are made into a milk-dish, and not into the milking-pail.

Stritch-stick, n. C. The bar connecting the traces of a leading horse in a cart.

Strong, adj. C. (pr. stthrong and stthrang). Hard (of frost), numerous (of people, esp. of a family), heavy.

> Ex.—*There was a stthrangish frost last neet.—It 's a bad job Hannah Smith lossin' er husband, sha 's sikan a stthrong fam'ly an' all.*

Strunt, n. C. A tail ; also commonly used as a verb in the sense of to cut the tail.

Struts, strut-sticks, strut-stower, n. C. The first two forms are applied to the posts or beams in a roof of a house, &c., which act as supports to the 'centre backs,' by being fixed into the foot of the 'king-post.' The last form is a more general term for a support, the principle of which is similar to that described. This word is found in place-names, being applied to projecting crags, e. g. Strutt Stear.

Stunt, n. C. Obstinacy, a state of obstinacy ; also used as a verb, and frequently as an adj.

> Ex.—*He teeak stunt,* i. e. He took to being obstinate.— *He started to stunt.—T' lad 's as stunt as owt.—If ah says owt tiv her she 's as stunt as stunt can be.*

Sturdy, n. C. (pr. sto'ddy). A disease in sheep, something like water on the brain, and from which they seldom recover. This word is also used as an adj. to signify stupid.

Sump, n. C. Any wet, boggy place. Dan. En Sump (a swamp, a pool).

> Ex.—*Ah flang it inti t' sump-hooal.—As wet as sump.*

Sumpy, adj. C. Boggy, moist, wet. Dan. Sumpig (boggy).

> Ex.—*Yon 's a varry sumpy spot.*

Sup, v. C. To drink (not necessarily in small quantities). Swedish Supa (to drink).

Ex.--*There was nowt ti sup.—He was set i t' langsettle suppin' yal.*

Sup, n. C. A quantity of liquid, more or less ; a 'drop.'

Ex.—*Wa could deea wiv a sup o' rain.—Wilt tha tak a sup o' yal.*

Supping-watther, n. C. Spring-water, drinking-water.

Sup off, v. C. To drink up, to drink what remains in a glass, &c.

Ex.—*Noo then ; sup off*; i. e. empty your glasses—commonly said by a host to his guests.

Surfeit o' cold, n. C. A severe cold in the head or chest.

Swad, swat, n. F. A portion, or measure, or quantity ; esp. of liquid.

Ex.—*Wilt ta tak anuther swad ?*

Swads. n. C. The outer shell of peas, beans, &c. Dan. At svöbe (to wrap round).

Ex.--*Ah gi'es 'em t' peea swads, bud they nivver eeats 'em* (said by a servant lad, blamed for hungering the pigs).

Swag, v. F. To roll as a boat; to sway to and fro as an overloaded vehicle. Dan. At svaie (to swing to and fro).

Ex.—*Deean't swag t' booat seea.*

Swaimish, adj. R. Shy, diffident.

Ex.—*Thoo maun't be ower swaamish.*

Swale, v. F. (pr. swaale). To throw a cast from oneself.

Ex.—*Ah swaal'd it awaay.*

Swang, n. F. Low-lying marshy ground. O. N. Svangr (a hollow place); Dan. Svang (the hollow of the sole of the foot).

Swanky, adj. C. Strong and large of its kind.

Ex.—*Your Tom 's a lang swanky chap gotten.*

Swape, n. C. A long oar or other contrivance where the fulcrum is considerably nearer one end than the other, though not necessarily that at which the force is applied ; e. g. as in a pump-handle, which is commonly called a swape. Also used as a verb. Dan. At svcie (to bend) ; Norse At sveive (to turn round by a crank handle).

Ex.—*Noo, my lad ; swaap her roond*: i. e. turn the boat round by means of the long oar.—*T' pump swaap 's brokken.*

Swarth, n. C. (pr. swath). The outer skin, rind, or covering, esp. of bacon, &c.; also the outer covering (so to speak) of land, i. e. that which has a permanent covering in the shape of grass upon it ; grass-land generally. Dan. Svær (rind of pork) ; Grönsvær (greensward).

Ex.—*Give t' bairn a bit o' bacon swath ti suck.*—*Oor swath 's gitten sadly bo'nt up.*

Swatch, n. F. The use of this word is peculiar: thus, if a person is not to be trusted, the caution is given to *keep a swatch on him.* This language is figurative, and has reference to a custom in use at the time when home-spun cloth was sent to the dyers; on these occasions a *swatch* or wooden tally was given, so that when the cloth was sent for after dyeing it might be at once recognised.

Swathe, n. C. (pr. sweeathe and swaathe). The reach of the scythe in cutting grass.

Ex.—*Thoo taks a lang sweeathe.*

Swathe-bauks, n. C. The long strips of grass or stubble left standing at the end of the *swathes*, the grass or corn being never quite so closely cut at the finish of the stroke as in the course of it. When an actual tuft of grass was left, the lasses would often chaff the mower and tie it in a knot, when it was left bare by the rakers.

Swatter, v. F. To splash water about; hence to waste or squander, esp. money.

Ex.—*He 'll varry seean swatter his bit o' brass awaay.*

Sweel, v. C. To gutter (of a candle). Norse Svælle (to swell).

Ex.—*What 's t' matther? T' cann'l sweels sadly.*

Swidge, v. C. To tingle with pain. This word is generally coupled with *smart,* from which it differs but little in meaning: possibly a burning sensation is implied by the word *swidge.* Dan. At svide (to burn or scorch; also, though rarely, to smart, burn, ache).

Ex.—*Mah finger swidges an' smarts weeantly.*

Swill, n. F. A light basket, generally made of willow twigs. This word is in use in the Wold district as well as in Cleveland.

Swing, v. R. To set up sheaves of 'line' on the ground.

Swingle, v. F. To beat flax, i.e. to rough-dress it. Dan. En Svingel (a bar).

Swingle-tree, n. C. The wooden rod which is attached to the traces and keeps them in their place when the horses are ploughing, harrowing, &c.

Swipple, n. F. The shorter part of a flail, viz. that by which the corn is beaten: this is usually made of tough wood, e.g. blackthorn. Dan. At svippe (to crack, to flick, as with a whip).

Switch, v. C. To fling or throw with force.

Ex.—*Sha com ti t' deear-steead an' switch'd a pail o' mucky watther reet inti t' hoos.*

Swizzen, v. C. To singe. Dan. At svide (to singe).
　Ex.—*Be sharp, Polly, them cleeas is swizzenin.*
Sword-dancers, n. F. (pr. swud-dancers). Those who dance the sword-dance, i. e. a dance with crossed swords on the ground; it is of very ancient origin and peculiar form. It is not often seen now; the only time when the performers go their rounds is about Plough Monday.
Syke, n. F. A large gutter or ditch, a streamlet; this was till lately the common word in the neighbourhood of Sessay for the thing described.

T.

Ta'en, part. C. (pr. ta'an). Taken. This abbreviation is universal, and as pronounced is more euphonious than the uncontracted form.
　Ex.—*Ah 've ta'en it.*
Ta'en ageean, part. C. The past participle of to *tak' ageean*, i. e. to hold in aversion, to dislike; similarly to *tak tiv*, or *tak til* (part. ta'en tiv or til) signifies to like, to be fond of, to become attached to.
　Ex.—*Oor maastther 's ta'en ageean ma, an' ah 's seear I can't tell what for.*
Tacket, n. F. A tack or small nail.
Tak, n. C. A taking or a holding of land for a fixed rent.
Tak, v. C. To take. Icel. Taka (to take).
　Ex.—*Tak ho'd on 't.*
Tak, by, C. By the piece, as distinguished from by the day, i. e. in engaging labour for any work that has to be done.
　Ex.—*A'e ya ta'en it by tak?*
Take, n. C. A flavour.
　Ex.—*It hes a queer tak wiv it.*
Tak off, v. C. To run away from an engagement or situation; to undertake a journey, esp. when a certain amount of secrecy is implied. A somewhat similar expression is used in Danish, e. g. Han tog til Helsingör would mean, He went off to Elsinore.
　Ex.—*He went ti pleeace; bud afoor a week was owered he teeak off.*
Tak on, v. C. To fret, to lament.
　Ex.—*Whisht, honey; thoo maun't tak on leyke that; thi mother 'll be back i noo.*
Tak on wi, v. C. To engage oneself to another, esp. in service or with a view to employment.
Tak tent, v. C. To take watchful care of; to pay close attention to.
　Ex.—*He 'll tak mair tent on 't 'an onny on 'em.*
Tak t' hig. Vide **Hig**.

C C

Tallow-cake, n. C. (pr. taller-keeak). A cake in which the inner fat about the kidney of a beast or sheep is an ingredient

T' ane, t' yan, pron. C. The one; as opposed to another. The corresponding expression to *one another* is *t' ane t' other* (or *t' ither*).

> Ex.—*They bazzaked t' ane t' other.*

Tang, n. C. The tongue of a buckle. Dan. En Tange (a tongue of land).

Tangle, n. C. (pr. tang'l). The long fibre of a root, e.g. the potato.

> Ex.—*When t' tang'ls is brokken they can't taatie.*

Tantle, v. C. To waste time, to dawdle.

Tastrill, n. F. A saucy, impudent child; one who is badly behaved; a rascal.

Tatchy, adj. C. Cross, irritable, fretful.

Taum, n. C. A short line, generally made of twisted horse-hair or worsted, to one end of which the fisherman's hook is attached, and the other joined to the principal line, which generally has several of such *taums* fixed to it; these are about nine inches long. They are commonly used for eel-fishing. Norse En Töm (a bridle, a rein).

Teegle, v. C. (pr. teeagle). To raise timber on to the waggon by means of tripod, pulleys, horses, &c.

> Ex.—*Wa mun start ti teeagle 'em up wi t' hosses.*

Teem, v. C. (pr. teeam). To pour from a vessel either liquids or solids; to unload, e. g. a cartload of coals, turnips, &c. To pour with rain. Dan. At tömme (to empty). At tömme en Flaske (to finish a bottle).

> Ex.—*Teeam t' watther oot o' yon can.—It fair teeam'd down* (with rain).—*Com an' help us ti teeam this keeak.*

Tell, v. C. To recognise, to distinguish.

> Ex.—*Them 's varry good 'uns ti tell*; i. e. those are easily distinguished.

There is not much difference between *tell* and *challenge*, except that the former is more general in its application, *challenge* being mostly used of persons.

Tell-pye, tell-pyet, n. F. A tell-tale.

Temse, n. F. A sieve, commonly made of tiffany, and used formerly for dressing flour, &c. Dan. En Timse (a coarse hair sieve).

Teng, v. C. To sting.

> Ex.—*T' wasp teng'd t' dog, an' t' dog hanch'd at t' cat.*

Tengs, n. C. A pair of tongs. Dan. En Tang (a pair of tongs), pl. Tænger.

> Ex.—*Whya, bairn, it 's a tooad; bring t' tengs.*

Tent, v. C. To keep watch over; to look after, esp. cattle in

the lanes, and birds in the corn-fields ; also, but not so
frequently used as a noun.
Ex.—*He 's tentin' bo'ds.--He 's coo-tentin'.*—*Thoo mun
tak tent on 'em.*
Teufit, n. C. (pr. teeafit). The common lapwing.
Tew, v. C. This word is used in a great variety of ways,
and is of most frequent occurrence. The root meaning is
to work in some way, and especially against time or
under difficulties ; hence it commonly implies to overtax
one's strength as the result of being always on the move.
Other meanings are, to strive hard in life, to work hard
and more than usual, to fidget, to lie restlessly, as a sick
person often does, or as a wakeful child.
Ex.—*Sha 's had ti tew hard, sha 's browt up a stthrong
fam'ly.*—*Noo thoo maun't tew thisen wi t' job*; i. e. you
must not overtax your strength.—*Ah can't bahd ti be
rowin an' tewin as ah used ti deea.*—*T' lahtle lass tews
hersen sadly i bed.*—*It's tewin 'deed*; i.e. it is hard work.
—*Thoo 's awlus tewin thisen,* i. e. fidgeting.
Thack, theeak, n. C. Thatch ; also commonly used as a verb.
Dan. At tække (to thatch). Jutl. D. Et Tække (a roof).
Ex —'*Mah haay hez all been steck'd an' theeak'd this
monny a day.*'—' York Minster Screen.'
Thack or thack-bands, n. C. Bands for tieing on thatch in
order to secure it.
Thack or theeak-prods, n. C. The hazel or other prods
used in thatching to which the bands are attached.
Thacker, theeaker, n. C. A thatcher. Jutl. D. En Tækker
(a thatcher).
Tharfly, adv. F. Slowly, shyly, unwillingly. The adj.
Tharf is also, but not so commonly, used. Dan. Tarvelig
(frugal, scanty).
Ex.—*T' rain nobbut cums tharfly.*
Them, pron. C. Those.
Ex.—*Them 's good uns.—Them 'at wants onny may lead
'em for thersens.*
Thills, n. R. Shafts of a cart, &c. Vide **Shills.**
Think long. v. C. To be long expectant.
Ex.—*Ah thowt lang o' ya comin'.*
Think on, v. C. (the stress is always laid on the latter
word). To remember, to bear in mind. This, though
allied to the Biblical expression ' think on these things,'
is not identical with it.
Ex.—*Thoo mun think on.—Ah lay t' lad 's clean forgot, he
can nivver think on.*
Thoff, conj. C. Though.
Ex.—*It leeaks as thoff it wer boun ti raan.*

Thondill, n. O. A measure of land. I have not seen this word in any glossary, but it has been repeatedly heard by me from the lips of an old man with whom I have conversed. He, however, only spoke of the word as having been used in his younger days; and therefore it is probably now obsolete. From what I could gather, plots of ploughing land on unenclosed commons were of three sizes, 'broads,' 'narrows,' and *thondills*, these latter being intermediate to the other two and about three roods in extent.

Thorpe, n. C. (as a place-name; pr. tthrup, the initial *t* being exceedingly lightly touched, and thrup). A hamlet. Dan. Torp, Drup, and Up (a hamlet).

Ex.—*Tholthrup, Helperthrup, Lowtthrup, Fridaythrup, Ugthrup, Fraistthrup, Tibthrup,* &c.

Threap, v. C. (pr. threeap). To assist or maintain obstinately, generally followed by out; to force down by argument.

Ex.—*He threeap'd oot 'at he hadn't deean it.*

Threed, n. C. Thread.

Threeve, Thrave, n. F. (pr. threeav). Twelve loggins or battens of drawn straw for thatching, each tied with two bands. For this work sixpence per *threeve* is the usual payment, and when so, or similarly paid, the men are said to work 'by threeave.' Formerly this word was applied to a 'stook' of corn. Dan. En Trave (twenty sheaves of corn); Travchob (a shock of corn).

Thriver, n. C. Anything that thrives well.

Ex.—*Noo them 's been good thrivers, a'en't tha ?*

Throng, adj. C. (pr. throng, sometimes thrang). More than ordinarily busy; in a state of confusion. Jutl. D. En Trynge (a crowd).

Ex.—*We 're throng weshin' ti-day.—Ah 'll a-war'nd it there 'll be throng deed at Pockh'ton sittins ti-morn.— It 's throng with it teeth* (said of a young horse at a time when its teeth were undergoing change).

Thropple, n. C. The wind-pipe, strictly speaking; but the word is sometimes used for the throat.

Throw, n. F. (pr. thraw). A lathe for turning.

Throw-back, n. C. A relapse (in sickness).

Ex.—*He had a throw-back last neet.—Ah 've had some sad throws back sen ah seed ya last.*

Thrummy, adj. C. Fat, bulky.

Ex.—*Sha 's a thrummy 'un.*

Thrumm'l, n. C. A loop in a rope tightly bound round a grooved iron ring, so that another rope may the more easily slip through it.

Thumml-teea, n. F. The great toe.

Thysel, Thysen, pron. C. (pr. thïsel, thïsen). Yourself. Of these two forms *thysen* is the commonest, and is used very generally, *thysel* being mainly confined to parts of the N. R.

Thrust, v. C. This word is always used in preference to push, to which it is equivalent.

Ex.—*He's thrussen't thruff.*

Ti, prep. C. To. Vide **Til.**

Tie, n. C. (pr. tah, or tahi). A band for tieing the hind legs of cows at milking time, generally called a *coo-tie*. It is made of horse-hair for the most part, with a spliced loop at one end and a knob of wood at the other ; it is placed round one leg, twisted, brought round the other, and if need be, twisted again, and the knob secured in the loop.

Tie, v. C. Used in the passive voice only with the signifi-cation 'to be obliged,' 'to be compelled,' but without any idea of physical force. Also used impersonally with the sense, 'it must,' 'it is sure to be so,' 'it is certain to happen.'

Ex.—*Ah's tied ti leeak efter t' meer.—He's tied ti loss his-sen ; he dizn't knaw t' rooad.—It's tied* ; i. e. It's sure to be so.—Q. *Is 't boun ti rain?* A. *It isn't tied.*

Tiffany, n. F. Stout gauze, from which sieves are made for dressing flour ; the name also given to the sieve itself.

Tike, n. C. Vide **Tyke.**

Til, tul, prep. C. To. Dan. Til (to). The dialectical varieties of this preposition are four in number, viz. *ti, tiv, til*, and *tul*. The two latter are seldom heard except in the N. R. ; *ti* and *tiv* are universal in the E. R., and are common also in the N. R. *Ti* is pronounced short, and the same may be said of the *u* in *tul*. *Til* corresponds exactly with the Danish prep. in form, and *tul* seems to be merely a corruption of it. But in Denmark *til* is pro-nounced colloquially, precisely as we pronounce *ti* in the dialect. *Tiv* is only, and in the E. R. generally, used be-fore a vowel or *h*, the *v* being added for euphony. With an infinitive mood, however, *ti* is used in all cases. The fol-lowing examples will best illustrate the various usages :—

Ex.—*Thoo mun gan til* (or *tul*) *him.* N. R.—*Thoo mun gan tiv him.* E. R.—*Ah's coom'd ti hear him.* E. and N. R.—*He dizn't want ti ax him nowt.* E. and N. R.—*He gav summat tiv* (or *ti*) *ivvery yan on 'em.* E. and N. R.—*He gav summat tiv 'em all* (never *ti 'em*). E. and N. R.—*When he cam tul*, i. e. came to his senses. N. R.—*It 'll nivver com ti owt* (and sometimes *tiv owt.* E. and N. R.

Timersome, adj. F. (pr. timmersome). Timorous, appre-hensive of danger.

Ti-morn, adv. C. To-morrow. Vide **T' morn.**
Tipe, v. C. To fall over.
　　Ex.—*He's tiped ower.*
Tipe-trap, n. C. A trap of which the floor hangs on a pivot and is evenly balanced, so that the weight of the animal entering it causes the door to fall.
Tite, adv. F. Soon, willingly. The comparative of this word is *titter,* and is more rarely used. Dan. Tid (time).
　　Ex.—*Ah 'd as tite deea t' job as not.—Titter up ca'* ; i. e. the soonest up in a morning call the rest.
Tiv, prep. C. To. Vide **Til.**
Tivvy, v. C. To run about in play.
　　Ex.—*T' lads is awlus tivvyin aboot.*
T' morn or **Ti morn,** adv. C. To-morrow. There can be no doubt that *t' morn* is an abbreviation of *ti* (or *to*) *morn.* 'To-morrow morning' would be expressed by *t' morn 't morn* or *ti morn t' morn;* this latter abbreviation might be either *at morn* or *i' t' morn,* but I incline to think that the former is correct. Similarly, 'to-morrow night' is *ti morn at neet,* or, for shortness, *t' morn 't neet.*
Toon, n. C. Vide **Town.**
Toon-street, n. C. Vide **Town.**
Top-coat, n. C. A great-coat, an overcoat.
Tottering, adj. C. (pr. tottherin). Changeable (of weather).
　　Ex.—*It's a tottherin tahm been this last fo'tnith.*
Tottle, v. C. To toddle ; frequently applied to elderly or in- firm people who walk with difficulty.
　　Ex.—*Ah 's nobbut waakly ; bud ah can just tottle aboot a bit.*
Town, n. C. (pr. toon). A village, of whatever size ; a col- lection of habitations ; a hamlet ; a town ; the main road through which is always called *t' toon stthreet.* Norse Tun (provincial town) ; Icel. Tun (a farmstead).
　　Ex.—*Ah seed him i t' toon a bit sen.—Iv oor toon.*
Towple, v. C. To fall over ; to double over.
　　Ex.—*To towple ower tail;* i. e. in fig. sense to double, as money might do at compound interest.
To you, I'll be, F. I will come to you.
Trail, v. C. To draw or pull along the ground, commonly with the idea of difficulty accompanying the action ; to trail oneself is to walk slowly and with difficulty.
　　Ex.—*Ah 's that badly, whahl ah can hardlins tthraal mysen across t' fleear.—Sha com tthraalin efther him* (said of a tired wife).
Trailtengs, n. C. An idle, gossiping female.
Trash, n. C. A good-for-nothing person.
　　Ex.—*He 's a complete bad trash.*
Travel, v. C. To walk, to move along. It is difficult to

describe the usage of this word, which is quite peculiar. To *walk* is commonly used, as e. g. when a man says he would prefer walking to riding, or when a man is seen walking on the road ; but if the road is difficult to walk along, as from snow, &c., then it is not said to be 'bad walking,' but *bad tthrav'lin.* Again, if an old man, stiff from rheumatism, wished to express that the stiffness somewhat wore off after he had begun to *walk* a little, he would say, *Ah isn't seea bad when ah git agait o' tthrav'lin.*

Trig, v. F. To fill with food, to give food, to feed (trans.), esp. animals.

Ex.—*He 's trig'd hissen,* i. e. He has eaten greedily.

Trigger, n. C. One who supplies with food, a feeder ; e. g. a *bullock-trigger* is the man who feeds bullocks.

Trod, n. C. A foot-path. Norse En Trod (a footpath). This word is invariably used instead of path.

Troll, v. C. (pr. between troll and trowl). To roll, esp. down a slope. Dan. Trille (to roll). This word is often used in speaking of the custom of rolling eggs on the grass on Easter Monday, that day being frequently called *Troll-egg Monday.*

Tup, n. C. (pr. toop, but slightly shorter). A ram.

Turve, n. C. A piece of cut turf from the moor, which is used as fuel. Dan. Törv (a turve, or piece of turf for fuel).

Turve-cake, n. C. A cake commonly made in the moorland districts. The cakes are put into a pan and covered over with a tightly-fitting lid ; the pan is then put upon a turf fire and covered all round and at the top with the burning *turves,* and so the cakes are baked.

Tweea, adj. C. (pr. almost as one syllable). Two.

Ex.—*Ah see'd tweea on 'em.*

Twilt, n. C. A bed coverlet, a quilt.

Twilt, v. C. To flog ; the corresponding noun *twilting* is also in common use.

Ex.—*He gav him a good twiltin.*

Twiny, adj. C. Fretful, peevish, hard to please.

Twitch-bell, n. C. The common earwig. Vide **Forkin-robin,** with which it is synonymous. Dan. Örentvist (the earwig).

Twitters, n. F. A state of impatience, nervousness, or anxiety.

Ex.—*He 's all i twitters ti be off.*

Tyke, n. C. A low character, a mean fellow ; commonly used as a term of disdain. This word is generally thought to be of Scandinavian origin : it seems to me more probable that it is a British word, and may be connected with the Welsh *taeog* (a villain).

U.

Unbeknown, part. C. Unknown. This word is in common use in the Pickering neighbourhood.

Unbethink, v. F. To think over again and find out a mistake. To call to mind, to recollect.

Ex.—*Ah can't unbethink mysen.*

Underdraw, v. C. To cover the underpart of a floor or roof with lath and plaster.

Underhanded, adj. C. (pr. un'erhan'ed). Of puny growth, undersized, not fully developed.

Ex.—*It 's nobbut a lahtle un'erhan'ed thing.*

Ungain, adj. C. Inconveniently situated, difficult of access.

Ex.—*Yon 's a varry ungain spot o' yours.*

Unmenseful, adj. F. Unfitting, unseemly, indecent. Vide **Mense**.

Up account of, prep. C. On account of. An abbreviation of 'upon account of.'

Upgang, n. F. A road or track up a hill. Dan. En Opgang (an uphill way).

Up-grown, adj. C. (pr. up-grawn). Grown-up, adult. This form of the word is quite universal, the ordinary form, grown-up, being never heard.

Ex.—*Sha 's an up-grawn woman noo.—All 'at ah seed was up-grawn folks.*

Uphold, v. C. (pr. upho'd). To answer for, to aver, to maintain, esp. in argument or in life.

Ex.—*Aye! bud ah 's seear on 't; ah 'll upho'd it.—That 's reet eneeaf, ah 'll upho'd it.—Ah doubt he weean't upho'd hissen mich langer.*

Upset (or **upsetten**) **with**, part. C. Elated, highly pleased with.

Ex.—*He 's weeantly upsetten wi gannin ti skeeal.*

Up of, C. Grown up; arrived at (maturity). This very common expression is equivalent to *upgrown*, q. v.

Ex.—*He 's ommost up of a man noo;* i.e. he has now nearly reached man's estate.

Ure, n. C. Vide **Yuer**.

Use, to no. C. Of no use, useless.

Ex.—*It 's ti neea use; ah can 't finnd it.—Them 's ti neea use; they 're good ti nowt.*

V.

Varry, adv. C. Very. (This pr. is universal.)

Varry weel, adv. C. Very much. Vide p. 170.

Vast, adj. C. A large number; commonly used as a noun of multitude.

Ex.—*A vast o' folks thinks seea, an' all.—Sitha, what a*

vast o' craws there is i yon pastur.—There 's a vast on 'em cum'd.

Viewly, viewlysome, viewsome, adj. C. Of good appearance, fine, handsome.

Ex.—*Them 's as viewly a pig as onny man need wish ti see.*

W.

Wa, pron. C. (pr. very short). We.

Wad, v. C. Would. (It is difficult to describe the pr. of this word, it is neither such as to rhyme with *had* nor yet with *rod*, but more like the former than the latter.)

Ex.—*Ah wadn't gie ya a haupenny for 'em.*

Wae 's t' heart, R. An abbreviation for '*wae* (woe) is to the heart,' an exclamation that was formerly commonly used on hearing of anyone's misfortune, affliction, &c.

Waff, v. C. To bark as a dog. This word is probably merely another form of Yeff.

Waffy, Waufy, adj. C. (pr. almost as wahffy, but not quite so open in the *ah* as ordinarily). Weak, feeble, esp. after an illness.

Ex.—*T' au'd man 's as waffy an' waakly as owt.*

Waft, n. C. (pr. waft). A puff or sharp blow of wind.

Ex.—*A waff o' wind.*

Wag, v. C. To beckon with the hand or finger.

Ex.—*He wagged ti ma as he passed.—Let 's wag on him.*

Waint, adj. and adv. C. (pr. weeant). Great (when applied to quantity). It is also commonly used as an intensive, being equivalent to very or greatly.

Ex.—*A weeant deal on 'em.—Ah 's weeant an' glad on 't,* i. e. very glad.

Waintly, adv. C. Very greatly, exceedingly.

Ex.—*Ah 's weeantly pleeas'd.*

Waintly off, C. In great trouble.

Ex.—*Oor Jack 's weeantly off aboot it.*

Wait of, wait on, v. C. To wait for.

Ex.—*Thoo maun't wait of us.—Ah can't wait on' him neea langer.*

Wake, wakely. adj. C. (pr. waak). Weak.

Ex.—*Sha 's nobbut a varry waakely soort ov a body.*

Wakken, v. (act. and neut.) C. To awake.

Ex.—*Ah nivver, yance wakken'd up.—Ho'd thi noise or else thoo 'll wakken t' bairn.—Lad! thoo 's asleep, wakken up.—' They 're wakken'd at Eeasby ! The Lord is amang 'em.'*—Castillo.

Wakken, wakkensome, adj. C. Easily roused from sleep, lively.

Ex.—*He 's varry wakken.*

Wale, v. F. (pr. waal and weeal). To flog with a whip or stick.

Waling, n. C. (pr. waalin' and weealin'). (1) This word is applied to the horizontal planks or beams which are fixed to piles on a river side or elsewhere to strengthen and protect the work; originally the word meant a rod: hence, (2) a flogging. Old Friesic Walu (a rod); Icel. Völr (a round stick).

Walk with, v. C. To court.
> Ex.—*They 've been walkin' wi yan anuther a good bit, ah lay they 'll be gittin' wed i-noo.*

Walsh, Welsh, adj. F. Lacking in flavour, watery; also sour.
> Ex.—*It tastes varry walsh*; i.e. it lacks flavour.—*T' milk 's welsh.*

Wangle, v. F. To shake, to totter, to waver; to be in a sensitive state. Dan. At vakle (to shake, or totter).
> Ex.—*Thoo mun put it varry wangling* (in setting a trap).

Wankle, adj. F. Unsteady, wavering, unsettled; esp. of weather, e.g. showery. This word is another form of *wangle.*
> Ex.—*It 's a wankle tahm been.—We 've had nobbut wankle weather.*

Wankling, adj. R. Shaky from weakness.
> Ex.—*Ah feels weeak an' wanklin.*

Want, v. C. The dialectical use of this word is very peculiar, and is not confined to any particular class, but is heard more or less with people of all classes. *Want,* followed by a present participle, forms a kind of middle voice unlike other constructions in our language. It will best be understood by one or two examples: thus, *Do those letters want posting?* is equivalent to 'are those letters to be posted?' or *I want my hair cutting*, is the same as saying 'I wish my hair to be cut.'

War, v. C. Was. Dan. Var (was).
> Ex.—*Ah warn't boun ti ax him nowt.*

Warbells, n. F. (pr. wahrbills). Swellings on the 'rigg' of a beast's back, caused by the larvæ of the gad-fly being embedded there.

Wardays, n. C. Every day in the week but Sunday. Dan. Hverdag (every day except Sunday).
> Ex.—*Ah 's awlus working, Sundays an' wardays, it 's all t' seeam wi ma.*

Wards. A common suffix signifying direction.
> Ex.—*Ah seed him cumin fra Newton-wards*; i.e. I saw him coming from the direction of Newton. In Cleveland the word *way* is inserted between the place-name and the suffix, e.g. *Ah seed him ganning Danby-way-wards.*

Ware, v. C. To spend (money).

Ex.—*He dizn't ware a deal o' brass i cleeas*, i. e. doesn't spend much on clothes.—*He wares nowt, for he addles nowt*, i. e. he spends nothing because he earns nothing.

Wark, v. C. To ache, also commonly as a noun. Dan. At værke (to ache); Hoved-værk (head-ache).

Ex.—*Mah heead warks weeantly.—It 's a back-warkin job. —Ah 've gitten t' teeath-wark.*

Warp, v. C. To bring water over land by artificial means in order that a deposit may be left upon the surface when the water recedes. This can only be done in places which the tide reaches. Through the constant ebb and flow of the tide, new soil, several inches in thickness, is thus formed in course of time, and land which was before worthless becomes valuable. The same term is of course applicable to the same process which takes place by natural means. This new soil is termed *warp*.

Warridge, n. C. (pr. warridge and warrish). The top of the shoulder-blade of a horse.

Ex.—*He 's weel up* (or *low*) *iv his warridge.*

Warse, adj. C. (pr. wahs). Worse. There is also another pr. of this word, viz. between *woss* and *waus*.

Warsen, v. F. To grow worse, esp. as to health. Dan. Forværres (to grow worse).

Ex.—*He 's neea better ; he warsens if owt.*

Warzle, v. F. To creep along softly in and out, like the motion of a snake ; hence to wheedle, to obtain by flattery.

Ex.—*They warzled him up*, i. e. they flattered him.

Wastrill, n. F. A spendthrift.

Wath, n. O. (except as a place-name). A ford across a stream. Dan. Et Vad (a ford).

Watter, n. C. (pr. watther, the *a*-sound here approximates to that in *what*, but with less of the *o*-sound ; the pr. in fact lies between this word and *bat* : there is nothing of the *au*-sound in the pr. of watter).˙ Water.

Wax-kernels, n C. Swellings in the hollow of the jaw, neck, &c. ; so called because they are thought to be commonest among young people who are still growing.

Wax, v. F. To grow, often used redundantly. Dan. At voxe (to grow).

Ex.—*Sha waxes an' grows.*

Way-corn, n. F. Oats or barley.

Ways, n. C. Way ; only used in such expressions as *cum thi ways, gan thi ways, git thi ways wi tha*, &c.

Wear in, v. F. To accustom to anything. This expression is used in identically the same sense as to break in, except that it is used of people as well as of animals.

Wean, n. F. (pr. wecan). A female. This word is another form of queen, and is used for the most part in a bad sense. Dan. En Kvinde (a female).
    Ex.—*Sha 's a meean weean.*

Weaky, adj. F. Moist ; the opposite of *ask.*

Weeks, n. F. Corners (of the mouth). Dan. En Vig (a creek, inlet) ; Mundvig (corner of the mouth).
    Ex.—*They 've awlus gitten peyps i t' weeks o' ther mooths.*
This word has the same derivation as *wyke,* a not uncommon termination in one form or another to place-names on the Yorkshire coast and elsewhere.

Weight, adj. C. (pr. wite). Many.
    Ex.—*There was a girt weight o' folks theer.—There 's neea girt weight on 'em.*

Well, very, adv. C. (pr. weel). Very much.
    Ex.—*He leykes it varry weel.*

Welted, part. C. Vide **Rigged.**

Wengby, n. R. Skim-milk cheese ; commonly applied to anything very tough and hard. This word is probably connected with *wheng.*
    Ex.—*That cheese is reg'lar wengby, it 's nobbut fit ti put inti ratten hooals.*

Wer, pron. C. (pr. wer, short, and oor, the former generally when it occurs in the middle of a sentence and the latter when it begins a sentence ; though this rule is by no means without exception). Our. There is also another common use of this word, viz. to express the fact that the person to whom the pronoun is applied belongs to the family of the speaker : e. g. *Our Jack* would mean our son or brother Jack. Dan. Vor (our).
    Ex.—*A'e ya seen owt ov oor Bet.—Wa like wer new spot varry weel.—Oor maasther com'd an' tell'd ma.*

Werrick, v. F. To laugh in a semi-suppressed manner.
    Ex.—*What 's ta werrickin' at ?*

Wersens, wersells, pron. C. Ourselves.
    Ex.—*Wa s'all a'e ti fend for wersens.*

Wether, n. C. A male lamb from the time of castration till it is weaned, after which it is called a *hog.*

Wet-shod, adj. C. Wet as to the feet.

What for ? adv. C. Why ? This interrogation is universally used throughout the district : it corresponds to the Fr. *pourquoi.*
    Ex.—*What for a'en't ya deean it ?—Ah deean't knaw what for he nivver tell'd ma.—What for not ?*

Whatsomivver, pron. F. Whatever. Dan. Hvadsomhelst (whatever).

Wheea, pron. C. Who. Another very common form of this pron. is *whau.*

Ex.—*Whau is 't?* i. e. Who is it?—*Wheea see'd 'em?* i. e. Who saw them?—*Whau 's yon?* i. e. Who is that?—*Ah can't ken wheea sha is,* i. e. I can't recognise who she is.

Whemmle, v. C. To totter, to shake, as before falling; to fall over, to upset. To *whemmle* seldom, if ever, is used to signify the act of falling simply, the premonitory symptoms of falling being also included in this expressive word.

Ex.—*It whemmled ower*: this expression is equivalent to it tottered and fell.

Wheng, or **whang,** n. C. A long strip of leather. The word is now generally used for the tough white leather made of horse-hide, commonly employed for uniting the ends of machine straps, or for the end of a lash.

Ex.—*Put a bit o' wheng at t' end on 't.*

While, adv. C. (pr. whahl). Until (the correlative to *so*).

Ex.—*Thoo mun wait whahl t' lad cums.*—*T' meer wer that full o' play whahl ah could hardlins ho'd her.*

Whins, n. C. Gorse bushes. The adj. *whinny,* i. e. covered with whins, is in use. Wel. Chwynd (weeds).

Ex.—*T' whinny garth* (a field-name).

Whisht, interj. C. Hush, keep quiet.

Ex.—*Whisht, or ah 'll skelp tha.*—*Whisht wi ya.*—*Ho'd yer whisht,* i. e. keep silence.

This word is also commonly used as an adverb in the sense of noiselessly.

Ex.—*Sha gans varry whisht.*

Whistle-jacket, n. F. A mixture of gin and treacle, used by old-fashioned people as a cure for a cold. An E. R. word.

Whoats, n. C. Oats. It is not clear how best to give the orthography of this word: the pr. is something like a short *oo* followed by *ats*; thus *oo-ats,* pronounced rapidly as one syllable, will perhaps afford the best idea as to the correct pronunciation.

Whya, interj. C. Well! at the beginning of a remark; also very well, in assenting to anything.

Ex.—*Whya! ah decan't knaw; they mebbe mud.*—Q. *Noo, thoo mun think on.* A. *Whya.*

Wi, prep. C. (pr. wi, short). With; always used before a consonant and sometimes before a vowel or *h.* Vide **Wiv.**

Ex.—*Wi sum on 'em.*—*Gan wi 'em* (or *wiv 'em*).

Wick, adj. C. Alive, living; also lively, sprightly. This word is another form of *quick* (living).

Ex.—*Is 't wick yit?* i. e. Is it still alive?—*Them 's varry wick 'uns,* i. c. Those are of a very lively sort.

Wickens, n. C.   Another form of wicks, the common couch-grass.
> Ex.—*Sha 's getherin wickens.*

Wicken-wood. n. F.   Vide **Witch-wood**.

Wicks, n. C.   (1) The common couch-grass, esp. the roots. (2) Quickset hedge seedlings, or young plants of the same.
> Ex.—*Q. What are they bonnin yonder?   A. Ah laay they 'll be wicks.—Them wicks 'll mak a good hedge eftther a bit.*

Widdy, n. C.   A willow shoot of a year's growth.

Wike, n.   Vide **Weeks**.

Wilf, n. F.   The willow; an E. R. word.

Wind, to loss, F.   To die.   Wind is not unfrequently used for breath in this and other phrases.

Winder, v. C. (pr. windther).   To winnow.

Windering machine, n. C.   A winnowing-machine.

Windle-straw, n. C. (pr. winn'l-stthreea).   A dead stalk of grass, &c.
> Ex.—*There 's nowt bud a few winn'l stthreeas*, i. e. a very poor crop.

Winge, v. C.   To threaten or begin to kick, to show signs of kicking, esp. of a horse.
> Ex.—*Noo thoo mun mahnd, he 's wingein.*

Wingey, adj. C. (pr. *g* soft).   Inclined to kick, having a tendency to kick, esp. of a horse.
> Ex.—*T' meer 's varry wingey.*

Winter hedge, n. F.   A clothes-horse.

Witch-wood; also called **Wicken-tree**, and **Wicken-wood**, n. F.   The mountain-ash.   This wood was commonly used as a charm against witches.

Wiv, prep. C.   With, by.   Only used before a vowel or *h*.
> Ex.—*Ah seed him stannin' wiv hissen.—He 's cumin' yonder wiv au'd Matty.*

Wivoot, prep. and adv. F.   Without, unless.   *Widoot* and *bedoot* are commoner forms of this word.
> Ex.—*Ah deean't knaw, widoot it 's t' cat 'at 's deean it.*

Wold, n. C. (pr. wau'd; or, at the end of a word, as e. g. in Easingwold, almost as wood).   A hill or rising ground, more or less flat at the summit.   The Wolds form an extensive range of such hills in the East Riding.   Dan. En Vold (a mound),

Woomle, n. F.   An auger.

Wrang, adj. C.   Wrong.   Dan. Vrang (wrong); Icel. Rangr.
> Ex.—*Thoo 's wrang.*

Wreckling, n. C.   Vide **Reckling**.

Wringe, v. C.   To scream like a pig; to whine like a dog; to utter a loud noise, as if in pain.
> Ex.—*T' pigs gans wringein aboot weeantly ti-daay.*

Wrong with, To get, C. To get across with, to be at variance with anyone.

Wrought, v. C. (pr. between rote and rout). Worked. The perfect tense of 'to work.'

Ex.—*Ah wrought an' tew'd mang t' taaties.—Ah 've wrought hard i mah tahm.*

Wye, n. C. A heifer under three years of age. Dan. Kvie (a young heifer).

Ex.—*We 've gitten anuther wye cauf.—Is 't a bull or a wye?*

Wyke, n. F. A small bay on the sea-coast. A place-name. Vide **Weeks.**

Y.

Yacker, n. C. Acre; commonly used as a plural also.

Ex.—*We 've nobbut fahve yacker mair ti plew.—Neenty yacker.*

Yah, yan, C. One. These two words are sometimes confounded by strangers to the dialect. *Yah* is a numeral adj. and always has a word agreeing with it, e. g. *yah pleeace, yah neet,* &c.; *yan* is an indefinite pronoun, and a numeral adj. when used singly, the noun being understood.

Ex—*Yan on 'em.—Yan said yah thing an' anuther said anuther.—Yah neet as ah com yam.*—Q. ' How many are there?'—A. *Nobbut yan.—Yah daay yan o' t' lads com ti ma wi nobbut yah hoss ti be sharp'd.*

Yaiting, n. R. Vide **Gait.**

Yak, n. C. Vide **Ak.**

Yakkron, n. C. Acorn.

Yal, n. C. Ale. Dan. Öl (ale).

Ex.—*A sup o' yal.—T' yal aals nowt;* i. e. The ale is good.

Yal-hoos, n. F. Ale-house.

Ex.—*Ah seed him i t' yal-hoos suppin yal.*

Yam, n. C. Home. There are no less than three distinct pronunciations to express *home,* viz. yam, heeam, and wom. The latter, which is very common in the E. R. seems to be a corruption of the Std. Eng. form, *home*; the other two approach more nearly the modern Danish form, Hjem, which is pr. almost as *yem.*

Yam, v. C. Vide **Aim.**

Yan, num. adj. and indef. pron. C. One. Jutl. D. Jen (one). Vide **Yah.**

Yance, adv. C. Once.

Ex.—*Ah mahnd yance 'at,* &c; i. e. I remember once that, &c.—*Nivver bud yance.*

Yannerly, adj. and adv. R. Solitary, alone, lonely. This very expressive word also conveys the idea of fond of retirement, shy. It is derived from *yan* (one). The word is seldom if ever heard now.

> Ex.—*He left her all yannerly at yam.*—*He's varry yannerly.*
> —*Whya! yoor maistther's geean doon ti Whidby;*
> *you 'll be quiet yannerly.*

Yap, n. R. An opprobrious epithet.

Yark, v. C. To inflict a blow; to flog: also commonly used as a noun.

> Ex.—*Ah 'll yark yer rigg.*—*He gav him a yark ower t' back.*

Yat, adj. F. Hot. It is to be observed that this word is never applied to the weather, no matter how high the temperature may be ; even 90° in the shade would only be termed *wahrm* or *varry wahrm*. To other things of high temperature *yat* is frequently applied, e. g. *a yat fire, a yat yewn,* &c.

Yat, n. C. A gate. Dan. En Gade (a gate).

> Ex.—*T' au'd yat 's fit ti fall fra t' creeaks.*—*Sneck t' yat.*—
> *T' yat-stoup 's lowzen'd at t' boddum.*

Yat-steead, n. F. The part covered by the 'sweep' of a gate in opening and shutting.

Yaud, n. C. A horse; sometimes restricted to a riding-horse, or applied to an animal in poor condition.

Yedder, n. C. (pr. yether, *th* soft). A pliant twig or young shoot in a hedge, which may conveniently be utilised for strengthening a fence by twisting it in and out along perpendicular stakes. Hedging down in this fashion is said to be *i stake an' yedder,* and the expression *nowther a stake nor a yedder* signifies the same as 'neither one thing nor the other,' and is frequently applied in that sense to a person of whom nothing can be made and who succeeds at no kind of work.

Yeff, v. F. To bark as a dog. Vide **Waff.**

Yenk, v. F. To flog, to thrash. An E. R. word.

Yet, adv. C. Still. This usage is universal; e. g. 'Is the man here *yet*?' would not mean Has the man arrived? but Is he still here ? 'Does it rain *yet*?' would not mean Has it begun to rain? but, Is it still raining? &c.

Yeth, n. C. Earth.

Yeth-worrm, n. C. An earth-worm.

Yetling, n. F. A pan or pot made of iron and used in cooking. An E. R. word.

Yewn, n. F. Vide **Yown.**

Yocken, yotten, v. C. To gulp; to swallow greedily or with a noise.

> Ex.—*Sitha! he 's yockenin' it doon.*

Yoke, v. C. (pr. yauk). To join a horse to a cart or other carriage by means of harness of some kind.

> Ex.—*A'e ya getten t' meer yauk'd?*—*We 've yauk'd tiv.*

Yon, pron. C. That (over there) ; used demonstratively of persons or things.

Ex.—Q. *Whau 's yon?* i. e. Who is that there? A. *Yon 's yan o' Tommy Otch'n ba'ans.—Whau 's owes yon hoos?*

Yorken, v. C. To swallow ; another form of *yocken*.

Yow, n. C. A ewe.

Ex.—*Wheea 's owes them yows?*

Yown, yewn, n. F. An oven. Dan. En Ovn (an oven).

Ex.—*T' yewn isn't yat yit.*

Yuer, ure, n. C. The udder of a cow. Dan. Et Yver (an udder) ; also commonly used as a verb, to express the swelling of the udder prior to calving.

Yuk, n. F. A hook ; also the top of the femoral bone.

Yuk. v. F. To beat, to flog; the corresponding noun being *yukking*.

Ex.—*Ah gav him a good yukkin.*

Yule-cake, n. C. A plum-cake made specially for Christmas-tide. Dan. Jule-kage (Christmas-cake).

Yule-candle, n. C. (pr. yule-cann'l). A candle of extra large size, specially burnt in houses on Christmas Eve, according to an old custom.

Yule-clog, n. C. A log of wood burnt in houses on Christmas or New Year's Eve.

D d

INDEX.

—◆—

D d 2

THE END

OXFORD: HORACE HART, PRINTER TO THE UNIVERSITY